PENGUIN BO

ONE IS A WAND

Francis King spent his childhood in India, where his father was a government official. While an undergraduate at Oxford, he wrote his first three novels. Then he joined the British Council, working successively in Italy, Greece, Egypt, Finland and Japan, before retiring in 1964 to devote himself entirely to writing. His books include: the novels *The Action*, *The Needle*, *Voices in an Empty Room* (Penguin, 1985) and *Act of Darkness* (Penguin, 1985), chosen by the *Yorkshire Post* as Novel of the Year 1983; five highly praised volumes of short stories including *Hard Feelings* and *Indirect Method*; and two non-fiction works, *E. M. Forster and His World* and *Florence*. For some years he has been Drama Critic of the *Sunday Telegraph* and he reviews fiction regularly for the *Spectator*. He is a former winner of the Somerset Maugham Prize and the Katherine Mansfield Short Story Prize. He has also edited and introduced *Writings from Japan* by Lafcadio Hearn, published in the Penguin Travel Library.

Francis King has been active on behalf of writers. A founder member of Writers' Action Group, which was involved in the final battle for Public Lending Right (PLR), he has been President of English PEN.

FRANCIS KING

One is a Wanderer

PENGUIN BOOKS

Penguin Books Ltd, Harmondsworth, Middlesex, England
Viking Penguin Inc., 40 West 23rd Street, New York, New York 10010, U.S.A.
Penguin Books Australia Ltd, Ringwood, Victoria, Australia
Penguin Books Canada Limited, 2801 John Street, Markham, Ontario, Canada L3R 1B4
Penguin Books (N.Z.) Ltd, 182–190 Wairau Road, Auckland 10, New Zealand

This collection first published by Century Hutchinson 1985
Published in Penguin Books 1987

Made and printed in Great Britain by
Richard Clay (The Chaucer Press) Ltd,
Bungay, Suffolk

Two's company, three's a crowd, one is a wanderer

Contents

Voices   1
The Tree   15
The Mouse   30
Appetites   38
The Brighton Belle   49
I Lived for You   64
Mess   76
Home   104
Hard Feelings   116
Loss   132
A Corner of a Foreign Field   161
The Goat   186
The Festival of the Dead   196
Indirect Method   218
A Scent of Mimosa   238
So Hurt and Humiliated   251
Sundays   266
The Soutane   275
Unmaking   284
The Silence is Rest?   298
His Everlasting Mansion   307

Voices

1

In the years of dubious fame, of fretful travel, of the hours spent in the heat of television studios or the chill of laboratories, lying alone or lying in the arms of Krishna, Pearl would always remember the exact moment when she first knew that she could do It. A duckling takes to the water, a nestling takes to the air. A moment of doubt, followed by a moment of terror; and then the new element embraces her as though she had entered it a hundred times already. . . .

A child of eight, in the summer dawn, Pearl stands, nacreously pallid and gleaming in her night-dress, behind the net curtain of her attic window. There is sweat on her forehead and her bare arms. There is sun already in the long narrow garden, that same sun that day after day has made her feel enervated and listless; but during the night (or did she imagine it?) she heard the far-off rumble of thunder, as though some giant's hammer were beating on the ground. She yawns, she watches, one fragile hand lifting a corner of the curtain. The two women, her mother and her aunt, also in their night-dresses, walk together down the garden, their arms linked; and dark on the dew-sprinkled grass their footsteps melt and merge. They are going down to the orchard and as they sway and sidle, their plump bodies colliding with each other, unresisting flesh against unresisting flesh,

1

their heads bend towards each other. But from high up here, under the steeply sloping roof that retains the heat of the day all through the restless nights, Pearl cannot hear what they are saying to each other. Her mother's hair is a jet, gipsy black; Aunt Marion's is streaked with grey, hanging loose down a neck that has a little creased cushion of fat just above the shoulder blades. Pearl imagines the swish of their night-dresses as they make their way from the close-shaven lawn (yesterday her father had at last been bullied into mowing it) into the long, wet grass of the orchard as though they were wading arm-in-arm into a shallow sea. Pearl knows where they are going. Against the far wall, crumbling like one of those dry sponge-cakes that Aunt Marion makes for tea, stand the peach trees, their branches heavy with fruit. The women approach them, loosening their hold on each other as though they were nearing some mystery or rite. The sun glimmers along an upraised arm. That is Aunt Marion, tiptoeing up as she plucks the huge ripe peach from one of the highest branches. For several days she has marked it down and waited, patient yet persistent. Pearl's mother now goes up on tiptoe too and feels, feels, feels among the fruit, her fingers wary not to bruise or pluck until she is sure that the precise moment has come. Pearl leans out, the ledge of the high window pressing against her flat, bony chest. Sweat beads her upper lip and, when she runs her tongue along it, it tastes salt and brackish.

There has been a strange, aimless kind of languor in all the women's movements as each has plucked a fruit; but now, with impetuous greed, they bite into the flesh, the juice running down their chins and staining their night-dresses. Aunt Marion squints up at her sister, the rising sun stabbing at her weak-sighted eyes behind their gold-framed glasses; the glasses catch fire. Mother says something and both women laugh. If only she, Pearl, glimmering high above their heads at the window of the attic bedroom, could hear them! She is always conscious of this secret world of theirs, in which the languorous plucking of the peaches is only yet another rite from which they exclude her. If only. . . . Then all at once the duckling takes to the water, the nestling takes to the air. A moment of doubt, followed by a moment of terror; and then she can hear them. . . .

There's nothing else for it. (Aunt Marion flings the peach stone from her into the long grass.)

Yes but. (Mother is again on tiptoe, reaching among the leaves, jumps, yanks.)

You've got to face. (Aunt Marion also reaches up, feels, rejects, feels again.)

2

But the child, for her sake.

She'll come to far more harm if you stick with him.

Yes but.

He's never been any good to you and he never will be.

Oh but.

No, Eileen, never any good at all.

Well but.

Run through your money, made a slave of you, can't hold down a job.

Yes but.

Half-cut most of the time, lazy, hopeless, hopeless, hopeless.

Pearl could now even hear the disgusting champing noises of their teeth, the salivation and the sucking of the juice, as they wolfed, talked, wolfed. But she no longer wanted to hear. She had heard enough. She ran back to the bed, jumped into it and pulled first the sheet and then the pillow over her head. But the voices went on.

Got to face up to it.

Oh but.

Not fair to the child, not fair to yourself. It's now or never. Leave him.

Yes if only.

There's no if only about it. Tell him this morning. That's my girl. Just as soon as he comes out of that drunken sleep of his. Tell him.

Oh, Marion.

Tell him.

However tight she pulled the pillow over her head and however deep she burrowed down under the sheet, she could not stop hearing. She had launched herself into the new element and now, carried out on the long, brimming tide, the hot upward thrust of air impelling her pinions forward, she could not escape from it.

2

That was when she first knew that she could do It. Soon, she was to learn that she sometimes did It without wishing to do It; and soon, too, that it was better not to let anyone, not even Mother and Aunt Marion, know that she could do It.

They leave that house and years later Pearl's only recollection of the place is of a cramped attic bedroom, a window so high that its ledge presses against her flat, bony chest and two women, at the start of a summer day, leaving a dark trail behind them on silvery grass and then reaching up, with languorous movements, to pluck the ripe peaches from the trees at the far end of a rankly overgrown garden. There was a man in the house, who was often described as 'ill' and whom Pearl would often be forbidden to approach in the study in which he spent so many of his hours since he had ceased to go out to work. He had been a jolly man, once, long ago, and he could still be jolly, even if with a jolliness that made Aunt Marion and Mother watch him warily, drawing in their breaths with a sharp hiss when his fun became too strident; but the jolliness of those last months seldom lasted, petering out in an aftermath of sulks and headaches or exploding in an orgy of shouts and broken crockery. Sometimes he would hold Pearl close to him, his breath heavy with the smell of pipe smoke and that other mysterious smell that she so much hated; and Mother or Aunt Marion would then order him to let the girl be, it was disgusting, the poor wee thing, had he no shame? I'll do what I bloody well please in my own house, he would yell, flinging the child from him; and Mother, icy and acid, would then query, Your own house?

Well, whoever owned the house, they leave it, first for a smaller one in a meaner suburb; and then for a flat, damply cavernous, in a mansion block south of Clapham Common.

Coming home from school, as she watches the bus approaching, Pearl has a sensation of gentle pressure inside her forehead and a sensation of a wind blowing against her fragile throat; and she is doing It, without wanting to do It. She can hear the two women, who at that moment are drinking their dark, bitter tea together two miles away, a letter open on the table between them.

He says there it's a death sentence.

Don't you believe it, it's nothing but a bid for sympathy.

But the doctor.

Who knows if he's ever seen any doctor at all?

But cirrhosis.

It's no more than he deserves.

Yes, but I feel.

Now you don't want to get mixed up with him again, after you've managed to get free.

Oh, but one can't help.

Think of Pearl . . .

Perhaps they are thinking of Pearl, shimmeringly nacreous schoolgirl, for then there is a silence; and Pearl, seated alone on the top of the bus, is thinking of them and of the father who used to hold her so tight against his chest as he breathed over her those fumes of pipe smoke and alcohol. He is dying? In need? On his own? She longs to be with him. Smooth his sheet. Carry a tray and tell him, It's such a lovely day outside. Take his temperature. She longs to hear his voice. But try though she may, a vein throbbing, throbbing, throbbing at a corner of her forehead, somehow she cannot do It. Perhaps he is too far for her to reach him.

She runs down the street from the bus stop and dashes into the house. What's all the hurry about? Aunt Marion asks; and Mother, slipping the letter under the tablecloth, says, You must have known that your auntie had baked one of her cakes. (The yellow wall crumbles in the early morning sunshine behind the peach trees; the peaches are gravid with juice.) Pearl cries out, Is he ill? I want to go to him. Where is he? Why didn't you tell me? The two women look at each other in shock and astonishment and then they both look at her in anger.

You've no business to eavesdrop.

And how did you get away from school so early?

Pretending to have just rushed in off the bus and all the time.

I've told you before.

All this hanging about outside closed doors listening to things that are no concern of yours.

Let this be the last time.

But I. Pearl does not continue. She knows that she must never, ever tell them that she can do It.

Yet slowly the women guess; and it frightens them, so that they never dare to put it into words to each other. Such a funny little thing. (Aunt Marion creams the butter and sugar with frowning concentration.) Almost as though she could read one's thoughts. One can't hide anything from her, Mother agrees, woefully totting up figures (electricity, gas, rates) on the back of an envelope that contains another of his scrawled, pleading letters (even a quid or two would help). It's quite creepy, it really is. So artful.

He dies at last; and though Aunt Marion tells Mother, I shouldn't say anything about it to her, why upset her, what's the point? she hears them from far away in the baker's shop where she has gone to buy a loaf and she rushes into the house and screams, Why didn't you let me see him? Why didn't you? Just once, only once! And now I'll never see him again! The two women look stricken and frightened and, more to her sister and herself than to the child, Aunt Marion commands, Now pull yourself together.

Krishna became their lodger two or three years after that. He came between the Turk whom Aunt Marion had to ask to leave because he wet his bed and the Arab who used to try to fondle Pearl's nascent breasts whenever he found himself alone with her. (This is our secret. You must never tell your Mummy and your auntie, Bearl. He could never pronounce a P.) Krishna was beautiful, pliant and sickly, like some exotic plant, perhaps a plant from his own native India, that stands in a northern sitting-room with its weak branches reaching out towards the distant sun; but the core of the plant was extraordinarily fibrous and resilient. His was the attic room opposite hers and he had it strewn with the components that he used for his work. He was a student, on some kind of scholarship, at Imperial College, but he was far cleverer than any of his fellow students, Pearl was sure of that. His palms, when he took both her hands in his hands, were strangely soft and cool. He wore a gold bracelet round one girlish wrist. His shoulder-length hair swung from side to side when he was working at his table. If she shut her eyes as she touched that hair, it felt exactly as if she were touching grass. He had a small beaky nose, as of some bird of prey, and huge eyes, ringed as with bruises, that seemed to look deep inside her and plumb her secret from that first moment that they met. He knew at once that she could do It. She had never had to tell him.

It could be hyperaesthesia, he speculated in his soft sing-song voice.

Hyper what?

He explained. There was Gilbert Murray. He would go to the other end of the house and then, when he was summoned back, he would know what people had been saying.

But this isn't just the other end of the house. Or even the other end of the street. It can be, oh, miles.

He smirked; he did not really believe her when she said that; he thought she was boasting, in the way that children do. (After all, she was only fourteen.) But he began patiently to test her, forcing her to concentrate while she felt that increasing pressure within her forehead and that wind that, on the stillest day, blew against her throat; and miraculously she would tell him what her aunt had been saying to her mother or what he had been saying to either of them while she had been far away at school or at the shops or in the park. He was puzzled then, as the doctor had been puzzled when for several days she had run a temperature without any other symptom. He would look at her, with a wondering insistence, sometimes holding both her hands in his (the palms so cool, so soft) and he would tell her, You're an odd one, without a doubt.

But I don't want to be odd. I just want to be normal.

You can't help it. Can you? That's how you're made.

Oh but.

You're a very exceptional person, Pearl. The whole world will be interested in you. You'll see.

4

Now the whole world is interested in her. At first Mother has doubts about it. You don't want to be a freak, you don't want to be like something in a fun-fair. But this nacreous freak earns money and her fun-fair is the world. There are articles about her in the news-papers. She appears on the television, the two plump sisters leaning hungrily towards her flickering image as countless people are doing the whole length and breadth of the country. Other children claim to have the same power, but of course they haven't. She spends several weeks at an American university, Krishna always with her. There are articles about her in the journals of psychic research. Her photo-graph appears on the covers of two Sunday supplements simulta-neously. She feels perpetually tired, as though she were bleeding, on and on and on, from an invisible wound. But she owes it to science and to herself to continue with the experiments, Krishna tells her; and she knows that she also owes it to Krishna, whom she has come to love, and to her mother and her aunt, who no longer have to take in lodgers and who have moved from Clapham to Chelsea. Krishna tells her and anyone else who is interested that she has taken a step ahead of the rest of the human race in the process of evolution. Some day, sooner or later, everyone will be able to do it. But since for the moment she alone has the capability, she must endure all this travel, all these questions, all these tests, all these people, all this tiredness.

She becomes pregnant while on a visit to Zürich. This is some-thing that Krishna, who plans everything for her, did not plan; but he is always businesslike and, telling her that nothing must be allowed to get in the way of their 'work' – later, he says, of course they will get married – he arranges for her to go into a clinic, one of the most expensive in Switzerland if not in the world, and the foetus is removed from her. Has It somehow been removed with the foetus? She does not know; she is really too tired to think clearly about it. But there is the fact, which she and Krishna must face together in the burnished Zürich laboratory: humiliatingly she can no longer do It. Soon there will be an article in a Swiss scientific journal to say that under stringent conditions the subject was totally unable to produce any phenomena at all. In the overheated, luxury hotel Krishna shouts at her, You stupid cow. What's the matter with you? Why don't you try? She feels totally drained of blood. It must have all flowed away, a black, sticky river, when their child was ripped from her.

Well, never mind, we'll have to think of something. Krishna is, after all, a genius in his own way. True, he can't hear what people are saying unless they are in earshot but his professor did say that he was one of the most promising students ever to have come to him from India. Krishna works hard in the work room that he has at the top of the Chelsea house, while Pearl sits watching the television with the two sisters who, sensing that she can no longer do It, for the first time for many years feel a sense of community with the nacreously pallid child-woman.

After many weeks Krishna produces an electrode about the size of a penny, which is covered on its operative surface with a thin film of mylar. He tells the bewildered Pearl that they are going to Barcelona, where a cousin of his practises as a dentist. The cousin is, in fact, the husband of a second cousin; and though he is a good dentist, he has found few patients in the country of his exile and has many debts.

But I don't need a dentist.

Krishna says something about her needing 'prosthetic dentistry'. She has no idea what this can mean. Trust me, he says; and though he is the least trustworthy of men, she trusts him because she loves him. It is only in the Barcelona hotel that he tells her, a soft and cool palm sliding over her fragile forearm, that he and the dentist are going to give It back to her.

What do you mean?

He explains but, since she is not very bright, she has difficulty in understanding him. An element for receiving electromagnetic signals at radio frequency. Transducer element coupled with receiving element and with live nerve ending of a tooth. Electromagnetic signals converted to electric signals at audio frequency for transmission to the brain.

8

But I don't understand all this! And I don't want all this!

Perfectly simple. You wouldn't want to have to sell the house, now would you? Turn out Mother and Auntie? And how otherwise can we ever get married and have the baby that we want? Won't hurt. Easiest thing in the world to operate once you get used to it. Tongue like this. (He demonstrates, pressing a long, sinuous tongue against a molar, mouth ajar. Horrified, she peers into the crimson cavern.) Tongue presses against exposed terminal on back tooth. The amazingly soft and cool palm continues to rub her forearm, with hypnotic persistence.

She screams. It's horrible. A hateful idea. I don't want It to happen like that.

Now you're getting all excited about nothing. Let me give you one of those pills that the Swiss doctor.

No!

But she eventually swallows the pill and soon she is feeling sleepy and wholly dissociated from all that he has planned for her, as though Pearl, who once could do It and now can no longer do It, is someone totally different from this Pearl spreadeagled on the rumpled double bed in the Barcelona hotel.

The next day they go to the dentist, who is furry and agile, his simian mouth cracking open in repeated smiles that reveal his gold inlays, as though to say, See how rich I am, here is all my treasure! He gives her an injection in her arm that makes her feel even more sleepy and dissociated than the pills of the night before, and then he gives her two injections in the mouth. The drilling and placing of the gold filling and the rectifier crystal take a long time and the dentist mutters imprecations under his breath in a language that is common to him and Krishna but that Pearl cannot understand. At one point he drops the tiny amplifier and the two men go on their hands and knees, two monkeys in quest of a fallen nut. They are now far more agitated than she.

Pearl is lying motionless in the chair, a tear glistening on either nacreous cheekbone.

At one point she says, I don't want.

But the two men appear not to hear her.

After that there were times when she forgot that It had gone from her and that her only gift was Krishna's gift of the ingenious piece of metal hidden under a toothcap. When the voices now came to her, she hardly noticed that they had grown oddly blurred, ebbing and flowing as though brought to her on wave after wave of some invisible but circumambient sea. Even her fear of being found out began to recede and she no longer awoke, sweating and with furiously thumping heart, in the loneliness of hotel bedrooms with Krishna asleep beside her, to think, Some day someone will realize. And then no one will ever believe that once I could really do It. They'll say that I always had Krishna to help me. They'll say we always cheated.

Krishna told her, We've only substituted one miracle for another, my dear. My miracle is every bit as extraordinary as your miracle, you know. They were growing very rich.

Krishna used to laugh at all the scientists. They just don't know how to observe, he would say. Conjurors know. But scientists are children. Worse than children. Even children observe more. She frowned in bewilderment and he went on, In the world of science most people are trying to prove the truth of a hypothesis to which they are already committed. The hypothesis is more important to them than any evidence.

Only once is Pearl convinced that someone who claims to believe that she can do It, really does not do so. He is a short, shrill American television personality, with spidery overactive hands and popping eyes and she appears on a series of his shows that are concerned with the paranormal. He holds her so tightly by the elbow that later that evening, in her New York hotel bedroom, she finds bruises on the nacreous skin. His breath is slightly sour as his face approaches hers and she notices that there is a faint rash on his forehead, just below the hairline. He talks very fast and from time to time stalks about among the audience, followed by the camera, like some hungry, impassioned animal in an invisible cage.

There are gasps of amazement from the people packed before her. He exclaims, Fantastic! Incredible! Extraordinary! The scientists nod their heads ruefully and one says, Well, you've got me beaten. I've seen nothing like this, says another.

But when he says goodbye to her, taking her cold hand in his sweating one, the famous interviewer gives her a glance of sardonic complicity. He silently seems to be telling her, We're both fakes. We understand each other. That glance frightens her and makes her feel ashamed. She does not wish to have any community with that shrill, prancing, self-intoxicated figure.

He guessed something, she tells Krishna as she slips out of her dress.

Nonsense. You were perfect. I was perfect too.

He guessed something.

Not a chance. But thank God no one suggested total body X-radiation again. Krishna has had to refuse that twice – at Göttingen University and at Heidelberg University. The Germans are so thorough.

6

Now there are months of success even wilder than in that period when she really could do It, and Krishna is delighted with her. She grows even more etiolated, thinner, vaguer; but he tells her that once they have got through this year ahead of them, then they'll take off on a holiday, perhaps a cruise round the world (they have already circled the world more than once). But before that they will marry. She wonders why he keeps putting off something that they could do any afternoon. Perhaps back in India he has a wife and children? But she does not want to think about that.

Then something strange and alarming begins to happen. She is asleep after lunch in preparation for an appearance on Rome television and Krishna has told her that he must go out for a breath of air. Suddenly she is roused by the sound of voices, there in her head. But she has not activated the tiny amplifier and it is unlikely that Krishna has activated his tiny transmitter. She listens, aghast, to a woman whom she does not know and a man whom she does.

What's she doing? (The voice is American.)

What she usually does. Sleeping. I've never known anyone who sleeps so much.

It must take it out of her.

Well, I suppose so. But living with her takes it out of me. Thank God, there's you to put it back.

Why on earth did you ever take up with her?

I often ask myself that question. But, oh well, it's fascinating. In its way.

And lucrative.

11

And lucrative.

She doesn't want to listen to the voices of the woman whom she does not know and the man whom she does. But on and on they go, there inside her head. She cannot stop them. She cannot sleep.

When Krishna comes back she does not tell him that she has listened to the whole atrocious conversation; but she says, I have a feeling that there's something wrong with this thing in my mouth.

What do you mean?

Well, from time to time I . . . hear things.

Hear things?

Scraps of conversation.

He pooh-poohs that as he combs his long, sleek hair before the mirror. He combs the hair as though it belonged to someone whom he loved, with long, languorous strokes from the crown of his head to the glistening ends. Impossible, he says. You can't hear anything unless I'm transmitting.

She shrugs in resigned agreement. But intermittently she goes on hearing scraps of conversation between him and other people. She learns the full extent of his contempt for her, even loathing.

She cannot sleep, becomes hysterical, on one occasion even makes a half-hearted effort to cut her wrists with one of his razor blades. Finally, knowing that she is no use to him or to anyone in her present state, he agrees that yes, they'll have the implant removed. They go to Barcelona and once again the agile, furry dentist gives her an injection in her arm and two injections in her mouth. This is the end, baby, Krishna says. After this we're washed up. Since he met that unknown American woman, he has begun to talk in these Americanisms.

7

But it wasn't the end but only a rebeginning. Where once there had been Krishna's device, there was now a clumsy amalgam filling; but she could again do It. Even when she did not want to do It, she would hear the conversations; not only Krishna and the American woman, or Krishna and Auntie and Mother, or Auntie and Mother between themselves, but also a host of other people, in whom she had no interest but who insisted on making themselves audible to her. Like actual physical masses, the identities of all these anonymous others pressed on her and crushed her. She could hardly breathe for them.

Did you really have that horrible thing removed?

Yes, of course I did. And now by some miracle the gift has come back to you. What could be better than that?

Silence, she might have answered. But she did not do so, since now she had grown afraid of losing him. As long as she could do It, he would never leave her.

At any time of the day or night the voices now torment her, a babbling murmur that slowly rises to a crescendo in her head, as though a hibernating swarm of bees had been stirred into angry life. But still the two whizz about the world, the pallid girl and her panthcrine 'manager', and more and more people acclaim her, Astonishing, Marvellous, Incredible, Miraculous.

In a Tokyo hotel she refuses to go to a party, given by one diplomat and his wife and attended by a number of other diplomats and their wives, even though Krishna tells her, You've got to go. The party's for *us*. Don't you understand? All those people will be coming for us.

But she clutches her head, that head that is now ceaselessly throbbing with the insistent identities of others, and cries out, I can't, can't, can't! All I want is somc pcacc. Some peace, some peace.

He knots his black tie and arranges the handkerchief in his breast pocket. He is angry with her, she knows that, but he says nothing of his anger. I'll have to go. It'll be better than nothing. Then he adds roughly from the door, For God's sake, now pull yourself together. It's no fun being with you, you know. They have not made love for a long time. He walks out into the late violet dusk, smelling so strongly of scent that the diplomat who is his host will later say to his wife in bed, Dreadful man, that. Reeking of some bazaar perfume. Did you notice?

Pearl lies on the bed in the gathering darkness and one by one the voices creep into her head. At first they are English or American.

Oh, I feel so.

Oh, I want so.

But of course I.

But of course you.

Well, yes if.

Well, no if.

Oh, I wish I.

I wish.

I wish.

Then there are other voices, French voices, German voices, Italian voices, even Japanese voices. The whole hotel is talking in her head. Her head tries to contain them all but it is not big enough. Her head will burst.

She jumps off the bed and goes to the window, holding back the curtain with a fragile hand as she peers out. The violet dusk has now deepened to night. Opposite the hotel, they are excavating the foundations for another, even more expensive hotel, a skyscraper. The men are working on under arc lights that reveal their puny, half-naked bodies. From here they look so small, so very small; but their voices in her head are loud, so very loud. Everyone else in the hotel has been complaining about a huge machine that rhythmically thumps on the earth with a terrifying tremor. But the voices are so noisy that she can hardly hear it. She sees it, however. Up and down goes its giant's hammer, up and down, and the men swarm about it.

She pulls on her coat over her underclothes and she goes out. She runs into the street and she then runs across it. The voices are getting louder; that vein is throbbing at one corner of her forehead; the wind is blowing, hot and dry, against her fragile throat. One of the puny men, who is in fact not puny at all, sees her and attempts to grab her. But before he can do so her head and the voices inside it have been thumped into the dust by that giant's hammer, to be silenced forever.

Her suicide horrifies everyone in Europe and America but secretly delights the Japanese.

They are, after all, connoisseurs of that kind of thing.

1977

The Tree

1

How I loathe the W.C. It has its uses, of course; civilization would be unthinkable without it. But it's so unreliable in performing its necessary functions. It's so unaesthetic. And, let's face it, it *stinks*. . . .

An old, famous, rich politician thinks these things as he lies out in the late afternoon, distended from too much food and depleted from too much conversation, after a Sunday luncheon party. They are the kind of thoughts that an English politician only acknowledges to himself when he is still half-asleep and that he will never acknowledge to others. *How I loathe the W.C.* How I loathe the working class.

Dry thoughts of a dry old man in a dry season.

He had said goodbye to the last of the guests, a simpering newspaper columnist and his broad, energetic opera-singer wife, crunching with them down the gravel drive and, firm hand shading firm eyes against the glare, watching them as they squeezed themselves into their Mini. Then, not wishing to go back to the disorder of half-filled ashtrays and quarter-filled glasses and coffee-cups (the women, his women, could see to all that), he walked round the Georgian house, past his youngest grandchild's tricycle and his oldest two grandchildren's bicycles, past the garden shed (one of his

15

wretched women had left the door open again), the greenhouse and the outdoor lavatory that no one ever used now that Mrs Parkin no longer came to 'do' for them, and down to the tree. Just as the women were his women, so the tree was his tree. It was a lime and at this time of year it seemed to him always to be enveloped in a cloud of scent. One of his women, his daughter-in-law, had told him only that morning that she could smell nothing at all – 'You're imagining it,' she had said. But how could she expect to smell anything so subtle and exquisite when she was always puffing at those filthy Gauloise cigarettes? The chair was there for him, because another of his women, the Spanish *au pair* girl who would so often sigh inexplicably when the two of them found themselves alone together, had been told to see that it was there on any day of fine weather. Sometimes, although the chair was there, he did not use it, because he was kept at the House, because he was attending some committee meeting or because he was opening a charity bazaar or a hospital or an antiques fair.

He stretched himself out in the chair and looked first around him at the long grass undulating as the warm breeze slid caressingly across it, and then up into the black branches, with the brilliant green leaves crowded about them. He could hear, since despite his age his ears were still preternaturally acute, the bees buzzing in the lime flowers. He liked that sound and the absence of any other sound of any kind whatever. Though the house was in Canonbury, the road was far away; and the grandchildren had mercifully been taken by the Spanish *au pair* to the swimming baths. 'You might be in the depth of the country,' the simpering newspaper columnist had gushed. His own pad (that was the word that he used as he spoke about it) was an eyrie above Shaftesbury Avenue, from which he never ceased to be aware of the unending turmoil of motion and emotion down there far below him. A rubbishy little man, the big man had thought; but the big man had none the less been charming to the little one, with the charm of someone for whom charm is a habit acquired from the best of parents, nannies, schoolmasters.

Lynton loved that tree as much as he loved any of his possessions; and when he was disheartened, fearful or depressed, its consolatory power was quite as great as that of his Rembrandt, his string of racehorses or his two pointers. Rembrandt, racehorses, dogs, tree: in his life of fretfully conscientious usefulness it was not often that he could pay attention to any of them. But he was not sure that that tree did not mean more to him than any other of his possessions.

Beautiful tree. The breeze made a gentle susurration in the branches as he looked up, up, up, through a pulsating tunnel of green to the eggshell blue of the sky above it. As a child he had played in its shade; as a boy he had read under it, lying out, not in a chair placed there by one of his women, but in the deep grass; as a young man, late one evening, the tree a shuddering mass above him, he had held in his arms the woman whom he had loved but who had failed to become his wife because she was a divorcée at a time when that mattered, because she was so many years older than he and because she was poor and (comparatively speaking, of course) of humble origin. He would like to die under that tree, exhaling his last breath as the tree exhaled its perfume, on some late summer afternoon, at once distended and depleted. . . .

It was as he was thinking that, that he heard that horrid common voice.

'Excuse me, your lordship.'

Mrs Parkin, who had lived for so many years in that house, the last of a mean, squat row, and whose husband had helped to tend the garden until a stroke had felled him, had always called Lynton 'your lordship'. But that had been in respect, with none of the irony that this old cow's mooing contrived to insinuate into the phrase.

'Yes, Mrs Sparks.'

She was the other side of the wall, in the narrow alley in which the residents of that row of slum houses dumped their lidless bins, their shopping-bags overflowing with rubbish, their cardboard boxes, broken crates, rusty tins. Sometimes the stench of all that garbage would mingle with the scent of his tree; but miraculously, even on a day as hot as this, it could never completely overpower it. She was on tiptoe, her brown, shiny face peering between the trailing arms of the Albertine rose; and even today, in the middle of August, she was wearing that knitted pixie-bonnet. She was ageless, shapeless, charmless; she was also unappeasable.

'That tree,' she said.

'Yes, Mrs Sparks.'

He could see her fingers, cracked and deformed from years of peeling potatoes, scrubbing floors and washing up for others, gripping the top of the wall. She's hanging on by her fingernails from the window-ledge of life, he thought; she always has. He liked that image, it amused him.

'Yes, Mrs Sparks?' he prompted again, since she was still peering at him silently, as though she had forgotten what it was that was on

17

her mind. But, in fact, both of them knew, he quite as well as she.

'That tree. All that sticky stuff is coming off it worse than ever. Everything's sticky in my garden. The bushes are coated with it. Like a kind of slime. I daren't put my washing out. I said to Mr Sparks only this morning that that tree has made our yard quite uninhabitable.' The voice whined on, mingling now with that consoling buzz of the bees and that even more consoling scent of the lime flowers. He had heard it all before, so often. He closed his eyes, his hands joined over his slightly protuberant stomach and his chest rising and falling as he breathed evenly and deeply. He might almost have been asleep.

'Are you listening to me, your lordship?'

He opened his eyes. The green, green leaves flickered above him. He made an effort, and then, with that elaborate courtesy of habit, replied: 'Yes, Mrs Sparks, I am listening. I've been listening to every word. I wish that I could do something to help you. But as I have already told you, that tree has a protection order on it. Even if I did want to lop it, prune it or have it cut down, I couldn't do so. I'm forbidden to do so. If I did so, I'd be liable to a fine.' What he did not explain was that he himself had sought the protection order just as soon as she, that oaf of a husband of hers and those two hulking brutes that were her sons had started their moans. 'I'm extremely sorry but there it is.'

'I don't understand about these protection orders. Who are they protecting?' Her hands moved at the top of the wall almost as though she were preparing to heave herself over.

'They are not protecting any *person*. They are designed to protect trees.'

'It strikes me that it's we who need some protection. Against that tree of yours. Mr Sparks was saying only on Sunday last there's nothing will grow in our yard. It stands to reason. No sun can get through.'

He wanted to say, 'The weeds seem to grow well enough.' He wanted to say, 'Mrs Parkin and her husband had no difficulty in creating a charming cottage garden.' (Often his guests, the politicians, journalists, writers, bankers, artists, actors, would peer over the wall and say how pretty it all was. None of them would be caught growing those giant dahlias in their own gardens, of course, but somehow they were just right for nice old Mrs Parkin and her husband, two Cockneys full of sly obsequiousness and quaint homespun wisdom.) He wanted to say, 'Somehow, Mrs Sparks, it seems rather appropriate that that once charming cottage garden should now be all overrun with loosestrife. Loosestrife: that strikes me as an excellent indication of the kind of sloppy, malevolent lives that you and your family lead.' But instead he smiled at her and said, 'I do feel awfully sorry for you. But there it is. If you want to have a word with them down at the Town Hall, do please do so. If you can persuade them to agree that the tree should go, then of course. . . .' (Hideous, ignorant woman, determined to amputate the one beautiful thing that redeemed that shocking row of houses.)

'I think that's for you,' she said.

'What's for me? What's for me, Mrs Sparks?'

The hands at the wall now reminded him, in their intrusive greyness and rubberiness, of the tentacles of an octopus in an aquarium. If one took a bill-hook and hacked one of them off, at once seven would sprout in its place.

'To see those Town Hall people. After all, it's your tree.'

Pointless to argue with her. But the habits of charm and courtesy persisted: 'I'd certainly speak to them if I thought that any good would come of it. But I know that it wouldn't.'

The pixie-bonnet bobbed as she tossed her head; there was a rustle from the trailing arms of the Albertine as she nudged a shoulder between them. 'They'd not be likely to send you away with a flea in your ear. They'd do what you told them.'

He laughed. 'I'm afraid, Mrs Sparks, that you're very much exaggerating my importance and influence.'

'You was a Minister, wasn't you?'

He nodded. 'Yes, Mrs Sparks, I was.'

'Well then?'

'There's no "Well then?" about it, I'm afraid. The fact of my having been a Minister doesn't mean that I can set aside a preservation order.'

'So you won't do anything?'

There must be some gipsy blood there, he thought, as he had often thought before when enraged with her. Her skin and that of her two sons, though not of her husband, was almost Indian in its swarthiness. Although she must be, oh, at least sixty, the thick eyebrows that met across her forehead were jet in colour, as was her hair.

'It's not that I won't do anything. I can't do anything.'

The tentacles uncurled from the wall. There was a flash of sun on the bilious green of the pixie-bonnet and then she had retreated, back past the overflowing bins and bags of rubbish and through the gate, fissured and creaking, that led into her yard. The gate slammed. He heard her speaking to one or more of her invisible menfolk, in a voice that was, he was sure, pitched purposely loud so that he should hear her. 'Stupid ole cunt! No change out of *him*! Might have guessed it!'

'Sh!' That must be her husband, a decent enough man when she was not there to goad him on.

He looked up at the tree, still now in the perfectly still air but for those eager bees that drank at its flowers. Beautiful, beautiful tree, so unlike that hideous, hideous woman. He closed his eyes. Sighed. Dozed off. It was as he awoke from that doze, like some diver emerging from the depths of ocean, that he began to think: How I loathe the W.C. . . . .

2

Her face puffy, the wiry hair falling across it, old Mrs Sparks ('Ma Sparks' to Lynton's cool women) emerges from slumber like some deep-sea creature hurled floundering and gasping up into the light of day by a depth-charge. Ooh, oh, oh. . . . She clutches at her head, the vee of her nightdress falling away to reveal udder-breasts streaked with purple veins. Mr Sparks ('Steptoe' to Lynton's cool women) sleeps on, humped and gently snoring, beneath a mound of bedclothes, a trail of saliva glistening down his chin as though a snail had crawled there. How can he bear the thick woollen pyjamas and all those army-issue blankets ('fallen off a lorry') at the start of an August scorcher like this? He is always chilled, wearing layer upon layer of vests, pullovers and cardigans even when he is playing bowls with his cronies. This morning, as on every other morning, he does not have to get up. He will kip on until the pubs open.

Ooh, oh, oh. . . . Mrs Sparks staggers to her feet and almost falls, inadvertently kicking out as she does so at the chamber pot, its enamel pitted and scratched from generations of scouring, that stands beside the bed. What looks like a strong solution of iodine splashes the rug. 'Fuck!' She pushes away her hair and waddles to the window, raises a flaccid arm and tugs the curtain aside on its bangle-like brass rings. It is so dark here; but beyond the tree the sun is brilliant. Now she raises the net curtain and peers beneath it. The yard is in shadow except for a dappling, as though a handful of gold coins had been scattered as largesse about it, where the light falls, hot and bright, through the crowding leaves. The breeze gently pulls the loosestrife, leggy and etiolated, now left and now right. There are some tenuous pale pink blooms on the murderously trailing arms of the rambler roses. She fumbles for the rusty catch of the window and then pushes it outwards, letting the freshness invade the frowstiness of this dim, dank lair.

She can now hear voices but, because of that bloody tree, she cannot see the children from whom the voices, as sharp as knives newly honed, are coming. The knives slash at her. Children. . . . She frowns, still holding the edge of the curtain up with one hand, and begins to remember. Her dream. She was a child again, barefoot and in a grubby pinafore, and she was stooping among the bluebells, snatching at them with a ravenous greed for their unexpected brilliance. The sun rested like a warm palm on the back of her neck as it filtered down through trees. The bluebells are against her chest and in the crook of her arm and on the ground all around her. 'You silly girl! You shouldn't be picking those.' She hears the voice and tilts up her head in an effort to see more than a pair of legs and a walking-stick. Then she gives a little scream because a dog with a long body and long drooping ears is sniffing at her. 'She won't hurt you,' says another voice, this time a man's. It is kinder but it, too, carries with it a certain disdainful authority. Plus-fours, another walking-stick. 'But do leave those bluebells alone. If you pick them, they'll only die. If you leave them, all of us can enjoy them.' The bruised stalks tumble from her as she clambers to her feet. Her hands are green and sticky. 'There's a good little girl,' says the woman, who is dangling the leash of one of the dogs from her firm, competent hand. 'Isn't anyone with you? You shouldn't be all by yourself in the woods, should you?' The little girl squints up; she cannot see the face because the sun is in her eyes now, like a warm palm pressing on them. 'My bruvver . . .' she says vaguely, gesturing up the path. The two walkers, with their two dachshunds, pass on. . . .

A dream or a memory? Or both? She cannot be sure. The uncertainty of it disquietens her. She never had a brother.

Again she stares out, trying to penetrate that screen of leaves to see what is going on beyond it. The mystery of it tantalizes her. There is a glint, which she knows, from what she has seen in the winter, to be an oval-shaped pond, stocked with goldfish. There is a blur of grey which must be the flagged path. There is the red and white of the canvas chair on which the old geezer lazes away his afternoons when he has nothing else to occupy him. She wonders what the children are doing to make their voices so excited and shrill. Once, on a winter's afternoon, she caught them trying to throw the Siamese cat into the pond. She was glad when the cat scratched the cheek of the older boy. If that cat ever finds its way over the wall, as once it did, she knows what she is going to do to it.

She stares down now into the yard. Well yes, it would be nice to have something growing there other than that purple weed thing and those unpruned roses and those giant clumps of rhubarb. Now that spuds are so dear, they could have some of those. Carrots. Broccoli. Or geraniums. Geraniums would cheer things up. But she can understand why Dad and the boys don't want to put in any work on the yard. What would be the point with that bloody great tree sucking up all the goodness out of the ground and shading all the light from the sky? Below her, she can see the two Yamaha motor-bikes, each gleaming and glistening within its caul of plastic. Behind them lies the rusting carcass of a Norton Villiers. Lynton, director of a number of ailing and failing companies, would find a facile symbolism there. But that is beyond literal Mrs Sparks, who sees only two new motor-bikes and an old one.

She drops the net curtain and, leaving her husband to go on snoring under the mound of bedclothes, she makes her way downstairs. She puts on the kettle, having decided that she need not call the boys for another ten minutes (the boys are, in fact, men in their thirties), and then she wanders out in her bare feet into the yard. Her toes are oddly crumpled, the nails brown and horny. Suddenly she feels the tackiness under her soles; and when she pulls at a head of loosestrife, that too is tacky. Disgusting. The tackiness reminds her of something nasty but she prefers not to speculate what it might be.

'Children! Children! Breakfast!' One of the cool women, either the one with the blonde hair to the shoulders or the other with the dark hair piled up on top, is calling through the swelling heat of morning. 'Come along! At once!'

She would like to see which of the two cool women it is. She would like to see the children hurrying up the path from the pond. She would like to see if they are eating their breakfast on the terrace, if the *au pair* is waiting on them and if the old geezer is there too. She would like to see the garden, with its regular patterns of rose beds and, beyond them, its brilliant herbaceous border. But that fucking tree is always there. As she now confronts it, it is like some high, high wall; or like a net woven of green and dark-brown cords.

Beyond it is the mystery that it guards; the secret rites that she can never join.

Each day the tree seems to approach nearer and nearer to the house. One day, she knows (though her reason tells her that it is only a silly fancy), it will come so near that it will begin to push against the brickwork, slowly tilting the house backwards until the walls crack, the windows buckle and rain down their glass on to the loose-strife below them, the plaster starts to trickle like sawdust to the ground and, behind their own house, the house of old Mrs Emerson begins also to disintegrate. The tree presses harder. The tree is inexorable. The roof rises, like a hat plucked off by a gale, and then crashes downwards. There are fissures snaking up the walls of Mrs Emerson's kitchen. . . .

She shakes herself and smiles. Silly. What an idea! But as she still confronts the tree, she feels once again that it is somehow advancing forward. But this time it is pressing not against the shoddily built little house but against her own fat, unlovely, sixty-six-year-old body in its fluttering baby-doll nighty.

3

Two or three days later, as he lay out under the tree with a book, open but unread, propped on his stomach, Lynton heard from beyond the wall, the alley and the other wall, the sound of steel ringing out on stone and deep men's voices saying things that he was just too far away to catch. Still half-asleep, he thought: What are they doing? Digging a grave? That sound of steel ringing out on stone had reminded him of the burial of his wife in the Dorset churchyard where, for many generations, all his family had been put to dignified rest. He lay back and listened with a strange feeling of trepidation. He had experienced that same trepidation when, many years before, he had felt the first faint judder of an earthquake while holidaying on one of the Ionian islands.

Eventually he got up and, wading through the deep grass, he ascended the slope on which the tree stood. From there, the trunk firm against his back, he could see what he wanted over the wall, across the alley and over the other wall. It was those two sons, who would never even give him a sulky good morning unless he forced it from them, and who would never look at him unless he stared at them insistently. He had never discovered what work they did.

Sometimes singly and sometimes in pairs they would be absent for several days on end; and then they would again be hanging about their home for periods no less lengthy. When at home, they spent hours on end tinkering with their motor-bicycles. They seemed to have no other interest – though the Spanish *au pair* had once said (giggling, not really minding it at all) that they had been 'cheeky' to her when she had been walking past the house. Now each was stripped to the waist to reveal long, muscular arms, the skin Indian in its darkness, and no less dark chests, broad and with heavily defined pectoral muscles, on which the nipples stood out like pennies and the hair grew thick. Each had a beaked nose, predatory under a low forehead; each full, very red lips. They were digging at the garden, hurling their spades into the earth with a murderous ferocity. It was a long time before they realized that Lynton was watching them and then, without gazing at him, they muttered to each other.

Lynton called at last from the protection of the tree against which he was leaning:

'I see you've made a start on the garden.'

The two men looked up reluctantly, their spades poised. Again one muttered something to the other. Then one of them replied, 'That's right, squire. We thought it was time.'

'What are you going to do?'

'Well, the first thing's to get rid of all this.' An arm, glistening with sweat, indicated a pile of leaves, bruised grass and trailing stalks. 'Then level. Then lay the concrete.'

'You're going to concrete it all?'

'Yep.'

'All of it?'

'That's right, squire. Seemed the best thing.' Neither of the men had ever smiled at him before but now the speaker did, revealing brown, broken teeth behind those full, red lips. 'Nothing'll ever grow here right. Not with that tree of yours. So we decided to make things tidy.'

Suddenly Lynton was aware that Ma Sparks had come out from the kitchen and was standing, legs wide apart and arms on hips, on the top of the steps that led down into the garden. From their two eminences they surveyed each other, as the men resumed their work, with that din of hacking, chipping and scraping. Then she gave a seemingly jolly smile, raised an arm and waved to him. 'Morning, your lordship!'

He had never known her to be so pally to him.

24

4

All that stifling day, as his voice had echoed around him in a half-empty hall, as he had pretended interest in what he was being told over luncheon at the club by a boring American businessman, as he had shopped for a birthday present for one of his women and had gone round a gallery with another of them, he had thought of the tree. The chair would be out under it and the children would be away, staying with a grandmother. It would be cool and silent there and Concepcion, dear little Concepcion, heaving her inexplicable sighs, would bring him a glass of iced China tea with a slice of lemon in it, just as he liked it. He would read that book of political memoirs; or he would do the *Times* crossword; or, better still, he would do nothing at all.

At first, it was all as he had promised himself. The air was fresh and faintly perfumed under the spreading branches; Concepcion hardly spoke, since she knew that, when he was tired, he preferred to be left in silence; and the Earl Grey tea was deliciously chill and astringent on his tongue. The book and *The Times* lay in the grass beside him; perhaps later he would pick up one or the other but not now, not now.

He lay back, the half-empty glass icy in his grasp, and stared up through that pulsating tunnel of green to the eggshell blue of the sky beyond it. Peace. Perfect peace. But then he saw the brown, like rust graining the sides of that tunnel here and there. Leaves dying or dead. Curled up. Brittle, juiceless, lifeless. Christ! He jumped up from the chair and hurried into the house, still clutching the glass of tea.

5

The man called himself a 'tree surgeon' and he was recommended by one of Lynton's friends, a professor of forestry. He was not a very impressive man, timid and inarticulate, with small womanish hands and a pear-shaped body; but the professor, whom Lynton trusted, had said that there was no one better.

'Well, there's certainly something wrong.' Which seemed obvious. 'What do you think it is?'

A shake of the head, a blinking of the eyes. The lashes of the eyes were short and thick and sandy. 'We've had a very dry summer. Haven't we?'

'Yes, we have.' Which also seemed obvious.

'I'd recommend soaking the roots. For several hours each day for a start. And I'll give some nutrient.'

'Nutrient?'

'I've got it with me.'

'But you've no idea otherwise. . . .?'

Again the short, thick, sandy eyelashes blinked. 'Limes are usually immune to disease. Not like elms. I can see no indication of any kind of disease. The tree looks healthy. Very healthy. Except for that dying-off of branches here and there.' He fell silent. He did not often say so much at one go.

Lynton stared up into the beautiful, ravaged tree, 'You don't think . . .' The tree surgeon, who was getting something out of his canvas rucksack, looked up in enquiry. 'You don't think that the tree could have been, well, poisoned?' He lowered his voice to ask this question since he had no wish for old Ma Sparks or one of her menfolk to hear him.

'*Poisoned?*'

Lynton put a forefinger to his lips, since the man had said the word quite loud. Then he indicated the house the other side of the alley and, in a whisper, told the story. 'I suspected something when I saw them digging up the garden. After all, that would have made it easy for them to get at the roots. The roots must reach that far, mustn't they? They could have dug during the day and then have put down the poison – weedkiller or whatever it was – during the night. Easy.'

The man was looking oddly at him, almost as though he suspected some paranoiac fantasy. But of course he did not know that evil old woman and her brood. 'Well, it's possible,' he agreed at last grudgingly, hitching at the trousers that rested low on his childbearing hips. 'But I shouldn't have thought. . . . There's no way of telling.' He stooped now and began to fumble in his canvas rucksack. 'Have you got some steps?'

'Steps?'

'I have to get up high on the trunk. The nutrient.'

'Oh yes. The nutrient.'

Lynton began to call for Concepcion. (That morning the Spanish girl had said that she was sure that Ma Sparks was a witch and that she had put some kind of spell on the tree.)

26

The tree surgeon climbed up the ladder and hammered into the trunk a number of small aluminium pipes that each had a plastic phial attached to the end of it. 'If anything will do the job, those will.' The tree no longer looked beautiful, its trunk stuck with those plastic phials and its branches drooping and withering here and there.

As he looked up at it, Lynton experienced exactly the same desolation and despair that had overwhelmed him when his wife had gone into the London clinic for the first and least cruel of her operations.

6

Mrs Sparks has been standing for a long time at the bedroom window, the net curtain raised in a swollen hand and her body bent low to peer out from under it, so that her back has grown stiff and aches. 'Come away from there!' Mr Sparks has told her from time to time. Once or twice he has joined her for a few seconds of her vigil, sucking ruminatively on his false teeth in a way that always gets on her nerves. But now he has put on his stained and battered trilby hat and tottered off to the pub where shortly, sweaty and grubby, the two tree fellers will also be calling in for a jar. Mrs Sparks's 'boys' are away on a job. She has heard from old Mrs Emerson, who heard from the lady who does for the big house, that the old geezer is away in America. He gave orders for the tree to be cut down while he was abroad.

It is thrilling to hear the mechanical saw rip through the branches and to see them tumbling downwards. At a safe distance, the three children, the two pallid boys and the plump girl, are standing watching. The Siamese is stalking up and down before them, her ears cocked and her tail erect, as though indignant at the destruction of the tree beneath which she has so often skulked in the long grass in ambush for birds. It is thrilling to feel the light grow brighter and the air grow warmer as yet another limb is amputated and falls away. She suggested to the old geezer that the 'boys' might do the job for him; but he answered coldly, in his most la-di-da manner, that he thought that it would be better if he got 'professionals' in. The 'boys' could have made a good thing out of it, getting paid for the work and then selling the wood. Mrs Sparks wonders if the old geezer has ever suspected how the tree died. But she does not really care. No one can prove anything. After all, people can spill what they like in their own yards.

That younger of the two men is not bad looking. Golden hair on his chest just like Dad's all those years and years ago. Nice, long golden hair on his head. Nice narrow waist. Briefly she is lost in an erotic reverie, in which she is somehow the tree up which the man is shinning, its branches her arms and legs, its leaves her toes and fingers. Nice.

'Come away from there! Don't stand so close!' It is one of the cool women, the one with the dark hair piled on top, emerging from the house, a hand raised to shield her eyes.

'They're all right there, ma'am. Nothing to worry about.' Mrs Sparks now despises the man over whom she has just been gloating; she does not like that note of deference in his voice.

Another branch crashes downwards and the youngest of the children, the little boy, gives a squeal of excitement.

There are two cool women now, walking together down the path. Mrs Sparks hears, or thinks she hears, one say to the other, 'It's so sad. He loved that tree. So terribly sad'; and the other answers, 'I'm glad he's not here to see it. He must have planned it this way.' Mrs Sparks finds that thrilling, too. It gives her a feeling of power, such as she has never had before in her life. She has not only caused that giant of a tree to be razed to the ground but she has driven a famous lord across the Atlantic.

The tree is now little more than a pole, smooth and straight, with some tufts of leaves sticking out from it here and there to break that smoothness and straightness. The room, usually so chilly even on the hottest days, now seems full of scorching air. Her cheeks are burning, as are her bare arms and her forehead. She leans far out, no longer caring if they see her, the ledge of the window pressing into her flabby belly. The men have placed that savage saw of theirs against the trunk. This will be the end.

The teeth gnash deep and deeper, spitting out sawdust in all directions. The three children and the two women watch, bemused into silence. There is sweat gleaming along the spine of the man stooped to the saw beneath her. For a moment she has another erotic reverie of her lips brushing away that sweat. The teeth grind and champ. The grass all about the tree is thick with the yellow sawdust. Her heart is beating uncomfortably fast and she feels a curious pressure in her forehead, just at the point where the jet eyebrows meet each other over the short, blunt nose. There is a strange guttural yell from one of the men, as though he were exploding at a climax of pleasure or agony. There is a crackling, tearing sound and then what is left of the tree veers over, slowly, slowly, slowly, and crashes into the grass.

'That's it,' one of the women says.

'Yes, I'm glad he didn't see it,' says the other.

Bored now, the children are already moving off, followed by the cat.

One of the men says, 'Phew! It's hot!', wiping his forehead on his forearm. The other straightens. 'Let's go round to the pub for a pint.' He turns to the two women: 'We'll be back to clear all this up.' But the two women appear not to hear him. They, too, are now making their way, arms linked, back to the house.

Soon Mrs Sparks is all alone at the window, looking out to the place where the tree once stood. The sun bounces in sharp splinters off the new-laid concrete of the yard. There are two tubs in it now, in addition to the two Japanese motor-bikes and the carcass of the English motor-bike, and one day, when she has time to get round to it, she will put some geraniums or perhaps two hydrangeas in them. Everything seems strangely open and strangely glaring. (A small girl in the bluebell wood lifts up a stone and worms wriggle convulsively away from the light, insects scuttle and scrabble in all directions.) She has a sense of falling, because the tree is no longer there to prop her up. She has a sense of the house itself falling, that green retaining wall suddenly removed from it.

She can see the whole garden now, surveying it from end to end: the symmetrical pattern of the rose beds; the pond, with the water lilies floating their fleshy discs upon it; the flagged path; the brilliant herbaceous border; the terrace with its white tables and chairs and its blue-and-white striped awning; even the old house itself. But it now all looks so small; and there is no longer any mystery in it. It might be her own house, her own yard.

She still feels triumphant over what she has achieved; but there is an undertow of disappointment, regret, sadness, fear. Yes, most of all she is afraid.

'Well, that certainly makes a difference,' Mr Sparks grunts, as he breathes the fumes of several pints over her at the window.

'Yes, it makes a difference,' she agrees. But she is still not quite sure what kind of difference it is and whether she really wants it or not.

1972

The Mouse

Vernon Thurible loved his wife, Stella, as much as their daughter, Mavis, loved the white mouse which they gave her for her seventh birthday. Mavis had herself asked for the mouse, insisting that it was one mouse only, and not a pair, that she wanted: 'It won't be lonely,' she said, 'because, you see, it will always have me for its friend. I don't want it to have other friends,' she added. Vernon and Stella thought this explanation charming, and they repeated it widely in their Blackheath circle. They both adored their child.

On the day when they bought the mouse in the pet department of a large London store, they had one of their many quarrels; and, as usual, money was the cause. For a man who affected to despise money, Vernon spent an inordinate amount of time thinking how he could make it, or make his wife borrow it. It was when they came to pay for the mouse (it was handed to them in a small wicker cage which was wrapped in brown paper) that Vernon had to face the disagreeable discovery that Stella had nothing but a single ten-shilling note in her bag; so that, as they walked to the underground, he spent the time either chiding her for having spent so much that week or urging her to ask her mother for more. Vernon despised Stella's relatives, who were in business, while his were in trade. 'You were always talking about your rich uncles and aunts before we got married. But now, when it's a question either of keeping your pride or of letting your child starve, you prefer to keep your pride.'

'You know it's not that, Vernon darling.' Stella, who was small and thin, with a delicate pink and white colouring and prettily weak features, slipped her arm through her husband's. 'But it's so awful to have to ask and ask and ask. And we still owe Mummy that fifty pounds we borrowed last year.'

'If she'd had any generosity, she'd have made it a gift. She's supposed to be so fond of Mavis, isn't she? And yet if it comes to helping us over a bad patch, she won't lift a finger.' The life of the Thuribles was made up of 'bad patches'.

So Vernon continued to nag; but the curious thing was that, as he did so, his voice was never anything but friendly and reasonable, and his intelligent, humorously vivid face never ceased to smile. But for Stella's look of distress any passer-by would have assumed that they were at that moment on the best of terms.

The Thuribles were now standing on the platform, and Vernon was saying: 'Oh, I'm sick of this endless living from hand to mouth. No wonder I can't write music, when I have to worry about money day after day after day. Little did I guess what a millstone I was putting round my neck that evening I proposed to you.' When he saw the tears in Stella's eyes, he gave a good-natured laugh, to show that he was joking: no one could say that Vernon was lacking in a sense of humour. 'How wonderful it would be to have my freedom again! Do you remember how you used to say that two could live as cheaply as one? You've never been much good at addition, have you?' He swung the cage back and forth, apparently forgetful of the terrified animal that was being rolled from side to side with feebly convulsive claws that scratched on the wicker. 'Really, one day I think I shall have to get rid of you.' Stella, head lowered, was blinking away the tears with her long, flaxen eye-lashes. He came up behind her: 'Just one push' – his hands were on her shoulders – 'gently – like this.' His green eyes were flashing with merriment, and as he spoke he laughed; but Stella (who tended, as Vernon often said, to hysteria) wrenched herself free and shot through the tunnel to the opposite platform from which trains went north, instead of south. There was a train just leaving, and she was able to squeeze herself in before the doors closed on Vernon's outraged face.

At the next stop, Stella got out, and caught the bus to Blackbeath; and there at the bus stop, waiting as if she had told him how she would come, Vernon was standing, with the mouse's cage still in his hand. Stella laughed as she climbed off the bus and Vernon laughed too, putting an arm round her shoulder.

Mavis was delighted with her present, and next day, at her birthday party, she amused her seven little friends by taking the mouse out of its cage and making it run up and down the sofa by prodding it with a pencil. But when a little boy attempted to prod it with his own stubby finger, she gave him a kick. She was devoted to her mouse, and wouldn't have anyone else tease it. At tea she fed it on cake crumbs and made it say 'Thank you' by pinching it between her thumb and her forefinger. She was a child with all her father's looks and good humour.

The mothers who were present were charmed by Vernon and decided that any talk of noisy quarrels or even of 'differences' must have been malicious gossip. They noticed, in particular, how lovingly Vernon stroked Stella's ash-blonde hair as he perched on the arm of the sofa beside her, and they agreed that any man who could dress so elegantly and offer them glasses of sherry at six o'clock, could not really be as badly off as their husbands maintained.

But the day after this successful tea party Vernon felt ill; he always said that the mere thought of money made him feel ill, and perhaps it was indeed this that sent him to his bed with a couple of aspirins. It was, as he pointed out to Stella, particularly unfortunate that he should be indisposed at this moment, as a music publisher had sent him a book for which an index had to be prepared by the end of the week. 'He'll never send me anything again.' Vernon groaned, and added: 'Oh, do draw those curtains. The light hurts my eyes.'

'Couldn't I do it for you?'

'The index? You, darling?' He gripped her small hand in his own large one; one would have thought that with a single squeeze he would be able to crush those fragile fingers. But Vernon was always gentle. 'How can you? You know you hate that sort of thing.'

'But we do need the money, don't we?'

'Oh, the money!' He sighed deeply and covered his face with his hands. 'Yes, we certainly need that.'

'Then don't worry. I'll do what I can with the index.'

Mavis had come in during this conversation and had thrown herself on the bed; the mouse was inside the sleeve of her cardigan and from time to time she peered down to see if all went well.

'You are angelic, darling. I don't know what I would do without you.'

But really, Vernon decided, as Stella came back and back to him with her fatuous, uncomprehending questions about the index, it would have been far simpler to do it oneself. Mavis was playing on the floor of the bedroom, and he liked to lie and watch her, as she urged the mouse up and down a staircase she had made for it out of matchboxes; but how could he be at peace and get well if Stella kept coming in to ask what should be included in the index and what left out? Not that he wanted to hurt her feelings – in fact, when she began to cry because he pointed out to her (in an entirely friendly manner, of course) that he had already explained the same point to her at least three times, he at once pulled her down on to the bed and began to kiss her neck. But, oh, he did so wish that he had married a woman of some intelligence! . . . However, she *did* persevere, there was no doubt of that; so that somehow, by staying up late for a week, she managed to complete the work, and cash a cheque for fifteen pounds with which Vernon was able to buy, among other things, the claret which the doctor had recommended so strongly for his health.

Meanwhile, by the end of that same week, Mavis had taught her mouse to scuttle up and down the matchboxes, for the reward of a piece of cheese rind. 'He's really awfully clever,' she said to her father. 'I think I could teach him anything.'

But still they needed money; soon the publisher's fifteen pounds had been spent on what Vernon would call 'the bare necessities of life' and inexplicably none of Stella's relatives would help them with a loan. Even Stella's mother, usually so generous, would do no more than treat Stella and Mavis to tea at Harrods and buy Mavis a new cage, of silver wire, for her mouse. Vernon was in despair. How could he write music? he would demand. Oh, he was sick of this life. For four years he had laboured at his symphony and now, for lack of bread, he would never get it finished. He would have to take a job. But of course, he hastened to add kindly, he didn't blame Stella.

Fortunately, however, his symphony was saved by the arrival in the flat below of a retired prep-schoolmaster. This man, who had suffered a slight stroke after his wife's death, needed someone to help with his cooking and cleaning, and Vernon put it to Stella that it would be an act of charity to help the poor old boy in his hour of distress. Stella received, of course, a token payment; for the man was not poor, and as Vernon pointed out, 'He'd probably much rather keep his independence. One must think of such things.'

The arrangement was not, however, wholly satisfactory. Often when Vernon needed Stella to copy music for him, to run an errand or to make him a cup of tea, she would be downstairs. He began to feel that the old man imposed on her; and it was no use Stella saying that he was really most kind and paid her extra if she stayed for more than the hour, for Vernon would only answer: 'You are a sweet-natured little thing. Anyone can get the better of you.'

Mr Errin (for that was his name) also had a dog, of indeterminate breed and sex, which was so old that it spent its whole day stretched out asleep on one of the flower-beds of the garden which was shared by the two flats; the poor creature appeared to like the warm moisture of the earth. Vernon himself did not work in the garden – it brought on his fibrositis – but Stella did, and it upset him to see the dog crush the flowers which she had planted with so much care. More than once he had to complain (of course in his usual friendly fashion) to old Mr Errin. Mavis also disliked the dog, being afraid it would eat her mouse; though on the rare occasions when, by accident, the animals came face to face, they appeared to feel nothing but a mild curiosity towards each other.

'Do you really *like* the old chap?' Vernon asked Stella.

'Yes, of course, I do. He's awfully sweet and kind. . . . By the way, he said he would lend us that twenty pounds for the rent.'

'You didn't ask him, did you?' Vernon said, horrified.

'Well – yes . . . I did.'

'Have you no pride?'

'But I thought . . . you said . . . As we were going to be turned out of the flat if we couldn't pay.'

Vernon ran his fingers through Stella's luxuriant hair: 'Silly!' he said. 'No one minds borrowing off relations. That's what relations are for. But from someone we hardly know –'

'Oh, Mr Errin's a real friend,' Stella protested. She saw the smile fade from her husband's face, and she added with a note of fearfulness in her voice: 'Isn't he?' Vernon's fingers tightened in her hair, so that it felt as if an electric current were shooting among the roots.

A week later Vernon was going to have lunch with a publisher; he was already late, as he had had to talk to Mavis severely about not teasing her mouse (she loved it, of course, and didn't mean to hurt it; but he couldn't bear to see her pulling it along by its tail, or pinching it between her fingers until it emitted its shrill, frightened squeaks)

34

and now he found that a button was missing from the suit he wanted to wear. It was a suit barely three months old and he felt angry with the Savile Row tailors who had made it for him, and even more angry with Stella for not having noticed that the button needed sewing, when she put the suit away for him. 'Stella, old thing!' he had shouted amiably. But Stella was not in the flat.

He looked at his watch and saw that it was ten past twelve; Stella was supposed to finish her work for Mr Errin at twelve o'clock precisely. So he went down in his dressing-gown and rang at their neighbour's bell. 'Oh, Mr Thurible!' Mr Errin exclaimed. 'Do come in, won't you? Stella – your wife' – as Mr Errin corrected himself, he blushed like a schoolboy – 'that is – we are just drinking a cup of coffee together. Won't you come in and join us?'

Vernon gave his frank and charming smile. 'It's awfully decent of you, but I'm afraid it'll have to be another time. I'm dashing out to meet my publisher, and the button has come off my one and only suit. I don't want to hurry Stella, but if she *could* sew it on for me –'

'But of course, darling!' Stella had overheard the conversation and now rushed out of the sitting-room, in an overall and with her hair bound up in a scarf. 'I'm so sorry. I couldn't have noticed when I put it away.'

The Thuribles both thanked Mr Errin for his offer of the coffee and apologized for leaving so hurriedly. Vernon put his arm round Stella's waist and squeezed her as they went upstairs. but (no doubt from the haste with which he had dressed) he was trembling from head to foot.

'You look just like a little charwoman,' he teased.

'Do I, darling?'

'Which, of course, is what you are now!' They both laughed together.

When they had shut the door of their flat, Vernon said, 'I'm going to be at least half an hour late. I'd better call the whole thing off. It'll look better than keeping him waiting all that time.'

'Oh, darling!' Stella looked at him in horror. 'But I thought you were hoping to persuade him to give you an advance.'

'Well, I shall have to persuade him to do that some other time. It'll take you at least five minutes to sew on that button. You're not exactly a needlewoman, are you, poor dear?' He kissed her on the forehead.

'Couldn't – couldn't you wear another suit?' Stella suggested timidly.

'You talk as if I had a dozen to choose from.'

'Well, you have got the grey flannel –'

'*Light* grey flannel at the Athenaeum!' He laughed indulgently. 'And I can't wear the blue, it needs pressing. You remember I asked you to take it –'

'Oh, dear!' She remembered, appalled. 'I've been so busy.'

'Yes, I know. That's why I really think you'd better stop working for Mr Errin. I've noticed that you've been looking awfully run down and seedy just these last few days, and obviously the whole thing is becoming far too much for you.'

'But I *enjoy* going,' Stella protested; and at once, from the tightening of Vernon's mouth, she noticed her mistake.

'Oh, I've no doubt you do. But that doesn't alter the fact that you can't hope to run two households at one and the same time. However much you *enjoy it*.' He gave the last two words the faintest and most subtle of emphases. 'I don't like to think of Mavis being neglected – and particularly neglected for an old bore like Errin. He'll have to find himself a daily woman.'

'But I don't look on him as an employer, he's a –' she broke off.

'Yes, my dear?' She was silent. 'Well, what is he?' Stella made no answer; her large blue eyes were filling with tears. Vernon once more put his arm round her: 'Anyway we can discuss all this later – when we're a little calmer, eh?' He gave the smile which the wives of their little circle found so irresistible. 'The immediate problem is this damned lunch party. Would you ring up the old man and tell him that I've got another of my migraines? I expect he's still at his office – otherwise leave a message at the Athenaeum.'

'Oh Vernon! Couldn't you possibly – if you take a taxi –?'

'Look, my sweet, do let me decide what I should, or should not do.' He picked up the telephone receiver and handed it to her, himself dialling the number. Stella, who had been well rehearsed in such falsehoods, told his lie for him in the tone of worried innocence which she usually adopted on such occasions. Then she put back the receiver and burst into tears.

'Now what's the matter?' Vernon asked, surprised.

Stella sobbed loudly, making strange gulping noises in the back of her throat. 'Oh, for God's sake!' Vernon said rather than shouted. 'Darling!' Now he was putting his arm again about her. 'What on earth is the matter?'

'Oh, I'm so hopeless – so useless –! I know it's all my fault.'

'It's just your kindness,' Vernon said. 'That's all it is, darling – that excessive kindness of yours. I know it's simply that you feel sorry for Mr Errin, and that of *course* there's nothing else – on your side, at least. Oh, darling – please!' Stella was now howling. 'Darling! For God's sake, be quiet! You know that I hate scenes.'

At last he picked up the latest number of the *Connoisseur* from his bureau and decided to go to the garden; one's nerves could stand just so much, and then no more. 'Darling!' he remonstrated once again as he passed out of the door. But Stella either did not, or would not, hear him. Really, she was so emotional, he told himself, as he took the stairs in twos. And a scene like this quite ruined one's appetite for lunch – apart from making it impossible for one to work.

But in the garden there was no peace either. Mavis was sobbing hysterically and battering some object, again and again, with a stone from the rock garden. Vernon went across: 'What on earth are you doing?'

Mavis continued to beat the stone wildly on the earth while the old dog, his mangy head raised, blinked glassy eyes at her from the neighbouring flower-bed.

'My God! It's – it's your mouse,' Vernon said.

'I told it – and told it – and told it,' Mavis cried between each stroke. 'I said it was not to go near the dog.' Her hair was falling about her face, and there was blood on her pinafore. Then suddenly she looked up at Vernon with a glance so cold and so penetrating that he found that he could not hold it.

'Where's Mummy?' she asked.

1951

Appetites

To the high, gleaming catafalque at one end of the ward they all bore their offerings. Come my treasure, my little doll, my little bird, eat, eat, *eat*. That was Aunt Sotiria, who was not really an aunt but a distant cousin, the arthritic joints of her fingers swollen as though from the constriction of her many knobbly rings, stooping over Maria and pleading. But I made these *dolmadakia* myself, try one, just a single bite, a single little bite. The *dolmadakia*, as lumpy as her fingers, lay piled one on top of the other in a grey plastic box filched from the disordered kitchen of one of the many disordered women, wives of television producers, journalists or publishers, for whom she cleaned and cooked in Camden Town. She tilted the box and an emerald slime, collecting in a corner, glittered evilly. Eat, eat, eat.

Uncle Kostas, who was not really an uncle but also a distant cousin, related to Aunt Sotiria by a nexus of relationships as tenuous and tough as a spider's web, suggested all the delicacies that he thought might coax Maria's appetite. *Taramasalata*, just a little of it, spread on a cracker? A salt herring, a salt herring was the best cure for nausea, he knew that from his days, oh many years ago, on the Athens–Crete run. Or how about some liver, thinly sliced and fried for a few seconds in the finest olive oil? There was nothing easier for the stomach to digest than liver. Now the two of them, the aunt and the uncle who were really only distant cousins, each leant over Maria, their faces vaguely affronted and uncomprehending at her lack of all response.

Soon Takis, another cousin, who was studying mechanical engineering at the North London Polytechnic, joined them with his English girl-friend, Sue. At first Sue remained indifferent, huddled into a coat of simulated fur which, hands deep in pockets, she kept wrapped tightly around her plump body as though she were hugging herself in self-congratulation at having such a healthy appetite. Come my treasure, my little doll, my little bird, eat, eat, *eat*. Takis used the same words but gave them a slightly hectoring edge. He had brought a round wooden box of *loukoumia*, with a little wooden fork that he jabbed into the gelatinous, pink-powdered cube that seemed largest to him. Come, come. He was a handsome boy, with a high-bridged nose and thick, arched eyebrows above it. He smelled of Greek cigarettes, pungent as burning hay, and of the hair oil, sweetly sickly, that gleamed in a line on his forehead where the black, curly hair sprang upwards. He held out the cube on its fork and fragments of pinkish sugar drifted down, a sunset snowfall, on to the pillow. Sue roused herself, her protuberant, previously vacant eyes focusing themselves on the catafalque. You must eat, you know. You have to force yourself. Once you've started again, you'll find it easier and easier. That was how the nurses also spoke to Maria. They felt sorry for her, one couldn't help feeling sorry for her, so fragile and so pretty and so undemanding, but they also felt exasperated. There was even a Nigerian nurse, with a high bosom like a bolster, who told her that among her people there were children who starved not by choice but because there was no food for them. Sue got up and approached the catafalque. I'm not surprised that that turkish delight turns her off. What she needs is some fruit. Grapes. Or a banana. Or a nice crisp Cox's. She was now speaking as though the girl on the catafalque could either not hear her or not understand her. But Takis again extended the gelatinous pink cube and again the sunset snowfall drifted downwards.

Widowed Kyria Papadopoulou arrived, her wide-hipped, deep-bosomed body balanced miraculously on the slimmest of legs, the most fragile of ankles, the highest of heels. She owned the City restaurant at which Maria had been working. Her son, whom she henpecked as she had once henpecked his father, served as her chef. I've brought you a chicken wing, I know you like chicken as my Petros does it. The skin is all crisp, see, and there's just the faintest flavour of *rigani*. Come my treasure, my little doll, my little bird,

eat, eat, *eat*. She tore at the chicken with long, red-lacquered fingernails and held out a sliver. Come, come, *come*! Then, rejected, she
turned away with a shrug of plump shoulders under her coat of real,
not simulated, fur. What's the matter with the child? What's one to
do? She too spoke as though the girl on the catafalque could either
not hear her or not understand her.

Eventually they all forgot the girl, the reason for their visit, and,
ranged in a semicircle about the catafalque, started themselves to
devour the food they had brought.

Kyria Papadopoulou, please try these home-made *dolmadakia*. I
am sure you have better in your famous restaurant but please try
one, please.

Some chicken, Sue? Try some of Kyria Papadopoulou's chicken.
I bet you've never eaten anything like it.

What would really tempt me is just the teeniest bit of that turkish
delight. I don't usually like it. My figure. But. (A gelatinous fragment glued itself to one of Sue's front teeth, softly pink on its
enamelled hardness.)

I was saying a salt herring. *Taramasalata*.

Fried liver.

Well, just another teeniest, weeniest piece.

Plenty of chicken here.

The girl on the catafalque stared motionless up at the ceiling.
Soon a sister trotted up, like a mettlesome, broad-beamed pony. I
really must ask you. Too much noise here. Disturbing the other
patients. Some of them very sick. Shouldn't really be so many of
you. Only two at a time.

When at last all of them had gone (I'll leave the *loukoumia* here, you
may be tempted later), it seemed only a few moments before the
Nigerian nurse rattled up with a tray. Now then, dear, you won't
have any difficulty in getting this lot down. She peered enviously
into the still open, round wooden box. Fancy bringing you sweets
like that. Silly. (In her flat, beyond the Archway, her mother was
minding her infant son; that turkish delight would be just the present for them.) There's simple broth here, can't upset you, and a
macaroni cheese and a nice milk pudding. But Maria turned her
head away, with a gasp and a little groan. The Nigerian nurse
banged down the tray (Well, please yourself, she thought but did not
say) and hurried off to attend to another patient. She hadn't got all
day, take it or leave it, she wasn't going to be late off duty yet again.

By now the restaurant would have started to fill. I could do with a real good blow-out. Well, you'll get that here. There's not much finesse in the way things are served but for value for money. Sweat on flushed foreheads. Saliva in the rubbery folds of mouths. Phew! Teeth tear at the leg of a duck, grease dribbling down a chin. Glutinous rice is piled on to a fork. A roll bears a smear of lipstick as though it were blood. Maria! I say, Maria! A fist like a ham splashes greenish oil from a cracked bottle on to a heap of plump courgettes. Some more of this vino, Maria. To your very good health. Poured gurgling from dusty demijohns into carafes that look like hospital bottles, the wine (red to the English customers, black to Maria) seems to clot on the tongue, its first sweetness sharpening to acid. Maria, be an angel, some more butter! In this heat the yellow trails of butter on the dish are deliquescent. A fork whirls a fragment of bread round and round in a pungent orange sauce. A mouth opens, closes, masticates with grunts and snorts. An American woman's voice, metallic and high: If I eat another morsel, I'll just throw up! Truly I will. Nonsense! You must try these profiteroles. Speciality of the *maison*. Out of this world. Fabulous. Maria! Maria my sweet! Where are you? *Parakalo!* (On a previous visit he had asked her how to say 'please' in Greek.) In the kitchen Petros puts a finger into the mayonnaise, takes it out, licks it. Too much vinegar, he scolds an underling. I've told you before. The underling ladles the mayonnaise out over some cold fish, indifferent to the criticism. Maria!

The girl on the catafalque still lay out motionless. Not eating, love? It was the woman on her right, shapeless and friendless, who habitually devoured Maria's food as well as her own, as though by sating the monster greedily and mortally at work within her, she could somehow appease it and lull it to sleep. Maria did not answer and the woman crept out of bed, a famished and furtive cat, and quickly exchanged her empty tray for the girl's full one. Waste not, want not. She had fed five children (two dead now) first from the breast and then from the meagre sums doled out to her by a drunkard husband. Now she fed herself with the same desperate, obsessive persistence.

Maria closed her eyes, open so long on the bare, white ceiling.

. . . Now she is back in her native Cyprus, in the village that no longer exists, minding the sheep that no longer exist on some rocky hillside or in some barren ravine. The sheep are thin, she is thin. The year has been a bad one, first ruinous storms, then a summer-long drought. She is hungry, she is often hungry, but she puts off the moment when she will unwrap the piece of newspaper that lies at the bottom of the tasselled bag slung over her shoulder. Not yet. No, not yet. She can hold out another ten minutes, fifteen minutes, half an hour. The bread is hard and coarse; she might be chewing on some friable excrescence plucked from the rocks sticking up all around her. The *feta* cheese might not be cheese at all but a slab of chalk as it crumbles in her mouth. Both are miraculously clean and astringent. She bites into a pear, her strong white teeth crunching on its strong white flesh. Juice trickles down her chin and on to the palm of her hand, following the dirt-seamed cracks. She bites again. The pear is gravid with the thick, musky summer air. She gets up, wiping her hands down on the coarse black folds of her skirt, and begins to leap downwards from rock to rock, the sheep baaing and blathering around her. There is a spring at the bottom of the ravine, oozing out from a dark jagged mouth with a beard of emerald moss. The water is ice-cold and clear. Clean. She cups it in her hands, lowers her head, gulps. The water tingles on her tongue and behind her nose. It seems to tingle in her brain, clearing spaces there until it seems as light as an empty honeycomb.

Cocoa, dear? The nurse who now approached the catafalque had recently begun to resent Maria after some days of feeling affectionate and protective towards her. She won't respond, I hate patients who will simply make no effort. She was a nurse who took each death as a personal affront to her; who bored her flatmates by bringing the hospital, with its stinks, agonies and bereavements, into their own heedless, happy-go-lucky lives; who ordered her patients 'Now recover!' and expected them to obey her.

Maria gulped, turned aside her head.

No?

No.

The psychiatrist, a dumpy middle-aged woman with stumpy fingers, wearing a leather jacket that had the sheen of pork crackling to it and a woollen skirt of the texture and colour of curdled milk, sat down, lumpy legs wide apart, beside the catafalque. Her eyes, palest of blue irises surrounded by a liverish yellow that looked like mutton fat, brooded on the girl. What to say?

Any better, dear?

Haven't you been able to force yourself to eat even the smallest bite?

The Viennese accent reminded Maria of the cake shop in Golders Green to which the Swedish boy, met at the language school, used to take her. There were éclairs that oozed a pus-like custard, chocolate cakes of a glistening blackness that suggested, suggested. . . . Better not to think of them.

Is something on your mind?

Repeat that: Maria, is something on your mind? Try to answer me, dear.

A shake of the head.

Homesick?

Shake.

Lovesick?

Shake.

Life-sick?

Shake.

The psychiatrist's stomach rumbled mournfully, a tube train shuddering deep in the bowels of the earth. It had been a long day and she looked forward to sitting down with her friend to a pot of tea, scrambled eggs on toast, Danish pastries, the telly. She might stop by at the deli and buy some smoked salmon as a treat. Be extravagant. One had to spoil oneself now and then.

You do awfully little to help yourself, you know, my dear.

It was not what a psychiatrist was supposed to say; but after a long day, when she was hungry and felt the first premonitory throb of a headache, the words came unbidden.

No one can help you if you don't help yourself. (Kyria Papadopoulou had told Maria, when she had first come to work in the restaurant: Now, Maria, whenever you feel you want to eat something, just help yourself. Kyria Papadopoulou had been kind.) That's the lesson we all have to learn.

But Maria was beyond learning lessons.

The psychiatrist got to her feet, tugging down that shapeless skirt the colour and texture of curdled milk and buttoning up that leather jacket that had the sheen of pork crackling. Well, dear, I'll come by again tomorrow. And before that I want you to do something for me. Will you do something for me? Maria?

Maria stared at the ceiling, which was as hard and smooth as the icing of one of Petro's wedding cakes.

Maria?

No answer.

I want you to do something for me. A favour. A special, a very special favour.

43

Eat.
EAT.

Motionless on the catafalque in the darkened ward, her neighbour grunting and snoring and sometimes emitting a strange, whinnying cry beside her, Maria dreamed.

There are huge, shark-like mouths, the teeth murderously serrated, and the saliva loops down from them in shiny ropes. The teeth masticate with a crackling and crunching. Blood spurts, arrow-heads of bone fly out in all directions. Marrow squelches. Sounds of gulping, slurping, choking, eructation. Maria, bring me. Bring me. More. Another. A plate of. A bottle of. Do you call this a helping? A long tongue unrolls itself around a finger smeared with a mud-like chocolate. A toothpick probes a gigantic molar in which a sliver of chicken nestles, a glistening mollusc in its shell. Bite. Chew. Swallow. Belch.

Oh, no, I can't, can't, can't!

The night nurse, a little Filipino with wide, startled eyes, hurried out.

What's the matter?

Oh, no, no, no!

The neighbour stirred from a dream of a delicious pork pie. Fancy waking everyone in the ward. Does it night after night. Ought to be in a loony bin.

Now, Maria, swallow this pill.

Swallow.

NO!

They gave up trying to wheedle, coax and bully. There were tubes of plastic and rubber, coiled like intestines. There were syringes that looked like the implements used by Petros to ice his cakes. Maria threw herself about, the hands that first gently restrained her growing impatient and brutal. She wailed in protest. She thrashed like a landed fish. That'll tranquillize her. There was sweat on the doctor's forehead, glistening like that sickly-sweet hair oil on Takis's. He might have been a diner at the restaurant, overheated with too much food and drink. Stupid cow, he muttered. It was not what a doctor, even one so young, was supposed to say. But he had been to a party the night before, he had quarrelled with his girl-friend, each time that he exerted himself, it was as though a mallet were thumping down on the back of his head. The Nigerian nurse's arms were more muscular than his. If you'd be sensible and eat, you'd save yourself and us a lot of trouble. The needle homed deep.

But just as her mouth and her teeth and her tongue and her throat and her stomach rebelled, so now even the cells of her ever-diminishing, ever-dwindling body rebelled and refused inexplicably to feed on what the young, sweating, red-faced doctor and his assistants gave them. I dunno. Can't understand it. No response. Weird. The grey, world-weary consultant did not know either; but he was able to find some elaborate scientific synonyms for his ignorance.

Even when she weighed less than five stone and was so light that the Nigerian nurse could have rocked her in her brawny arms as she rocked her infant son, Maria's beauty, so far from withering, seemed only to blossom further. Even the young doctor, with his bloodshot eyes and his throbbing morning head, noticed it. Walking away from her down the long white corridor in his lisping suede bootees, he is all at once trailing, a small boy, behind his doctor father and an obesely waddling spaniel dog on the downs behind their Brighton home. Under the bushes he sees a bone, violin-shaped, chalk-white with tinges here and there of emerald. He picks it up with his nail-bitten fingers, turns it over and over, stares down at it. It is hard, clean and pure. It is beautiful. He wants to take it home with him. But his father turns impatiently and calls, Oh come *on*! And then his father wanders back, followed by the dog, and asks: What on earth have you got there? A bone, he says, just a bone. His father takes it from him. A rabbit's head, he says. I should think. Or a cat's. Anyway, we don't want to play around with something like that. Unhygienic. An arm swings, the miniature white violin glitters momentarily in the sun. Then it is lost. The boy wants to cry but he knows the kind of voice, contemptuous and cold, in which his father will demand, *Now* what are you blubbing about? So he runs ahead. The dog stays with his father.

The bone, hard, clean and pure, lay out on the catafalque. He stared down at it and again, as so many years before, he wanted to cry. But someone – perhaps the grey, world-weary consultant or the Nigerian nurse with the high bosom like a bolster – would ask him, *Now* what are you blubbing about? and he didn't want that to happen. So he hurried away down the corridor, his suede bootees lisping on the highly polished floor.

That day they closed the restaurant.

I loved her like a daughter, Kyria Papadopoulou said. It's the least I can do for her now. She had never had a daughter of her own, much though she had wanted one; and though she nagged incessantly at Petros to marry this or that girl that she found for him, he, so obedient in every other respect, remained inexplicably recalcitrant in that.

Why, why, why? cried Aunt Sotiria.

Why? They all took it up.

Homesick?

Lovesick?

Life-sick?

They all had their indefatigably voracious appetites; they were bewildered and abashed by her loss of hers.

Uncle Kostas sobbed noisily at the funeral, thinking of a wife coughing out her lungs in the starved years of the Occupation, of a daughter bleeding to death in childbirth and a son swallowed up, and therefore as good as dead, in the insatiable maw of the New World, of comrades shot by Germans or their fellow countrymen, lost at sea, crushed on high roads, burned by fevers in the crowded wards of hospitals. Kostas bit his lower lip until he thought it would bleed. Petros wondered if the cake, a marvel of the confectioner's art, had been taken out of the refrigerator by his snotty underling. Sue twitched her coat of simulated fur closer about her, peered disdainfully into the newly dug grave and wished that she could afford a coat of real fur, expensive fur, like that old trout's over there.

Back at the restaurant they huddled for a while around the cast-iron stove, holding out fingers mauve with cold and feeling the skin of their faces tauten and tingle. Then, bit by bit, their desolation melted from them, as their dully aching bodies thawed out. Petros hurried into the kitchen and they could hear his voice, high-pitched and nasal, upbraiding the snotty underling. I told you. Why didn't you turn down the gas? I told you. Why didn't you open the wine? I told you. Why didn't you take the cake out of the refrigerator?

But everyone agreed that it was a wonderful spread. Kyria Papadopoulou always did you proud. She spared no expense, you'd have to go far to find a cook as good as her Petros. They slurped from bowls of steaming *avgolemono* soup. They tore at the fresh-baked rolls and shoved chunks of them into their mouths, so that Sue, one cheek crammed, looked as though she had toothache. They picked up the lamb chops in their fingers and their teeth tugged at them, while fat dribbled down their chins and even on to the *broderie Anglaise* of Aunt Sotiria's crisply starched blouse. They drained their glasses, their mouths leaving messy imprints on their rims, and, as soon as they had done so, Uncle Kostas would at once brandish yet another bottle and pour out from it, spattering the clean linen cloth as though with blood. Petros, usually so ladylike, picked up a *keftedaki* in his fingers and rammed it between his teeth. His mother sighed, belched, muttered, Excuse me, and settled herself yet more deeply in her chair, her plump elbows resting on the table with the dishes all around them. There were other relatives, other friends, other people whom no one really knew, all guzzling, swigging, gulping, sozzling.

Suddenly, with a shooting pain under the heart like a stab of indigestion, Aunt Sotiria was transfixed by the thought of Maria, their own little Maria, lying out there in the dark and cold, the earth heavy upon her lightness. Tears began to roll unchecked down her cheeks, even while she was intent on gnawing at the leg of a chicken.

What is it, Sotiria *mou*? Uncle Kostas asked.

Crunch, crackle, suck.

What is it? What is it?

That child. That poor child.

Ah, Maria! Kyria Papadopoulou's face became tragic as she ladled out more of the *stifado* on to her plate.

Maria!

Sue murmured, Poor darling, as she picked out a fragment of meat from between her front teeth with a red-lacquered fingernail.

How she loved Petros's cakes! Kyria Papadopoulou groaned, as much from the weight of her grief as from that of the food that was now lying heavy on her stomach.

I took a cake to the hospital for her, Petros said, nodding his head sadly, but she was so ill she wouldn't eat a slice. The other patients had it all. I hadn't the heart to bring it back.

Uncle Kostas got shakily to his feet, his grizzled hair in a tangle over his forehead and his face all flushed and sweaty, as though he had been running a race. Let us drink, he said and raised his glass high. Let us drink to the memory of Maria, our little Maria!

Maria!

Maria!

Our little Maria!

Sue's pointed fingernail eased a cherry off the cake, causing Petros to squint in anger. She popped the cherry into her mouth and then she too said, Maria!

If only she could be here eating this feast with us now, Aunt Sotiria cried.

If only!

Oh, if only!

The snotty underling, breathing asthmatically through his perpetually open mouth, tottered in, to the cheers of the whole assembly, with a suckling pig on a vast platter awash with grease. It weighed even more than the body in the cemetery.

1977

The Brighton Belle

She was the daughter of an earl, she had been rich, she had been beautiful. I think that it was I who first gave her the nickname 'the Brighton Belle'.

She reminded me of one of the old first-class Pullman coaches, once elegant but now dilapidated and ramshackle, that make up that train: its opulent upholstery beginning to sag and to exude a smell of spilled food and drink; its tarnished brass and cracked mirrors boldly stating the meretriciousness at which they had only hinted in their glory; its passage seismic with sudden jolts and tremors.

She lived a few doors up from me, and before we had met at a party, I had often seen her making her unsteady way down the hill, thrusting before her a shopping basket on wheels and stopping from time to time to peer over a fence or hedge into a front window. I used to wonder who she was; and even then, in spite of the soiled and shabby chothes, the large hats with the abundant fruit or feathers on them, and the anklestrap tart's shoes below the bulging legs, I was certain that she must be someone of distinction. She had a habit of talking and of grimacing to herself as she moved along. Her face was a curious mauve shade, with deep-set eyes around which the mascara was heavily smeared, a small retroussé nose and a pointed chin above a wobbling subsidence of fat. Her hair was fuzzy, an improbable shade of orange, brushed forward over her cheeks to conceal (so our mutual friend Robin Charles, the antique dealer, maintained) the scars of a face-lift performed, as he put it, 'in the dark ages'.

'I only live on the ground floor now. I find it difficult to manage all the stairs. So I let off some rooms – not for the money, of course, but because I like to have young people around me and it gives me an interest in life.' Her cat, a huge neutered Russian Blue, jumped into her lap, which was already streaked with its hairs. She looked around her, kneading its head: 'Yes, I'm afraid that this room is really overcrowded. But I don't like to leave my really valuable bits and pieces in my lodgers' rooms. They don't appreciate them in the first place, and they damage them in the second. . . . Is this tea all right for you?'

'Oh, yes, thank you.'

The tea was so bitter and black that I suspected that she had merely poured more hot water into the pot she had prepared for her breakfast.

'It's a special blend which Jackson's used to make up for my father and for his father before him. It's difficult to get them to do it for me now – they say it's too much trouble. But I drink nothing else.' She sipped and sipped again, drawing the tea between her lips with a curious suck and click. 'A biscuit?' She held out the plate. 'That's a pretty design, isn't it? Chinese. You'll recognize it of course. I had a set of twelve given to me by General Doi when I was in Japan just before the war. You know who I mean by General Doi – the Chief of Japanese Intelligence? This is the only plate that survives.' She examined it from all angles; then she said firmly, as though to defy any secret doubts I might have about its beauty, its date or its provenance, 'It's very valuable.'

After she had poured me out a second cup of the tea, ignoring my insincere plea that I never drank more than one, she continued to talk of her travels in the East. 'Yes, those were the days! When I think how I and my second husband – he was a painter, you know – squandered our money! I remember that in Peking these Chinese friends of ours, such delightful people, related in some way to Sun Yat-sen, lent us their mansion and we gave a party for more than five hundred guests. We all wore Chinese costume and I had this oh, so lovely embroidered robe-thing of the ninth century, a fabulous shade of peacock blue, and these rubies the size of. . . .' After China, it was Japan. 'The Japan we knew disappeared with the war. *Your* Japan must be entirely different. The Emperor, as you probably know, had and still has this interest in marine biology, and my husband, who was Russian, White Russian, had a marvellous idea of ordering for him from Canada or Iceland or somewhere this very, very rare species of crab – two of them to be precise, male and female. And when we were received by the Emperor, I presented the crabs to him. Oh, we had a good laugh about that later.' At that she proceeded to have a good laugh again, throwing back her head, so that the sagging chins were drawn taut, and closing her eyes, as though to squeeze out of them the tears which eventually began to trickle down her cheeks, tinged with mascara. 'You see' – she plucked a handkerchief, far from clean, from the recesses of her bodice – 'you see, the English language press, the *Tokyo Times* or whatever it was called, had this priceless headline with a photograph of little me and his Imperial Highness: "Earl's daughter exchanges crabs with Emperor".'

Could the source of the 'good laugh' be what I suspected it to be? Only later was I to be certain that it was.

'I see that you are admiring my darling table.' In fact, I had been eyeing, not the table, but the mildewed banana skin which I could glimpse beneath the papers littering its top. How long had it been there? How long would it stay? 'Yes, it's a lovely little piece – a real gem.' The 'gem' was made of boarding-house bamboo, with dragons clumsily lacquered on to every available plane. 'It came from the Pavilion originally, you know. And that chair too – the one with all those clothes on it. Of course they've been in my family for years and years – since long before I was born. But I've made arrangements in my will that eventually they are to go back. . . .' She broke off, at a knock at the door. 'Poop!. . . . Yes? Who is it?' A plump, brown face appeared. 'No, I'm sorry Mr Barzengi, I'm busy at this precise moment.' She enunciated with extreme care, giving an equal value to each syllable. 'I'm busy. Later, please.'

'But, madam, my electric light. . . . It is impossible for me. I am now waiting three days and I cannot continue with my preparation and my teacher. . . .'

'Later, my dear. Let us talk of it later. I've called the electrician, I really can't do more. Now can I? Later, later.' She got to her swollen feet, waddled across the room, and gently closed the door on him. 'Oh, these people! It's just not worth one's while to have them. I do it because all my life I've been interested in international understanding. There was a time, you know, when I took a leading part in the World Government Movement. But I feel that to provide a decent home for half a dozen foreign students is really of far more value than any amount of sitting on committees. Don't you agree?'

She had gone to the huge break-front wardrobe in one corner of the room and had begun to tweak out of its drawers one crumpled piece of clothing after another, dropping each on to the floor. 'There's something here that I know will interest you. A bowl, a Sung bowl. It was also a present. From the Governor General of Kyoto. We travelled there, you know, in the Imperial Train. The Emperor put it at our disposal. I shall never forget it! There was this little teahouse actually on the train – can you imagine? – and a lovely young girl, a real geisha, passed the time for us by initiating us into the tea ceremony. Oh, they don't do things like that now! I bet that you never enjoyed the tea ceremony on a train. Now did you? . . . Ah, there we are!'

She began to unwind a tightly wrapped bundle, which slowly revealed itself to be a night-dress, grey with grime. 'There now!' She dropped the night-dress and held the bowl out to the light. 'Now isn't that just the most exquisite thing you've ever seen?'

'Yes, it's rather nice,' I said, compromising between good manners and truthfulness.

'I am right in thinking that you collect Oriental art? That's what Robin told me.'

'I don't really know much about it,' I deprecated.

'Robin tells me that you have a quite marvellous collection.' Robin so rarely praises any objects other than those he himself has for sale that I was sure that he had never said anything of the kind. 'Sung,' she said, turning the bowl round and round before my eyes. 'Exquisite. But what use is it to me? I have nowhere to display it. As you see, I've already got far too many objects. So it lies in this drawer. If you're interested,' her manner at once became both wheedling and anxious, 'if you've really fallen in love with it, then perhaps. . . . I'd like it to go to someone who would appreciate it, really appreciate it, and know its true worth.'

Later I was to become inured to the Brighton Belle's attempts either to sell me objects which both of us knew to be of no value, or to borrow off me money which both of us knew would never be repaid. But on this occasion I was acutely embarrassed. Stammering that of course it was a most remarkable piece, and that it was kind of her to think of me, I concluded that its purchase would, I was afraid, be far beyond my means.

But 'Name a price,' she pursued relentlessly. 'There's no harm in naming a price. As I told you before, what I'm chiefly interested in is finding the right kind of home for it.'

I was glad that at that moment the bell rang and went on ringing until, again making that curious exclamation 'Poop!', she had to go out to answer it.

'Lady Dorothy Pawson?' I heard a girl's voice drawl.

'Yes.'

'Oh, Lady Dorothy,' the voice rushed on, 'you won't know who I am. But a friend of mine, Sonia Smith-Borrows, was lodging here with you last year. Remember? Well, she told me about lodging here, and so I wrote you a letter last week asking if you. . . .'

'A letter? What letter? Don't know what you mean.'

'Perhaps you never got it. Anyway, Lady Dorothy, I'd so much like to lodge with you. And now that I'm in the Old Fashioned Music Hall on the pier, I'd be awfully grateful. . . .'

'The Old Fashioned *what*? The house is quite full.'

'Oh, I don't mind where I sleep – just anywhere, any odd corner. And I love housework, there's nothing I enjoy more than pottering around the house. So I'd willingly help you. Can't you really find room for me? Please!'

'Well. . . .' There was a long silence. Then: 'Well, come in and we'll talk about it.'

Of all the Brighton Belle's friends it was therefore I who first met Cynthia.

Cynthia was no longer young, but she had all the optimism with which the young console themselves for the lack of talent or success. None of us ever learned her age: but references to being in the chorus of this revue with Hermione Gingold or of that pantomime with Nellie Wallace suggested that she was well into her thirties. Her hair, which had a metallic reddish glint in its brown, was loosely waved and usually worn over a ribbon which she tied in a girlish bow in front. She had a wide mouth, which tended to remain half open to reveal teeth with a gap in their middle, a small, beaked nose and eyes set close together under finely pencilled eyebrows. There were times, usually in conversation with male strangers, when she affected a lisp.

'She's a monster,' Robin pronounced. 'What can the poor Brighton Belle see in her? It's a mystery, an absolute mystery.'

Robin's wife, Helga, stopped polishing a table. 'There's no mystery about it. Cynthia believes every word that Dorothy tells her.

And none of Dorothy's other friends can do that.'

'She pretends to believe.'

'Well, if she pretends, then she pretends better than we can – any of us. And that's what Dorothy wants. If the Brighton Belle says that a table has come from the Pavilion, then as far as Cynthia is concerned, that's where it came from. If the Brighton Belle says that an Imari bowl is Sung, then for Cynthia Sung it is. It's as simple as that.'

Things always were simple to Helga's German mind.

'But what does Cynthia get out of the relationship?' I asked.

'She's a little snub.' To Helga the words 'snob' and 'snub' have always been interchangeable. 'And to be on terms of friendship with the daughter of an earl. . . . Besides, she probably has her eye on a legacy.'

'What has poor Dorothy got to leave except her debts?'

'As far as Cynthia is concerned she has a lot to leave – a Sung bowl, a Chinese Chippendale table and countless other treasures.'

'She's a monster,' Robin repeated. 'And we have to accompany the Brighton Belle to Eastbourne tomorrow to see the monster perform in what the *Argus* calls "a happy family seaside show". Oh God!'

I did not, at that time, know Dorothy (or Dotty, as her oldest friends from the pre-war days would call her) well enough for her to attempt to bully and wheedle me into joining that particular party. But in the months ahead I was often to be her victim on similar excursions. With the same persistence with which she pursued anyone who seemed likely either to buy one of her 'heirlooms' or to lend her money, she would telephone or call at my house repeatedly to force me to accompany her.

'. . . Cynthia has a part in *Ladies in Retirement* at Westcliff-on-Sea,' she would announce. 'It's a semi-professional production. Not quite what one would wish for her, but I tell her that this is the beginning for her in the legitimate theatre.' She giggled. 'Why do they call it the "legitimate" theatre? Those two recent plays by Osborne and Pinter to which you took me might really be called "illegitimate". . . . Now I know that you are fearfully busy, my dear, but would you escort me? I hate the idea of going to a benighted place like that all on my own. And the poor child does so value your support and criticism. She calls you "the sea-green incorruptible", you know. "When Francis says that a thing is good or bad, one always knows he means what he says," she remarked

only yesterday. Yes, do come with me! I count on you! Please!
I really couldn't face that awful journey on my own. And after the
show we can have dinner at a marvellous little restaurant run by
a charming Spanish couple – a discovery of Cynthia's. You'd never
imagine that a place like that could exist at Westcliff-on-Sea. Just
the three of us together.'

She knew my interest in food and shamelessly she was now prepared to play on it. But I doubted if the restaurant existed at all; and
if it did, I should certainly be left with the bill.

'I'm so busy,' I protested feebly. 'I really can't. . . .' But I knew
even then that I should have to give in.

Half an hour later Robin was on the telephone.

'Westcliff-on-Sea?'

'You too?'

'Yes. And Ruby Lamont and Irvine and Delia Morrow and the
Quinceys and, well, all the crowd.'

'Dinner at a marvellous little restaurant?'

'Just the three of us together – yes, that's right. Cynthia insists I
see her performance. She values my criticism so much.'

'Does she call you "the sea-green incorruptible"?'

'Yes. How clever of you to know that!'

In the course of the next year the Brighton Belle persuaded us to visit
most of the seaside resorts of southern England. We saw Cynthia
smiling fixedly at us from the front row of the chorus on this pier
and at that hippodrome; we were present at her first 'starring' performance in a village hall on the Downs, we clapped, when there was
no one else to clap, as she pranced forward, simpering, to take a
curtsy after rendering 'Somewhere over the Rainbow' in *Aladdin* in
East Croydon. Each performance served only to harden us in our
conviction that she had no talent at all; but at each performance the
Belle herself was enraptured.

'If a Victorian sofa can become a Louis Quinze settee, then why
shouldn't poor little Cynthia become a Mrs Siddons?' Robin asked
bitterly when we were returning, tired and depressed, from a performance of *The Circle* in Bognor.

The Brighton Belle's final aim was to achieve a West End debut
for her protégée, and since one of Robin's most extravagant customers was Sir Charles Otley, the famous actor, she now began to
scheme for this eminent if disagreeable man and 'the little girl' – as

she had recently begun to refer to Cynthia – to be brought together.

'He would be far more interested in a little boy,' Robin commented when approached. But being basically good-natured (in spite of his venomous tongue) and having a genuine affection for the Belle, he eventually arranged a meeting in his house.

Dorothy, on that occasion, both flattered Sir Charles and astounded the rest of us by managing to remember a host of roles played by the last of the great actor-managers in the thirties and even twenties. . . . 'Oh, I shall never forget that marvellous Joseph Surface in the Komisarjevsky production. It was definitive – that's the only word for it – definitive. And of course it was the same year that you did the second of your Romeos, wasn't it? What an *annus mirabilis*!'

The rouged and raddled old queen told Robin afterwards that he had found Dorothy 'delightful, quite delightful – a *grande dame* of the old school'; but when Robin inquired, 'And what did you think of her protégée?' he said, 'Who?' and then added, 'Oh, you mean that writer fellow who sat glum and said nothing.'

Cynthia, who had also sat glum and said nothing, he had obviously not noticed at all.

But that first failure did not deter the Brighton Belle; nothing, where Cynthia's career was concerned, could ever deter her. She invited Sir Charles to 'an intimate supper' at which I was also present; she went round to his dressing room at the Haymarket Theatre, pushing Cynthia into it before her but leaving me to wait for them outside (as I much preferred to do in any case); repeatedly telephoned to him and sent him messages by Robin and wrote him letters in a scrawl of green ink.

By this time Cynthia had taken to calling Dorothy 'Auntie', and was playing the part of devoted niece to the old woman far more convincingly than any part she had ever assumed on the stage. She seemed to take a rare pleasure in saying the words 'Lady Dorothy', savouring them as a ham actor might savour 'To be or not to be' or 'Tomorrow and tomorrow'. 'I'm ringing up for Lady Dorothy – Lady Dorothy Pawson. Lady Dorothy's sherry has not arrived yet and her guests are already here.' The 'guests' were merely myself and my dog. 'Lady Dorothy would like the sherry at once – as soon as you can make it. . . . Thank you. Yes, I'll tell Lady Dorothy.' Often what she had to tell Lady Dorothy was that no South African sherry could be delivered until a bill had been paid.

It was no longer possible ever to see Dorothy without 'the little girl' unless it was on a night of a performance; and even then it might well be that Dorothy had decided to go for yet another time to see *Ladies in Retirement* or *Dear Octopus* or *The Corn is Green*. No longer did Dorothy stay on and on when one had invited her to a drink before Sunday lunch, so that the joint began to shrivel and flake away and one grew groggy with hunger and too much alcohol. Cynthia saw to that, and one was grateful to her for doing so. But nor did the Brighton Belle now have the opportunity to regale one with those libellously indiscreet accounts of her earlier life or of the lives of our Brighton friends. Cynthia, who was a prude, also saw to that: with a shocked 'Oh, really, Auntie, no! No, don't listen to her! Isn't she awful?' Once, in an aside to me, after she had stopped Dorothy from telling some particularly scurrilous and risqué story, Cynthia whispered: 'You'd never think from some of the things she says that she came of such an aristocratic family, would you?' Evidently Cynthia did not know that an eighteenth-century squarson ancestor of the Belle had been one of the most outspoken and scandalous of English diarists.

Helga and Robin, whom I invariably consulted when anything baffled me in Brighton, explained Dorothy's theatrical ambitions for Cynthia as a compensation for her own frustrated ones in the distant twenties. Dorothy had, after all, been one of Mr Cochran's Young Ladies for a few months, before she had married the first of her three husbands; and years later her friendship with Ivor Novello had brought her a walking-on part in one of his musicals. Probably she had had no more talent then than poor Cynthia now; but at least on the evidence of the fashionable photographs, taken through draped fishnet, ropes of paper wistaria or yards of fine gauze, she had been exceptionally beautiful.

Through ceaseless badgering and coaxing, through the halfhearted intervention of Sir Charles and through the last-minute illness of another actress, Cynthia at last got her chance in the West End. The play was a comedy thriller in which a once famous star of the wartime screen had for some time been touring the provinces. From the way in which Dorothy and even Cynthia spoke of the part, I assumed that it was almost as important as that of the former film star. 'In terms of actual lines it's not of course the leading role – Madam has seen to that!' the Brighton Belle announced. 'But in terms of dramatic effectiveness – well, you'll see for yourself.' But before the opportunity came to see for myself, I had to hear for myself too. Dorothy insisted that I should 'run through' the role with Cynthia.

It was useless to say that this was a task for which I was wholly unqualified. 'No, my dear,' Dorothy brushed aside all my objections. 'As a writer, you have this marvellous feeling for words. What you can teach her will be invaluable.'

For the words of the play, unfortunately, I had no feeling at all. They were totally undistinguished.

Cynthia's reading of them on the other hand, did have bizarre distinction, as she mouthed, grimaced, threw her arms about and showered both the script and myself with spittle. The part was a minuscule one – she appeared briefly as a secretary, taking dictation from the hero in the first act and answering the telephone in the third. But it was apparent that both she and Dorothy regarded this peripheral character as having the same kind of artistic significance as the Gravedigger in *Hamlet* or the Porter in *Macbeth*.

'Isn't she splendid?' Dorothy exclaimed, as I polished the moisture off my glasses. 'I feel that this will be her breakthrough. Madam's going to regret that she ever allowed her in the show.'

This I could well believe.

For days before the first night Dorothy was busy rallying her friends and the friends of her friends. A couple whom she had met for a moment in my house – they were going out as she was entering – were astonished to receive first a leaflet about the play with a green ink scrawl across it ('Do come! We're counting on You!') and then a whole succession of telephone calls, each more insistent than the last. A schoolmaster and his wife, whose lives were devoted to the cultivation of orchids, they seldom went to the theatre more than once each year. To many of us she sent out letters couched in terms so ambiguous that those who did not know her well (by now I was not one of them) assumed that they were being invited to attend the first night as her guests. When, having accepted, they received a notification from the theatre that an early remittance would oblige, they made far from obliging comments.

I felt myself to be to blame, at least in part, for the accident. If I had not been so eager to escape Dorothy, it might never have happened. She knew that the drama critic for one of the weekly reviews was an acquaintance of mine and, since he lived not far from Brighton, she had been telephoning me almost daily to ask if I had done anything about bringing him and 'the little girl' together. I had made vague promises, but these were not enough for Dorothy, who, as always, insisted on action.

Helga and I had just emerged from the butcher's, when Helga clutched my arm: 'Oh, my lord! There's the Brighton Belle – with Cynthia.'

'And there, thank God, is my bus!'

'And mine,' said Helga, who in fact lived in the opposite direction.

'Can't stop, Dorothy dear. Must catch this bus.' I shouted at her, as she waved from halfway across the road, the traffic swerving and braking around her. 'I'll call you.'

Her swollen legs wide apart and a pink silk umbrella raised in one hand, she shouted: 'Wait! Take the next one! Wait! Important!'

I pretended not to hear, as Helga and I scampered for the bus.

When I swung myself on after Helga, I realized that the Belle was hobbling behind us, still shouting my name, while Cynthia, lurching under two heavy shopping baskets, brought up the rear.

Approaching from the back of the bus, where neither the driver nor the conductor could see her, Dorothy raised a foot on the platform and gripped at the rail. But simultaneously the bus jerked off. 'Oh, poop! The fool! The bloody fool!' Dorothy bellowed. Frantically I rang the bell, while Helga screamed, 'Let go, let go!' But with astonishing persistence, Dorothy continued to cling on, as she was dragged, one leg on the platform and one on the ground, forwards by the bus. I tried to catch hold of her and pull her aboard; and simultaneously Cynthia raced up from behind and began to push.

It was all so quick – a matter of seconds. The bus began to halt, passengers jumped to their feet; the Brighton Belle's grip weakened on the rail, I made repeated efforts to cling on to her and drag her aboard the platform, as though she were a stranded dolphin, while she herself kept gasping, 'Bloody fool, bloody fool!' – her huge floral hat askew and one shoe now off the foot which was being dragged along the road.

Then she was away from the platform altogether, her knees bumping horribly along the road and her hands going down with a slap, slap, one after the other.

When we hauled her to her feet, she seemed dazed, but otherwise all right apart from some superficial cuts and bruises.

'You shouldn't have started, you bloody fool!' she panted at the conductor, as a crowd collected around her on the pavement. 'You might have killed me.'

'And you shouldn't have got on to a moving bus from behind the platform.'

'I did nothing of the kind! The bus hadn't started. Had it?'

She turned to me for the confirmation which I could not in good conscience give her; but a red-faced woman in the crowd took up: 'That's right. The bus hadn't started. Criminal! You might have killed her, the poor old lady.'

'Well, take my number then. Take my number.' The young conductor histrionically pulled forward the lapel of his jacket. 'Take it, if you want to. Go on.'

'How can she take your number, the state she's in?' the red-faced woman demanded, squaring her shoulders. 'Write it down for her.'

Eventually we got Dorothy home in a taxi. Cynthia bathed the grazes on her knees, elbows and palms, Helga made a cup of the 'special' tea (which appeared to come in bags), and I kept urging the Belle to allow me to call a doctor.

'No, no. . . . Not necessary, not necessary at all. Helga sweet, do put the teeniest, weeniest dash of rum in this tea. That's all I need. In the Regency chiffonier over there. That's an angel! No, just a little bit more than that. I want to be able to taste it, after all.'

Eventually she had recovered enough to return to the subject of the critic.

'Wouldn't you like to call him now – from here? Why not?'

'Oh, he never gets home until the evening.'

'Well, call him in London – at his office.'

'He doesn't have an office.'

'Well, call him where he is.'

I gave a sigh and called him. Fortunately no one answered.

Perhaps the accident really had nothing to do with the stroke; perhaps it would have happened anyway.

I had just gone to bed, shortly after one o'clock, when I was brought to the door in my dressing-gown by a repeated ringing of the bell. Cynthia was there in pyjamas and a raincoat, her face shiny and creased and her eyes bleared with sleep. 'It's Auntie,' she moaned. 'She's had a queer turn. I'm awfully worried about her. She doesn't seem able to talk at all – I can't get anything out of her. Oh, do come quickly.'

So for the second time that day, I had to attempt to heave up Dorothy, whom I found propped against her bed, her puffy, blue-veined legs outstretched before her, with the skirt of her night-dress rucked above the knees, her chin on her raddled chest, and her mouth horribly twisted. But this time Cynthia and the frightened Mr

Barzengi, wearing a checked cap and with a blanket draped about him, were there to help me. Even so the weight was formidable.

The Brighton Belle kept trying to say something; but each time all that emerged was a kind of hiccoughing gasp.

Then suddenly, my ear to her mouth, I realized what she was croaking: the name of the critic to whom I was to introduce 'the little girl'.

The next day Dorothy was able to enunciate an occasional word with the greatest of difficulty. 'Theatre . . . rehearsal . . . rehearsal. . . .'

'Yes, what about your rehearsals, Cynthia? I can stay with Dorothy – I can bring my work over here – if you have a rehearsal in London.'

'Oh, I've withdrawn from the play,' Cynthia replied in a rush of embarrassment. 'I've already told them. I rang up this morning.'

'Withdrawn!'

'It won't be all that inconvenient – it's such a small part, they were probably quite relieved. I wasn't much good in it.'

Dorothy's eyes, the skin around them streaked with mascara as though with coal dust, all at once became frantic in the terrifyingly immobile face. She made a sound as of retching and repeated it three times before she got out: 'Go. Must go. Rehearsal. Go.'

'Now, shush, Auntie, shush!' Cynthia got to her feet. 'I'm going downstairs to get you some supper, while Francis sits with you. All right?'

Dorothy scrabbled at my hand and then gripped it tighter and tighter. 'Make – her. . . . Must – make – her. . . .'

But from then on no one could make 'the little girl' leave the Brighton Belle for more than a few minutes on end.

Robin, always cynical in his ascription of motives, said that it was obvious – of course 'the little girl' was determined to get all Auntie's money. 'She daren't let her out of her sight for a moment. Even when that cousin called to see her, did you notice how Cynthia watched her like a lynx? And Helga – who after all has known the Brighton Belle longer than any of us – says that she and Dorothy are never left alone together for even a moment. . . . Well, that poor creature is going to get a nasty shock when she realizes that Auntie's heirlooms are, in fact, quite valueless.'

'You talk as if Dorothy were going to die.'

'Well, isn't she?' Robin retorted brutally.

*

Robin was, of course, right – he usually is; Dorothy died after a second stroke, some four months later, having spent the last three weeks of her life in a coma during which Cynthia, with the assistance of the district nurse, attended to all her needs. Many of her friends joined the doctor in urging that the Belle should be placed in a hospital; but Cynthia would have none of that. 'No, she hated hospitals,' she would say. 'She hated illness. I'm certain that she would like to stay here.'

'But Cynthia, she's taking nothing in – nothing in at all,' I argued. 'It doesn't matter to her whether she's. . . .'

'I think that she'd rather be here.'

Cynthia raised a cigarette to her mouth with a hand that trembled slightly and puffed at it, exhaling the smoke as soon as she had drawn it in. She had asked me for the cigarette; she never smoked as a rule. 'Filthy habit,' she used to say, as she swept up the ash scattered by the Belle over the lacquer dragons on the table reputedly from the Pavilion. 'Why do you have to do it?'

'It's the only pleasure left to me,' the Brighton Belle would answer.

Cynthia choked and began to cough, banging with her knuckles on her bony chest, until tears came to eyes already red-rimmed with the ones she had shed that morning. 'Poop!' she spluttered. 'Poop!' I had never heard her use that expletive before.

She was wearing trousers and a dark blue polo-neck sweater, and her hair, no longer flashing those curiously metallic glints of red, hung straight in a bob, its brown streaked with grey. 'I like a womanly woman,' Dorothy used to say, glancing at her. But poor Cynthia was no longer that. The months of constant attendance on her dying friend had both aged 'the little girl' and given her a masculine toughness and hardness.

'So that's it, Francis,' she said. 'That's it.'

Quite what was what, I was not clear.

'Now you must start your career again,' I said encouragingly, if fatuously.

'My what? Are you off your nut?' She puffed again, two or three times in rapid succession, at the shrivelled end of her cigarette and then stared down at its tip. 'I have no "career" and you know that.' She seemed to enjoy my embarrassment. 'So Auntie wanted to believe that I had. Well, why not? But I was never good enough for anything but the chorus – and the back row at that. Right?' She gave a hoarse laugh. 'Oh, I could see what all of you thought of my dramatic ambitions – or, rather, the poor old dear's ambitions for me. Of course I could see! Well, you were right. Just as you were right about all that furniture, which anyone in their right senses could tell had come from a junk-shop. But if she wanted to believe. . . . Well, she had to have something. There was so little left for her. Three marriages and all of them unhappy – no children – precious little money. Nothing really but that handle to her name. And what good was that? It didn't even get her any more credit.' She stubbed out the cigarette. 'I shall be sick if I go on with that. . . . No, not even a single bottle of South African sherry.'

'Then what are you going to do?'

Cynthia slumped yet lower in the chair and covered her eyes with a hand on which the veins stood out. 'Do, oh, God knows! I don't want to *do* anything any more.' She shook herself, straightened in the chair and, with an effort, smiled at me. 'All I want to do is sleep, and sleep, and sleep. . . . But I miss the old girl, you know. There was something – she had something. . . . You could tell at once. See her, staggering down the street, half-drunk, and you could tell at once. She was a lady, a real lady. I suppose that's what got me.' She put a little finger to the corner of an eye, to wipe away the tear that had formed there: the ladylike gesture of someone who would never be a lady.

'I'll go on running the lodging house,' she said. 'Because that's what it was – a lodging house. If she could make a little money out of it, then I can do much better. That's what I'll do. We'll continue to be neighbours. That'll be fun won't it? But – oh dear. . . .' – again the little finger brushed the eyelashes – 'It won't be the same without the Brighton Belle. It won't be the same for any of us.'

It was the first time that I had heard her use the nickname; she was to call Dorothy nothing else from then on.

1964

I Lived for You

'*I* don't mind at all,' Mrs Parrish said. 'But it's just the sort of thing that would upset poor Gerald. We have to think of Gerald.'

Her granddaughter, Caroline, saw no reason why they should think of the coloured servant at all; but it was better not to exasperate the old woman, to whom exasperation came more and more easily with the passing of the years. She therefore went out into the garden at the rear of the house and shooed her two young children, both of whom were entirely naked, back through the open french windows into their bedroom. 'You must never, *never*, do that again,' she said in a loud, cross voice. Then she added more quietly, so that Mrs Parrish should not hear: 'At least not in this house.' At home, the children, who were two and four, were used to running about without any clothes.

There were many things that they and their mother were not allowed to do in the Brighton house because of Gerald. There were many things that Mrs Parrish did not allow herself to do because of him. She no longer swore, as in the presence of her former house-keeper, Miss Carfrae, now dead; she no longer slopped around the house in her dressing-gown until lunch-time and even later; and her bouts of drinking had become increasingly furtive and guilty.

Gerald, her relatives all told each other, had done the old woman a world of good; he had given her a new lease of life; they could not

64

imagine how she had ever managed without him. But neither these considerations nor the abstracted saintliness of his manner could make them like him. He was, each of them was convinced – though they never mentioned this to each other – after Mrs Parrish's money; and since they were after it themselves, an unacknowledged rivalry was bound to exist.

Gerald came from the West Indies and, when asked his age, used to answer with his benignly remote smile, 'Now you'd better ask my mother that, hadn't you?' As said by him, the reply could not be taken as an impertinence; but it secretly annoyed those who had put the far more impertinent question. His hair was a wiry black streaked with grey, and he brushed it straight back from his bulging, unlined forehead, over his ears, to make a bush at the back of his head. Perhaps it was this bush of hair, always slightly redolent of macassar oil, which made his neck seem so fragile and long. His liquid eyes were beautiful – everyone agreed on that – and so were his hands. One of the grandsons claimed, on the flimsiest of evidence, that Gerald used the hands to massage Mrs Parrish when she had her bouts of fibrositis; but this seemed unlikely. Gerald was always so fastidious, he always shrank from any contact with others, perching himself on the edge of the back seat of the car so that no part of his person or even his clothes would have to touch either of the two children when Caroline and her husband gave him a lift to the market. Waiting at table, he wore gloves.

'I can't see the point of the gloves,' one of Mrs Parrish's sons remarked. 'In Florence my Bruno puts on gloves, and that's just as well, because he has such awful hands and the nails are never clean. But Gerald's hands are marvellous.'

'Perhaps it's because they are so marvellous, that he wants to protect them,' his mother replied.

Gerald had now been with her for almost a decade.

After the death of Miss Carfrae there had been a bad period of almost a year. Mrs Parrish had first employed a former buyer from a London store, whose hair was dyed an improbable shade of orange and who never stopped talking, either to Mrs Parrish or to herself; then a succession of sluttish daily women, who left her either because she found them dishonest and dirty or because they found less exacting and better paid work in the hotels; and finally a Scots couple who each night banged around in the basement set aside for them and each morning emerged from it bleary and indiscriminately scarred and bruised.

The couple left after a scene, in which they had discovered to their amazement that 'the old girl's' language was a match for their own; and Caroline had then come down for a week 'to help out'. But she found Mrs Parrish, as she wrote to her husband, 'Impossible, quite impossible', and not even the thought of the legacy which would, they hoped, eventually pay for them to send their elder child to Eton, could persuade her to stay. So she put an advertisement for her grandmother in the *Brighton Argus*, explained that she really must leave because she didn't like to entrust the children to Nanny for too long, and returned to London, vindictively glad that the old woman would now have to cope for herself.

A number of applicants for the job appeared; but either Mrs Parrish told them point-blank that she considered them unsuitable or her tone, hectoring and peevish, made them decide that they themselves would be better suited elsewhere. The house grew dustier and untidier; an indefinable smell, both musty and sour, began to envelop it; the milkman was annoyed to find a greenish sediment in the bottles left out for him and the dustmen were surprised to find that often no dustbins were put out for them for several weeks on end. From time to time Caroline or one of the other relatives would come down for what they called a 'blitz'. All of them were secretly convinced that, like the beautiful old Regency house, the once beautiful old woman was entering on her final dissolution. She was drinking heavily and blatantly, with no attempt, however perfunctory, at concealment; she was eating hardly at all.

Then Gerald appeared, in answer not to the advertisement in the *Argus* but to one, put up many weeks before, on a newsagent's board and now grown faint and streaky from the rain which had seeped into it.

'It's no use your applying,' the old woman panted crossly, as she swayed before him on the doorstep, one ringed hand raised – there was some ink on the bony wrist and the nails were far from clean – preparatory to slamming the door shut. 'I said quite distinctly – I mean, I wrote, my granddaughter wrote, quite distinctly – "Housekeeper".'

'I wish to be housekeeper,' Gerald said. 'That is my wish.'

It was then that he gave that benignly remote smile of his, the full lips slowly parting to reveal first the teeth, white against purple, and then the pink gums above them, while the black eyes grew oddly unfocused as though at the advent of some deep-seated pain, not for himself nor even for his interlocutor, but for the whole of the suffering and striving world at large.

Mrs Parrish hesitated; then she said, 'Well, come in for a moment. Though it's really no use. I had a woman in mind.'

'I can do anything that a woman can do, madam,' he replied in his deep, sing-song voice, pressing against the door to click it shut, since she had failed to close it properly.

He mounted the stairs behind her to the first-floor sitting-room; then rushed ahead of her on the landing to pull open the door.

She was disconcerted by the way in which, as she interrogated him, he automatically began to tidy the coffee table before his chair: tipping the contents of all the ashtrays together into the largest of them; folding up the papers; and then placing the magazines one on top of the other, with a rapid glance at the date to make sure that he had them in the right order.

Yes, he could cook; at present he could prepare only simple dishes but he was willing to learn. No, he had never done work of this kind before, but he was sure that he could do it to madam's satisfaction. A reference? He frowned at the pile of magazines, biting on his lower lip. Well, of course, there was the chief nurse at the hospital.

'The hospital?' Mrs Parrish took up, alarmed. She was convinced now that he was a madman, either escaped or discharged prematurely from a lunatic asylum.

Yes, he explained gently, he had been working at a hospital; he lived in the male nurses' hostel. 'But I do not care to be with those people. Such a life does not suit me – such a life in the hostel. And I have been unlucky in my lodgings – when I have lived in lodgings.'

As he continued talking, Mrs Parrish inspected him surreptitiously: the frayed but neat blue pin-stripe suit, its trousers sharply creased but a little too short for him so that even when he stood up his socks remained visible; the black tie and the shirt with the old-fashioned detachable collar, cream against the white; the belt with the silver snake clasp. But even then she had the uncomfortable feeling that it was not she who sat in judgement on him, but he on her. Her hair, she realized, was a mess; and glancing at her reflection in the lid of a silver cigarette-box at her elbow, she saw to her horror that the lipstick was smeared at one corner of her mouth.

'My only desire is to serve. Please allow me to do so.'

To her own amazement, but not to his, she acceded to a request which, she was soon to learn, was totally sincere.

To serve did, indeed, seem to be his sole desire. She would go down to the kitchen at eleven o'clock at night and find him on his hands and knees, scrubbing the floor. On his days off he would often tell her that he had decided to remain at home in order to prepare some dish for a dinner party on the following evening. He had asked her to buy him a number of cookery books – the only extravagance to which he subjected her – and from these, not from any instruction she or Caroline or any other of the children or grandchildren had been able to give him, he had learned to become a superb cook. Mrs Parrish offered to get him in a woman for the rough, but he invariably replied that he preferred to have the house to himself.

Mrs Parrish and her family were all curious about Gerald; but they discovered little. He spoke of a brother in the vaguest of terms – he had some unspecified business in Barbados and every six months or so a flimsy letter would arrive for him, so thin that, as she fingered it, Mrs Parrish used to wonder if the envelope contained anything at all. Gerald apparently had no friends, though he would chat with assistants who served him at the shops. His room – both Mrs Parrish and her family would peep into it from time to time when he was out – contained nothing personal: no photographs, no ornaments except those that Mrs Parrish put there, nothing except a calendar, the date neatly torn off each day, an inkwell and a dipper pen, a canvas garden chair which he had bought for himself, evidently preferring it to the armchair provided by Mrs Parrish and, most important of all, his religious books.

What was his religion? They never discovered. He had second-hand volumes on Zen Buddhism and theosophy and Gurdjieff and Subhud; he had tracts, also usually second-hand, containing instruction in the Roman Catholic faith; he had ancient parish magazines and copies, often with their covers missing, of *The Divine Word* and *Spiritual Healing* and *Psychic News*. Mrs Parrish would turn over the new acquisitions, shaking her head in wonder; her children and grandchildren would giggle over them and tell each other that Gerald was 'really quite dotty'. He never went to church, as far as any of them knew.

Mrs Parrish had never, until then, been a tidy woman. With the prodigality of those who have had money all their lives without ever being obliged either to earn it or safeguard it, she allowed food to rot in the larder until it had to be thrown away; newspapers and magazines to accumulate unread on occasional tables, chairs and even the carpet; clothes to grow musty in soiled, jumbled heaps in cupboards or the corner of drawers for lack of a single button or because of a seam that needed stitching. To all that, Gerald put an end.

He seemed to enjoy nothing more than to wash, iron and repair her clothes, so that garments the existence of which she had wholly forgotten would suddenly appear, as though new, on hangers or neatly folded. He also spent patient hours on bringing order to the chaos of her dressing-table, her bedside table and the two desks, one in her bedroom and the other in her sitting-room, into the drawers of which she had the habit of stuffing any papers too complicated or too tedious for her to deal with. She became furtively ashamed of the squalor and untidiness which she created, to be removed each day by this gentle, perpetually smiling servant; and the very fact that he never complained or showed the slightest exasperation or disgust seemed not to alleviate her shame, as one might suppose, but merely to intensify it.

'Caroline, dear,' she would say, 'do take care where that cigarette ash is falling. It makes so much more work for poor Gerald.' Or: 'Children – you'd better ask poor Gerald for a dustpan and brush and do something about that mud you've brought in.' Or, to the eldest of her sons, a brigadier in his fifties: 'Can't you clear up some of the mess in your room? I hate to have Gerald see it like that.'

There were, however, curious periods – so widely spaced apart that each of them came to Mrs Parrish with the shock of a disagreeable novelty – when the smooth precision of this process of tending both to the house and its octogenarian mistress would suddenly suffer unaccountable checks and hesitations. Gerald would become absentminded, forgetting Mrs Parrish's bedtime glass of milk with a dash of brandy in it, or omitting to lock and bolt the front door last thing at night, or leaving a shopping bag on the counter of a shop; his hand would tremble as he stooped over her with a dish of potatoes and he would give a series of peculiarly extended sighs while he moved about his cleaning; his clothes would look dishevelled and even dirty, he would stammer and swallow as he talked to her, and in his eyes, usually so placid in their indiscriminate benignity, would lurk an expression of anxiety and even panic.

Such occurrences, of which there were one or two each year, always reminded Mrs Parrish of the occasional breakdowns of her dishwasher. This was an expensive machine, the best on the market, and day after day it carried out its tasks without any trouble. But then, suddenly and inexplicably, its quiet murmur would become a sequence of strident moans and grunts; it would shake as though in rage or terror; and the dishes which were taken from it emerged covered in bits of macerated food, detergent and grease. A mechanic would come round and at once the machine would resume the ordered tenor of its existence, its brief aberration forgotten. But there was no mechanic for whom to send to deal with Gerald.

'Do you think he drinks secretly?' Caroline's husband asked, when a visit to Mrs Parrish had coincided with one of Gerald's 'turns' (as Mrs Parrish called them).

'Nonsense! Gerald never touches a drop.'

'Perhaps he gets homesick from time to time?' Caroline suggested.

'This is his only home. He has told me that more than once.'

The smell of burning potatoes crept up the stairs. Normally Gerald never burnt anything in the kitchen.

Mrs Parrish had been to London for the christening of one of her grandchildren. Gerald had, as usual, driven her to the station in her old but capacious and comfortable Armstrong Siddeley and had settled her in the first-class Pullman carriage with a pile of magazines, most of which she would leave unread on the table when she reached Victoria. One of her sons was to meet her.

'Don't forget that the carpenter is coming in to mend that window frame.'

Gerald said that he would not forget; and Mrs Parrish herself knew that it was unnecessary to remind him.

'Well, then, have a good rest for the three days,' she dismissed him. But she also knew that, whether she was present or absent, Gerald would never rest.

Gerald met her again at the station and, as he dropped her hatbox while taking it from the carriage – gaily it rolled on and on ahead of them, with Gerald making no attempt to retrieve it – Mrs Parrish realized, with the mixture of shock and unease she always experienced on these occasions, that this was the beginning of another of his 'turns'.

In the car she questioned him about the weather in Brighton, but his answers were almost inarticulate. Turning round to stammer an answer to another of her questions – this time about the window frame – he all but drove into the back of a van in front of them. Mrs Parrish decided that it would be better to be silent.

It was then that she noticed his neck. It was a cold afternoon – the month was March and an icy wind was blowing off the sea – but in spite of that the brown skin under that out-thrust bush of hair was glistening with sweat. She watched fascinated and yet obscurely horrified, as a trickle ran down the line of his jaw and then fell, with a plop, on to his collar, which – she also now noticed – was far from clean.

They drew up at the house in Brunswick Square – although there was plenty of room, it was some time before Gerald succeeded in getting the car alongside the kerb, between a lorry and a motor-bicycle – and Mrs Parrish then waited for him to open the door for her, as he usually did, and to help her down. But he was carrying out the luggage.

'Gerald!' she summoned him sharply; until at last, with dragging footsteps, he came to her. His face at the window, as he stooped to open the door, shocked her both with its expression of despair and with its greyish pallor. He supported her to the top of the steps, unlocked the door, pushed it open, mumbled something and then ran back to the car. Mrs Parrish went in, first pulling the pins out of her hat and then removing it from her head, which had unaccount-ably started to throb. She put her hat down and knew even then that something was amiss, though she failed to realize that it was the carriage clock which had disappeared from its place on top of the hall table where the hat now rested. Fearfully she went into her bedroom, on the ground floor, switching on the light although it was far from dark, as though in an effort to dispel a premonition.

The photograph, the photograph of her long-dead husband in its silver frame! The ivory and gold brushes! The little Fabergé box in which she kept pins! She put her hands to her lips to stop their idiot trembling and, aghast, gazed around her, her fur first twitching on her shoulders as she swung hither and thither, and then writhing to the floor.

'Gerald!' she called weakly. Then she screamed, 'Gerald! Gerald! Gerald!' on a note of shriller and shriller panic.

But Gerald did not come.

She tottered out into the hall and saw the two suitcases and the hatbox standing in one corner. The front door swung open on a gust of icy wind. She went to it, picking her way over the parquet as though it were treacherous ice, and peered out. The car was still outside; there were some children playing beyond it on the lawns; an old man limped by with a mongrel dog on a length of rope. But she could not see Gerald.

She shut the door and called again.

Breathlessly she began to mount the stairs to the upstairs room, his name now becoming a kind of plaintive mewing as she continued to repeat it. 'Oh – oh – oh!' Again, in the sitting-room, she pressed

71

her hands to her lips. All at once she had experienced a terrible lurching sickness in her stomach and her throat. The cigarette-case – the cigarette-case which Auntie Janet had given them! The three miniatures to the left of the fireplace! The. . . . the. . . .

At last she reached Gerald's room, at the top of the house. She pressed a hand to her side and then, with the same hand, knocked on the door. Her rings rattled and scraped on the wood. But no answer came. She fumbled for the door handle, turned it and peered in.

Gerald sat on a straight-backed chair, one hand on either knee and his eyes fixed on the empty grate. Mrs Parrish had never seen the room in such disorder: bedclothes lay on the floor, one of the two curtain rods hung down from a corner of the window, with the curtain trailing, its velvet thick with dust and plaster; the bedside lamp lay in fragments, its shade crushed to a plate-like oval.

'What *is* all this? What on earth has happened? Gerald, tell me! Speak to me!'

Gerald said nothing and Mrs Parrish began to whimper anew: 'Oh, Gerald, what is it? How did it happen? Tell me, Gerald!' while her eyes picked out one fresh horror after another.

Suddenly Gerald slipped off the chair, gliding down on to the curtain at his feet as limply as a doll. Mrs Parrish thought that he had fainted; but he began to writhe on the floor, burying his face in the folds of the curtain and sobbing incoherently 'I can't . . . I can't . . .' while Mrs Parrish looked down at him in amazement and horror.

The police eventually arrived, summoned not by Gerald but by Mrs Parrish. It was also Mrs Parrish who opened the door to them. The bell rang three times, while she waited for Gerald to answer; then she made her way slowly down the stairs herself and let them in.

The senior of the two detectives had a chilly, even contemptuous manner and he made no attempt to restrain his irritation when Mrs Parrish gave way to tears. He surveyed the places from which this or that knick-knack had been looted with the detachment of a dentist examining the gaps in a row of teeth.

Finally he asked to see Gerald, having already enquired what staff Mrs Parrish employed.

Mrs Parrish called, 'Gerald, Gerald!' forlornly up the stairs, after she had repeatedly rung the sitting-room bell without receiving an answer. Gerald did not come.

'Perhaps he's gone out?'

Mrs Parrish shook her head.

Again there was no answer when Mrs Parrish knocked on the door. Gerald was standing by the window, and when they went into the room, he did not turn round.

'Gerald, here are the police. They want to ask you one or two questions.'

Gerald leant further out of the window, as though he were about to retch into the street below. He was standing on the end of the curtain, with his arms crossed over his stomach and his shoulders hunched.

The detectives spoke in turn to him, but he would not answer them any more than he would answer Mrs Parrish. At last, still speaking calmly to him though plainly exasperated, they asked him to go with them to the police station. Mutely he followed them down the stairs, his arms still crossed over his stomach and on his face a look of dazed terror.

Mrs Parrish went downstairs with them, let them out and then descended to the basement to make herself a cup of tea. She sipped at it; then she poured in first one finger and then a second of brandy. She began to cough and as she did so, she suffered an attack of giddiness, so that only by clutching at the side of the kitchen table was she able to prevent herself from falling down.

It had long since grown dark when the bell rang again. Mrs Parrish was by then seated hunched, still in her coat, before the empty grate in the drawing room, the curtains undrawn and only a single lamp burning on the table beside her.

It was the senior of the two detectives. She wished that it had been the other one, who was younger and plainer and obviously more stupid. The detective said that they had questioned Gerald carefully and that they thought they had got to the bottom of the business. At first he had been uncooperative but, well, at last he had given them the answers to their questions.

'But surely you can't think that he would ever have –'

No, it was not precisely *that* that they thought.

He leant forward in his chair, fussing at the same time with the bowl of the pipe he had asked her if he might smoke.

'Did you realize that your servant was a homosexual? . . . Excuse me putting it so bluntly.'

The idea had never occurred to Mrs Parrish. But with marvellous dignity she straightened herself in her chair, fixed her clear blue eyes on his face and answered: 'Well, of course, I guessed that he must be. Would any other sort of man become a woman's servant?'

The detective gave a small smirk; it was a smirk of embarrassment, tinged with disappointment.

He went on to explain how the theft had taken place, and now the chilliness of his demeanour began to thaw out, he gave off a kind of wintry sparkle.

Gerald had 'picked up' (that was the phrase the detective eventually selected after some deliberation) an Irish labourer from a building site in Western Road and had brought him back to the house to spend the night. The labourer had gone berserk, had attacked Gerald – oh, yes, he was quite extensively bruised – and had then looted the house before he had got away.

'Of course, the poor wretch was terrified of calling us in. But I don't know how he expected to hide the thefts from you.'

'I wonder why he didn't tell me at once, instead of allowing me to find out for myself,' Mrs Parrish said quietly.

'It wouldn't be an easy thing to tell.'

'Not all that difficult.' She gave herself a small shake, drawing her pointed chin down on to her breast and then breaking into a sigh.

She barely heard what the detective said after that. '. . . Not to worry. . . . Now we have our lead. . . . Dare say we'll get our man. . . . Not to worry. . . . All come out in the wash. . . . Get our man. . . .' Nor did she see him out.

More than an hour later, as she still sat hunched, shivering and hungry, before the empty grate, she heard Gerald come in. But by the time she had tottered out on the landing, he was already racing up the stairs. She called his name; at the sound, his face, distorted and streaked with sweat or tears, was briefly turned towards her as he hissed: 'Please! Don't talk to me! Don't!'

She deliberated; then she climbed yet again up to his room. But though she knocked on the door repeatedly, cajoled, and rattled the handle, he would neither let her in nor speak to her.

Wearily, she went downstairs, and without eating, got into her night-dress and slipped between the icy sheets. 'My hot-water bottle,' she thought. She gave a little moan. 'My milk.' She buried her face in the pillow. 'The curtains.' At that time these three trivial omissions seemed to be far worse betrayals than anything of which the detective had told her.

Many hours later, half awake and half asleep, her whole body shivering in spite of the central heating and the blankets piled on top of her, she heard a faint creak and then another on the stairs outside her room. 'Gerald!' she called. For a moment she imagined in panic that the Irish labourer had returned. She swung her legs out of the bed and scrabbled with an arm in the sleeve of her dressing-gown as she tottered to her feet.

At the same moment that she opened the door of her bedroom, the front door clicked shut.

She hurried over to the front door; an icy wind whipped at her as she managed to pull it open. Trees plunged like gigantic stallions, their hooves battering the night to whirling sparks, and under them, cringing as he ran, was Gerald, a suitcase in either hand and his raincoat billowing out behind him. She shouted his name; she even ventured out into the road, clasping the folds of the dressing-gown over her shrunken breasts and feeling the hardness and coldness of the pavement beneath her naked feet. But the drumming hooves had beaten him into the darkness of which, without her guessing it, he had always been a part.

Then, passing the hall table (the sobs rising in her throat like terrible effortful hiccoughs) she all at once saw the note lying where the carriage clock had stood for three generations, and would now stand no longer. The paper, blue and lined, seemed to be heavy with the ink in which it was saturated. He had used large capital letters, which had bitten deep.

Mrs Parrish read, sitting on the edge of her bed with her bare, blue-veined feet crossed one over the other and her whole body shivering:

SORRY. I LIVED FOR YOU BELIEVE THAT. BUT I
CAN'T GO ON. SO ALL THE BEST. FORGIVE. SORRY.
    GERALD.

She went to the uncurtained window, an old woman in an old, empty house (now at last she saw herself as that, with an access of self-pity) and looked out through the uncurtained window at the thrashing trees, at the empty lawns and at the black sky above them.

'I LIVED FOR YOU BELIEVE THAT.'

But now she knew, after so many years, that it was she who had lived for him.

1966

Mess

Myra, in the over-large quilted dressing-gown that had belonged to a dead aunt, put her head round the door of the attic room.

'Aren't you coming down, dear?'

'I've already been down,' her fifteen-year-old son answered, without looking up from the work-bench across which he was sprawled.

'Been down! Then you've had your brekkers!'

The boy shook his head, still not looking up as his mother now shuffled into the room, rubbing at her eyes with one hand while the other held the dressing-gown together over her shallow breasts.

'Aren't you hungry?'

'I'll wait until lunch. Whenever that will be,' he added on a note of quiet fury.

'But, darling, we always have brekkers late on a Sunday. You know that. You can't expect us to get up at eight-thirty after a party. And such a party!' The hand that had been rubbing her eyes now went to her temples.

'Yes, I heard it,' he said, pouring a dark brown liquid carefully from one test-tube to another.

'Surely you can get your own breakfast once in a while!' Myra's voice was now no less accusatory than her son's. The boy went on pouring. 'Roger! Surely!'

'I took one look at all that mess and decided I couldn't face it.'

'What mess?'

'All that mess in the kitchen. And elsewhere. Everywhere. Except in here.'

'Well, *of course* there's a mess after a party. You expect a mess after a party. Everyone has a mess on their hands after a party. . . . What are you smiling at?'

For the first time the boy raised his head, overlarge for his skinny body; his spectacles glinted at her as they caught the sunlight through the window. 'There's always a mess in the kitchen – party or no party. You know that, Mummy.'

'Is it my fault that Patty decided to take off like that without a day of notice? Or that that wretched *au pair* woman decided to be so unhelpful?' She waited for an answer. 'Is it?' The boy shrugged. 'These days people have no sense of responsibility. Think of all we did for Patty. It makes me sick.' She put a hand on her son's shoulder, leaning more and more heavily on him while he scowled down at the test-tube. Then she put a cheek against his, so that he could smell the sour alcohol on her breath. 'Don't be cross, darling,' she coaxed. 'What's been the matter with you these hols? You're no longer the sweet-natured boy you used to be.'

'You've been drinking,' he said.

'Drinking?' She straightened, squinting angrily down at the test-tube in his hands. 'Of course I drank last night. Everyone drinks at a party.'

'I mean drinking now. This morning.'

'Roger, I *haven't*! How dare you say such a thing!'

'I can smell it.'

She made heavily towards the door. 'Well, if you want any break-fast you'd better come down.'

'There's no bread.'

'How do you know?'

'I looked.'

'Bloody hell!' She hesitated; then she said in a coaxingly artificial voice: 'In that case, darling, couldn't you be an angel and jump on your bicycle and go down to the delicatessen and –'

'No,' he interrupted her. 'Can't you see I'm busy? Why can't Daddy go? He could go in the car!'

His mother no longer drove, after an accident when, drunk, she had all but killed an old woman.

'Daddy's not feeling well. He's still in bed.'

'What's the matter with him?'

'He's not feeling well.'

'Then Marje.'

'She and the American seem already to have left the house.'

Myra seldom referred to her daughter's boy-friend in his absence except as 'the American'.

'Perhaps they never came home.'

Myra had already guessed that they had never come home; but she now preferred to ignore this supposition. Twisting the handle of the door she coaxed again: '*Please*, darling. Just for once be helpful. You don't expect *me* to get on your bicycle and go instead? Do you?'

Roger began to snort with unexpected laughter at the idea.

Enraged, his mother stared at him; then all at once she put the fingers of both hands to her lips, letting the dressing-gown fall open on her black lace nightgown, wrinkled up her face and let out one gulping sob after another.

'Mummy! *Please!*'

It was the one thing he could not stand; to see her cry filled him with pity, embarrassment, hatred and shame all at once.

'*Mummy!*'

She had put her forehead to the door; her whole body was shaking.

'Oh Mummy!' He jumped up, ran to her and put an arm round her wildly jerking shoulders.

'What's come over you?' she got out between sobs. 'I don't understand. I just don't understand.'

'All right,' he said. 'I'll go. All right.' First he was consolatory; then in a sudden rage he shouted 'All right! I've said I'll go! All right!'

She clutched at him still; even her tears, smearing his cheeks as well as her own, seemed to smell of whisky.

'You're really a very sweet boy,' she said. 'And we've all been such pals. I don't know what I'd do without you. Such pals.'

Gently but remorselessly he freed himself from her grasp and made for the stairs.

'Oh, darling,' she called after him. 'One other thing. Daddy's *News of the World*. You won't forget Daddy's *News of the World*? They seem to have forgotten to bring the papers this morning.'

'Perhaps they'd bring them if you remembered to pay the bill,' he shouted back over his shoulder. Then he added, pausing on the landing: 'Daddy can jolly well get his own *News of the World*.' As he continued down the stairs, he muttered, now to himself, 'I'll be damned if I'll get it for him.'

When Roger entered the delicatessen, he at once saw that Dick Harrap was standing at the counter. A young, fair-haired man with muscular shoulders and acne on the back of his neck, Harrap was wearing a blue pin-stripe suit shiny at the seat and elbows. In one hand he was carrying what looked like a prayer book.

'Yes,' he was saying, in a vaguely distracted voice. 'Yes. What else? What else do I need? Oh, some pork luncheon meat – a tin of pork luncheon meat.'

The Jewish owner of the delicatessen scratched at the thick black hair on one of his bare arms, said, 'No pork luncheon meat,' in a good-natured voice, and then added, 'I've got some nice tinned beef, if that's any use to you.'

'Oh, yes, yes. Sorry. Yes.' The acne-covered neck went scarlet. 'That'll be fine.' His purchases completed, Harrap almost bumped into Roger as he left the counter, calculating the change in a sweaty palm. 'Oops! Sorry!' Then he saw who it was and greeted him: 'Hello, Roger! Long time, no see.'

'I was at the baths on Tuesday. I was there all afternoon. You never came.'

'Oh, gosh! Yes. I had to put in some extra work – one of the other blokes ill.' He frowned in an effort at recollection. 'But I told your mother I couldn't make it. I met her coming out of the Druid's Head and I asked her to give you a message.'

'Mummy never gives a message.'

'On principle, you mean?'

Roger, who suspected that his mother had no principles, shook his head. 'She forgets.'

'Anyway, I'll be seeing you this afternoon, won't I?'

'Will you?'

'Of course I will.' By now they were standing beside Harrap's motor-bicycle, Roger resting a hand on its worn seat. 'Your mother asked me to pop in for a cuppa.'

'Oh, good,' Roger said without enthusiasm. He always preferred to see Harrap away from home.

Harrap straddled the machine and kicked its engine into loud, throbbing life. His cheeks and lips trembled at the vibration, his large hands gripped the handlebars. 'Expected to see you at church,' he shouted above the din.

Roger did not confess that he had been to the Roman Catholic Church up the road, but instead merely shrugged his shoulders and pulled a little face.

'Bad boy!' A black-gloved hand waved. 'See you!'

'Don't come too early. We won't have finished lunch,' Roger shouted in warning. But the motor-bicycle had already screeched giddily round the corner.

Marje lay out in a deck-chair in the garden, picking tar off her brown suede boots with a twig. The prematurely middle-aged American, whom everyone called Mac, was asleep on the grass beside her, a thread of silvery saliva glinting in the sunlight as it stretched from his openly snoring mouth to his ear. 'That beach,' she said. 'It's a disgrace.'

'Oh, darling, I do wish that you'd cleaned those boots of yours a little earlier. Now we'll have tar all over the carpets yet again.'

'Eucalyptus oil. It only needs some eucalyptus oil. That always does the trick.'

'Fine,' her mother agreed, sucking deeply on the cigarette she held between thumb and forefinger. 'But who's going to go on hands and knees to deal with it? You really are a rather thoughtless girl.'

'Oh, *please*, Mummy! Must you always nag? You *know* that I'm not feeling awfully well.'

'I wish I knew what was the matter with you.'

'Oh, it's just the usual.'

'You really ought to have that little op.'

'Do shut up! When I decide to have the operation, I'll have it. Now let's drop the subject.'

'What operation?' Roger looked up to ask from the flower-bed he was weeding.

'None of your business.'

Perhaps she had to have an abortion, Roger thought with swift distaste. Serve her right! He would always remember coming on the two of them in the dining room, the curtains undrawn and that heaving and grunting, as though of some dying animal, from the shadows of one corner. 'Beat it!' Mac had said hoarsely and Roger had beaten it, taking the stairs in twos and threes. He had thought that, when Mummy and Daddy came home, he ought to tell them; but in the event they were in the middle of one of their rows and he preferred to sit, shivering with anger and disgust, before his test-tubes and retorts, their hysterically acrimonious voices reverberating up the stairwell, rather than go down.

Jack now came limping across the lawn, a silk scarf at his throat and his neatly crimped blond hair appearing as no more than an extension of the lined forehead below it. He was nine years younger than his wife and it was on her money that they lived.

'Where's my *News of the World*?' he demanded, in that parody of a military voice that Roger's schoolmates had been quick to take off.

'Roger forgot to buy it,' Myra said. 'You can have Mac's *Observer*.'

'Christ no! No thanks!'

'How's the head?'

'Hellish.'

'What about a little drinkie before lunch?'

'Well, that might help, I suppose. What's yours?'

'Some of that supermarket gin.' Myra raised her glass.

'Gut-rot,' he said. He stooped and pinched Marje's leg. 'How's our Marje?' he asked.

Marje scowled at him. 'Our Marje is not feeling well,' she retorted.

'Too many psychedelic experiences?'

'Oh, pack it in!'

'Anyway that pallor suits you. Yes, it suits you. Doesn't it, Mac?'

Mac had already opened one eye; now he opened the other, frowning up as he brushed away the thread of saliva on the back of a bony hand. 'Christ, I had such a dream!' he exclaimed. 'Wow!'

Roger straightened himself by the flower-bed and began to wander over.

'A nice dream?' Myra asked, lighting one cigarette from another and then tossing the used one over her shoulder.

'Nice? *Horrible!* I dreamed about that witch-wife of mine. And the two brats. Dreamed I was going on a long, long journey with them and they were always getting lost or wanting something. Horrible, just horrible.'

'Poor darling,' Marje said, stooping to run her finger through his thinning red hair.

'What about lunch?' Roger asked.

His mother looked up at him, hugging her trousered legs. He hated to see her in trousers; once she had even worn them when

81

visiting him at school – the other boys had been merciless about the size of her bum. 'What about what, darling?' she asked.

'Lunch,' he almost shouted. 'I'm famished.'

'Poor dear. Yes, I must do something about it.' She got to her feet, still clutching her glass of gin.

'It's gone three. If you put the joint in now, it'll *never* be ready.'

'Oh, let's forget the joint,' she said. 'We can have it for supper. Or tomorrow. I'll make an omelette Arnold Bennett – how about that? There's the haddock from yesterday.'

'From the day before yesterday,' Roger amended.

'I think your mother is fabulous,' Mac said, settling himself once again on the grass. As he said it, with a small sideways smile, it did not sound like a compliment.

'Do you want me to help you?' Roger asked. A moment before he had been thinking, Slut, slut, slut; but now as she waddled off across the lawn, with her blouse hanging loose around the trousers that constricted her thighs and buttocks, there was something so forlorn about her that he felt a sudden stab of pity. She was not a bad sort; not really. If Daddy had not had to leave Malaya, if she had not got that sugar-thing that made her have to inject herself, if she would only stop drinking. . . . He knew all the things she ought to do – leave Daddy for a start; and if only she would do them, then of course she could be happy. But she never would. Never.

'Well, that's sweet of you, darling.' She put an arm round his shoulder, splashing gin over his shirt-front without being aware of it, as she propelled him towards the house.

In the kitchen, with its piles of unwashed plates, its garbage bin that had overflowed on to the floor, and the two cats that set up an accusatory miaouing as soon as they entered, Roger asked: 'Hadn't we better clear up first?'

'Oh, *no*, darling. I couldn't bear it.'

'But it's so difficult. . . .'

'We'll do it all after lunch. Everyone will lend a hand. You'll see.'

She had said exactly the same thing the day before and no one had lent a hand and nothing had been done.

'The cats want some food.'

'Yes, I know, the poor sweeties! I meant to ask you to get them some tins when you went to the delicatessen. Never mind – we'll give them some of the haddock.' She took the fish out of the refrigerator, unwrapped it and held it to her nose. Then she extended it for him to smell. 'Do you think that fish is off? It shouldn't be, should it? I mean, salt fish doesn't go off, does it? Smell, darling.'

'I don't want to smell.'

'Oh, come on!'

He sniffed; there was a faint whiff of ammonia. 'Well, it *does* have rather a nasty pong.'

'I expect it'll be all right.'

'We don't all want to be poisoned, Mummy.'

For some reason that he could not explain and that caused him a strange unease, he found himself blushing as he said this.

'Poor Daddy feels queasy enough as it is!' she agreed. But she nonetheless began to prepare the haddock. 'He's rather hurt about your attitude to him,' she said.

'Hurt, Mummy?'

'You used to be such good friends.'

They had never been good friends; Roger had always hated his father and now he had also come to despise him. But he let that go, since he knew that it was important to his mother that the family should seem united.

'We still are,' he mumbled.

'Try to talk to him a little. He feels that you ignore him.'

'It's just – just that I have so much else to think about.'

'You and your stinks! Yes, darling, I know. But Daddy *can* be fearfully interesting. Honestly he can.'

Roger, who had heard his father tell over and over again the same dreary stories about his adventures as a policeman in Malaya, secretly doubted that. But he merely nodded now as he began to collect the knives and forks to put on the table.

'He's not an intellectual. I know that. But you could learn a lot from him. You give the impression of – well – looking down on him.'

'Oh, I don't do that,' he lied quickly. 'But we have so little in common.'

'Things have not been easy for him,' she said, as though in extenuation of his shortcomings. 'Having to leave Malaya like that really wrecked his life.'

'Even if that's true, that gives him no right to wreck yours,' he wanted to answer. But he restrained himself. 'What *are* his interests?' he asked instead. 'I've never really known.'

'What do you mean?' Myra was almost angry. Put point-blank like that, it was a question difficult to answer. She could hardly say, 'Sex and drink.' 'Well, there's his golf, dear,' she said at last. 'And he's very interested in politics. And horses. And the countryside. And - and his photography. Oh, you know all this!'

'He never uses the darkroom. It was just a waste of money. I could have had it for a lab.'

'Well, if you're nice to him,' she coaxed, 'then he might give it up to you.'

At that moment the door bell rang.

'We'd better not answer!'

Roger, who knew that it must be Harrap, was ashamed that his friend should find both his father and his mother tipsy and the lunch still uneaten at nearly four o'clock.

'Of course we must answer it.' Myra could never bear not to pick up the telephone as soon as it rang, not to open every letter as soon as it reached her, not to attend every function to which they were invited. She seemed to live in perpetual expectancy of some surprise that would at a stroke change all their lives.

Mac had loped to the front door. They heard him say, 'Hi!' and then Harrap's 'Good afternoon,' followed by some nervous clearing of the throat. Mac appeared:

'It's that schoolteacher pal of Roger's,' he announced in a voice obviously audible to Harrap, who could be seen through the two intervening doorways, a hand tugging at his collar as though it were too tight.

'Oh, Mr Harrap! Lovely to see you!' Myra hurried through the dining room, her glass again in one hand. She waved it in the air and more of the gin splashed out. 'We're fearfully late - we're just about to have our *lunch*. Do forgive us. Isn't it awful?'

'Would you like me to come back later?'

'Heavens no. You can share our omelette Arnold Bennett. Or I can make you a cup of tea. Whichever you prefer.'

'Well, I think I'd really rather have a cup of tea. If that's no trouble.'

'Of course you would! Roger - be an angel and put on the kettle.'

'Do let me help,' Harrap volunteered. 'Living alone, I'm really very domesticated.'

'One day you must show us your flat.'

'"Flat" is far too grand a word for it. It's only a furnished room. . . . How are things, Roger?' But Roger sensed an absence of warmth in the routine question, as always when Harrap spoke to him in the house. Outside it was different; then the schoolmaster's voice took on a lingering, almost caressive quality and he had the habit of staring at the boy with his pale blue eyes for seconds on end.

Harrap now joined Roger in laying the table; but to the boy's shame there were not enough knives and forks until Myra ran some of the dirty ones under the tap and then wiped them off on a cloth that was used indiscriminately to dry both the crockery and cutlery.

'You must think us a real slum family,' Myra remarked as she handed him the still greasy silver.

'Not at all,' Harrap assured her; but he had been shocked to discover that people whom he had always regarded as rich should live in far worse squalor than his own family in Doncaster, his landlady, or himself.

When at last they had all sat down at the table, Marje raised a forkful of the omelette Arnold Bennett and then put it down again. 'This is off,' she said decisively.

'Oh darling, is it?' Myra wailed.

'Of course it is.'

Mac lifted his whole plate and sniffed at it. 'It smells *very* odd.'

'What do you think, Dick?' It was the first time that Roger had ever heard his mother call Harrap by his Christian name and it gave him a jar. She held out her plate.

Harrap sniffed in turn; then he said with nervous diffidence: 'Smells all right to me.'

Myra jumped to her feet. 'Bloody hell!' She began to gather up the plates, crushing the servings of omelette as she placed them one on top of the other. 'Well, well, we'll just have to make do with bread and cheese and fruit. At least this wine is good. . . . Roger, *do* give me a hand.'

In the kitchen Roger said to her, 'Oh, I'm sick of it!'

'Sick of what?'

'All this – this *mess*!'

'What mess?'

'Never mind.' He was on the verge of tears. Angrily he swallowed and swallowed yet again, his throat aching and his eyelids feeling as though grit were lodged beneath them.

'He's nice,' Myra said, as she unwrapped some cheese.

'Who's nice?'

'Dick.' Roger could see that she was now really drunk. 'I once knew a limerick about someone called Dick. How did it go?' Balancing the cheeseboard on the uplifted palm of one hand, like a waiter with a tray, she waddled back into the dining room, tripped and sent Gruyère, Camembert and Cheddar tumbling across the carpet. 'Thanks, Dick. Thanks,' she said, as he stooped to help her retrieve the fragments. 'Thanks a million.' Still kneeling, she dusted a piece of Cheddar on her blouse. 'I was trying to remember a limerick I used to know. About a young man called Dick. Do you know it?'

Dick shook his head.

'How did it go?' She thought, the hand clutching the piece of Cheddar raised to her cheek. ' "There once was a fellow called Dick, Who was known for the size of his prick. . . ." '

'*Mummy!*'

'What's the matter, darling? You know far worse words than that, I'll bet. . . . Roger! *Roger!*'

But the boy had fled into the garden.

'Now where's he gone to?' Myra asked, lumbering to her feet.

'Leave him,' Marje said. 'Don't worry.'

'What's the matter with the child?' Myra demanded, at last putting the cheese on to the board. 'Did I say something so bad?' she asked Harrap; but, flushed, he did not reply.

'He's a silly little prig,' Jack remarked, pouring some wine into his glass. 'I don't know what they've done to him at that expensive school of his. He usedn't to be like that.'

'We-ell, I can understand it,' Mac drawled.

'Can you?' Myra heaved a sigh. 'I wish I could.'

'Sure I can.' The American cracked the joints of his bony fingers one by one as he began his exposition. 'Reaction. That's what it is. We all – all of us here – reacted against the oppression – and – er – *sup*pression of our family backgrounds. Right? That's what makes us tick. Right? We believe in individualism and a healthy contempt for authority and the need to call a spade a spade – or a prick a prick.' Harrap's flush darkened even further, but the rest of them laughed. 'But Roger here – as I see it – is reacting against our permissiveness. He craves authority. Discipline. Order and conformity and convention and all the rest of the crap we flung out of the window.'

Myra was staring at him in admiration, her pudgy chin cradled in a far from clean palm. 'Oh, Mac, you put these things so clearly. In perspective. Doesn't he, Marje?'

'Well, he ought to,' Marje said acidly. 'After all, he *majored* in psychiatry.' It was obvious from her tone that they were soon due for another of the spells of bickering that afflicted them like a recurrent hysteria.

'Doesn't he put it well, Dick? Don't you think?'

Harrap nodded unhappily. Then summoning courage, he cleared his throat and said, 'I've always regarded myself as a rather conformist person too.' He swallowed. 'Actually.'

'But you're not conformist! Not in the way poor Roger is!' Myra shrilled out. Suddenly on a drunken impulse she put a hand over his. 'Is that tea very horrid?'

It was. But he shook his head, staring fascinatedly into her blotchy but far from uncomely face.

Roger sat on a bench and gazed morosely now at the dull grey waves and now at the passers-by. His stomach rumbled with hunger but he had run out of the house without taking any money with him and so could not buy a hot-dog from the stall behind him. At first the smell of vinegar and burning fat had sharpened his appetite; but now it had become so nauseating that he kept telling himself that he would have to move on.

Oh, the mess of it, the *mess*! It hadn't always been like that: not when Daddy had been on his own out in Malaya because Mummy had only just started her sugar-thing and no one really knew what was wrong with her and they had that little furnished house at Bexhill with the sitting-room that had hardly any room in it for the whale-like sofa and two armchairs, all covered in the same curious, shiny grey material. Meals were on time then and the kitchen was clean and for a whole year they had had the same daily woman, that one with the cleft palate and the dyed orange hair, instead of a whole succession of Austrian couples and *au pairs* and chars who flounced out of the house saying that they had just about had enough. What had gone wrong? What had happened? Daddy had tried a number of jobs and, failing at them, had then put Mummy's money into a number of businesses at which he had also failed. Mummy had started to drink more and more and to care less and less what people might think of her. Using all those dirty words she had never used before. Chain-smoking. Not bothering to change the sheets or to wash his shirts for him or to buy anything *proper* to eat. No puddings, unless they were those awful stodgy pies that came in packets. Tins. Sausages. Frozen vegetables when everyone knew that they had far fewer vitamins than fresh ones.

If only she would listen to him he could put it all right. First, of course – pay off Daddy. What did they call it – alimony? That was usually paid by the husband to the wife but there was probably no reason why it shouldn't be the other way round. Sell the house – it was all very well to say that one couldn't live in anything but a Regency house, but who wanted damp in the basement and cockroaches and mice in the kitchen and all those stairs going up and up and up? What they should have was one of those modern flats along the seafront. Mummy would have to lay off the drink. And inject herself regularly. Marje would have to be told to behave herself. Or else. It was a waste of time for someone like her to go to the university, where all she did was to fool around. A secretarial course. Or she could train to work in a hospital. Discipline was what she needed.

Clutching his stomach, he swayed back and forth in mingled misery and hunger. What was the use? Mummy would never listen to him. He had tried to tell her something of what he felt often enough in the past and she would hug him and say, 'Poor little darling,' or 'You mustn't be so censorious,' or 'Darling you're so young – you must try to understand what it means to be grown-up.' If being grown-up meant never paying bills or keeping appointments or looking after things, then he preferred to stay as he was.

He jumped to his feet and began to wander aimlessly along the front. His head was throbbing now and, although he could no longer smell the hot-dog stand, he still felt vaguely sick.

Eventually he found himself trailing up the road of squalid rooming houses and boarding houses in which Harrap lived. He had not been conscious of making in that direction until all at once there he was, outside the narrow Victorian house with the extraordinary multicoloured art-nouveau glass porch and the rust-coloured paint that was flaking off like scalded skin. 'Petrada'. He had thought it such an odd name until Harrap had explained to him that the landlady's dead husband had been Peter and she herself was Ada.

Peering into the shed, constructed of tarred clapboard and rusty corrugated iron, that nudged the red-brick side of the narrow, mean-looking house, he was surprised to see Harrap's motorbicycle gleaming from the shadows. No doubt, shocked and disgusted by what he had found at Lewes Crescent, he had beat a retreat as soon as he could.

Roger wandered round the side of the house and on an impulse tapped on Harrap's ground-floor window. Then, regretting that he had done so, he began to hurry off.

'Hey! Roger! What are you doing here?'

'Oh, you *are* in!' he said feebly, turning. 'I didn't know. I knocked on the off-chance but you didn't seem to hear me the first time.'

'Come in. The front door's open.'

'But aren't I disturbing you? I'm sure you've lots to do.'

'I have. Thirty-three compositions to correct. But never mind. I can take ten minutes off.'

As Roger opened the front door, the landlady appeared from her sitting-room, gave him a stern, appraising glance and then said, '*Good* afternoon.'

'I – I came to see Mr Harrap.'

'That's all right, Mrs Mills. Thank you very much.' Harrap's voice had the same artificially jolly tone that it assumed when talking to Myra or Marje. 'This way, Roger.'

Since Roger had visited Harrap's room a number of times, he wondered why the older man should think it necessary to tell him the way.

Mrs Mills leant her sixteen stone against the front door. 'You haven't closed the door properly.'

'Oh, haven't I? Sorry.' The boy turned, flustered.

'All right, I've done it.'

When Harrap had shut his own door, he smiled at Roger and said, 'She's always in a disagreeable mood on Sundays. Don't ask me why.' He picked a box of chocolate peppermint creams out of a confusion of exercise books and papers and held it out.

'Thanks.' Roger munched. 'That's the first thing I've had to eat today.'

'*What?*'

'None of the others has any breakfast on Sunday. And I – I couldn't be bothered to get my own. And then – as you know – I rushed away like that before I'd had my lunch.'

'You'd better have a biscuit.' Harrap fumbled in a cupboard stuffed with clothes, most of them soiled, and eventually extricated a tin from under a rugger vest. It had a powder-blue poodle on its lid. 'They're a bit soggy,' he said.

He was right; but Roger did not mind the sogginess, so hungry was he feeling.

'Sit,' Harrap said, lowering himself on to the unmade bed.

Roger sat, not on the bed as Harrap seemed to indicate but on an upright chair, over which a tweed jacket was draped.

'I'm sorry this room is such a slum. I never seem to have a moment.'

'It's nothing compared to our house. That really *is* a slum.'

Harrap gave the boy that long, meditative stare of his, his pale blue eyes seeming to focus not on the eyes opposite to them but on a point somewhere between them and the mouth. 'Poor Roger,' he said at last.

Roger squirmed on the chair, at once touched and yet obscurely put to shame by the other's pitying tone.

'I shouldn't have run off like that,' he said.

'No, you shouldn't,' Harrap agreed.

'It's just that – that. . . .' He was at a loss for words, as one of his hands fiddled with a button-hole of the jacket against which he was leaning. 'All that – that *mess*,' he got out at last, with an involuntary grimace.

Harrap laughed. 'What about the mess in here?' he asked.

'Oh, that's different,' Roger said.

Again Harrap laughed. 'How different?'

Roger did not know; but different it certainly was. He shook his head, drawing his brows together so that his steel-rimmed spectacles edged further down his nose.

'You must be more tolerant,' Harrap said.

'That's what my mother tells me. I try to be tolerant.'

'But you don't really succeed. Is that it?'

Roger jumped off the chair and went to the window. The concrete-paved yard contained nothing but three dust-bins and, in one corner, a number of flowerpots, most of them lying on their sides, out of which vegetation trailed yellow and limp. 'I wish I could get away.'

'Where to?'

'Anywhere.' He turned: 'You know, I must be the only boy at school who prefers school to the holidays.'

'But that's awful, Roger.' Again the pale blue eyes fixed themselves on the boy's face with a curiously withdrawn, yet melting gaze. 'I'd no idea you were *that* unhappy.'

'I wouldn't care if the whole lot of them –' He broke off. He had been going to say, 'if the whole lot of them were dead,' but he now amended this to, 'if – if I were never to see any of them again.'

Something in the suppressed passion of the boy's declaration excited the schoolmaster. He got up. 'What a funny boy you are!'

'Am I?'

'Yes. You look so cool – and – intellectual – and in control of things. . . . And yet – really – behind that scholarly exterior. . . .' He stood close to Roger now, his large hands deep in the pockets of his creased grey flannel trousers and the weight of his whole body falling entirely on one out-thrust foot, as though in preparation for a spring. 'You say that now – about not caring if you never saw your family again – but what would you do if suddenly you were all alone?'

'I'd manage,' the boy mumbled almost sulkily.

'Would you? How?'

The boy shrugged. 'Oh, I'd manage. I'm not a baby.'

'You could make your home with me. I – I could adopt you.' Harrap's tone was bantering; but his lower lip trembled oddly until he bit on it. 'Yes,' he said, 'I could adopt you. Would you like that?'

Roger did not answer. He had picked up one of the exercise books and was turning the pages over.

'Would you? No great enthusiasm, I see!'

'I ought to go. Perhaps my mother is worrying.'

'You could telephone.'

'No, I'd better go, I think. Thank you.'

In a vaguely cross voice, Harrap said. 'Well, come again. Any time. Whenever suits you.'

He opened the door.

Roger caught his hand. 'Thanks,' he said. 'Thanks a lot.'

Then he was gone, hurrying past Mrs Mills's door, which creaked open as he passed it.

As he strode back along the front, his eyes blinking against the wind that whirled dust and scraps of paper in spirals at every corner, Roger felt at once excited and disappointed. Of course it had been only a joke, that suggestion of adoption. But he had been a real idiot, failing to respond. The truth was Harrap made him feel unaccountably shy; and when he was shy he knew that he sounded cross and – and censorious. Censorious. It was the word that Daddy now used about him often. 'Oh, don't be so bloody censorious!' he would shout. Or, 'You and those censorious airs of yours!'

Just before he reached Lewes Crescent he stopped and looked down from the Drive, first on the crowds on the promenade below, then to the beach, from which the last bathers were preparing to retreat, and finally out to sea. The dying sun had streaked the farthest crimped waves with an orange that faded at the edges of the horizon to yellow; and against this orange the silhouette of a ship slowly moved, its masts jabbing the sky like upended toothpicks. A woman's voice from the promenade was calling shrilly, 'Chang!

Come here! Come here this instant!' and as he listened to it he suddenly experienced a terrible thirst to be out there on that ship, moving off northwards into the silence and gathering darkness. He forgot that he hated the sea, that he could not swim and that the slightest swell invariably made him seasick; nor did he realize that the ship in question was, in fact, a dredger. He imagined himself lying out on a deck-chair, oblivious of the cold, and watching the waves roll away from either side of the stern, their tops glittering in the last light of the sun. A gong would sound out for dinner, all the other passengers would have already gone below; but he would be entirely content where he was. On and on moved the ship; and now, still on the deck-chair, he felt the shadow of the fiord they were entering falling coldly, thrillingly across his body and his eyes went up and up to scale the towering and wrinkled blue-grey rock that hemmed them in, on either side. 'Rock of ages cleft for me. . . .' The words came into his mind; and simultaneously, still lying out on the deck-chair, he felt a hand on his shoulder: 'All right?' It was Harrap's voice; and turning his head, he found him there behind him, his hand on the back of the chair, in a pair of white cotton shorts and gym shoes and a white cotton vest, at the neck of which the blond hair sprouted. (That was how he had first met him, at the public tennis-courts in St Ann's Well Gardens.)

. . . Roger shook himself. Again that voice, near now, shrilled out: 'Chang! *Will* you come here!' Then, puffing and with one ringed hand pressed to her side, an elderly woman emerged up the steps that led from the promenade to the Drive, her blue-veined legs bare and her arms covered in goose-pimples, with a Pekinese dog panting up behind her. 'The little monkey,' she said, either to herself or to Roger. She stooped with difficulty and attached a lead, while the dog gazed at her with huge eyes that smouldered like topazes in the slanting rays of the sun. She touched her purple hair, cut short in a fringe across her forehead, glanced at the boy and then waddled off with the waddling dog, admonishing him, 'Now walk! Just walk! Don't pull!'

When Roger looked again for his ship, it had miraculously vanished; and a moment later the orange swathe through which it had moved had darkened to mauve.

Myra was washing up alone. Apart from her, the house was deserted.
'Can I help you, Mummy?'
'Oh, there you are! No, I don't want any help. No thank you.'

She spoke in a cold, hurt voice, not looking up from the glass she was turning round and round as she polished it on a grubbily grey towel.

Silently Roger hunted for a clean cloth in the drawer of the dresser and then, having found one that was not actually clean but less dirty than the others, he no less silently set to work. Side by side they stood, Myra breathing heavily as though over some exacting physical task. Suddenly she burst out:

'What's the matter with you? For God's sake, what's the matter with you?'

He did not answer, fishing some knives out of the tepid greasy water in which they had been lying.

'What poor Dick Harrap thought I really do not know. When there are guests in the house you really might make an effort –'

'Well, what do you think he thought, coming in and finding us like that?' He spoke with the cold fury which, he now knew, always terrified her; and the fact that it terrified her filled him with an exultant sense of power, if also with shame.

'Like what?'

'Not having had lunch at nearly four o'clock. The kitchen full of filth. And that awful meal.'

'Really! How dare you say that! Everyone agrees that I'm a jolly good cook.'

'When you can be bothered. Anyway that fish was bad.'

'Was that my fault? If that bloody fishmonger gives me a piece of expensive finnan haddock which is no longer fresh –'

'He wasn't to know that you'd forget to put it into the refrigerator. And keep it for days on end.'

Myra set down the glass she had been ineptly polishing and put a hand to her forehead. 'Oh stop it, stop it! *Please!* Why can't you be a little more understanding?'

Stubbornly he made no response to this plea, though part of him ached to do so.

'Don't you realize – I'm *ill*!'

'Oh, I know that, Mummy – we all know that. But if you'd remember to inject yourself –'

'How would you like to have to inject yourself – day after day after day?'

'I wouldn't *like* to do it. But if I *had* to do it –'

'Oh, you're so marvellous, so bloody marvellous!'

'I wish you wouldn't swear like that.'

'I'll damn well do what I like.'

He knew that he only had to put a little more pressure on her to reduce her to tears and the prospect of those tears at once excited him and filled him with dread.

'As you wish,' he said.

'You don't know how much I have to worry me.' Her voice broke on the word 'worry'. 'You just don't know.'

'Well, tell me.'

'You're still just a child. You've no idea what I have to go through. Oh, you're so hard. And so – self-satisfied.'

When she spoke of what she had to go through, he knew that she meant his father; but in that case, why not leave him?

'You could make a new start,' he ventured, at last, without looking up at her.

'What new start? What are you talking about?' With sudden violence she turned on him, her face, already glistening with sweat, darkening and growing oddly congested.

'You've got yourself into this rut,' he said with a new gentleness. 'If you could only get yourself out of it. Begin again. It wouldn't be difficult.' He swallowed. 'I'd help you.'

She stared down into the greasy washing-up water; then she jerked out the plug and continued to watch the water as it eddied away. 'There are no new starts,' she said, still staring down. 'That's where you show how young you are. New starts don't happen. They just don't happen.'

Mac and Marje had one of their recurrent quarrels and Marje took an overdose of the sleeping pills prescribed for Myra. Mac wept by Marje's bedside – passing in the corridor, Roger stopped and with tingling scalp and rising gorge, listened to his abrupt, hiccoughing sobs – and two nights later they borrowed some money, never to be repaid, off Myra and went to Amsterdam with a group of friends from the university.

The next week it was Myra who fell into a coma because she had failed to inject herself.

'But why, Mummy, why?' Roger asked her, when he had summoned the doctor – no one else was in the house – and she had at last been brought round.

Wearily she replied, 'Because I had so much else on my mind.'

'But did you *want* to die?' he demanded, kneeling by her bedside and clutching at a corner of the eiderdown as though he were about to jerk it off her.

Tears trickled from under her eyelids and coursed slowly down her cheeks. She was wearing the black net nightdress and he noticed the curious crease, like a red scar, that ran from between her breast almost to her left shoulder-blade.

'Did you? Mummy, did you?'

Still she did not answer, only turning herself over and away from him with a deep sigh and then drawing the bedclothes up to her chin.

Three days later it was Jack who was in trouble.

Roger returned home from a visit with Harrap to the King Alfred Baths and, as he slipped into the hall, hoping that no one would hear him so that he would be able to get on with some work in his room in peace, he was assailed by the voices of his mother and father from the kitchen. It was always a source of astonishment to him that they should spend so much time in that room and yet perform so few of the usual kitchen tasks. Hugging the damp roll of his towel and bathing trunks, he leant against the front door and listened.

'But how could you? How *could* you?' his mother was demanding, as Roger had so often heard her demand in the past; and as in the past his father seemed incapable of explaining. 'You said the last time,' she went on. 'You promised. Have you no control of yourself?'

His father mumbled something too low for him to catch.

'It'll be in all the papers,' Myra went on.

'Don't be a bloody fool! Who's interested in reading that kind of thing in the papers? Happens every day. I'm not that famous.'

'It'll be in the *Argus*.'

'To hell with the *Argus*!' Jack was slowly working himself into a self-indignant rage, as so often when she caught him out. 'I don't care a damn.'

'*You* don't care! Of course you don't. But what about us? I suppose that you don't care a damn about us either. I just can't understand how you could *stoop* to anything so – so squalid and – sordid – and, oh, puerile.'

'Now that's an end of it!'

'What do you mean – an end of it? It's only the beginning. You might go to gaol. Of course you might! Don't grin at me in that idiotic way. Of course you might! They're not likely to take such a lenient view now that it's the second time.'

'Well, at least in gaol I'd get a bit of peace.'

'Oh, I don't know, I just don't know,' Myra had begun to moan, almost inaudibly from the hall. Then suddenly she was shouting hysterically: 'Oh, don't just stand there! Can't you ever be of any use? If you'd *do* something, you'd have less time to get yourself into trouble. For God's sake do something! Stoke the boiler – or – or lay the table for supper – or peel these bloody potatoes for me.'

Roger stiffened suddenly as he heard the unmistakable sound of a slap, though at first he did not know who had slapped whom. Then he heard his father say: 'Steady, old girl! Steady!' in the threateningly craven voice of a man who feels obliged to challenge an opponent and yet has no intention of fighting. 'Steady on!'

'Let me go! You're hurting my wrist! *Will* you let me go!'

At that point Roger appeared in the door and Jack, hurriedly releasing Myra, began to rub one cheek. 'Your mother slapped me,' he said.

Roger looked from one of them to the other. 'What's it all about?'

His mother had turned to the cupboard she was tidying. 'Nothing,' she said. 'Nothing to do with you.'

'I heard you shouting at each other.'

'All right. We were shouting at each other. That's something married couples do – shout at each other. All right.'

Jack began to wander unhappily towards the door. 'Your mother's temper gets worse and worse,' he said. 'She ought to watch it.'

'If anyone ought to watch it, it's you,' Myra turned to scream at him.

Jack bolted.

'What *is* all this, Mother?'

'Nothing. I've told you, nothing.'

'When I came in you were saying something about – gaol.'

Myra, now kneeling by the cupboard as she savagely pulled out jars and tins and then thrust them back again, did not answer.

'You were, weren't you?'

'You'd no business to be listening to our conversation. It was private. Something between the two of us.'

'I could hardly *help* hearing. You were shouting so loudly.'

'Oh, for God's sake let me get on with this job in peace.'

Roger stared down at her; he had never noticed before that she had a small bald patch, the size of a sixpence, at the crown of her head. One of her shoulder-straps had slipped.

Hitching at it with one hand, she held up a jar with another.

'You're always so snooty about the *mess* in the kitchen, but what about this? What's this doing here?'

'It's my killing-bottle.'

'Your *what*?'

He would like to have added, 'Yes, I'd like to put the lot of you in it.' But he merely repeated, 'My killing-bottle. For killing my specimens – my butterflies.'

Myra pulled a face and put the bottle down among the others that contained coagulated grains of demerara sugar, sago, tea to which age had given the colour and consistency of chopped straw, prunes and haricot beans.

Roger was often to wonder later why he had not taken up the jar and carried it to his room.

'Oh, do go away!' Myra ordered irritably. 'Either lend me a hand or go away! I hate being watched.' Again she hitched at the shoulder-strap.

'Tell me what's the matter,' he pursued.

'Nothing's the matter!' she turned to shout at him, her rage against Jack transferred, as often in the past, to the tall, trembling boy.

'But I heard –' he persisted.

'Well, you'd no business to hear. Now – go away! Go – a – way!' Each isolated syllable was like a blow at the pit of his stomach.

Slowly he went.

Harrap was on his way to the laundromat on foot when Roger passed him on his bicycle. The schoolmaster was carrying a huge polythene bag stuffed with dirty clothes. The brakes of the ancient bicycle – Roger had repeatedly asked, in vain, that Jack should buy him a new one – squealed agonizingly as he came to a halt, one foot kicking at the edge of the pavement.

'Where are you off to?'

Harrap was wearing khaki shorts, smeared with grease, and a pair of sandals that flopped as he walked. Grease was also on one cheek-bone, on his hands and on a knee.

Roger had in fact been to Mass but he did not tell Harrap that. 'Oh, just taking a ride,' he mumbled.

'The motor-bike has packed it in again. I've been struggling with it for the last hour and a half.'

'Would you like me to look at it for you?' Once before Roger had been able to mend the motor-bicycle when Harrap had been incapable of doing so. But the other man had seemed almost to resent the assistance then, as he seemed almost to resent its offer now.

'Oh, I'll let the garage have a look at it,' he said. 'I think that one sometimes does more harm than good by trying to put these things right oneself.'

'Anyway let me take that bag for you.'

'It's only around the corner.'

'Never mind. I'll take it.'

Roger dismounted and placed the polythene bag across the handlebars of the bicycle, which he then began to push. The bag had the same animal odour that came from Harrap's body after they had played tennis together or had gone for a long walk; the same odour that clung to his room, even when he was out of it. Through the polythene he could see the soiled socks and the tennis vest and the grubby pyjamas and pants, and the sight of them all there, pressed against each other, filled him, not with distaste, but with a curious exaltation.

'It's hotting up,' Harrap said.

Roger swallowed and nodded his head.

'We might go for a swim today,' Harrap went on. 'Except that that wind has brought in a lot more tar. I'm going to teach you to do the crawl if it's the last thing I do. You can't go on doing that ladylike breaststroke.'

Roger blushed.

As they sat waiting in front of the washing machine, Harrap asked: 'How are things at home?'

Roger shook his head; he did not want either to think or to talk about them.

'Funny your father doing a thing like that. He doesn't seem the type. . . . Oh, well,' he went on charitably, 'I suppose that at a certain age any of us might make that kind of slip-up. That's why the magistrate asked for that medical report.'

Roger listened in mounting panic. Since he had overheard that conversation between his mother and father in the kitchen he had known that something was seriously amiss; but neither of them had said anything to him and, in spite of their anxious comings and goings, the visit of Mr Bird, their solicitor, and a number of other visits from men he had never seen before, he had, all unconsciously, made no further attempt to discover what was happening. Day after day he would sit up in his room working at what his mother called his 'stinks'; and at meal times he would merely allow himself to become another particle in the web of boring, viscous silence in which his parents were entrapped. He noticed how his mother seemed to be making up her face with even greater boldness and how – a sure sign that she was deeply unhappy – she would eat more than he and his father ate between them; he also noticed the curious twitch down one side of his father's face, causing him to screw up his mouth as though at some sudden, brief stab of pain.

'Do you prefer not to talk about it?' Harrap asked, leaning forward in his chair, grease-stained hands clasped, and looking into the flushed but expressionless face of the boy.

Still Roger did not answer.

'There's nothing to worry about,' Harrap went on. 'As I said, any man of that age might do the same thing. *I* might at fifty. *You* might,' he added with a laugh.

'Daddy's only forty-four.'

'Really? He looks much older. Doesn't he? Then your mother –'

'She's older than he.'

'Oh, I know it's difficult to imagine how anyone could do a thing like that. You probably think that it's – rather sordid. But honestly it's happening all the time. You mustn't take too serious a view of it.' The boy's curious withdrawn apathy had begun to worry him.

'I think your things are ready,' Roger said quietly.

Harrap leapt to his feet, relieved at the distraction. 'Oh, good show! So they are!'

'Yes, it was in the papers,' Myra said. 'In the *Argus*.' The trowel in her hand tossed up not merely some weeds but also a clump of pansies, which she at once tried to push back into the soil. 'I wasn't going to point it out to you. The less you knew about it the better.'

'Will he go to prison?'

'No. I don't think so.' She frowned, shook herself and then snapped: 'Of course he won't! Don't be idiotic!'

'He might.'

'They'll say he must have medical treatment. That young man at the Brighton General – that psychiatrist – he seems awfully nice. He'll fix it.'

'But what did he *do*?' Roger was standing over his mother as she knelt beside the flower-bed, her knees on a cushion which Jack had long ago ruined by being sick on it when drunk.

'Oh, it doesn't matter what he did! You saw the paper.'

'I never saw the paper. I heard about it from Harrap. And he never told me what he actually *did*.'

'Then why didn't you ask him?'

The answer was that his shame had prevented him. But he did not confess this to her, merely insisting, 'Mummy, do tell me. What did he *do*?'

She got to her feet, rubbing first one of her knees and then the other. A soil-covered hand went to the hair that was sticking in damp wisps to her forehead. 'Well, if you must know,' she said, with what was almost hatred in her voice, 'it was what is called indecent exposure. You know what *that* means?'

He nodded slowly, horrified. The sunlight glinted on an edge of the trowel as she turned it in her hands, peeling off the soil that clung to it.

'Your dear father was loitering on the beach – and there, it seems, were these girls from the High School – and he – he just –'

She broke off; one muddy hand went to her lips to check the sudden tears and simultaneously her mouth widened as though to bite on it.

'Mummy! Please!' He caught her by the arm and shook her. '*Please!*'

'Your dear father –' she began again. 'Your dear father –' Then in sudden hysteria she shouted: 'I want to die, I want to die!'

'You must try to understand.' Jack's voice was at once haughty and quavering. 'You're no longer a little boy.' He drew on one of the Gauloise cigarettes with which the house now always reeked and then started to cough, the back of his small, freckled hand to his neat moustache. 'You must see these things as – as an adult.'

'But how could you? How *could* you?' Without realizing it, Roger reproduced both his mother's words and her exact tone of voice. 'It's all so disgusting.'

'I agree it's not very – pretty.' The fingers that carried the cigarette to the slack, pink mouth trembled. 'But you really mustn't be such a little prig. You'll do worse things in your life, I'm willing to bet. Just you wait and see.'

'Poor Mummy. . . .'

'Your mother has been very understanding about the whole affair,' Jack said with an attempt at dignity. 'She's stuck by me. As any wife worth her salt *would* stick by her husband. As any son would stick by his father for the matter of that,' he added on a sudden vicious note. 'After all, what I did – though stupid – was hardly a crime. A temporary aberration.' He was quoting from Mr Bird, the solicitor. 'Could happen to anyone, as I said. These things – they – they just come over one. Just like that. Good God,

Roger, you must at some time in that blameless life of yours have had some impulse you couldn't control!'

Roger merely stared at his father, who was now stubbing out his half-smoked cigarette in the saucer of his late-morning cup of coffee.

'Why are you looking at me like that?' Jack demanded. 'As though I were an insect or something. Oh, you think yourself above all human failings, don't you, Mr Prig? Don't you? You make me sick!' He turned away petulantly on the sofa on which he was sitting, kicking out with his pyjamaed legs in the violence of his disgust.

'*You* make *me* sick,' Roger said quietly, as he left the room to his father's impotent shouting of 'How dare you speak to me like that? How dare you!'

At least his own room at the top of the house was quiet and orderly and clean. The books in the bookcase, which he himself had painted white, were arranged by subjects and by authors, and there was a catalogue to them as to the gramophone records – mostly of Bach and Byrd and Mozart and Haydn – that he had recently begun to collect. On the wall he had framed in black passepartout the four Dürer prints given to him by Harrap for Christmas. His work-table gleamed with jars and retorts and test-tubes.

It was such a hot day that even the white candlewick bedspread felt hot and sticky against his body as he threw himself upon it. No breeze came through the wide-open window.

Mess, mess, mess! There would never be any end to it; it would only get worse and worse, in the same way that the beautiful Regency house gathered more and more dust in its corners and crevices, more and more rubbish in its attics and more and more cockroaches and mice in its basements. The mess was self-perpetuating. And it was not even as if they were happy in their mess, like some of the boys at school. Mummy wanted to die, she had said so over and over again; and though Daddy was outwardly cocky, his despair was really even deeper than hers. What future could there be for them? They would go on drinking and spending money until, in the end, they would have to sell up the house. Then, in some smaller, more squalid house, they would go on drinking and spending money until it, too, had to be sold. 'I'd be better dead.' Mummy had said that more than once. Daddy had never said it but it was even more true of him. Roger stared up at the light that trembled like a distant wave on the ceiling of the room and then the thought came to him, suddenly powerful and vicious: 'And Marje would be better dead too. And Mac. The pair of them.' He raised his head on an elbow and brooded darkly. Then he got up from the bed, put Byrd's *Ave Verum Corpus* on the gramophone turntable, returned to the bed and, half-listening half-thinking, continued to stare up at the quivering wave on the ceiling above his head.

The whole house was stinking of curry. The smell had even crept up to his room and wrapped itself around the curtains and the two drip-dry shirts he had hung in a corner, a towel spread beneath them.

'Won't you really have some lunch with us, darling?'

Roger shook his head. 'It'll make me too late.'

'I've made a lovely curry,' Myra pleaded with a pathos that for a moment made him want to rush to her and hold her in his arms. 'You know you love curry.'

'I'll be late. I'll buy myself some sausage rolls at Clark's.'

'Can't you keep your darling Harrap waiting for a little?' Marje asked. 'One would think you were meeting a girl-friend.'

Roger was about to turn on her; but then he told himself, 'It doesn't matter. Let her say what she likes.'

Jack, who was already half drunk, his face covered in crimson blotches and his eyes dull, shouted, 'Let him go! If he doesn't want to have a civilized meal with us, he damn well doesn't have to! Does he?'

Mac drawled, 'I suppose this English passion for curry is a legacy of the Indian Em*pah*.'

'Aren't you going to kiss me goodbye, darling?'

But Roger had already gone.

For a while those last words of hers pursued him; he almost went back. Then he felt a strange, glacial calm spreading over his body; his nerves relaxed, his mouth ceased to feel dry, he no longer had to control the trembling of his hands and jaws. Gaily now he bicycled towards the sun and the King Alfred Baths and Harrap.

It would be all right. Of course there would be extensive enquiries; they would search through the dust and grime and disorder for a clue; they would wonder how the killing-bottle found itself on a shelf between a jar of demerara sugar and another of haricot beans; they might even question him with a mixture of suspicion for a potential murderer and pity for the only survivor of a terrible family tragedy. But they would be baffled by the lack both of motive and clues. They would decide in the end that somehow, inexplicably, a fatal mistake had occurred.

There were other ways he might have done it, of course; he had pondered them all. But the important thing was that with cyanide there would be no mess. On no account did he want any mess.

1964

Home

'Elizabeth and I have shared our lives for more than a quarter of a
century,' Eleanor was in the habit of saying. What she meant was
that Elizabeth had shared the expenses of the house for that period,
even though she seldom lived in it. 'Why on earth don't you bring
the arrangement to an end?' Elizabeth's friends, who were seldom
also Eleanor's friends, would ask her; and she would then explain
that she was really very fond of Eleanor, that she preferred to leave
her bits and pieces in the house than in store and that one day her
years of wandering would be over and she would wish to settle
down. But the true reason was a mixture of kindness and weakness:
she shrank from hurting others partly because she did not like to
inflict hurt and partly for fear of retaliation. So in Taos or in
Taormina, in Dubrovnik or in Delhi, she would regularly, every
month, inspect Eleanor's account and then write her a cheque for
rates, repairs, utilities and the wages of whatever 'treasure' was at
that moment in the process of turning into 'a dead loss'.

The two women were so unlike in every respect that people were
puzzled that they should ever have come together, much less continued together for that quarter of a century in which Eleanor took
such pride. The most common explanation was that Elizabeth, who
had been an orphan brought up by a succession of unloving relatives, found in Eleanor, her senior by sixteen years, a mother figure;

and certainly Eleanor was like many mothers who become fixed points in their children's lives but ones to which the children become less and less inclined to return.

'Elizabeth has to be abroad for her painting,' Eleanor would explain. But there seemed no reason why the watery watercolours of potted plants or bowls of fruit or the façades of houses or churches should not be as easily executed in St John's Wood as in some remote corner of the globe.

Two or three years would pass and then Elizabeth would return, to find that Eleanor had had her sofa re-covered with a particularly hideous chintz, or her room redecorated with a particularly hideous wallpaper. 'I know it's not *quite* what you'd have wanted. But as you probably saw from the account, that little man gave us an absolutely bargain price.' There were innumerable little men in Eleanor's life, who by a process similar to that which turned treasures to dead losses, progressed from being 'wonderful finds' to being 'rotters' or 'utter crooks'. 'You must be delighted to be back,' Eleanor's friends would say to Elizabeth – her own friends usually knew better – and she would agree that, yes, it was wonderful to be back. But after five or six weeks Eleanor would announce to all and sundry, 'Well, Elizabeth is off on her travels once again,' and, after a wine-and-cheese party, Elizabeth would vanish for a further two or three years.

But this time Elizabeth had been away for less than five months; she had come back because the family doctor had told her to come back.

'It's typical of that woman to take herself off just when I need her most. When I think of all that we've done for her. All that trouble with her son, getting him out on bail. That holiday we gave her in Cornwall.' It was Eleanor alone who had decided on the gift of the holiday; but it had nonetheless subsequently appeared as an item of expenditure in the monthly account between the two friends. 'These people are all alike. No sense of gratitude or responsibility.'

Pink-cheeked and white-haired, her large capable hands resting outside the bedclothes, Eleanor did not look like someone for whom it had been, as the doctor put it, 'touch and go' less than a week previously. Perhaps because she had nursed a deaf father for many years until his death, her voice had always seemed pitched to an invisible public meeting; and now, miraculously, it had lost none of its resonant timbre.

'I'll go to the agency tomorrow,' Elizabeth said. 'Anyway, what's the urgency? I can manage on my own for a while.'

But Eleanor refused ever to believe that Elizabeth was capable of housework, let alone cooking.

'I've made you an oxtail stew. I got up after breakfast and did it. As soon as that hopeless home-help had gone.'

'You *what*! But Adams said you weren't to get out of bed except for absolutely essential things.'

'It's not only *you*, dear. It's Miss Saarinen and Bob Graham. I had to think of them.'

'I could have dealt with them.'

'You know you loathe cooking.'

In fact, Elizabeth enjoyed cooking and cooked better than Eleanor; but the older woman had for so many years told all and sundry 'Elizabeth loathes cooking' that in the house in St John's Wood Elizabeth went into the kitchen only to do the washing-up. This Eleanor was always prepared to leave to her.

'They could eat out,' Elizabeth said.

'Then we'd have to give them money for it, wouldn't we? After all, they're supposed to get full board.'

'Eleanor dear, is it really necessary to have these lodgers?' One was a Finnish philologist at the Institute of Education; the other a distant male cousin of Eleanor's, who was working in a King's Road boutique while labouring at a novel.

'It's not *necessary*,' Eleanor said. 'But I do feel that it's, in a way, a duty. After all, they couldn't afford to live anywhere else in central London and we *do* have this big house, which is usually half empty.' Eleanor liked to maintain the fiction that, though she charged the lodgers twenty-five pounds a week for bed and board, it was only out of kindness that she kept them.

'But if you're ill,' Elizabeth said. 'They must understand.'

'Oh, I shall be up and about in a day or two. These little turns never leave me any the worse for wear. You know that.'

The little turn had, on this occasion, been a massive heart attack.

'But, Eleanor, Adams says you *must* take things easy. For a long, long time.'

'He's an old fusser. . . . You don't mind, do you, dear, that Bob is using your sitting-room for his study? After all, you can always use mine.'

Elizabeth did mind, especially since her permission had not been sought; but she decided that, with Eleanor so ill, it was better to make no opposition. 'Oh, that's all right,' she said. 'He's welcome to it.'

'That bedroom's so poky. He must have somewhere to spread himself – for his writing, I mean. And he's been paying extra for the use of the sitting-room, you know. I insisted on that.'

Elizabeth wondered for a moment why, if he were paying extra for a sitting-room that belonged to her and not to Eleanor, she had received none of the money; but that resentment too she put away from her, as though it were something soiled and soiling.

'You look much better than I'd hoped.'

'Oh, I feel perfectly all right. I can't think why that idiot Adams sent you such an alarmist bulletin.'

'Well, I was coming back anyway,' Elizabeth lied. 'I was getting bored with Greece.'

When she had left Eleanor – who had insisted that she must deal with some correspondence – Elizabeth set about exploring the house before the lodgers returned. A few weeks previously Eleanor had written to tell her that 'this perfectly marvellous little man,' an ex-marine, had painted the staircase from top to bottom; and now gloomily Elizabeth examined the paint encrusted like inexpertly applied icing to the banisters, the white splashes on a corner of a Bokhara rug inherited from an uncle, and the dents, obviously made by a ladder, on the William Morris wallpaper. It was the only wallpaper in the house that Elizabeth could bear to look at; she had been present at its choosing and for once had held out obstinately against Eleanor's demands for 'something a little less sombre – something gay and cosy'. Presumably, following the usual pattern, another little man would eventually have to be called in to repair the damage caused by the first little man; and so little man would follow little man, on and on *ad infinitum*. Elizabeth sighed, drawing her small pointed chin down on to the neck around which she always wore the same rope of pearls, a long-ago present from Eleanor.

At the top of the large Edwardian house was the attic room in which Miss Saarinen lived. It was typical of Eleanor to favour a man, however young and silly – and her cousin was both – at the expense of a woman, however elderly and worthy. Elizabeth had never met Miss Saarinen, but as she gazed round the neat, chill room, with its low ceiling and its white-wood furniture and its single-bar electric fire, she imagined someone equally neat and chill to match it. No doubt Miss Saarinen had herself knitted the pale blue cardigan that rested over the back of a chair; and no doubt Eleanor had persuaded her, as she persuaded all her female paying guests, that in lodgings in England it was customary to make one's own bed. On the dressing-table there was a photograph of a young naval officer with a wide, rectangular face and irregular teeth. Not a son, obviously. And, equally obviously, not a boy-friend. A favourite nephew, Elizabeth decided. She pulled open a drawer and glanced down at a pile of sanitary towels. Somehow she had imagined Miss Saarinen as long past the menopause. Then, feeling ashamed of herself, she pushed the drawer shut with a slam.

The boy's bedroom, which faced south and had two beds in it and received the benefit of central heating, smelled of cigarette smoke, of stale sweat and of something, acrid and vaguely cloying, that was less easily definable. The bed was unmade, because in this case the now vanished treasure had no doubt been instructed to make it for him and he was now waiting for someone to replace her; his pyjama trousers lay on the floor and his pyjama jacket had been festooned over the French nineteenth-century ormolu clock that had mysteriously travelled from the mantelpiece in Elizabeth's sitting-room to the bedside table. There were fag ends everywhere: in a tea-cup on the floor beside the bed, in the fireplace, in an empty soap-dish and even on the window-sill. For a moment Elizabeth decided that she had better do out the room; if she did not do it, then in a moment of madness Eleanor might attempt the task. But she was tired from her flight and tired from the innumerable, complicated mental adjustments she seemed to have to make as soon as she stepped over the threshold of the St John's Wood house.

The sitting-room – her sitting-room – was as untidy as the bed-room. A caster had come off one of the legs of her pretty little Victorian serpentine-backed sofa and someone, presumably the boy, had used her *Oxford Dictionary of Quotations* to prop it up. There were cigarette ends here too; three lay in a Sèvres bonbonnière that she had always particularly treasured. It was too bad of Eleanor not to see that her things were properly looked after, Elizabeth thought with sudden anger; but then she relented, reminding herself that Eleanor had no interest whatsoever in 'things': Sèvres or Doulton, Meissen or Denby, it was all one to her.

The boy had cleared Elizabeth's desk of everything on it: the little silver clock, shaped like a church, that she had inherited from a nanny; the large silver inkstand, encrusted with ink, that her mother had once used; the ugly twisting brass candlesticks that she had brought back from Benares; even the blotter and the lamp and the tray of pens. All had been ranged about the floor to make way for the typewriter and the papers scattered about it. She peered at the sheet actually in the machine and read, with bewilderment, 'I was a child and she was a child in this kingdom by the sea, She is older than the rocksss.'

Elizabeth felt slightly sick when she left the little room, crammed with possessions either inherited or collected during her wanderings. It's too bad of Eleanor, she thought again. It's not the first time either. This is *my* room. She's no business to let anyone else use it without asking me. But she always shrank from a clash of opposing wills and now the excuse that Eleanor was in no fit state to take on an argument made her decide that she would have to 'put up with it'. Putting up with it was something for which Elizabeth had a talent.

When abroad Elizabeth had always thought sentimentally of the house – it was, after all, the only permanent home she had ever known – but now, as she continued her exploration, a curious feeling of suffocation allied with one of despair began mysteriously to come over her. Nothing in the house seemed to belong to her any more, even though everything of any value was in fact hers. All the invisible nerves that had joined her to the Sèvres bonbonnière in which the boy had stubbed out his cigarettes, to the serpentine-backed Victorian sofa or to her desk and everything on it now seemed to shrivel up like the tendrils of a creeper when thrown on a bonfire. She had become all at once a stranger among things strange to her.

In an access of growing panic she pushed open the french windows of Eleanor's sitting-room and went out of the airless house into the airy London garden. A hand to her greying hair, a dumpy middle-aged woman with a beautiful, pale, oval face and weak eyes behind gold-rimmed spectacles, she breathed in deeply again and yet again the scent of the phlox from the herbaceous border that ran along one wall. When they had first come to inspect the dirty and dilapidated house just after the war, with its boarded-up windows and its damp-stains and its obscene scribblings on the tattered wallpaper, it was only this garden, dark green, mysterious and whispering, that had attracted her. Everywhere there had been overgrown shrubs; and between them huge docks and towering clumps of cow-parsley with the trailing, murderous arms of wild rose-bushes, festooned with bindweed. It had seemed then to be not a small back garden in London, but the heart of some secret place in the secret heart of the country. 'We'll have our work cut out getting this in order,' Eleanor had said; and the words had even then given Elizabeth a pang. Month by month Eleanor and her helpers – for a time Elizabeth was one of them – hacked and burned and trenched and planted; and long since the former wilderness had shrunk into this neat little jigsaw of herbaceous borders and triangular rose-beds and zigzag crazy paving.

Worst of all to Elizabeth had been the destruction of the drunken circular wooden summer-house at the remotest and darkest end of the garden. Apparently a novelist, long since forgotten but once successful, had lived in the house and had built himself this little revolving hut in which to work. Part of the roof had rotted away; birds had built their nests inside; and it was only by pushing hard that one could persuade the tottering little box to rotate on its rusty track. But Elizabeth – she could not have said why – adored it. 'We *must* have it repaired,' she used to say, and Eleanor would answer, 'Oh it'll cost a fortune, dear. Let's leave it for the moment.' Then Elizabeth went away and when after several months she came back again Eleanor said to her, 'Come and see my surprise for you.' She took Elizabeth into the garden and there in the place of the round wooden summer-house was a sensible square one, of red brick with leaded window-panes.

Elizabeth was appalled. But she rallied and said, 'Oh, Eleanor, how lovely!'

'It's useful too, because I had a shed made at the back for the mower and the garden tools. I knew you'd like it.'

Elizabeth never used the new summer-house except on the rare occasions when Eleanor carried tea out there. She used to wonder if Eleanor noticed her hatred of the place. Probably not, since she was observant only of things, never of feelings.

Now Elizabeth walked over to it and leant against its door, so that she could look back and up at the house. She could see a shadow move across Eleanor's curtains. That meant that she had got up for something or other. She ought really to go and see what she wanted, but with a brutality that surprised her she told herself: Well, let her get on with it. If she's so foolish, at her age, as to disobey the doctor, then she'll have to take the consequences!

Again she touched her close-cut greying hair, brushing a tendril of it away from her cheek. Was Eleanor going to die? The thought suddenly hit her. The tone of the doctor's letter – 'not at all happy about the long-term prognosis . . . defective valve . . . essential you should . . .' – suggested that she might. Reading the remote, measured phrases in a hotel bedroom overlooking the Lycabettus, Elizabeth had felt a rising nausea that had eventually made her stretch out on the bed, the letter still in her hand and her cheek pressed deep into a pillow. Then she had jumped up and rushed out into the afternoon glare to book a seat on the earliest plane back to England. From then until her arrival she had been unable to force more than a mouthful or two of food down her throat.

But now, her back against the door of the hideous, squat summerhouse, she found that, as she asked herself that question 'Is Eleanor going to die?', she could consider it calmly, even coldly, with none of that former flurry of panic and desolation. Eleanor had always seemed so firmly rooted in life, with her positive gestures and her positive decisions and that firm, loud voice of hers. It was hard to think of her as mortal.

Again the shadow moved behind the curtains. Elizabeth straightened and then forced herself to go in to see what her friend was doing.

Supper with the silent Miss Saarinen and the loquacious Bob was over.

'Oughtn't you to be trying to go to sleep, Eleanor dear?'

Eleanor was still propped up in bed, letters scattered everywhere around her. Her glasses were low on her long, bony nose; the grey hairnet she was wearing looked like a cobweb across her forehead.

'Must get through this lot first,' she said.

'Can't you leave them till tomorrow? I could help you. You could dictate to me on the typewriter.'

'I'm hopeless at dictating.' She might have added that Elizabeth was hopeless on the typewriter. 'No, dear, I feel perfectly all right. What you could do is make me a cup of Ovaltine.'

'Eleanor – do please stop.'

But Eleanor picked up another letter, her lips moving soundlessly as she read it to herself. Then she looked up over her glasses: 'How was the oxtail?'

'Delicious,' Elizabeth lied. The meat had been glutinous, as it had shredded from the bones; the gravy had been edged on the plate with a hardening frill of yellow fat.

'I sometimes think that I'm the only person who knows how to cook oxtail properly. The secret is in the time, of course. It must have at least six hours. . . . What about Miss Saarinen?'

'What about her?'

'Well, is she all right?'

'Oh, yes. She wanted to look in and see you but I put her off.'

'Why did you do that, dear? You go on as though I were seriously ill. I'd like to have had a little chat with her.'

'She doesn't seem exactly a chatty sort of person.'

'And Bob?'

'Oh, he chats away all right.'

'Such a nice boy. Oh – that reminds me. He hasn't yet given me his cheque. The rent. Perhaps you could remind him?' She threw down one letter and picked up another. But instead of reading it she again looked over her glasses at her friend: 'It's so nice to have you back, my dear,' she said.

'It's nice to *be* back.'

'I hope you're not going to go gadding off again too soon now. We want really to see something of you.'

'Oh, you're going to have me here for a long time,' Elizabeth said. 'You're going to get sick of me.'

At half past ten Elizabeth again entered Eleanor's room.

'Now, Eleanor, you really *must* stop! Please!'

'But it's only just gone ten.'

With unwonted decisiveness, Elizabeth began to gather together the letters, papers, magazines and books scattered about the bed.

'Dear – you're muddling them all up! Elizabeth!'

'We can sort them out again tomorrow.'

Eleanor sighed. 'So impractical. What's the good of my putting them all in order if you then muddle them up?'

'Now I'm going to bring you a wash-basin here. No, Eleanor, Adams said you were on no account to get up to wash. It's quite unnecessary now that I'm here. I can bring you everything you need.'

Elizabeth began to bustle around, while Eleanor shouted instructions at her. 'No, dear! Not that soap! . . . Don't squeeze so much toothpaste on the brush, just half an inch. . . . If you'd put down the basin, you'd find it easier to manage the jug. . . .' Eleanor had the faculty of always being able to make Elizabeth feel incompetent.

It was when Elizabeth was soaping her friend's hands and then sponging them – usually so strong-looking, they now seemed oddly helpless as they lay limply, one after the other, in hers – that the tenderness that had eluded her out in the garden suddenly returned. Elizabeth was relieved: she had feared that all her devotion to

Eleanor had suddenly and mysteriously dried at its source. The wedding ring – Eleanor's husband had been killed in the war, after they had been married for only a few weeks – was reassuringly tight on the finger. Even though she had been so dangerously ill, she had obviously lost no weight.

'Such a fuss,' Eleanor was muttering. 'Quite unnecessary.'

When Elizabeth had finished, she asked, 'Now have you all you need for the night?' She plucked away a pillow and began to plump it up. It was strange to be looking after Eleanor, in this total reversal of usual roles, and the unwontedness of it made her feel clumsy and somehow embarrassed.

'Everything, thank you, dear.'

'I've put the bell here. Now ring for me, if you need anything. I'm a light sleeper, as you know, and I'm certain to hear you.'

'Oh, I won't need anything.'

'Would you like one of my pills?'

'Heavens no!' Eleanor disapproved of 'drugging', as she called it.

'Well then – good night, dear.'

'Good night.'

Elizabeth put her lips to Eleanor's forehead. She had always hated physical contact and in the early days of their friendship she would involuntarily stiffen when Eleanor touched her or kissed her, or she had to touch her or kiss her back. But now she had grown used to it.

'Sleep well.'

'It's you who need the sleep. After that long plane journey of yours.'

Elizabeth had told Eleanor that she would bring her breakfast in bed at nine o'clock, after she had got Miss Saarinen off to the Institute and the boy off to the boutique in the King's Road. Miss Saarinen had left promptly at twenty to nine, but the boy, obviously in no mood to hurry, had chattered to her in his pale blue silk dressing-gown, a cigarette dangling from his loose mouth, while she washed up the breakfast things. He had eaten three fried eggs and a number of rashers of bacon.

'How ill *is* Eleanor?' he asked in a loud voice.

Elizabeth lowered her own voice as she answered, 'Very ill, I gather. Far iller than she knows.'

'Don't you think that doctor's got himself into a needless tizz? She doesn't strike me as all that bad.'

'He's a good doctor,' Elizabeth said, wishing the boy would go. She began to set out Eleanor's tray.

The boy put out his cigarette in one of the unwashed plates stacked by the sink and then, whistling under his breath, left the kitchen, taking with him the copy of *The Times* that Elizabeth was about to take to Eleanor. Elizabeth went in pursuit, but he had already gone into the lavatory.

There was no answer to her first knock on Eleanor's door and so she knocked a second time, balancing the tray awkwardly on a raised knee in order to free a hand to do so. After that she struggled with the door-handle and gave the door a gentle push with the toe of her shoe.

'Eleanor!'

Slamming the tray down on to the dressing-table, so violently that a brush shot to the floor, she rushed over to the bed where Eleanor lay sprawled across the bed-rest. The curtains were closed; the bed-side lamp was burning.

The counterpane was covered with papers and there were also papers on the floor, making a dry crunching noise, like insects, when Elizabeth trod on them in her panic.

Elizabeth grabbed Eleanor's shoulders and tried to pull her up and back on to the pillows. But even before she saw the swollen purple face, something about the still warm but stiffening flesh under the flimsy night-dress told her that her friend was dead. 'Oh, Eleanor!' she cried out once more, in what was half a moan and half a sob, letting the head fall forward again on to the bed rest.

She put both hands to her temples, swaying from side to side in a terrible access of grief. Until, suddenly, that undying worm that is present at almost every death bed, however deeply mourned and however little expected, raised its head in the deepest and darkest recesses of her being and whispered, 'Free! You're free! Your bond-age is over!'

Carefully she again attempted to raise Eleanor and this time, shrinking from that obstinate flesh and yet forcing herself to handle it, she at last succeeded. Eleanor's face lay back on the pillows; but it was a subtly different face, not merely because of its dreadful puffiness and its dreadful colour, but because the glasses had fallen off the long, crooked nose.

What on earth had Eleanor been doing? What were all these papers?

Elizabeth peered, picking up first one and then another.

All of them were bills for the last month; and on the bed-rest – a fountain pen had left a smear of ink on the counterpane beneath it – there was the beginning of an account in Eleanor's large, clear handwriting, as of a clever child. Elizabeth read:

June 2nd	Wages to Mrs. Turton	£8.00
	Window cleaner	1.50
June 3rd	Bulb for Miss S's room	0.35
June 4th	Early-morning tea service	12.00

Early-morning tea service! Elizabeth read no further.

In a fury that obliterated all her previous emotions of horror, shock and grief, she thought: Why the hell should I have to pay half for her early-morning tea service? I've never had early-morning tea once in this house.

1966

Hard Feelings

'Has my – ahm – nephew got here before me?'

Sometimes, as now, Adrian would describe Mike as his nephew or even as his son; but more often – since he was a snob in spite of his repeated protestation 'I can truthfully say that I haven't an ounce of snobbery in my make-up' – he would describe him as his secretary. Though he was never conscious of it, his choosing of one of these designations or the other depended on whether Mike was at that moment in favour or not. Mike was very much in favour that weekend, after a long period of being out of it.

'Your nephew, sir? No, sir, no one has asked for you.'

There had been a time when Adrian would take pains to mention to any desk clerk that the reason why he and Mike shared a room was that he had this dicky heart and his doctor had told him that he must always have help within call. But in recent years he had come to realize that whether he and Mike had adjoining rooms or shared a room was a matter of total indifference to the staffs of the anonymous London caravanserais in which on such occasions, forsaking Brown's or Bailey's, he would always put up.

'When he arrives, send him up, would you? Say that I'm waiting for him.'

'Very good, sir.' The desk clerk, who was not used to receiving tips from customers when they checked in, or indeed at any time, blushed as Adrian pushed a fifty-pence piece towards him. 'Er – thank you, sir.'

'Is that a Rifle Brigade tie you're wearing?' There was a variation of this worn ploy, in which Adrian asked if the tie were an Old Etonian one.

'This, sir? Oh, no, sir.' The young man fingered it delicately. 'Well, it may be, but if it is, I didn't know it. I bought it at Simpsons.'

'It gives you a vaguely military air. Which suits you. I like to be welcomed by a young man who's clean and well dressed and has hair that's a reasonable length. And polite. I stopped going to the rival establishment up the street after being cheeked by a night porter whom one could only describe as a hippie. Perhaps he was one of these revolting students out on strike.' When Adrian laughed, the clerk decided that he must join in too. 'Well, anyone can see that you're going to go places in this organization. I have a friend in the hotel business – one of the biggest men – and he tells me that the right kind of personnel are worth their weight in gold. Well, it stands to reason. We've built all these hotels but we've done damn little about finding the right people to staff them.'

The clerk was flattered by Adrian's attention, as simple people were usually flattered by his policy of what he called 'building-up'. The opposite of building-up was, of course, pulling-down – a process that Adrian confined only to those people not present to defend themselves against it. 'Yes, I make it my policy to build up. That's the way to get the best out of others.' Getting the best out of others meant getting out of them what was best for Adrian.

The diminutive page with the bags whistled in the lift and continued to whistle as he conducted Adrian down the corridor to his room. Adrian, who was unmusical, did not realize that the boy was whistling flat; but he was none the less irritated by the sound, regarding it as yet another indication of a decline in the quality of service in English hotels.

However, true to his building-up policy, he jingled the change in the pocket of his greatcoat, produced a ten-pence piece and held it out: 'There you are, my lad. . . . And how old would you be?'

The boy had just heaved Adrian's suitcase on to the luggage rack, an exertion that had left him surprisingly breathless. 'Sixteen, sir,' he said, in an adenoidal voice so high-pitched that Adrian assumed it had still to break. 'Thank you, sir.' He palmed the coin with none of the embarrassed hesitation of the desk clerk.

Adrian noticed with distaste that the boy's shoes were scuffed and his fingernails grubby and bitten, but he resolved to persevere. 'Sixteen! You're very tall for sixteen, aren't you? I should guess from your accent that you're a Geordie like myself.'

'No, sir. I'm a Scouse.'

There were times when Adrian, whose family had come from Northumberland, also claimed to be a Scouse, but it was too late to do so now. 'And how do you like it in the south?'

'It's not so bad.'

'But you don't get the same kind of folk. Not the same matiness. That's what I miss. The matiness. Give me the North Country' – he pronounced 'Country' as a stage Yorkshireman would – 'every time.'

When the boy had gone, Adrian began to unpack the suitcase that his sister Pamela had packed for him. Though he was to be away from Tunbridge Wells only for the night, she had put in three of everything: three pairs of shoes; three of the shirts, one of them silk, that she herself washed and ironed for him, since he was adamant that they should never be sent to the laundry; three of the silk-and-wool vests and pants that he always bought from Harrods, because wool alone chafed his skin; three pairs of socks and three sets of cuff-links and three ties. The cuff-links were larger and more ornate and the ties brighter and wider than one would expect this military-looking middle-aged man, with his neat, bristling white moustache and his brogue shoes and his conservatively cut tweed suit, to wear. Drat the woman! Adrian searched everywhere but there was no sign of his Floris Malmaison toilet water. She always contrived to forget something on these trips.

Although his shirt was spotless after the journey – he had put it on for the first time that morning – he nonetheless decided to change it for another. He would wear the purple tie, he decided, with the matching purple handkerchief peeping out of the breast pocket of his jacket. Mike had given them to him, with some subtle prompting, as a birthday present only a few days before the trouble had broken. Adrian had never worn them since. But now all that was behind them at last and it was somehow symbolic of the change to have decided to take them out of the drawer again and to put them to use. Mike should be pleased.

Adrian, who was obsessive about cleanliness – in the early years it had been difficult to persuade Mike to have a bath at least once a day, to change his underclothes regularly and to wash his hands

118

before meals – went into the bathroom in his pants and vest, to soap his neck and forearms and armpits and splash water over his face. Then he brushed his teeth vigorously and gargled with Listerine, throwing back his head and rolling his protuberant blue eyes from side to side. If only he had that toilet water! But at least he had the deodorant spray. It was the only brand of deodorant that he found he could use; every other kind brought him out into a rash.

He deliberated whether to squat on the lavatory; but he had already tried twice on the train, to no effect. It was odd how some people complained that excitement made them loose; with him it had precisely the opposite effect. He had better make sure that Pamela had remembered to pack the fruit salts.

Turning over the various medicaments in the suede leather pouch with which he always travelled, he was so absorbed that he did not hear the first knock at the door. At the second he felt a curious leap of panic, even though he had been telling himself for days how much he was looking forward to this reunion.

'Come in!'

The door opened and Mike entered, his suitcase in his hand. It was odd, Adrian had often reflected, how at these hotels there was always a page at hand to help him with his bags but Mike was usually left to lug his up himself.

'Hello, Adrian!'

'Mike! Marvellous to see you.'

Adrian pulled on his blue silk dressing-gown, and then hurried over. 'Let me look at you!' He gripped Mike's shoulders, holding him at arm's length. 'You look wonderful, Mike. Wonderful. Not a day older. God, it's good to see you again. Here, give me that case of yours.' But though he extended an arm, Adrian made no attempt to pick the case up. 'No, I shouldn't put it on the bed, if I were you. There's a rack contraption for it over there. Tell me all about yourself. You got my letter saying that I thought it best if we met here? You know what it's like getting across London. Otherwise I'd have met your train at the station.'

'That's OK, Adrian,' Mike said in a hoarse, subdued voice that seemed to belong to someone totally different from the exuberant Mike that Adrian had once known. 'I got a taxi. No time at all.'

'Oh, Mike! Extravagant as ever!'

'Well, I'm just getting over this flu. Don't seem I can shake it off. I told you in my letter. I've got no energy.'

Illness frightened Adrian. If he himself were ill, he rushed at once

119

to the doctor; if others were ill, he would either rush away, ignore the fact, or say that it was 'only nerves'. 'Well, you look in terrific health.'

'I wish I felt it.'

Adrian hoped that Mike was not going to be in one of his 'down' moods. They could last for several days, and no exhortations to 'snap out of it' or to 'look on the bright side, for God's sake' were of any avail.

'Poor Mike!'

Mike was about to stretch himself out on Adrian's bed, his shoes still on; but Adrian was quick enough to stop him just in time: 'Actually I thought I'd take that bed, as it's nearest to the door to the loo and you know how I often have to get up in the night. Do you mind?

'All the same to me.'

Mike stretched himself out on the other bed, putting his hands behind his head and emitting a couple of yawns so wide that Adrian could see his uvula.

'Don't tell me you're tired.'

'Like I said – I'm recovering from this flu.'

'Because I've planned an exciting evening for us,' Adrian went on, ignoring all mention of the flu. 'Two seats in the third row of the stalls for *No Sex, Please – We're British*. Pamela saw it and said that Evelyn Laye was terrific – didn't look a day over forty. And then I've booked a table – guess where?'

'Veeraswamy's?'

'You know I can't eat Indian food since I had that tummy trouble. No. I'm going to take you to Chez Pierre. Remember it?'

Mike remembered it. 'Yep,' he said without enthusiasm.

'You look terrific, Mike.'

Adrian always imagined that if one said a thing often enough and with enough conviction, it would eventually be true. In fact, Mike looked so far from terrific that his appearance after these five years had given Adrian a disagreeable pang, instead of the uplift he had promised himself. Drink sometimes had the same kind of effect on him these days: he would sip at a glass of brandy and find that, instead of his spirits rising, all that rose was a recalcitrant heartburn.

'Well, that's nice to know.'

'As handsome as ever. I bet you've been breaking hearts galore in Sheffield.'

In the past Mike had liked Adrian to flatter him about the good looks and the physical strength which he had possessed so conspicuously and, even more, about the business acumen in which he had been wholly deficient. But now he merely turned his head to one side on the pillow, emitting a long sigh.

For a moment Adrian was appalled as he looked at him. God, how he had aged. His face had fallen in – could it be that he was wearing false teeth? – and instead of that marvellous ruddy colour, recalling the boyhood spent on a farm near Taunton, his complexion had a greyish sheen, as of lard. The hair had not merely thinned, retreating on either side of the widow's peak so that the forehead looked disproportionately high for the features beneath it, but it had lost all that rich, oily, blue-black vitality that Adrian had once found so exciting. Mike had always spent an inordinate amount of time caring for two things: his hands and his figure. But the hands now looked raw and rubbed, many of the fingernails broken, with a nicotine stain on the right one that made it appear as if he had spilled iodine over forefinger and middle finger; and his figure had, quite literally, gone to pot, the abdominal muscles which he used to exercise each morning with innumerable press-ups now sagging to give him a little paunch.

But he was still good-looking, Adrian hurriedly assured himself; and those violet bruise-like shadows under the brown eyes – how odd that the eyes no longer sparkled – were probably only the result of that old trouble of *overdoing things* (the euphemism that Adrian had always used). None of us got any younger; one had to remember that five years had passed and Mike was now – what was it? – well, at least thirty-one.

'It's marvellous to see you again. As though it was not five years but only five days. Yet what a lot has happened.'

'It certainly has.'

Adrian went over to the bed and sat down on it, one hand cupping Mike's knee, while with the other he reached for his hand. (Yes, those nails certainly were ugly; but he had probably broken them at his work.) Mike did not move, one hand still behind his head, the other limply in Adrian's, and his eyes searching the ceiling.

'I think what you've done is a marvellous thing,' Adrian said. 'I always knew you would. Not many people would work their way back like that. I don't mind saying that I'm proud of you, Mike. Damned proud. You're a free man again. That's how I look at it. Because all these years you were like someone in prison, weren't you?'

'I don't want to talk about it.'

'No, of course, you don't. And we're not going to talk about it. But

I just wanted to say how – how *proud* I am of you.' Adrian squeezed the kneecap. 'You realize – don't you, Mike? – that I did it all for your own good? It wasn't revenge. You realize that, don't you? But I had to make you get back your self-respect. That was the important thing. If a man loses his self-respect – well – he's done for. Finished. Isn't he?'

'I don't want to talk about it, Adrian.'

Adrian leapt off the bed. 'Now not another word. It'll all be as if none of it had ever happened. We had such good times together before – before that nightmare. And we're going to have lots and lots of good times now. You'd better get off that bed and start getting ready, or we're going to be late.'

Mike sat up, rubbing at the inflamed lids of his eyes; but he did not rise to his feet. Again he gave a huge yawn. 'I'm ready,' he said.

'But wouldn't you like a shower?' Adrian persisted. 'Or a bath. I asked for both.' He noticed that Mike's shirt was grey around the collar and hurried on: 'And why don't you wear this shirt I have here?' He pulled open a drawer and held up a pale green silk shirt. 'I got it in the sales – at Austin Reed – only last week. Pamela thinks it too young for me, but we know how conservative she is! You can borrow it now and, if it really suits you, perhaps I'll give it to you.'

For the first time Mike showed some animation as he examined the shirt. 'It's a beauty,' he said. 'Real silk. I thought at first it was one of those terylene jobs. You know how terylene makes me sweat. Can I really borrow it?'

'Of course. But why not have a shower first?'

'I had a bath this morning.'

'After that long train journey it'll freshen you up. Go on. You'll find a cake of Chanel Gentleman's Soap in there. I brought it specially. I remembered how you like it.'

'So it's the life of luxury again,' Mike said, more as a question than a statement, as he stripped off first shirt and then vest. The sight, after all these years, of the dark pelt on his chest, narrowing to a line that ran down his navel and then again widened, filled Adrian with a sudden longing and sadness. Poor Mike! He was really a good boy, a very good boy! It was that Danish *au pair* slut and that whole Bayswater crowd that had really been responsible. He was weak, that was the trouble with him. A country boy, who couldn't resist the temptations that others put in his path.

'Dear Mike. Dear, *dear* Mike.'

Naked, Mike came over and stood beside Adrian. Then with a

nervous, tentative gesture, like someone making up his mind to stroke a dog that has the reputation of biting, he put out one of his hands and laid two fingers on the back of Adrian's neck. 'I've missed you,' he said.

'Have you really? Have you really, Mike?'

'Yep.' He looked down at Adrian, with a small, melancholy-bitter smile that Adrian could not remember ever having seen before. 'Sheffield was very different from Tunbridge Wells. And the factory was very different from the shop.'

Adrian sighed. 'There were often moments when I relented, Mike. I hated to think of you going through all that. But then I said to myself, "No, it's for his own good." And it was, Mike. Wasn't it?'

The younger man did not answer for several seconds. Then he seemed to shake himself: 'Yes, I guess it was, Adrian. Yes, I'm grateful to you.'

He went into the bathroom and as Adrian continued to sit there on the bed, listening to the sounds of splashing water, there came back to him, he did not know why, Mike's voice telling him about his father: '. . . He was a right old bastard. Hardly a day passed when he didn't take the strap to me. But I suppose I should be grateful to him. He made me what I am. There's many a kid nowadays, who needs that kind of treatment – just as I needed it – and who'll spoil for want of it.' They had been lying side by side – in Amsterdam, was it? – and Mike had been a little drunk as he talked up at the ceiling with Adrian's arm across his chest, pinioning him affectionately to the vast double bed.

'Yep, this is a super shirt, Adrian.'

Naked, Mike had returned to the bedroom, rubbing briskly at his hair with a towel, and peering down at the shirt.

'Oh, Mike! You silly boy! That's not the hotel towel, that's mine! Why on earth didn't you ask?' But then Adrian relented; it was a pity to spoil things at a time like this. 'But it doesn't matter. Go on! Use it! Use it!'

In the darkened theatre Adrian found himself stealing surreptitious glances at the face beside him. Occasionally Mike would laugh at some joke on the stage, but for most of the time his expression remained unhappy, even despairing, the eyes dull and the corners of the mouth – there was a small cold sore on one side – turned slightly down. In the interval he did not want a drink – 'No, don't let's bother,' he said, shaking his head when Adrian suggested one – though in the old days he always liked his double gin and tonic and the opportunity to quiz the audience.

'Not feeling too good?'

Mike shook his head. 'I'm feeling fine.'

'We've so much to talk about. Over dinner, not here. I've all kinds of ideas for the future.'

Mike stared emptily ahead of him, the knee that had been restless throughout the performance now once again beginning to jerk up and down.

In the restaurant Adrian said, 'I know exactly what you'll like,' and proceeded to order for Mike exactly what he liked himself. 'This is a celebration and only the very best will do,' he summed up, as he handed the menu back to the waiter. 'We must fatten you up, Mike. I don't think they feed you properly in those digs of yours.'

'Oh, the grub's not too bad. Plenty of it. But like I said, I've had this flu and I don't seem to be able to shake it off.'

'What shall we have to drink? Champagne? Yes, it must be champagne.'

After Adrian had dealt with the wine waiter at length, Mike leant forward, one large, raw hand supporting his chin, to ask, 'How's Pamela?'

'Pamela?' They had not yet talked of her. 'She's aged a bit, you know. But she keeps pretty fit and active. I wish *I* had her health and stamina, I can tell you that.' Although Adrian's sister had undergone a hysterectomy only a few months before, it was convenient for him to maintain the fiction that her health remained far superior to his own. 'She sent her love. And hopes to see you soon.'

'Thanks.'

Something in the intonation of the monosyllable made Adrian protest, 'You mustn't think that she doesn't like you, old chap. There was a time, I know, when she was – well – jealous. And of course all that business upset her a lot, it was bound to. Especially the loss of Aunt Bea's silver. But she shares my admiration for you now. It was an extraordinary achievement, paying us back through all these years. Quite extraordinary. I can't think of many other people who would have done it.'

Mike did not answer; he raised a *grissino* to his mouth and gnawed intently at the end with a dry, splintering sound, as though it were made of wood.

'I know you think that maybe I'd have been a bit more – ahm –

lenient, if it hadn't been for Pam. But you're wrong, you know, I'd have behaved just the same even if she hadn't had anything to do with it. I didn't *want* to put you through it. And the money wasn't *all* that important – or the other things. I've never been one who bothered much about possessions. Now have I? But I felt that you must get your self-respect back, like I said. Otherwise – well, how could things ever be right between us?'

'Yep, Adrian. I see that, of course I see that.'

Mike's tone was still apathetic and he did not look at Adrian as he spoke.

'This smoked salmon is superb, really superb. My God, they do you well here.' Adrian gulped a mouthful, and then, fork and knife poised, ruminated, his eyes fixed on the third button of the shimmering, pale green shirt opposite to him.

He had first met Mike, then a marine, in one of the pubs in Portsmouth to which, telling Pamela that he was going to attend a sale in that part of the world, he would make intermittent visits in search of what he called 'a teeny adventure'. Adrian was experienced enough to know that Mike, like every other of his past pickups in that pub, was interested only in making money; but he had also sensed in the boy something unusual – a deep-seated and totally unconscious craving for affection and admiration. A visit to Tunbridge Wells, when Pamela was on a cruise, was followed by weekends in London and weekends in Paris and Amsterdam and then three weeks in Torremolinos in the house of a rich and idle homosexual who was probably Adrian's closest friend. When Mike had eventually come to the end of his term of service it had seemed natural enough to ask him if he would like to work in the antique shop which Adrian and Pamela shared. 'What does he know about antiques?' Pamela had demanded, and Adrian had replied acidly, 'He doesn't have to *know* about antiques. What we need is someone strong enough to do all the fetching and carrying that we can't do.' But Mike, though strong, had a dislike of manual labour and the part-time helpers with whom Adrian had hoped to dispense were soon back again. What Mike, with his charm and air of openness, could do to surprising perfection was to sell.

'He's changed my whole life,' Adrian would gush. 'Who'd have thought that he'd make such a marvellous assistant? A totally uneducated boy like that. It's a miracle. A real miracle.'

Adrian set about 'civilizing' Mike – that was the word that he used to his friends and sometimes even to Mike himself – and in this mission he was generally far more successful than he had ever dared to hope. True, Mike never learned to hold a knife other than as if it were a pen and there were certain vowel sounds that no instruction could eradicate; but Adrian was soon able to boast to all and sundry, 'You know, I can take him absolutely anywhere without a moment of embarrassment.'

Of course Mike could be a wee bit naughty. He would drink too heavily and what he drank was often whisky for which Adrian and Pamela had paid. Then there were the 'sluts' (Adrian's word) on whom he would spend far more money than he could possibly afford and whom, when Pamela and Adrian were away, he would even bring back to the house, though emphatically and repeatedly told not to do so. 'He's not really interested in girls,' Adrian would say. 'But he must have at least one in tow if he's to keep his self-respect.' In this Adrian, so wrong about so many things that concerned Mike, probably was right.

When the netsuke disappeared – Adrian had picked it up for ten shillings in a junk shop in Battersea and, delighted with his cleverness, had assured Mike, with some exaggeration, that it was worth at least a hundred times that sum – it was natural enough to accept Mike's explanation that some customer must have pocketed it when his back was turned; after all, every dealer suffered that kind of loss from time to time. When, a few weeks later, the shop was burgled, Adrian again suspected nothing, though there were some odd features of the break-in that made one of the two detectives in charge of the case speculate that perhaps it might have been an inside job. Less than a month afterwards it was the turn of the house – among the things taken was all Aunt Bea's Georgian silver, left to Pamela alone, since the old woman had never cared for Adrian; and this time, too, the same detective talked of an inside job and questioned Adrian about everyone in his employment. Adrian admitted that he had never been entirely happy about an Irish knocker with whom he sometimes traded; and when the police revealed that this man had had a conviction for receiving stolen goods, Adrian went round saying that the police knew the identity of the culprit but just could not get enough evidence against him.

It was Pamela who finally trapped Mike. From time to time she had been complaining that small sums of money had been missing from her bag, but Adrian had pooh-poohed the idea of any theft – the trouble was, he told her, that she just splashed money around and forgot where she had done so. But Pamela, without telling

Adrian, marked some five-pound notes; and one of these she found in Mike's wallet, which she searched one night while he was having a bath.

Adrian still would not have believed Mike to be dishonest – he had a rare faculty for disbelieving anything that he did not wish to believe – had it not been that Mike himself poured out his confession. Seated tearfully in nothing but a dressing-gown on the edge of his bed, with an implacable Pamela on one side of him and a horrified Adrian on the other, he admitted to everything. 'Christ, I hate myself!' he kept exclaiming, between one nauseating detail and another. 'You trusted me, Adrian, you did all this for me, and this is how I have to pay you back. I'm a shit, Adrian. You've got to face the fact that I'm nothing but a shit.'

Eventually he broke into gulping sobs, that sounded like an effortful kind of retching, his large hands clasped between his bare knees and a thread of saliva running down his open mouth on to his chin and then to one lapel of the dressing-gown. Adrian, strangely moved as he had not been moved since the occasion, many years ago, of his mother's death, would have liked to have touched him in comfort, but he was too frightened of Pamela to do so.

'You'd better call the police,' Mike said at last.

Adrian looked at Pamela. Then he said, 'You know I couldn't do that.'

'But Christ, you've *got* to, Adrian! I mean to say! I deserve all that's coming to me.'

'I couldn't do that to an old friend like you.'

What Adrian really meant was that he could not do that to himself. He had a terror of scandal.

'But look how I've treated you! The one person who ever took any real trouble with me in the whole of my life. You've got to call the police.'

It was as though his desire for punishment was as intense as Pamela's desire to see punishment inflicted on him.

Adrian and Pamela stayed up late that evening discussing what course of action they must take. Meanwhile Mike lay on top of the bed in his room, still in nothing but the dressing-gown but indifferent to the cold that made his large hands grow clumsy and stiff, his teeth chatter and his body shake. Pamela had always really hated Mike, though she had pretended to like him; and like so many people who pass over the threshold of middle-age in the bitter knowledge that they have never known a reciprocated love, she regarded her possessions as extensions of her own being, so that what Mike had, in effect, done in making off with Aunt Bea's silver was to amputate a limb from her.

Eventually brother and sister managed to reach a verdict and together they went into Mike's room – it was significant that, for the first time since he had come to stay with them, neither of them knocked or asked if they might enter – and told him what it was. They would take no legal steps against him; but he would have to sign a confession of all that he had told them and over the next five years, week by week, he would have to pay back their losses.

'But you can't do that, Adrian!' Mike had cried out; and at first Adrian thought that he was protesting because the terms were too harsh. But then he went on, 'You ought to hand me over to the police. That's what I deserve. I'll take my punishment.'

Adrian shook his head. 'Pamela and I have decided that we just couldn't bring ourselves to do that.'

Mike's face was pulled out of shape, like a child's when it is about to give way to a storm of tears. Head lowered, he staggered off the bed, approached Adrian and then threw his arms around him, his head on his shoulder.

'Christ! What have I done to deserve a friend like you!'

The next day Mike went north to exile and five years of hard labour; and now the five years were over and the total restitution had been made.

Adrian raised his glass. 'We must drink to the future, Mike. To our future together.'

Hesitantly Mike raised his glass. 'To our future together?'

'Why not? You'll come back to the shop, won't you?'

'Well. I – I don't know.'

Mike put the rim of the glass to his lower lip but did not sip.

Adrian felt an upsurge of irritation that his offer should have evoked, not the expected joy, but a response so ambiguous.

'Wouldn't you *like* to come back?'

'I'd like to come back. 'Course I would, Adrian. But would it – I mean would it – would it *work*?'

'Why shouldn't it work?'

'There's Pam.'

'So what?'

Mike shrugged unhappily.

'Pam and I have discussed it all.' The discussions had, in fact, been prolonged and acrimonious; but as usual Adrian had finally got his way. 'She's in full agreement with me. A hundred per cent.

We both want you back.'

'Well, I'll have to think about it, won't I, Adrian?'

'Surely you don't want to go on in those frightful digs, doing that frightful job?'

Mike shook his head, again holding the glass against his lower lip without sipping it.

'Well then?' Adrian put out a hand and covered the raw hand that was clutching the stem of the glass. 'It can be as it used to be in the old days, Mike. It needn't be any different.'

Mike gave a sudden, choking laugh, not of mirth but hysteria. 'It's *got* to be different. You wouldn't want all that to happen again, would you?'

'It won't happen again.'

In the taxi on the way back to the hotel Adrian felt tender and relaxed. He slipped an arm round Mike's shoulder: 'Oh, it's good, it's damned good to have you back, Mike. All those years. I don't know how I got through them. Perhaps it was silly of me, perhaps I ought to have forgotten the whole affair and told you to return. But it wouldn't have been fair to you, would it? Would it, Mike?' Mike did not answer, his face expressionless as he stared out of the window at the lights that whisked past. 'Dear Mike.' Now Adrian had a hand on his knee. 'You know, you're the only person I've ever loved. Yes, honestly.' Adrian had said this to other people but now, in a moment of devastating clarity, he saw that it was true. He had never loved anyone else, because he had never been capable of loving; but somehow Mike had given him that capacity. Then he thought, with a piercing jab of excitement, of the hotel bedroom that awaited them.

There seemed to be an ineluctable weariness in all Mike's movements as he stripped off his clothes, dropping them unfolded, one by one, on a chair. Naked at last, he sprang into one of the beds – the one that Adrian had assigned him – and tugged sheet and blankets up to his chin. He was shivering; his jaw was trembling.

'One moment, Mike.' Adrian suddenly felt that his bowels, obstinately closed all day, now wished to open. 'Hang on.'

His dressing-gown swished as he hurried into the bathroom. Then he came back; went awkwardly to the chair over which his jacket was draped; bent over; got something out, which he stuffed into his dressing-gown pocket; and disappeared again.

Soon he re-emerged, beaming: 'There we are! Now I feel much comfier.'

129

The dressing-gown was placed on a hanger on the door; the key was turned. Adrian was wearing only a pair of Y-fronted pants. It was his modest habit to wait to remove these until he was under the bedclothes.

'Dear Mike.'

But when he put his lips to the cheek on the pillow beside him, he was astonished to taste something damp and salt.

'Mike! What's the matter?''

'What did you get from your jacket?'

'When?'

'Just now. When you went to the toilet.'

'Only some Kleenex. You know how I hate tough lavatory paper.'

'You took your wallet.'

'What are you talking about?'

'You had all your money in your wallet. And you took it in case I should pinch it.'

'Nonsense!' But there was no conviction in Adrian's voice.

'Then let me look in your dressing-gown pocket. It must be there now. Or did you hide it in the toilet?'

'Well, yes, Mike, I did take my wallet. But that was because I didn't want to put any temptation in your way. Was that so bad of me?'

'You were right not to trust me. Perhaps I would have taken it.'

'Don't say such silly things. All that's behind you. We both know you've learned your lesson.'

Again Adrian tried to take Mike in his arms; but the younger man remained obstinately on his back, his arms behind his head and his eyes staring upwards.

'Mike! . . . You're not angry, Mike?'

A long silence.

'Mike?'

Mike then said in that hoarse, subdued voice so unlike the voice that Adrian had known, 'It wouldn't do, Adrian.'

'What wouldn't do? What *is* all this?'

'My coming back.'

'But I *want* you back.'

Mike shook his head. Then he said in the same hoarse, subdued voice: 'Will I get into the other bed or will you?'

'For God's sake, Mike!'

But Mike climbed slowly, shivering, out of the bed, his arms crossed over his thin, hairy chest and his shoulders hunched, to enter the other bed with a creak and a long, trembling sigh.

'I just don't know what all the fuss is about!' Adrian raised himself on an elbow and peered at the outstretched shape in the bed beside him. 'You really are incredibly touchy.' When, after several seconds, Mike had still not said a word, Adrian conceded, 'Oh, very well then! If that's how you want it! But I'm – ahm – I'm sorry, Mike.'

Still there was no answer; and when Adrian held out a hand across the space between the two beds, Mike did not stir.

'No hard feelings?' Adrian said.

Again there was silence.

1973

LOSS

Dr Nakamura was waiting for Eithne, as he usually waited for her but she never waited for him, on the platform of Falmer Station. She had often asked him why he did not choose some place more comfortable – he could, after all, far more conveniently pick her up outside her office – but the only answer was a hurried drawing in of the breath on the monosyllable 'Sa . . .' and a shrug of his shoulders. 'Perhaps you're ashamed of me,' she would sometimes add bitterly, when the day had been a particularly tiring one or when she was suffering from one of her migraines. For some reason, this suggestion always agitated the Japanese. 'Ashamed of you?' he would cry out. 'Why should I be ashamed of you? Why? I am *proud* of our friendship.' If she then still persisted, 'Then why do you hang about for me *here*?' he would mutter something about gossip and her reputation and the fact that he was a foreigner in England on a scholarship. The discretion that was so deeply a part of his nature always filled her with exasperation and, on occasions, even with rage.

This time, approaching him where he sat alone on his usual bench at the farthest and, as she often pointed out, the draughtiest end of the platform, Eithne had adopted the slightly knock-kneed, slouching walk, head lowered and hands deep in the pockets of her overcoat, that showed that the day had not gone well for her.

132

'Cold!' she called out, as though it were a greeting, when she was still several yards away.

Nakamura got up, hugging his scuffed black brief-case over a chest that Eithne knew to be far more muscular than his slight, even fragile, appearance in his clothes might suggest. 'You are cold?' he asked.

'Yes, I am cold.' She had a habit of imitating, not the accent, but the rhythms of his speech. 'Either that heating is turned up so high that one becomes a steamed pudding or else it's turned down so low that one becomes an ice-cream.'

Nakamura looked into her handsome, cross face for several seconds before he gave a delighted giggle. 'Ah, Eithne, I like the way you say things! So original,' he added.

Before she had met Nakamura she had never been conscious that she had any gift for self-expression. It was he, a foreigner, who had first discerned it in her, and taking confidence from his discernment Eithne had then set about developing the gift. As a result, suddenly, in her mid-thirties, she had found that she was able to make people listen to her and laugh at her.

The cold air, swept along the platform by the incoming train, brushed against them like a tangible presence. Eithne clung to Nakamura's arm, her other hand struggling with the hem of her skirt. 'Christ!' she muttered through clenched teeth. Nakamura, always polite, opened the door for her, held out a hand, saying 'Please,' and then gave a little bobbing bow as she stepped in.

Once she was settled in one corner of the long, open compartment, Eithne looked around her. Even when she was with Nakamura, she could not stop herself from looking around, so ineradicably engrained was the habit. Well, I wouldn't mind him, she told herself, glancing at the profile of an obvious student, with the kind of large hands and wide mouth and coarse black hair that she liked; but she recognized, now as on other similar occasions, with a perennial astonishment, that though she would not mind him – or, indeed, any of the other young men like him – it was Nakamura that she would always prefer. 'I suppose I'm in love with him really,' she would say to Rose, the girl with whom she shared; and Rose would then squeal, 'Oh, Eithne, no!'

'I have made progress today,' Nakamura announced, using a rotating movement of his forefinger and middle finger to make a little peephole through the misted glass of the window. 'You have probably heard it said that the first Christian book to be published in

Japan was *Sanctos Nogosagveono* in 1591, but I have always suspected that maybe – ' At that point the train entered a tunnel and Eithne was glad that his precise, beautifully modulated voice should be lost in the whoosh and roar. If he were mad about classical music, like Clive, or about politics, like Keith, she might be able to keep up with him. But religion had never interested her and the history of Christianity in the Far East just bored the pants off her.

'. . . Though the first work of *western* literature introduced to Japan was of course *Esopono Fabulas* – better known to you as *Aesop's Fables*,' Nakamura was ending as the train again emerged into the dimming light of evening.

'Now fancy that!' Eithne exclaimed, cuddling up to him, her hand drawing his own hand into the pocket of his overcoat. She got a secret pleasure out of using on him a gentle irony the existence of which he never even suspected.

'Yes, it is interesting,' Nakamura agreed solemnly, squeezing her hand in the pocket. 'And surprising.'

Eithne was staring at the young man in the corner. His face was averted from them; but she knew, as she always knew such things, that he was looking not out of the window but at her reflection in the glass. Probably, she thought, he was saying to himself, 'Now why should an attractive girl like that want to take up with a middle-aged coloured?' (To Eithne Japanese were 'coloureds'; and she herself, though now in her thirties, was 'a girl'.) That people should put that question whether silently to themselves or, as in the case of Rose, audibly, excited Eithne, she could not have said why. 'Yes, I suppose it *is* rather kinky of me,' she would sometimes admit to Rose. 'But honestly I go for him in a way I've never gone for anyone else. And that includes Jim.' Jim was the merchant-seaman husband that Eithne had not seen for almost six years.

Nakamura went on talking about his research; but Eithne, as usual, did not listen to him. It was enough to feel his muscular body so close to hers through the overcoat that muffled it, to press his hand and at the same time to dart an occasional glance at the face of the student, who had a curious way of sucking on his full lower lip as he frowned at her reflection in the window.

Nakamura was now explaining how, with the persecution of the Christians, people in Japan had come to fear that if they were seen with a foreign book, they might be thought to be converts and that, in consequence, *Aesop's Fables,* once so popular, had ceased to be read. He gave his dissertation without looking at her, his eyes on the spot, just above a framed sepia-coloured photograph of Little-hampton, where someone had scratched with a penkife 'J. Wright is a tart'; and all through it his hand never ceased to massage hers, sometimes so fiercely that she all but cried out in mingled pain and pleasure.

'That boy was watching us,' she said, as they got out at Brighton Station and hurried for the barrier.

'What boy?'

'That boy in the corner.'

It was typical of Naka (this was Eithne's nickname for him) that he should at once say in alarm, 'I hope he does not know me. I hope he is not in my department.'

'Silly!'

'But why should he stare at us?' Nakamura pursued.

'I expect he was wondering how I managed to pick up such a handsome man.'

Again the irony was lost on Nakamura.

'Do we go to my place or do we go to yours?'

'Let's go to yours,' Eithne said. 'We can call in at Food Fayre and get some stuff. We don't want to eat out, do we? Not in this perish-ing weather.'

'After supper I must work,' Nakamura said.

Arm in arm they were scurrying into the wind that swept up from the front.

'Work! But you're always working these days.'

'I must, I have only two more months in England. Once I return to Tokyo, I will have no time. Busy, busy, busy. At last, after ten years – no, eleven years – I am in sight of finishing my book. I wish to finish it before I leave England. That is my plan.'

'Will you dedicate it to me?' Eithne asked in joke.

Nakamura stopped in his tracks, the arm that was linked with Eithne's anchoring her to the pavement beside him. 'Ah, Eithne,' he said with genuine regret, 'that is what I should *wish* to do. Without your interest and encouragement. . . . But unfortunately – I regret – such a thing is not possible. I must dedicate my work to Professor Oda. Professor Oda is now eighty-seven, he is my former *sensei*. I owe the dedication to him. . . . Do you understand?' he finished anxiously.

Eithne laughed. 'I was only joking! What would your wife say if she saw my name at the beginning of your book?'

Still serious, Nakamura replied, 'That would be no problem. I would tell her that Mrs Eithne Morrow was my research helper – that she gave me great assistance.'

Evidently, Eithne realized, he had already worked that out.

'Besides my wife is not interested in my work,' Nakamura went on. 'She is not like you. She is a typical Japanese housewife. Children, home, cooking. You would say that she is an ignorant and uneducated woman. Though of course,' he added quickly, 'she comes of a good family. Her father was a baron. Not that there are now barons in Japan, but her father was a baron.'

Eithne had heard this often; but daughter of a baron or not, she had never felt jealous of Nakamura's wife – except at the beginning. During those first weeks, when she and the Japanese lay uncomfortably on the single bed – if one or other of them fell off it, Eithne would giggle but Nakamura would always seem genuinely distressed – there on the mantelpiece were the photographs of the woman in a kimono, of the little boy with the overlarge head and the overlarge girl with the little head; and when Eithne glanced at them, over Nakamura's naked shoulder or past his flushed cheek, she would experience a pang of dismay or exasperation. But after her fifth or sixth visit the photographs had suddenly gone and in their place was another photograph, cut from a newspaper or magazine, of an elderly and sombre-looking gentleman with an ill-knotted tie.

'Who's that?' Eithne asked.

'Arthur Waley,' Nakamura had answered.

'And who's he when he's at home?' Eithne pursued, between one bite at Nakamura's shoulder and another.

'Arthur Waley? You know who Arthur Waley is. He is a great man. A great scholar.'

'Oh,' said Eithne. And then in a different tone 'Oh, oh, oh!' as she felt the weight of Nakamura's body settling on top of her.

Now, as soon as they had let themselves into the cramped little flatlet that had been fitted into what had once been the huge reception room of a Brunswick Square mansion – the elegant sweep of the bow had been barbarously severed by a flimsy partition and, all proportions having thus been destroyed, the ceiling now yawned cavernously – Eithne at once put a match to the gas fire and then set about changing into what she always called 'something comfortable'. This was the heavy silk kimono that Nakamura had given to her, saying, 'This is really a man's kimono.' Its shade was that of pewter and it smelled of the Turkish cigarettes he had smoked in the days when he himself had worn it. At first Nakamura had been nervous of her removing any of her clothing in his flat, though, oddly, he never showed the same circumspection about removing his own clothing in hers. But now he had got used to the fact that neither his landlady nor the other tenants of the house had any interest whatever in what went on behind his locked door.

The kimono suited Eithne's monumental build. When she wore it she ceased to slouch: throwing back her shoulders and arching her spine, so that she all at once acquired a dignity and presence lacking in her day-to-day appearance as typist in a pool of nine girls. She would release her thick auburn hair from its bun at the nape of her neck, allowing it to cascade down her shoulders. Nakamura liked her hair; most men did, she found.

Usually, as on this evening, it was she who did the cooking, while Nakamura, content to leave to her a household task with which throughout his life in Japan he had never had to concern himself, squatted cross-legged on the bed, reading. But sometimes, in a sudden craving for the food of his own country, the Japanese would take over. On those occasions Eithne would balance this or that titbit on the ends of her lacquer chopsticks, would put her head on one side as she peered down in a miming of horror or amazement and would then scream out something like 'Raw fish! Revolting!' or 'This rice is *slimy*!' before she popped the object into her mouth.

'Would you like a drink while the potatoes are boiling?'

Nakamura shook his head, putting an arm round her waist as she leant slackly against him. 'No. I must keep my head clear,' he said.

'Clear? What for?'

'For my book.'

'Oh, you and that precious book of yours! You're like husband and wife. I believe you care more for that wretched book of yours than you do for me.'

Nakamura wriggled his toes uncomfortably; he had slipped off his shoes without undoing the laces before squatting on the bed. 'My book is very important to me,' he said. 'Though maybe to no one else,' he added with a small, self-satisfied smile.

'Of course it's important to you. I understand that. After all, I came into your life far later than that book. Ten years later. You've lived with it far longer than with me.'

Nakamura squeezed her waist. 'You are so understanding,' he said.

Although Nakamura would drink nothing, Eithne herself drank, both before supper and during the meal. Since even a single Martini would make Nakamura go red in the face, he never ceased to be astonished by her ability to swallow one after another without any observable effect other than the voluptuous langour, so at odds with her brisk everyday behaviour, with which she would recline on his bed, gorged with food, and then reach out for the cigarette she insisted that he lit for her.

'This soup is good,' Nakamura said, sucking at it with the noisy relish that she had never been able to teach him to abandon.

'Out of a tin,' she said. 'One day I'll make you a *real* soup.'

'The days are getting few.'

She put out a hand, her plump forearm rosy in the light of the lamp as the sleeve of the kimono fell away from it, to rest the backs of the fingers momentarily on his cheek. 'I shall miss you,' she said. 'What'll I do without you? No more of these cosy evenings, no more journeys back from Falmer.'

Nakamura continued to suck loudly at the soup, his head lowered. Eithne realized that she had embarrassed him, as she usually embarrassed him with too vehement a demonstration of her love; and with that realization came, for the first time in their relationship, a sudden annoyance.

'You don't care,' she found herself saying in a loud voice.

Nakamura looked up now, startled. 'Eithne! Of course I care. But what are we to do?'

She shrugged. 'Nothing.'

The meal over, she stacked the dishes by the tiny, cracked sink and then threw herself across the bed, lying on her stomach with her head supported on her hands. 'I'll deal with the washing-up later.'

Nakamura, standing by the folding card-table at which they had eaten, was staring at her while excavating one of his beautifully strong, white teeth with a toothpick. There was a curious expression, at once remote and embarrassed, on his handsome face.

'Cigarette,' she said, extending a hand.

Slowly Nakamura took a cigarette from the case she had given to him – it had belonged to Jim and she had found it at the back of one of her drawers – and put it to his lips; equally slowly, as though he were deliberating some problem, he fumbled for a match.

'Come on, slow coach!'

He handed it to her. Gulping greedily at it – most of her actions seemed to have that same brisk rapacity – she said between puffs, patting the eiderdown: 'Come.' Nakamura hesitated. 'Come,' she repeated.

The Japanese withdrew his feet slowly from their slippers, approached the bed and then placed himself beside her. She held out the cigarette and he sucked at it, both of them watching as the smoke curled up towards the ceiling and then, strand by strand, disintegrated.

'I wish I could go to Japan with you,' Eithne sighed.

Nakamura drew in his breath with a sharp hiss. 'Alas, that is not possible.'

'Of course it isn't possible,' she retorted fretfully. 'But one can wish, can't one? I'm sick of England.'

'England is a nice place to live.'

'You've said it – nice! Too nice! Too bloody nice!' She tossed and wriggled briefly on the bed as though she were uncomfortable.

Nakamura continued to stare silently at the ceiling, his arms to his sides and his jaw clamped together with what appeared to be the rigidity of conscious effort.

Eithne went on: 'What a hole this is!'

'What is?'

'This room, this flat. Like the whole of this awful country. Look at these houses from outside – you'd think they were full of rich people with butlers and chauffeurs and antique furniture. But behind their splendid fronts – did you know that the owners are made to paint them once every three years? – what do you find? Slums, just slums.'

'This is not a slum,' Nakamura said, so shocked that he jerked up to a half-sitting position beside her recumbent body.

'Of course it is. A nice slum. All England's a nice slum.'

'You should see a real slum in my country.'

'I wish I could. Oh, I do! I'd like to see a real slum. At least there'd be some life in it.'

'A terrible kind of life. No, Eithne, you should not say such things.'

Suddenly Eithne began to laugh, the sound gurgling in the back of her throat as she gripped the bed head with her plump hands. 'Have I shocked you then?'

Nakamura did not reply; in fact, she had.

'I'd just love to go to Japan,' Eithne went on. 'Do you think I could find a job there? Would they have any use for me?'

'Maybe an American or English firm – ' Nakamura began, anxiously slow.

'But I wouldn't want to be there unless I was with you, Naka.

Unless you could meet me each day at some station in Tokyo and we could come back together to some horrid little flat like this and I could cook you a meal or you could give me some raw fish and sticky rice.'

'Alas, that is not possible,' Nakamura said, dejectedly.

'No, alas, that is not possible,' Eithne concurred, again imitating not his accent but his intonation. 'Never mind. Forget it.'

She turned towards him, took his hand and guided it into the opening of her kimono.

But on this occasion, instead of dexterously unfastening her brassière as he always liked to do, Nakamura left his hand cold on her warm flesh, merely giving a little sigh.

'What's the matter?' Eithne asked.

Again Nakamura sighed, the merest puff.

'Well?'

Nakamura swung his legs off the bed, cradling his head in his hands, while his stockinged feet turned inwards, one on top of the other in a pigeon-toed stance. 'Eithne, I must work,' he said. 'I told you.'

'Work! At this hour?'

'Yes. Alas, yes.' He got up, feet still turned inwards, and made for the brief-case he had abandoned on the table when he had come in. Pulling up one flap and then another, he took out a pile of crumpled papers. 'All this.' He waved the papers in the air. 'Only two months. I must get them all in order.'

'But not *now*.'

'Yes. Now. Time is running short. Time and tide wait for no man. Unfortunately.'

Eithne got slowly off the bed, first kneeling on it and then lowering one leg to the floor, to be followed by the other. 'So you want me to go?' she said.

Nakamura stared unhappily at the papers in his hand. Then he looked up with an astonishingly sweet smile: 'Of course I do not *want* you to go. You can stay, Eithne, of course you can stay. But I must work and maybe that will be boring for you. And distracting for me,' he added.

'I'll go,' Eithne murmured, stripping the kimono off. Standing there in nothing but her brassière and pants she all at once felt chilled; her teeth began to chatter, her body to shake. Hurriedly she began to struggle back into her clothes.

Nakamura, watching her, asked: 'Are you angry with me, Eithne?'

'Of course not,' she muttered, her head diving into her jumper.

'You do understand?'

'Oh, yes, I do understand.'

'It's my book. That's what I came to England *for*. I must complete it. Ten years now I have worked on this book. Too long, Eithne.'

'Yes, too long,' she said, hitching at a stocking without once meeting his gaze.

'I owe it to my university – to finish this book. And to the foundation. All that money, Eithne!'

'Yes, yes!' Suddenly she was shouting at him in exasperation. 'Don't go on explaining! I understand! Of course I understand! It's the book, the bloody book, that counts!'

'Eithne!' Nakamura was appalled by her sudden violence.

But at that, surprisingly, Eithne began to laugh, going to him and putting her arms round his shoulders and her head on his chest. 'Don't worry, Naka,' she said. 'I'm a little disappointed, of course. But I understand, of course I understand.'

Nakamura, relieved, gave a little squeeze and a kiss on the forehead. 'I should *like* you to stay,' he began, but Eithne cut him off.

'No, no! No more of those explanations!' She broke free and began to finish dressing with the embarrassed speed of a patient before a hard-pressed doctor. 'There we are! Now where the hell did I put my bag?' Nakamura retrieved it from under the eiderdown and handed it to her. 'Thanks. . . . Well, work hard, Naka. Work hard.'

'I will try, Eithne. Hard work is my programme for the rest of my stay in England.'

She patted him on one cheek with mocking playfulness: 'That was interesting – all that about *Aesop's Fables*. Don't forget to put it in your book, will you?'

Taking her seriously, as he always did when she was teasing him, Nakamura gave a grin of pleasure: 'Of course I shall put it in my book. Thank you, Eithne.'

'Well, same time, same place.'

'Same time, same place.'

Briefly they kissed; but there was something perfunctory about the way in which Nakamura rapidly inserted his tongue into her mouth and then withdrew it, so that it did not surprise her that, as soon as they had separated, even as she opened the door and turned to say a last goodbye, his gaze had moved sideways and away from her to the pile of crumpled sheets of paper of varying size that lay on the table.

After he had closed the door on Eithne, Nakamura leant against it for several seconds as though in fear that she would return to attempt to carry it by storm. His thick, glossy eyebrows were drawn together, his mouth pursed. Then, with a sigh, he crossed to the table, picked up his manuscript and carried it to the desk. His eyes were on one of the closely written pages as his hand reached out, fumbled and eventually switched on the reading lamp. Jumping up, he then turned off the overhead light and returned to the desk. The brilliant circle of illumination in which he sat isolated, with the washing-up (Eithne had forgotten it), the bed and the card-table all excluded, brought him a curious sense of stability and peace.

In the same way, as a small boy, the youngest of a family of nine children, he would isolate himself in some corner, crouching with a book on the floor before him, while older voices argued and bickered above his head. In the same way, later, as a student, sharing a room with three of his fellows, he would escape from their incessant badinage about girls by concentrating in a small circle of light on some academic problem. In the same way, on his way to England, he would lie on his bunk in the cabin he shared with two Australians, and slowly slip away from them, their crude voices growing fainter and fainter and their gross presences in sweat-stained underclothes growing more and more insubstantial. 'Well, what do you say to that, eh, Prof?' One or other of the Australians would nudge him. But he had nothing to say to it, since he had heard nothing.

The tiny characters made his eyes burn and swim; but their very smallness was part of the magic that enabled him to escape. He drew a pen from out of the pocket of the jacket draped over the chair behind him and made one meticulous annotation in the margin and then another. On an impulse he jumped up and turned off the gas. When absorbed like this, he did not notice the cold; so why waste money?

Soon he had forgotten about Eithne: both about the brief pang of regret he had felt when deliberately denying himself the pleasures of her plump, ardent body, and about his subsequent guilt as deject-edly she had reached for the handle of the door before he could get to it, had slipped through with a mumbled 'Good night' and had pulled it shut behind her. He felt her slowly dim and then, wisp by wisp, vanish from his consciousness as, after his first few bitterly homesick weeks in England, his wife and two children had dimmed and vanished.

'*Exegi monumentum, aere perennius*. . . .' Well, that was putting it rather too strongly. But this would be the standard – and authoritative – work for a long time to come. There was no doubt about that. Oh, no doubt at all.

Meanwhile Eithne battled against the wind, her chin tucked into the collar of her coat and her head turned downwards and sideways. There had been a bus but she had decided not to run for it, preferring to make her way home on foot and so delay the moment when she would burst in on Rose, perpetually knitting before the gas fire, to be greeted by a squeal of 'Well – you're back early!'

A young man, a long scarf twisted around his neck, was standing outside the Curzon cinema, his muscular body supported on an umbrella that seemed on the point of snapping beneath his weight. It was not the young man seen in the train that evening but this one, too, had gazed at her on some occasion in the recent past, she could not remember when or where. Now, too, he gazed at her as she passed: first at her legs, then at her face, then at her breasts. Should she stop, making the photographs on display outside the cinema her excuse? For a moment she did so; and as she paused, the man himself straightened and began to wander over. But then, with a shake, she hurried on. Surprised, she realized that so far from this possible encounter filling her with excitement, it had caused in her a jolting kind of nausea.

Eithne had often described herself since the gradual crumbling away of her marriage as 'a bachelor girl'. When Rosie, who was seven years older and had long since acquiesced in a state of impregnable virginity, would give one of her shocked little squeals at the revelation of this or that of Eithne's adventures, Eithne would retort with a certain self-satisfaction, 'Well, I like to play the field.' But now, overnight as it were, there in the middle of the field she had played for so long had risen up this mountain – the Japanese whom at first it was rather a joke to 'lead on' and whom now, she realized, she could not do without. Oh, damn that book of his, damn, damn, damn!

'So that's what it means! I'm less important to you than that stupid book of yours. That's it, isn't it?'

Nakamura, who had on this occasion eaten supper at Eithne's

flat – Rose was out at one of her church meetings – quailed before the onset, cheeks sucked in and head lowered, while his fingers did up the buttons of the raincoat he had just put on. 'Eithne – you must try to be more understanding,' he said. He had the Japanese horror of scenes – they were crude, vulgar, ugly; but at the same time he could not help feeling obscurely moved by her impassioned voice and manner, as she confronted him with flushed cheeks and eyes that seemed to have grown suddenly small and sharp under the heavy, bluish lids.

'Every night it's the same,' Eithne rushed on. 'Do you think that I have nothing better to do than travel in that bloody train with you and then get you your supper?'

'If you prefer – ' Nakamura began humbly.

'What can I find to *do*,' Eithne cut him off, 'when at half past eight you announce that you want me out of the way so that you can concentrate on that wretched book of yours? It's too late to do anything. No one wants a date for an hour like that. I could have gone to the cinema with Clive – he asked me this morning – or I could have gone to Rose's meeting!' (Eithne had never in fact gone to a single one of Rose's meetings through all the years they had lived together.) 'But at this hour – ! It's hopeless.'

'I am sorry,' Nakamura said. 'Very sorry.' Part of him wanted to get away from the congested face thrust towards his own and the loudly accusing voice; but the other part was irresistibly attracted.

'If it were another woman, I'd have something worthwhile to be jealous of. But a book! And your time is running out. Only six more weeks.'

'Six and a half,' corrected Nakamura, who always liked to be accurate.

'Well, six and a half. Do you realize that it's more than ten days since we – since we – ' Eithne broke off, knowing that Nakamura shrank in shame and embarrassment from any discussion of their love-making or indeed from any reference to it. 'You can't be in *that* much of a hurry.'

'My mind must be clear,' Nakamura answered simply. Then with extreme difficulty, his hands twisting at the buttons of his raincoat, he got out: 'If we – we make love – then afterwards – afterwards I have no disposition for study. It is bad, I know, I should have better control of my mood. But alas, that is how it is, I cannot help myself. And as I have explained to you – '

She was staring at him, wondering how she could ever have

managed to fall in love with such a – such a cold-blooded, self-absorbed *creature*. But that she was in love with him she was now in no doubt at all.

Then, her voice suddenly going slack and her body going slack with it, she said, 'All right. Go.'

'Go?'

'You want to go. Go. Go,' she repeated, with a momentary revival of the old vehemence.

'I will see you tomorrow?'

She almost replied, 'Hell you will!' But instead she found herself saying meekly, 'Yes, I suppose so.'

'Same time?'

'Same time.'

'Same place?'

'Same place.'

'Eithne – I am sorry. Truly sorry.'

'Naka – I am sorry. Truly sorry,' she mimicked back at him.

As soon as he had closed the door, she flung herself on the sofa and burst into loud, gulping sobs. It was perhaps lucky that Nakamura had escaped having to witness this noisy paroxysm of frustration and grief. When he had left Tokyo, he had had to chide his wife for allowing the university colleagues who had come to see him off to witness her with tears trickling down her otherwise rigidly composed face.

Professor Armour, who contributed to the *Statesman* and *Encounter*, frequently appeared on television and was perpetually shuttling between Sussex and the United States, had never until then taken any notice of Nakamura. It had therefore been a surprise for the Japanese when he had been bidden to a dinner party to honour Dr Norfolk, on a visit from Berkeley; and even more of a surprise to find that of all the distinguished people present in the Park Crescent house – politicians, scholars and writers – it was with him, Nakamura, that Dr Norfolk seemed most eager to talk. The huge red-faced American and the little Japanese were separated at either end of the table; but throughout a protracted and curiously ill-cooked meal – the *poulet à l'estragon* shredding between the teeth, the mousse carrying a faint flavour of glue – Dr Norfolk would perpetually bawl down its length things like 'Now Professor Nakamura will no doubt confirm . . .' or 'I hesitate to embark on this topic in the presence of Professor Nakamura. . .'. When the ladies left the men to their port, it was beside Nakamura that Norfolk placed himself, striding down the room in order to do so, while demanding some whisky.

Until that triumphant occasion Nakamura had suffered during his months in England a curious whittling-away of his self-confidence, of which he had been almost unaware. His colleagues at Sussex either patronized him or ignored him. He was merely one of a number of foreign scholars who burrowed away in busy obscurity at some totally unimportant subject of research. From time to time some dons kinder than Professor Armour would ask the Japanese in a jolly, encouraging voice, 'Well, how are things going, Professor Nakamura?' but when Nakamura embarked on an answer full of his habitual qualifications and periphrases, the discussion would quickly be brought to an end. But here was a world-renowned scholar who was prepared to accord to him the kind of respect to which he had grown accustomed in Japan. Dr Norfolk had even read many of his papers, published in Japanese.

Professor Armour was unusually amiable as he said good night to Nakamura on the doorstep.

'You must visit us again soon. One sees so little of you.' He put his cigar to his babyish mouth and smoke wreathed out on the still evening air. 'It's all very well to spend all your time at your desk but you must have a thought for your colleagues too.' He put an arm round Nakamura's shoulder, as he guided him down the steps. 'Sure you don't want a taxi? Or I could ask the Liddles to drive you home.'

'No, no. I like to walk. Walking is good for me.'

'Splendid character, Harry Norfolk. He took to you. Thinks the world of you, one could see that at a glance. First-rate scholar. Absolutely first-rate.'

Beaming and waving, a portly but youthful figure in a heavily draped dinner jacket and elaborately pleated shirt, Armour remained on the bottom step outside his house until Nakamura had turned the corner.

Yes, it had been a gratifying evening; one might say a triumph. But as, elated, he trotted off to the bus stop – he had never been as late as this, might the last bus have already gone? – Nakamura found that all the details of what had passed in the sumptuous crowded house were fading from his mind, to be replaced by a joyful anticipation of returning to his book. The wheezing, watery-eyed American had asked him about it – 'We've waited far too long,' he had said in mock reproof, shaking a finger brown with nicotine, and when Nakamura had murmured, humbled, 'Yes, I regret. I am sorry,' the American had then retorted between snorts of seismic laughter: 'The real trouble in our game is not the scholars like yourself who take too long to get the stuff out but those who get it out too quickly.' He had then glanced at Armour, twirling his cigarette, one end sodden, between middle and fourth finger, in unmistakable malice.

Seated in the bus at last, opposite a woman either so sleepy or so drunk that she swayed perpetually from side to side in imminent danger of falling, Nakamura pressed his hands together between his knees in an effort to stop them shaking with the excitement that kept welling up inside him, like an onset of fever. He had felt like this in the early days when he used to sit at the end of the platform at Falmer Station, waiting for Eithne to appear; and in his student years on the rare occasions when he and some of his friends would visit a brothel and would have to wait, as decorously polite as patients in a dentist's waiting-room, for their turn to be called. Eithne was right, although during their recent scenes he had repeatedly denied it: the book really mattered to him far more than anything or anyone else, and the pleasure that he got from it exceeded any other pleasure known to him. Watching the saliva trickle out of one corner of the seamed mouth of the old woman swaying across the aisle from him, he saw it now with clarity.

When he opened the door of the darkened flat, pulling off his overcoat and dropping it over a chair before he switched on the light, it was as though he were entering the home of a beloved, whom he knew to be waiting in silence for him behind the closed bedroom door. He found himself moving on tiptoe, each of his senses sharpened to a thrilling alertness.

. . . The shock was at first like a stupefying blow. He stared down at the desk, feeling a strange icy trickling moving along his spine. Then he began to rush about the small, crowded room, turning over papers, flinging clothes and books to the floor and even stooping to peer under the bed, where the dust lay in swollen grey sausages, into the shoe-cupboard and behind the paper fan he had made to cover the empty grate. Suddenly, he whirled round, as though someone playing a practical joke on him were just behind his shoulder; then he tore the bedspread off the bed, and dragged the bedclothes to the floor.

His manuscript had vanished.

Who could have done such a thing to him? Who would want it?

Outside in the street, into which he rushed without his overcoat, he found two tall, ladylike policemen talking in a doorway. Breathlessly he explained what had happened, while they looked in turn down at him and into each other's pale, angular faces, wondering whether he was drunk or mad. 'My life's work,' he moaned; as he continued to moan when he had got them to enter the flat.

'Is anything else missing?' one of the policemen asked.

'I don't know, I haven't looked.'

'Well, may I suggest you look now?'

Both policemen seemed deliberately to refrain from calling Nakamura 'sir'.

Nakamura hunted among his belongings, pulling out drawers and then pushing them back, opening the little bamboo box in which he kept his cuff-links and studs and finally making sure that his camera and its accessories all still lay undisturbed at the bottom of the wardrobe.

'Well, it's a bit odd,' the less languid of the two policemen commented at the end of this search. 'Isn't it? Those papers of yours gone and everything else untouched.'

'What exactly *were* these papers?' his colleague enquired.

'Ten years of research. My book on Christianity in the Far East.' As he spoke the words, Nakamura had to resist an almost overmastering desire to burst into tears. He put both hands to his mouth, fingertips pressed to trembling lips.

'Now who would want something like that?' the same policeman asked, in a voice that carried with it a faint undertone of mockery.

'If they were *scientific* papers – ' his colleague took up knowingly.

'No, no, they were not scientific papers. No, not at all. They were, as I say, concerned with my research into the spread of Christianity in the Far East.'

The policemen stayed long enough to ascertain that no door or window had been forced and to make some notes. Then they left, telling Nakamura to call at the station in the morning.

'You are very kind,' he told them, still tremulously agitated, as he let them out. 'If the thief can be found, I know that you will find him. I have always heard that the English police force is the finest in the world.'

Nakamura stood on the doorstep, watching them as, two tall, thin shadows in blue, they made their way off up the square. How their boots squeaked, in exact synchronization as it seemed!

Back in his room, he again made another fruitless search of all the places he had searched already. For a moment he thought that a shoe-brush had also been taken and his heart rose at the possibility of a definite, if eccentric clue; but the brush was eventually revealed beneath the kitchen chair.

In a fearful access of desolation he threw himself on his bed, moaning against the sleeve that he pressed to his mouth: 'My book, my book!' Then, after what must have been several minutes of this keening, he jumped up again and began to scrabble his way back into his raincoat. He would go and see Eithne and tell her what had happened.

At that moment, if the thought had occurred to him that she might have had anything to do with the disaster, his conscious mind had repressed it.

Rose came sleepily to the door, leaving it on the chain as she asked, 'Who is it? What do you want? Who's there?' in a high-pitched, fearful voice.

'Nakamura.'

'Nakamura?'

They had met often enough, but Rose said the name as though she had never heard it before.

'Eithne's friend. Her Japanese friend.'

'It's very late.'

'I must see her.'

'Eithne's asleep.'

'Yes, but I must see her.'

Leaving the door still on the chain, Rose padded off. Nakamura had not seen Eithne for more than a week. Afternoon after afternoon he had waited for her on the platform in vain; until, taking courage, he had stood outside her office only to slink away, not sure whether she had seen him or not, when she emerged, vivaciously laughing, in the company of the young clerk she called Clive (or was it Keith?).

'What *is* all this?'

Eithne strode down the corridor, barefoot, in a pair of blue and pink striped pyjamas, the top two buttons of the jacket undone so that it seemed as though at any moment her ample breasts would burst out.

'Eithne – forgive me – but I must have your advice.'

'At this hour?'

Her implacable tone both repelled and intimidated him. It was then that the unconscious suspicion began to float upwards, like some greenly swollen corpse, into his conscious mind.

'Something terrible has happened.' He glanced at Rose, who stood at the farther end of the corridor, arms akimbo under her flat chest and eyes curiously bulging and defenceless without their usual glasses, in the doorway of her room. 'My book – the manuscript of my book. Someone has stolen it. It's gone.'

'Stolen it! Who would want to steal such a thing? What use would it be to anyone?'

'That's what the police said. But it's – it's *gone*.'

Eithne gave an impatient shrug of the shoulders. 'You must have put it away somewhere.'

'No, no, I haven't, I haven't!' he cried out, exasperated by her terrible, contemptuous calm. 'Do you think that I could put it somewhere and not know where I put it?' Again Eithne shrugged, doing up a button of her pyjama jacket and then raising the same hand to cover a yawn.

'Perhaps you took it to the university and left it there?' Rose suggested, advancing towards them.

'No, I never take it there – never! It is out of the question. Never would I take the whole manuscript there. Besides,' he added pathetically, 'it is too heavy.'

'Did someone break in?' Rose asked, feeling that she must provide the sympathy that Eithne was so mysteriously withholding. 'Is anything else missing?'

'That is the strange thing. My Canonflex camera is untouched. My pearl cuff-links – they are in fact Mikimoto pearls – are in the little box where I always place them. Who would leave such things and yet take my book? Who, who?'

'Who indeed?' Eithne said.

'You haven't let anyone have that key, have you? I mean,' he hastily corrected himself, 'no one has taken that key?'

'What key?'

'The key I gave you.'

'Of course not.'

'That is good.' But quite why it was good he could not have explained.

'It's ghastly for you,' Rose said. 'I see that. Would you like a cup of tea? Perhaps it'll cheer you up.'

'No, no. No, thank you. No tea.'

Again Eithne yawned, this time with no attempt at concealment. 'Well, I must be getting back to bed,' she said. Raising her arms

150

above her head, first one and then the other, she stretched luxuriously, the pyjama jacket rising with her rib cage to reveal the flesh of her diaphragm.

'Sure you won't have some tea?' Rose coaxed. 'It'll only take me a jiffy.'

'No,' Nakamura said in a broken voice. 'No. But you are very kind. Very kind indeed. Forgive me. Such an hour. Disturbing two sleeping ladies. But I was so upset. Forgive me, please.'

It was Rose, her rayon dressing-gown rustling with every movement, and not Eithne who saw him out.

In the parched and frantic weeks that followed Nakamura found himself producing a number of versions of the story of how he had lost his book. All of them were prompted by the general disbelief, first voiced by the two policemen, that any casual thief would mysteriously enter the flat without forcing the door or any window and would then make off with something seemingly useless and valueless except to its author.

At the university Nakamura had first tried out on a woman student, always pestering him and the unwitting object of his dislike in spite of her mania for all things Japanese, the version of having absent-mindedly left the manuscript in a café, from which it had disappeared when, half an hour later, he had hurried back to retrieve it. But the tone, half pitying and half contemptuous, with which she had drawled, 'Oh goodness, what an absolutely *mad* thing to do!' had convinced him that the story, if told in this manner, would only make him look ineffectual and silly. The next time, therefore, that he poured out the details of the tragedy – to Armour, who since the dinner never saw Nakamura without jovially asking him how he was getting along – he recounted how, travelling on the train from Falmer, he had, as he put it, been obliged to respond to a call of nature, leaving his brief-case containing the manuscript on the luggage rack above him; arriving at Brighton Station he had reached for the brief-case to find it was not there. 'I am afraid that the thief must have had a disappointment,' he concluded with a twitching smile. 'But for me it is a tragedy.'

Armour put a massive arm around the Japanese's shoulder, making him involuntarily cringe away from him. 'My God!' he boomed. 'Oh, what bad luck! Oh, I am sorry!'

The upshot of all this sympathy was that Armour eventually offered Nakamura a lift back into Brighton in his E-type Jaguar and once there, to his immediate regret, suggested that perhaps the Japanese would like a drink.

Nakamura, ill at ease with a bonhomie that even he could at once see to be factitious but at the same time not wishing to cause offence, lugubriously accepted.

Out in the garden – it was now spring and the day had been warm – Armour cradled a large glass of whisky on his chest as he lay, stretched out almost at full length, on a vast wicker chair. 'Yes, that *is* bad luck,' he took up again. 'The nearest I've ever got to that was when I dictated a broadcast talk and the little idiot of a stenographer somehow mislaid her notebook. Something comparatively trivial,' he added. 'Though annoying nonetheless.'

He went on to speak of T.E. Lawrence who had mislaid the original draft of *Seven Pillars of Wisdom* in not dissimilar circumstances – 'and frankly, in the case of that piece of fiction, one can't help wishing that that had been allowed to be the end of the matter' – and of Carlyle, who had bravely set about rewriting the whole of his *History of the French Revolution* 'after J.S. Mill's maid – sensible girl – had consigned it to the flames.' There were other equally heartless anecdotes. But what made Nakamura most uncomfortable, like a hinted accusation, was the catalogue that followed of the scholars who, for one reason or another, had found it convenient to 'lose' manuscripts which either had never existed or had existed in so chaotic or imperfect a state that publication of them would never have been possible. 'It's hard for a philosopher to say after twenty years of labour that his conclusions are balls. Far easier to have a tale of a master-work mysteriously lost or stolen. And the same goes for a novel. We all know of those individuals who have been said, for the best part of a lifetime, to have been working on an epoch-making novel. The fact that they are doing so appears to excuse so much that is otherwise unsatisfactory, drab and spineless in their lives. But as the day of reckoning approaches and the tattered sheets of paper in the bottom drawer of the desk lose even the surprise of contemporaneity, then what is the solution? Theft – loss – fire! What else? . . . Now this business of the Sibelius Symphony is an interesting one. The old boy, as you probably know, liked to excuse the complete artistic sterility of his final years by dropping hints to this or that visiting notable that he was at work on a final symphony. But when he finally shuffled off that substantial mortal coil – the cupboard was bare!'

Did Armour imagine, Nakamura asked himself, sick with

desolation, as he struggled on his homeward way, that he, too, had invented the loss of his manuscript? Was that what he was implying? Was that what his colleagues, seeming so ready with their sympathy, were thinking had really happened? It was monstrous! In his mind, Nakamura heard them chortle to each other with gleeful malice: 'Eleven years, was it, that he was supposed to have worked on that *magnum opus*? . . . And of course he got that award on the strength of it. . . . I suppose he realized that it was worthless. . . . *If* in fact a single paragraph had ever been written.'

It was when he wrote to his octogenarian *sensei*, Professor Oda, and to his colleagues in Japan, that Nakamura first formulated the theory that the manuscript had been appropriated by some rival scholar, either jealous of his reputation or eager to make secret use of his research. He had by now reached such a state of paranoia that there were long stretches of time when he managed to persuade himself that this unlikely hypothesis was in fact the truth. There was an elderly Chinese from Hong Kong, a Baptist minister with the name of Mr Ling, who was following at the university a course of research in a field not entirely dissimilar from his own. Since Mr Ling had, in the past, responded to all overtures of friendship with a baffling and humiliating coldness, it was not now difficult for Nakamura to adopt the suspicion that it was he who was the thief.

Occasionally Nakamura would also ruminate darkly on the possible role of Dr Norfolk in the mystery. Norfolk had visited Brighton on the night of the theft; he had known that the Japanese would be away from home, having dinner in Park Crescent; and he, perhaps alone of western scholars, would be in a position to appreciate the originality and importance of Nakamura's discoveries. Had there not been something false about the joviality with which, his face shiny and flushed with drink, he had bawled down the table his questions and compliments? Norfolk was known to be a rich man, quite apart from his academic salary; and for a man so rich it would be easy enough to find someone – an impoverished student perhaps – to execute the theft.

Unable to sleep and barely able to eat, Nakamura would lie out on his rumpled bed – it was days since he had made it, though he was usually so tidy – to give himself up to these fantasies, which at least had the consolation of allotting to him the role of tragically deluded protagonist in a tragedy of human vileness and betrayal. But then he would have to get up, to wander unhappily to the lavatory, and reality would supervene. Professor Oda might indeed believe that there had been some dastardly conspiracy – his letter, received that morning, bore witness that he did – but Nakamura himself could not believe it for any length of time. There was some other explanation; and the only possible explanation – though he shrank repeatedly from accepting it, pushing it far down into the abyss of his subconscious – lay in Eithne.

Since his late-night visit to her flat, Eithne had made no attempt to get in touch with him. On two or three occasions when he had seen her in the grounds of the university, it was obvious that she had deliberately avoided a confrontation. He telephoned her but Rose invariably said she was out; he wrote and the letters remained unanswered.

At last, having resolved to make a surprise visit at a time, soon after she had got back from work, when it was likely she would be in, he came face to face with her on her doorstep in answer to his ring.

'Yes?' It was the tone of voice used to a canvasser or a collector for a charity. Evidently she had been washing her hair; and the towel wrapped round her head like a turban gave her an appearance both androgynous and menacing.

'I want to talk to you, Eithne. May I?'

'Have we anything to say?'

Still she blocked the doorway with her ample, vital presence.

'What has happened? Why do you treat me like this? Have we quarrelled?'

She gave a disagreeable smile and raised an eyebrow. 'I got bored,' she said. 'That's all. You bore me.'

Nakamura looked nervously over his shoulder, terrified that one of the neighbours might be eavesdropping on this exchange. 'May I not enter?' he pleaded.

'Rose isn't in.'

'But I do not wish to see Rose. It is you I wish to see.'

Eithne considered for a moment. Then she gave an abrupt side-ways jerk of the head, so that water splashed from under the towel on to one eyebrow. Nakamura entered; the door clicked shut.

'Well?' she demanded.

'Why are we not friends any longer?' Nakamura asked, his voice still plaintive and abased. 'What have I done?'

'I saw that you had no more use for me – that you had other, more important things to occupy your attention. So' – she shrugged her shoulders – 'I decided to efface myself. It was as simple as that.'

'But of course I had use for you. Of course!'

'Yes. As your cook. But no other use.'

'As my friend,' Nakamura said.

'Friend!' There was a terrible scorn in the words as they emerged from between her clenched teeth.

'Eithne – do not be angry with me. . . . I came – I came to – to ask you – something. . . .' He faltered, his eyes gazing at her feet, and then cleared his throat with a dry, rattling sound, not once but twice.

'Well? Get on with it.'

'Eithne – my book – my manuscript. . . .'

Before he could go on, she shouted, eyes blazing under her towering headdress: 'Your book! I'm sick of your book! Your book doesn't interest me! Do you understand? What do I care about that precious book of yours?'

'Eithne. . . .' The sweat was cold on his forehead and between his shoulder blades; he could hardly get out the words. 'If – if you have my book – please – please – I beg of you –'

'*If* I have your book! Why should I have your book? Are you out of your mind? What possible interest might I have in that book of yours? Do you think I stole it? Do you?'

Head bowed, he let the words spark back and forth above him, in total submission to their sword-like swish and flash.

'I – I just . . .' he eventually managed to get out incoherently. 'No stone must be left unturned, every avenue must be explored. . . . As they say,' he added, in seeming apology.

'What an absurd idea! Why should your footling little work concern me in the least?' The towel was working loose with all this vehemence and she now plucked it off with a single gesture, allowing her thick, still damp hair to tumble around her shoulders. Ah, how beautiful it was – he had forgotten how beautiful! Suddenly he no longer thought about the book and wanted only to put out a hand and run his fingers through that hair, again and yet again. 'I'm sorry it's lost,' she went on, 'of course I'm sorry. Since I know how much it means to you,' she added on a nasty note. 'But if you're crazy enough to imagine that *I* had any part in its –'

'No, no!' Piteously he now denied it, his eyes still on that cloud of auburn hair. 'I just thought . . . wanted to make sure. . . . Maybe in joke. . . .'

'Well, in that case, I must get on with setting my hair.' Peremptorily she pulled the door open; meekly he went through it.

'Goodbye, Eithne,' he turned to say. 'Thank you. Please forgive me.'

But she had already closed the door and was pulling across the bolt.

Nakamura's colleagues eventually could not fail to notice how ill he was looking. Three parallel lines appeared mysteriously on either side of his mouth, which in turn seemed to have grown much wider and thinner as the flesh fell away from his face. His skin took on an orange hue, as though at the end of an attack of hepatitis. Usually so athletically erect for a man of his age, he had now started to walk with a curious shambling gait, eyes lowered, chin on chest and shoulders bowed. 'It looks to me as though the poor man's heading for a nervous breakdown,' Armour told a colleague, who nodded in sage agreement and gave the opinion that the sooner Nakamura got back to his own country the better.

An advertisement placed both in the local evening paper and in the Personal column of *The Times* brought as its only result a visit from a journalist so young that his voice seemed not to have broken. He questioned Nakamura about his loss, expressed sympathy and said that his story would appear in the local evening paper in a day or two. But no story appeared.

Distractedly, Nakamura went through the ritual of preparing for his journey back to Japan.

Then, a few days before his departure, two letters arrived by the same morning post to bring him a little cheer. One was from Dr Norfolk, who began by expressing his regret at the news of 'the theft' and then went on to say that he had persuaded the American foundation that had originally financed the Japanese's year in England to pay him a similar sum for another year, in order to rewrite what – as Dr Norfolk put it – 'would undoubtedly prove a major contribution to Far Eastern studies'. The second letter, from Professor Oda, brought the news that the university had decided that, if Nakamura should desire it, he must be given a further year of absence from his post at his usual salary.

But the pleasure that those two letters brought him was only temporary. As, that evening, he sat at his desk trying to compose two suitable replies, he suddenly realized that he was sick with a mortal sickness: homesick; sick of research; sick of the book; above all, sick of himself. For the first time in his whole married life he felt an intense longing to be back in his home; to be seated at the table while his wife submissively brought him his food; to be out in his own garden with the azaleas in bloom around him and the tree-frogs croaking out of the depths of the dripping and misty greenness beyond.

He must go back, first he must go back. Then he would decide.

Having reached this conclusion, he ate a large meal for the first time for many days and slept a deep sleep.

In Japan a visiting professor would have been seen off by all his colleagues and friends. There was no one to see off Nakamura. The night before, Armour had given a perfunctory dinner for him – no liqueurs were offered, as on the occasion of the dinner for Norfolk, and there were only six guests. Rose, of whom he had been seeing a little, had had dinner with him at a fish restaurant the night before that; they had both been embarrassed by their habitual inability to communicate with each other and it was with mutual relief, if also with a certain sadness, that they at last separated, before ten o'clock, Rose pressing into his hand a package that turned out to contain an Edward VIII Coronation Mug. 'It's rather special,' Rose felt obliged to explain, 'because, you see, he was never actually crowned.'

'You are very kind,' Nakamura said. 'Always kind to me.'

'What train are you taking?' Rose asked, embarrassment making her change the subject.

Nakamura told her.

'I wish I could come to see you off. But I can't get away from the school at that hour. I'm so sorry.'

'Never mind. I will send you a postcard from our first port of call.'

'Will you?' Suddenly she sounded eager and hopeful. 'I'd like that.'

The porter grumbled about the number of small bundles and bags with which Nakamura was travelling. 'You'd do better to buy yourself a couple of large suitcases,' he advised with brutal candour. 'This is the surest way to have something stolen.'

For a flash Nakamura imagined, with a revival of his paranoia, that this was a sly reference to the loss of the book.

The bundles and bags had been arranged on the luggage rack and on the next-door seat, Nakamura had divested himself of his rain-coat, neatly folding it up and placing it on a suitcase, and the porter had slouched off, examining the coin in his grimy palm with a look of sour distaste on his face, when all at once there was a peremptory knock on the window beside Nakamura's cheek. He turned.

'Eithne!' he cried; but outside the cry came to her as no more than a noiseless moving of his lips and a radiant smile such as she had never seen him give before. Half running, he made for the door at the end of the compartment.

As he neared her, her face upturned and the mouth drawn back to reveal the large, even teeth, his delight gave way to panic. How ill she looked, how thin, how grey! Her eyelids, bluish in the past, were now almost violet; her hair, usually so glossy, had grown brittle and dry; her neck looked scrawny and lined.

'Eithne!' Now the name he had cried out so joyfully the first time emerged on a soft note of pity and concern. 'How did you know? Oh, what a surprise for me!'

'Rose told me.' Her lips barely moved as the words came drily through them. She avoided his gaze. 'I came to say goodbye. And to give you a goodbye present.'

'A present! For me?'

'Yes, a present. For you.' Already he had noticed that she had a flat cardboard box under one arm. 'I think you'll be even gladder to have it than to have Rose's.' The stretched skin round her mouth cracked into a smile that was almost a grimace. 'Here you are, Naka. Here!' She thrust the box at him; and as, numbly, he took it from her, she called out 'Goodbye, Naka!' turned on her heel and began to hurry off.

'Eithne!' he shouted. 'Eithne!' He started to pursue her; but a whistle was blowing, a woman with a Pomeranian managed to lasso his legs with the lead, he could not leave his luggage.

'Eithne!' he shouted again, this time in the face of the guard who was hurrying the length of the train, slamming door after door.

Then, clutching the parcel, he clambered back into the carriage.

'Aren't you going into dinner, sir?' the elderly Chinese steward asked.

Nakamura shook his head.

'Is this rough sea worrying you?'

'No, no. I'm just not hungry. Thank you.'

'Very good, sir.'

Nakamura got off the bunk, feeling slightly giddy as he raised his head from the pillow, peered at the belongings with which the other occupant, a Cingalese businessman, had littered the floor and table, and then stooped to take the parcel out of one of his bags. Although he had not yet opened it, he had no doubt of what it contained.

Always neat, Eithne had made up a package that was a model of symmetry and tidiness. Nakamura unpicked the knot, carefully removed the green string and then made a roll of it, before slipping off the paper. Nursing the manuscript on his chest with both of his hands, he then slowly crossed back to the bunk, sank down on its edge and started to read.

At first, he felt nothing but pleasure: in the clarity of his style; in the lucidity with which he had organized so many intricately disparate elements into an artistic whole; above all, in the originality of so much of the material he had managed to unearth. But into the pleasure there slowly began to seep a bitter, hopeless melancholy.

Each paragraph carried with it a reminder, often of events long since forgotten. Here, for example, was the passage about the persecution of the Christians in Nagasaki: he had worked on it during his honeymoon in that city and he remembered now how his wife would patiently sit waiting for him back in the inn, while each morning and often each afternoon he would delve in the record office and in the museum. Here, beside a section about St Francis Xavier, there seemed to run, silently parallel, an account of his vexed journey to Peking, with the difficulties of obtaining a visa, the permission of the Japanese government and of his university, and the currency for his expenses. Here was that whole chapter written when his son was so ill with tyhoid fever: while he laboured at it, his wife, pale and trembling, would keep coming in to him to announce 'His fever's getting worse,' or 'He's still passing blood,' until, in fury, he had shouted at her, 'Why can't you leave me in peace?' Here, too, were the final finishing touches, the ink a fresher blue, put in, during the last weeks before the theft, on the evenings when Eithne had reluctantly left him. 'What will power you have!' she would taunt him savagely on those occasions.

Suddenly he stopped reading the manuscript, in a piercing access of horror. It meant nothing; *nothing at all*. Sometimes in the forests about his home town on the Kii Peninsula he would come, as a boy, on a mammoth anthill. But when he kicked at it repeatedly until it split open, the baked mud, mined with its labyrinth of channels, would contain no life at all. All the seething, relentless energy that had gone to its construction had vanished, who knew where. The intricate factory had become a mausoleum. His book was the same.

Here, in his hands, lay the story not merely of the Christians in the Far East, but of his own ambition and ruthlessness and singleness of purpose. Here also lay the story of the people who had suffered for him: the docile, undemanding wife, with her innumerable trivial ailments from which she was slowly dying with the same weary patience that she brought to everything she did; of the two children to whom he had always been a remote and minatory presence, to be avoided or placated; above all of Eithne, whose ample body had dwindled, whose eyelids had darkened with the weight of her grief, whose glossy coils of hair had dried like grass in the midsummer sun.

He jumped up off the bed and ran to the porthole, struggling to pull it open, while his breath came in gasps like an effortful sobbing. Wind and an icy spume lashed down at him. The pretty chintz curtains billowed out above his head, with a sound as though of ripping.

He went back for the manuscript; then struggled to throw it outwards into the plunging darkness.

But the wind that pressed against him like some vast invisible presence, clammy shoulders heaving against his shoulders, plucked the pages out of his grasp and spun them back across the floor and on to the bed and over the pitiful possessions of the fat Cingalese. Some even seemed to be mysteriously sucked under the doorway, even though the metal lintel was so high.

Going down on his knees, Nakamura attempted to scrabble the pages up into a bundle. Through the open porthole a stinging spray came spattering across them, making the tiny characters blur and drenching his hair and shirt.

'Oh, Eithne, Eithne, Eithne!'

Suddenly tears were joining the spray, falling in large drops on his hands and on the Cingalese's pyjamas and on the sheets of the book that had been his whole barren life and also, he realized now, a terrible and prolonged kind of dying.

1966

A Corner of a Foreign Field

In my profession, not of writer but of British Council officer, those who crave success must learn a superficial versatility. The colour-blind lecture about Matthew Smith and Ivon Hitchens; the tone-deaf about Britten, Tippett and Walton. The man with a pass degree in geography does not demur if he is represented as an authority on the British Constitution, and people who have never in their lives kept personal accounts know the appropriate subheads to which to charge their official expenditure on paper-clips, bus-fares or toilet-paper. When, therefore, I learned of the subject on which I was expected to speak at the Annual General Meeting of the Association of Japanese Teachers of English, I was able to conceal my dismay.

'Mr King, we are very honoured that you have consented to talk for us.' Professor Watanabe, the secretary, was seated opposite to me in my office.

'I am honoured that you have thought of inviting me.'

'Last year Professor Edmund Blunden was our foreign lecturer.'

'That makes the honour all the greater.'

'You are also a writer,' Professor Watanabe said, on a rising note of vague interrogation.

I nodded.

'And a graduate of Oxford University?'

'Yes, that's right.'

'A Master's degree, of course,' he said with an embarrassed giggle.
'It's all the same at Oxford and Cambridge.'

'Please?'

'Master's degree, Bachelor's degree, they come to the same thing.'

'I do not understand.'

'Yes, a Master's degree.'

He opened the brief-case which straddled his knees and took out a sheet of paper. He placed the paper carefully on the table between us, removed a pair of glasses from his breast pocket, held the lenses up to the light and peered into each in turn to make sure that they were clean, and then set the glasses on his nose. 'I have consulted our members about the subject desired. We are, you see' – he giggled again – 'very democratic. We should like' – he picked up the sheet of paper and stared at it – 'yes, we should like – *they* would like the theme "The Dawn of English Literature".'

'The Dawn? You mean – Chaucer and Langdale and so on?'

'A little earlier, please – if that is possible, Mr King.'

'Sir Gawain and the Green Knight?'

He drew in his breath on a long, flattened whistle.

'Well, we should really prefer – could you perhaps be a little earlier still?'

'Old English?'

Professor Watanabe nodded energetically, beaming his pleasure. 'That is what our members desire. Few of us know anything about Old English literature.'

I was glad to hear it; I was in the same position.

'There are other subjects which I should prefer. What about – "The Problems of a Novelist"?'

'I think that many of us have already heard that lecture – that very interesting lecture.'

'Yes, I was afraid so.' I pondered. Then "Somerset Maugham: The Writer and His Work"?' I suggested at last.

'Your "Writer and His Work" lectures are, of course, extremely popular. But Professor Higashi is conducting a seminar on Maugham for our Association.'

'I see.'

'Here is the title. I have written it on this paper. Excuse, please, the badness of my writing.' 'The Dawn of English Literature' had been inscribed in the kind of beautiful copper-plate hand at which Victorian governesses were adept.

'Very well,' I sighed. 'Then let us make it "The Dawn of English

Literature".' After all, I reminded myself, only the week before I had talked about Lord Baden-Powell to six hundred Girl Guides.

'About - about remuneration -' Professor Watanabe halted in the door of the office and in his embarrassment began to fumble with the straps of his brief-case. 'You will understand that our Association. . . . You will give us your sympathetic consideration -'

'Oh, no remuneration will be necessary. This sort of thing is part of my job. I'm not allowed to accept any money for lectures.'

'But we should like to express to you our -'

'No, no, please.'

'Our gratitude to you - and our - our -'

'No, please, please. It's not allowed. I can't. Please forget about it.'

'You are very kind, Mr King.'

'Not at all. It's just that my organization is unduly strict about such things.'

'You are joking. This is Oxford irony, I think. You are very generous to us.'

'Nonsense, nonsense.'

'Then - then thank you for your sympathetic consideration, Mr King.' He sighed. 'On Thursday we shall all be hanging on your lips.'

'And now,' announced Professor Watanabe, 'if any members wish to put questions to Dr King' - in Japan I have grown used to the honorific 'Doctor' or 'Professor' - 'he will be very pleased to answer. Any questions, ladies or gentlemen?' A timeless silence followed; row upon row of passive faces were turned up to mine, like sunflowers to the sun. 'Then in that case -' Professor Watanabe eventually began in melancholy resignation, until 'Yes? Yes?' he broke off eagerly, to point to a figure which had arisen far down the hall. 'Yes? Your question, sir? Ah, it is Professor Kuroda. That is Professor Kuroda, Dr King. He has a question for you.'

I peered into the distance. The face was a smudge; and it was therefore all the more surprising that the precise, resonant voice should roll its words, each distinct and separate, like multicoloured marbles, up to the platform, so that not one of them escaped me. 'You mentioned in passing, Professor King, King Alfred's translation of Boethius's *de Consolatione Philosophiae*. Have you any view about the dating of the Cottonian Manuscript?'

'The Cottonian Manuscript?'

'Otho A, Six.'

'Otho A, Six. Well . . . well, no. There has, as you know, been considerable disagreement between scholars about it.'

'Would you accept the first half of the tenth century?'

'Oh, yes. Yes I *think* so. Oh, definitely, yes.'

'But you would not care to be more precise, Professor King?'

'No. No, not really. Would you?'

The figure disappeared with a 'Thank you, Professor King.' A question from the lecturer, I have learned from experience, often puts a halt to questions from the audience.

'Any more questions – gentlemen, ladies?' Once again Professor Watanabe raked the room. 'Then in that case. . . .' The applause sounded like pebbles being rattled in a tin.

'Your lecture was quite interesting, Mr King,' said Professor Watanabe, when we had returned to a small anteroom to refresh ourselves with tea. I hastily reminded myself that 'quite' in Japan is often mistakenly used for 'very'.

'You opened up a new continent for us,' an ancient professor emeritus wheezed, as he prepared to bite into a cake.

The fourth member of our party announced: 'We now have forty minutes before our next lecture.'

'Was I too short?'

'Oh, no, no. But on such a subject – questions are difficult. When Professor Blunden lectured on Shelley, we overran our period by twenty minutes and many people still had questions for him.'

'I was afraid that my subject might be dry.'

'Dry subjects, like dry wines, are often the best.' Professor Watanabe giggled at his little joke.

The professor emeritus wiped his mouth with his handkerchief and said: 'It was a privilege to hear King's English.' Then in case anyone had failed to appreciate the pun, he added 'Professor King's English.' His joke, so much feebler to western ears than the one which had preceded it, sent his colleagues into delighted peals of laughter.

Professor Watanabe, the first to recover, got up and fetched down from the top of a bookcase a package almost half the height of himself. 'Professor King, we must ask you for your sympathetic consideration.' He bowed before me, placed the package on the table at which we had been drinking tea, and then bowed again. 'This gift is a token of our gratitude and respect. Thank you, Professor King.'

'How very kind of you! But I wish that you had not done this. Thank you very much indeed.'

164

'Thank *you*, Professor King. It is, I am afraid, a very small gift. We ask for your sympathetic consideration.'

But the gift, as I carried it down the stairs, seemed a very large one. I knew already what it was, even though Japanese etiquette forbad me to open it until I reached home. My unwanted family of dolls had now acquired its eleventh member.

I was surprised to find Pierre, a French friend of mine, waiting for me in the hall downstairs. Twice as tall and twice as handsome as the average Japanese, he was, as usual, wearing full Japanese dress; probably the only man in the building that day to do so.

'What is it this time?' he asked in the English which he had learned when serving with the Free French in London, pointing to my package. 'A tank of tropical fish?'

'I hadn't thought of that. I assumed that it was a doll. You weren't at the lecture, were you?'

'Of course.'

'But, Pierre, why? What on earth possessed you?'

'I'm a teacher of English,' he said. 'As well as French. Have you got a cigarette?'

'You know that I don't smoke.'

He looked around him and then put out a long, bony hand to stop a Japanese who was scurrying past us, eyes averted.

'Oh, Professor Nishimura.'

The Japanese bobbed up and down in greeting. 'I did not notice you, Monsieur Mollet.' It seemed impossible not to have noticed a foreigner so tall, and dressed in that fashion. '*Comment allez-vous?*'

'Fine, thanks. You don't happen to have a cigarette you can spare me?'

'Alas, no, Monsieur Mollet. I do not smoke between the hours of eleven and five.'

'Too bad. Thank you all the same.' As the professor scuttled on, Pierre added: 'And I suppose that at five he rushes out to buy himself a packet. The stinginess of it!'

'Do you *never* have cigarettes of your own?'

'Of course. I'm always buying them. But it's this guilt thing I have about them. I buy them and then I lose them. It's happening all the time. You must have noticed how often I buy them – . . . Ah, Professor Kuroda! Now Professor Kuroda smokes, don't you, Professor Kuroda? Do be kind and. . . .'

'Of course, Monsieur Mollet, of course.'

'State Express!'

'One of my extravagances. I fear that for me the pernicious weed is also the expensive weed.'

'You know Mr King, don't you?'

'No. But I am delighted to have this opportunity to congratulate you on your lecture. It was a true case of "nature to advantage dress'd"!' (It was only later that I recalled the line which follows: 'What oft was thought, but ne'er so well express'd'.) 'Please forgive me for asking that foolish question.'

'Professor Kuroda, as you will know, is the leading Japanese authority on Old Norse.'

Professor Kuroda smiled: 'The only Japanese authority, let us say.'

'But he knows much more about English literature than I do,' Pierre countered. 'Probably more than you.'

'May I perhaps invite you gentlemen to a cup of coffee?' Professor Kuroda asked. 'The next lecturer is to be Professor Takayama on Swift's use of the colon, or something of that kind. Perhaps you wish to attend?'

We followed our small, neat, genial host out across the campus. Unlike most Japanese professors he was, I noticed, a dandy: his shirt made of a cream tussore-silk, his suit of slate-grey mohair, his small feet shod in unwrinkled patent-leather moccasins. Bald except for a frill of white hair which circled the lower half of his skull from ear to ear, he swung in one hand a leather brief-case: not the usual scuffed object of the Japanese professor, its corners battered and its leather thongs curling up from the hasps, but one which appeared to have come only that day from the shop.

'I hope that we shall not find too much noise here,' he said, holding the door of the coffee-bar open and waiting for us to precede him. 'Yes, I am afraid that we shall.' The place was full of students. '"The loud laugh which speaks the vacant mind",' he murmured. 'Please, Mr King. A pew, Monsieur Mollet.'

As usual everyone was staring at Pierre, who had picked up the menu even before seating himself. 'An ice cream,' he said. 'No, an ice-cream sundae. No, an ice-cream parfait. And a cake. Two cakes. What about you, Professor Kuroda?' He searched in the sleeves of his kimono: '*Merde!* No cigarettes!'

'Here you are, Monsieur Mollet. Please. Please keep them.'

'No, no. Just two. Or maybe three. It's this guilt thing I have, you know. As soon as I buy cigarettes, I promptly. . . . Now what are you smiling at, Francis?'

'They stock cigarettes here.'

'Yes, I suppose they do. Nasty, cheap brands.'

'You graduated from Oxford, Dr King?'

'It's only Mr King, I'm afraid. Yes, that's right.'

'How fortunate! Your college?'

'Balliol.'

'Balliol! Splendid!'

'Shall we order?' Pierre asked. The stocky waitress was slouched patiently against our table.

'Of course, of course.' Professor Kuroda dealt with this task, and then resumed: 'But Bailliol – how interesting. T.H. Green, Jowett, Sidgwick. . . . And of course your present Prime Minister. I should like to have studied at Oxford. It is now my dream to visit there before I die.

'Oxford to him a dearer name shall be

Than his own mother University. . . .

Not that my mother University is not dear to me, quite the contrary. I am a graduate of Tokyo University,' he added.

'Can't you give Professor Kuroda a scholarship?' Pierre asked, removing his parfait from the tray before the waitress could set it down before him. 'What grubby little cakes!'

'I?'

'Well, your organization.'

'Unfortunately our scholarships are only for people between the ages of twenty-five and thirty-five.'

'Yes –' Professor Kuroda sighed ' – I am afraid that I have missed the boat – and the bus – by falling between two stools. Before the war I was *persona non grata* with the Japanese government; after the war I was a refugee from Manchuria – I went there during the war, to escape our abominable militarism. And now I am an old man, and who wants to indulge the dreams of an old man? What can an old man do but die?'

Pierre looked up from the parfait at which he was greedily scooping with a long spoon. 'But you can do many things. Your Old Norse grammar, your translation of *Emma*. . . . Don't be silly.'

Professor Kuroda appeared to be comforted. 'Can you imagine, Mr King,' he said, 'there is no translation in Japanese of *Emma*. Isn't that extraordinary? You can buy translations of almost every novel by Pearl Buck, but Jane Austen. . . .'

'Jane Austen never won the Nobel Prize.'

'That was delicious,' said Pierre, wiping his lips on his handkerchief. He picked up a fork and dug into one of his cakes. 'Stale,' he said. He munched. 'Surely you can do *something* for Professor Kuroda?' he said.

'I wish that I could.'

'He's a *real* Anglophile. You can see that at once. He even writes poetry in English. Don't you, Professor Kuroda?'

'Not poetry, Monsieur Mollet, jingles, mere jingles. Or does the word "jingle" suggest rhyme? Unfortunately my verses lack that rudder – the rudder of rhyme.'

'I should like to see some of your poems.'

'Ah, you are being too kind! I should feel ashamed to have you look over anything so – so jejune.' He selected the word with some hesitation, but seemed to be satisfied once he had spoken it. 'However, if you would perhaps glance at a small essay which I have been writing on *Where Angels Fear to Tread*. . . .'

'I'd be delighted.'

'I think that I'll have another of these cakes,' said Pierre.

'Please, Monsieur Mollet, please! It is not often that I have the pleasure of entertaining – of treating – two such distinguished guests.' He turned to me: 'I hope that we shall meet again, Mr King. I hope that we shall be friends. You say in English that the only way to have a friend is to be one, don't you? I wish to be your friend, Mr King. May I?'

In Japan I have found many intimate friends among the young; but Professor Kuroda is one of the few whom I have found among the elderly. The elderly seem to feel that it would be ill mannered to take too much from a friendship; and to give in Japan, where every obligation must be repaid, is often merely another way of taking. But Professor Kuroda, from that first time we met, was willing both to give and to take freely.

I had happened to mention in the coffee-bar that I was working on an article on Lafcadio Hearn in Matsué, the place from which Professor Kuroda had just told me that he came. He was delighted. 'I am glad,' he beamed, 'that there is some foreigner who is interested in our Hearn. You notice that I say "our". He has become ours because no one else seems to want him.'

'He is yours because he chose you,' Pierre said.

'Yes, but I am afraid that he is not the great writer we wish him to be.' He sighed.

'No one has understood Japan better,' I said.

168

Two days later I received a telephone call. 'This is Kuroda here.'

'Ah, good morning, Professor Kuroda.'

'We met after your lecture to the Association of Japanese Teachers of English.'

'Yes, of course.'

'You did me the honour of having coffee with me, if you recollect. With Monsieur Mollet.'

It was part of his humility to imagine that in such a short space of time I must have forgotten him.

Could he call to see me? he asked. He had something to show me which might be of interest to me. But he was afraid of intruding: 'Please be frank with me, Mr King. It may be that you are using your Sunday leisure to write, and in that case I have no wish to be a person from Porlock.' Eventually I managed to surmount these hesitations and he agreed to come at once.

It would have been discourteous, according to Japanese etiquette, for him to broach the purpose of his visit as soon as he was seated and he therefore spent several minutes complimenting me on my house ('a real home from home') and the wilderness which had once been its garden ('an English garden, a typical English garden!') before he began to undo his *furoshiki* – the handkerchief in which Japanese habitually carry personal belongings – and took out a pile of exercise books. 'I do not know if these will be useful to you. My great-uncle was a colleague of Hearn's at the school where he taught in Matsué, and they used to have many conversations together. My great-uncle unfortunately died young, at the age of thirty-two, of pulmonary tuberculosis, but he kept some diaries in which he recorded many of his meetings with Hearn. I found the diaries many years ago, and I translated some of the relevant passages into English. I intended to produce a little book – or at least an essay – but like so many intentions in my lazy and disordered life, nothing came of it. However, here are the translations – if you can read my poor hand. They may amuse you for an hour.'

'But this is fascinating!'

'Not fascinating, I fear. But not without a certain – a certain pathos, perhaps. My great-uncle had so much love for Hearn. And Hearn himself tended to repay love with contempt or indifference. That is always sad, isn't it?'

We wandered out into the garden, still talking of Hearn. Professor Kuroda tripped, as he peered up through the trees at the moon, and I had to catch his arm to prevent his falling. ' " I cannot see what flowers are at my feet", ' he said.

'No flowers, I'm afraid. Just weeds.'

'Well, then, "Long live the weeds and the wilderness yet". Please do not make this into a formal Japanese garden, Mr King – all twisted shrubs and twisting paths and stagnant ponds, the size of thimbles, to breed mosquitoes for you. Let this " corner of a foreign field" remain "for ever England".'

Eventually we sat on two rickety deck-chairs under my persimmon tree and continued to talk late into the evening.

'How will you go home?' I asked when at last he took his leave.

'Oh, I shall walk.'

'Let me get my boy to drive you back. I don't drive myself.'

'But that is totally unnecessary. We are neighbours.'

'Neighbours?'

'Certainly. You didn't know that? I live over there.' He pointed. 'You know the Korean School? I live just beyond it. Before I knew who you were, I often saw you exercising those ferocious dogs of yours. That is one English passion I cannot share – dogs.'

'Then I'll walk with you,' I said.

'No, please, Mr King. You will tire yourself. Please do not put yourself to the trouble. Please.'

'But I should like a stroll. If you don't mind my bringing the ferocious dogs with me.'

'The dogs?'

'Do you mind?'

'Do they bite?'

'They'd never bite you. They're terrible snobs, you know. You're far too well dressed and far too clean.'

'That is my little hut.' We had walked for five minutes, and now he halted to point to a small house standing in the grounds of a large one. 'The – the mansion belongs to my brother. He is in what you call "trade", he makes much more money than any professor. So he lends me my – my hut. Please come to visit me.' He seemed to read my thoughts: 'I live all alone.' He smiled. 'You will not have to endure or to inflict any domestic embarrassments. Like you, I am not married. In the West that is not strange but here in Japan everyone assumes that if one is not married, it is because of hereditary disease or something seriously amiss with one's character. Oh yes! My brother was once very concerned about my single state. But now, fortunately, I have reached an age when he ceases to urge me. I have some books which may interest you.'

'May I really come to visit you?'

'Of course. Please come. And you do not have to warn me in advance. I am usually here in the evenings.'

'Thank you.'

'Well, good night then, Mr King. Good night, Ben. Good night, Arabella. Good night, Puppy-chan.' Solemnly he bowed in turn to each of the dogs and then bowed again to me, before he went through the gate. 'It was a great privilege,' he said over his shoulder.

The house in which he lived consisted of only two rooms, a downstairs sitting-room and an upstairs bedroom which was also a study. Everywhere there were books: even in the lavatory there was a case of them. He owned many beautiful and valuable things – family treasures which he had brought from Matsué with him – and also a great deal of what we should term 'junk': a plaster statuette, found at the monthly Kitano Market, of the Queen as a young girl; two hideous Edwardian brass lamps; a harmonium at which he would sometimes play hymns although he was not a Christian; ancient, empty bottles of brands of whisky of which I had never heard, stacked on a shelf; photographs in frames of Thomas Hardy, George Meredith and the youthful Bernard Shaw; some Benares bowls, a chipped Wedgwood cup and saucer, a heap of Bryant and May's match-boxes and a garden gnome. I realized that the accumulation of Japanese objects in my own house must seem equally odd to native eyes.

Professor Kuroda's gaze followed mine. 'Does all this give you a nostalgia?' he queried. 'My friends all joke with me. "Where are you living, Professor Kuroda?" they ask. "In England or in Japan?" "I do not know," I reply. "I know only that I live in my own world." Now – please sit down. Here is an English rocking chair. Will you sit in that? Good. And I shall make some tea. You will drink some Lipton's tea, won't you?'

'Thank you. That would be very nice.'

He put two teaspoonfuls of tea into the pot and then added a third. ' "One for the pot" don't you say? Now please instruct me, Mr King. When I put in the hot water, should I stir the leaves or not? What is your advice?'

Having carried on an extensive correspondence not merely with scholars in his own field but with many of the English writers whom he especially admired, he now fetched down box after box of letters, often having to clamber up on to a chair in order to reach them, and emptied them out before me. 'Your E. M. Forster once wrote to me

171

in answer to a letter which I had the *audacity* to write to him.
Yes. . . .' He stood on tiptoe and strained to get a box down from
the top of his wardrobe. 'Ah, thank you, Mr King.' I had reached it
for him. 'Yes. . . .' He began to read the letter over to himself, smiling as he did so. 'What a charming letter. . . . delightful. . . . As
though he were talking to one. Please.' He held it out to me.

'You really *must* visit England,' I said at one point. 'You have all
these correspondents, you know so much about England. I shall
have to see what I can do.'

'You are very kind. But who is interested in financing an old
scholar whose teaching days are almost over? And I, unfortunately,
lost my – my *little all* in Manchuria. So there we are! No matter! I
have a small piece of England here around me. And you have given
me a bigger piece to add to it. . . . Did you see that postcard from
Bernard Shaw? Please – it will amuse you. I had written to protest
about some remarks he had made about Herr Hitler – complimen-
tary remarks, I'm afraid – and he replied to – to pull me over the
coals.'

A few weeks later I invited Kuroda to a cocktail party which I was
giving for a visiting English Member of Parliament. It was a foolish
thing to do and later I regretted it. At first he had been disinclined to
accept – he went out so little, he had lived so long ' "The world
forgetting, by the world forgot" ', he had 'no glad rags for such an
occasion'; and having at last accepted at my insistent persuasion, he
then telephoned me at least half-a-dozen times to ask me innumerable
agitated questions. How did one address a Member of Parliament?
What time should he arrive if the invitation said 6.0 – 8.0 p.m.?
Could I advise which of my 'potent concoctions' would be most
suitable for an old man who had 'like Cassio, "very poor and
unhappy brains for drinking" '?

Through the glass door of my sitting-room I was aware, as I
talked to one of my guests, that he was standing out in the hall, pretending to examine a Hiroshige print which he had long ago dated
for me. I went out to him.

'Ah, Professor Kuroda. How nice to see you. Do come in and
meet Mr Dalby.'

'Oh, no, no, no. Later, later,' he whispered in agitation. 'Such an
eminent man – at the beginning of your reception. . . . I should
have nothing to say to him. I should find myself totally – totally at
sea.'

'He is only another Tadpole or Taper.' We had been discussing Disraeli as a political novelist at our previous meeting.

'Let me gather my courage.'

'Then please gather it with a drink. Come.' I propelled him into the sitting-room.

'. . . You should really try Predonine. That terrible scratching sensation disappears at once.'

'At the Baptist Hospital they gave me an ointment.'

'An *ointment*! They must be out of their minds.'

'Greasy and *mauve*. I put it on in the morning and wash it off at night.'

Two male American teachers were standing just beyond the door, one of them holding a plate of canapés in his hand, from which both of them fed themselves as they talked.

'Harry, Joe . . . I want you to meet Professor Kuroda. Mr Van Groot, Mr Peterson.'

'Professor Kuroda – nice to meet you.'

'Good evening, Professor Kuroda.'

'But no one uses ointment these days. No one has used ointment for an allergy in fifty years.'

'It contains some kind of antihistamine, I guess.'

'You try Predonine. I had this allergy, had it for weeks. I got it after eating curry on an Indian ship. . . .'

By now they had both turned at an angle from Professor Kuroda.

'Enid, dear.' I caught hold of a plump English woman in a straw hat which looked like a huge loofah, as she left a group of people to put out a cigarette. 'This is Professor Kuroda.'

'Professor who?'

'Kuroda. K-U-R-O-D-A. . . . This is Mrs Evans, Professor Kuroda. She's Kobe's leading amateur actress.'

'Oh, Francis, it's a long time since you've said anything as nice as that about me! And what do you profess, Professor – er. . . .'

'Old Norse,' Professor Kuroda stammered, as I pushed a Martini into his hand. 'What is this?'

'A Martini. Excellent for you.'

'Old Norse! Well, fancy that! . . . My husband was posted to Oslo for seven months but unfortunately I couldn't accompany him. The children, you know. Old Norse! Well, fancy!'

'You are an actress?'

'Oh, Mr King's just teasing. He's a terrible tease, you know. . . . Well, yes, actually, I do act. I was a professional once, donkey's

173

years ago. But then I became a respectable married woman and had to give it up. Except for our amateur shows in Kobe. Ever come to them?'

'No, I very much regret. . . .'

'But you must! You'd enjoy them. We've just started to rehearse *The Mousetrap*. Do you know it?'

'*The Mousetrap?*' Professor Kuroda looked momentarily bewildered; then his face cleared. 'Ah, *Hamlet*, you mean?'

'*Hamlet!*' she shrieked, displaying teeth smudged with lipstick. 'Good lord, no! What a priceless idea! Agatha Christie, a thriller. I'm to take the Margaret Lockwood part. Lots of fun. Perhaps not intellectual enough for you or *Professor* King here, but it's the kind of thing our low-brow members enjoy.'

Professor Kuroda had taken out a notebook. 'Please – let me make a note of this. The title is *The Mousetrap?*'

'That's right.'

'And the authoress is a Miss Margaret Lockwood –'

'No, no, no, Professor Kuroda!'

At that moment I had to leave them to greet some other guests; and when I again looked for Kuroda, a quarter of an hour later, he was once more alone, his back turned to the room as he examined some of my books. I went over to him.

'Now you must meet Mr Dalby.'

'Oh, no, please, Mr King. *Please!*'

'You'll like him.'

'But I have no experience of the – the race of politicians. I – I have no idea how to –'

Mr Dalby was upon us.

'Ah, King, a splendid party this, splendid.' He gulped greedily at his Scotch. 'Just had a most interesting chat with the Mayor.' He indicated the Governor with his glass. 'Wonderfully humorous old boy.'

'The Governor,' I said.

'Yes, the Governor, the Governor. We were talking about my forthcoming speech in Asoka.'

'Osaka.'

'Yes, that's right. He gave me one or two pointers. Pretty useful pointers, as a matter of fact. We've met before, haven't we?'

He turned to Professor Kuroda who gave a nervous smile which was almost a grimace and then looked at me with panic-stricken eyes.

174

'Yes, I haven't managed to get round to reading your pamphlet yet, but I look forward to doing so. My PA – that's him over there, David Swinton – tells me that he's glanced at it. He's a bright boy, David, can always find time for everything. "The Missionary Universities in Japan" – you have quite a subject there.' He gulped again at his Scotch, and before I could intervene, went on: 'Now you're just the man, Professor, to give me some advice. As I see the situation in Japan – correct me, if I'm wrong – the war has brought about enormous improvements of every kind – a democratic way of life, a rise in the standard of living – but it has also destroyed something of the – the old moral fibre of the nation. . . .'

'I – I think that you are making a mistake –' Kuroda began, but Dalby overwhelmed him.

'No, no – *surely*! It's obvious to anyone with the eyes to see.'

At that point I had to leave them to say goodbye to a distinguished guest. When I next glanced in their direction, Dalby was still swaying before a hypnotized Kuroda. '. . . The supreme importance of the family structure . . . decay of belief . . . teddy-boys, beatniks and juvenile delinquents. . . .' The rich parliamentary voice was clanging away. Well, it was probably best to leave them together.

Pierre arrived at ten minutes to eight, sweeping into the room in a kimono which made everyone turn to gape at him. 'I'm late, I'm afraid. . . . Could this Martini perhaps be a little paler?'

I took the glass from him, and when I returned it, said: 'Is that the right shade? I added some water.'

He sipped, pulled a face and waved to Professor Kuroda, who waved his glass back. 'Is the Professor drunk?'

'I don't know. I hope not.'

'He looks terribly flushed.'

'That may merely be the effect of Mr Dalby's eloquence.'

'Your guest of honour?'

'Yes, come and meet him.'

'Later. First I must eat something. I'm absolutely famished. Do you think you could prepare me a sandwich – I mean a real sandwich, not one of these titbits?'

'We're going out to eat in a moment, and I was hoping that you would join us.'

'Of course. But you won't get rid of this crowd for at least another hour.'

This estimate was, in fact, an optimistic one, and it was nearly quarter to ten before we set off. Professor Kuroda had by then collapsed into a sofa, where he sat alone, from time to time nodding and smiling at nothing in particular.

'Let my boy drive you home,' I suggested.

'Excellent, excellent,' he said.

'He'll be back in a moment.'

'Excellent.' As though he were moving one of his Sung or Tang treasures, he used both hands to place his empty glass on the table before him. 'I am afraid that your potent intoction was altogether too concoction,' he said.

'Professor Kuroda, you are going to dine with us, aren't you?' Pierre flopped down on the sofa, so violently that Kuroda was bounced up into the air, as on a see-saw.

'I am about to return home.'

'Nonsense, you must join us for dinner. Mustn't he, Francis?'

'Of course. If he would like to do so,' I said reluctantly.

'There's nothing more miserable than going home at ten after a cocktail party. What can one do? Either one falls on one's bed and goes to sleep, to wake up an hour later, or else one opens a tin of baked beans. I'd hate to have you do either of these things, Professor.'

'Baked beans?'

'Well, if you're a Japanese, then I suppose that you take some fish-cakes from the ice box. Anyway – you must dine with us.'

There were seven of us altogether, the others being Dalby and his assistant, David Swinton, and Enid Evans and her husband, Bob. Dalby wanted to see 'some local colour'. Enid, suffering from 'a gyppy tummy', insisted that she must avoid Japanese food, while Bob pointed out to her repeatedly that most western restaurants in Kyoto closed at eight. Pierre contented himself with characterizing any suggestion made by the rest of us as 'gruesome' or 'macabre'. It was the usual futile discussion which follows a cocktail party – on this occasion carried on in the hall to the sound of water cascading from the lavatory, into which we each took turns to vanish. Only Kuroda was silent.

'I know!' Pierre exclaimed at last. 'Let's compromise and have a Chinese meal. There's this new Chinese restaurant. Everyone's talking about it. Called the "Champs Elysées".'

'Called the *what*?'

'What's in a name? Friends tell me that the food is absolutely excellent.'

'I don't know if my stomach is any more likely to survive a Chinese meal than a Japanese –'

'You can eat rice,' Bob said unsympathetically.

'Thanks.'

'How about it, sir?' Pierre appealed to Dalby.

'Lead on, Macduff!'

'Francis?'

'Anything you say.'

'You like Chinese food, don't you, Professor Kuroda? Professor Kuroda once lived in China. He can translate the menu for us.'

At this prolonged and complicated task Professor Kuroda was more adept than I had expected: evidently the car ride had sobered him. Everyone wanted something different, and every order was changed at least half-a-dozen times. As the head waiter returned to us at each new summons, the bead curtain which separated our cubicle from the main dining room seemed to clash with a fiercer and fiercer vehemence. While we waited for our food, Bob and Enid bickered in undertones, Pierre and Dalby began to argue about General de Gaulle, David Swinton asked me if I knew this or that celebrity, and Professor Kuroda snored gently and rhythmically, his chin on his chest.

At last the innumerable dishes were set down before us.

'Delicious!' Enid declared.

'Excellent,' said Bob. They seemed to like each other again.

'I wonder if, while you were in Helsinki, you were ever taken to a delightful little Chinese restaurant near to the Russian Church?' David Swinton asked me. 'Some friends of mine, Baron and Baroness. . . ,'

'. . . People say that the old boy's impatient of criticism, but that was not *my* experience. If I put something to him, straight from the shoulder, he might not like what I said but he'd always consider it – often I'd even get him to change his mind. Churchill unfortunately. . . .'

'Professor Kuroda, you're not eating,' Pierre said.

'Ah, yes, yes,' Kuroda aroused himself. 'I'm afraid that I – er – nodded, nearly napping. Please forgive me. This banquet is indeed Lucullan. Yes, indeed.'

It was almost midnight when we finished, the restaurant deserted but for ourselves, the head waiter and a boy who was sent from time to time to peer at us through the bead curtain.

'Well, I suppose that we'd better go,' I said, and I called to the boy, at his next sulky appearance, to bring us the bill.

I was talking to Dalby when the boy returned and did not notice that he had walked over to Kuroda and placed before him the silver platter with the folded bill upon it. Pierre tells me that Kuroda went first white, then red and then white again. At last he leant across the table and hissed at me in a voice of panic-stricken urgency: 'Mr King – I am extremely sorry – you must forgive me – I cannot possibly – I am afraid –' At that, Pierre jumped up from his chair at the end of the table and gaily snatched the bill from Kuroda's hands. 'Poor Professor Kuroda! He thought that we were going to make him pay! No, no, Professor. We wouldn't dream of playing such a trick on you. This is the man who's going to pay. He can charge it all up to the British tax-payer. Can't you, Francis?' It would have been discourteous to have denied this, and I meekly took the proffered bill. Having glanced at it, I too blanched, reddened and blanched again. Slipping behind the bead curtain, I arranged with the supercilious waiter for the bill to be sent to my office the next morning.

'Poor Professor Kuroda!' Pierre was still chaffing him when I returned. 'That was a nasty moment, wasn't it? You should have seen your face.'

After we had left Dalby and Swinton at the Kyoto Hotel, Kuroda and I travelled on in my car, in a silence which had grown inexplicably uncomfortable.

'I hope that you were not bored.'

'Of course not, Mr King.'

'You talked for some time to Dalby.'

'Yes.'

'He's said to be very able. But as in the case of many men of whom that is said, the ability is not at once apparent. Is it?'

No answer.

'The cocktail party is a wretched form of entertainment. That's one western custom you Japanese should never imitate.' Silence. 'I've discovered a new disease – the Cocktail Party Syndrome. Pains in the backs of the legs and the back of the neck and the shoulders, a craving for water, a craving for solitude.'

Nothing more was said until we drew up outside his gate. 'Thank you, Mr King. It was very kind of you. I enjoyed myself.' The polite phrases, accompanied by a taut smile and frequent bowings, seemed to be repeated automatically.

'I hope to see you soon. Come by for coffee tomorrow evening, if you feel like it.'

'Thank you, Mr King.'

'And don't forget the concert on Sunday.'

178

'Thank you, Mr King.'

But he did not appear for coffee, and when I telephoned to him about the concert, he had some excuse about his sister-in-law being ill. More than a fortnight passed before we met again, and more than a month before our friendship got back into its old, comfortable groove. What had gone wrong? How had I offended him? In some way not immediately apparent to me, he had felt he had lost face; and each time that I thought about it, I came back reluctantly to that incident of the bill. It must have been that.

Kuroda never cared to discuss the ways and means of realizing his dream of visiting England, even though the dream itself was often a topic of our conversation. 'It is too difficult, it is too complicated, I am too old, Japan is too far from Europe,' was his invariable response – infuriating to me in its abject fatalism. 'You want to go, don't you?' I demanded on one occasion.

'Of course I do.'

'Then you should do something about it.'

'But what *can* I do, Mr King?'

'Other professors get money from their universities or from the Ministry of Education.'

'They are young.'

'Not all of them.'

'Ah, the others are very eminent scholars – national treasures and cultural properties. Unfortunately I am not of their army.'

'Of course you are. You're an eminent scholar. Don't be silly.'

'You flatter me, Mr King.'

'Nothing of the kind. How did that old fool Professor Nozawa get to Europe?'

Kuroda pretended to look shocked, but he could not help being pleased at the same time: this colleague was one whom he despised and disliked. 'Professor Nozawa is not a fool, Mr King. He is the leading authority in Japan on Mark Rutherford.'

'Of course he is a fool. You know that he is a fool.'

Kuroda raised a hand and giggled behind it. 'Then I must suppose that your saying is true: "Fortune favours fools".'

'Where did he get the money?'

'What money, Mr King?'

'For his trip.'

'From many sources, I think – his university, the Ministry, from one or two foundations.'

179

'Why can't you do the same?'

'I have not been invited.'

'What has that got to do with it?'

'If I am invited, then possibly – *possibly* – I can procure some funds. It all depends on the invitation.'

'From whom must the invitation come?'

'From some university or college. Professor Nozawa is to give a course of lectures in California.'

'On Mark Rutherford?' I asked in amazement.

'Oh, no, Mr King. On Buddhism – Zen Buddhism.'

'What nonsense!'

'No, no, he is an expert on Buddhism, a great expert.'

'Couldn't you lecture on Buddhism?'

'I? You are joking.'

'So – if you were to get an invitation from some university or learned society, then possibly you could –'

'It might be a little easier. I cannot be sure. This is a very complex problem. I have few friends in the Ministry and at the university I have tended to – to hoe my own row. Is that expression permissible?' He was, I could see, already preparing to retreat from any action. 'I am afraid that really it is all too difficult. Please do not trouble yourself. You have too many other concerns.'

But I was now obsessed with the idea of getting him to England, and his reluctance to impose on me only goaded me to further efforts. I wrote to our London office; I wrote to my former tutor at Oxford and friends who had become dons there; I wrote to an assortment of authors, Members of Parliament and Japanophiles. All professed to be interested, all wished they could help; but for this or that reason none could do anything positive. Then to my astonishment and delight, I received an answer to a letter which I had written, several weeks before, to Henry Hunter.

I have known Henry ever since, more than twenty years ago, he published my first poem; and that kindness – it was a bad poem, one of several bad poems which I unloaded on to him – has been followed by many other kindnesses. Henry is – I almost wrote, has been – a poet himself; but he is now chiefly known to the world at large as one of those professional conference-goers and committee-sitters who dart from continent to continent now making speeches about Cultural Freedom, now adjudicating literary competitions and now acting as lecturers on Creative Writing at American Universities. Henry, inevitably, is on a number of British Council committees; and with his habitual generosity he will deliver a lecture at a Council centre to an audience of thirty Brazilians or Poles or Japanese for less than the money it will cost him to pay for the dinner which he insists on giving the director afterwards.

'. . . I was interested in what you wrote about your professor,' he began. 'But is he really as deserving of help as you so cleverly make him sound? One so fears another of your lame dogs, avid to bite the hands of those whom you talk into feeding them. Anyway, as you have probably learned already, I have been invited to attend the forthcoming PEN Club conference in Tokyo and your London office has suggested that I might at the same time give one or two lectures. If you would welcome this idea, then I could spend a night in Kyoto and you could perhaps arrange for me to meet your professor. If he is all that you say, then I have some ideas of how we might help him. You must let me know what subject (if any) you would like me to talk about. I thought "Committed or Uncommitted?" might be a possibility. . . .'

I at once hurried over to Kuroda to give him the news.

'You know something about Henry Hunter, don't you?'

'Oh, yes. In fact I have here a copy of his first volume of poems. It has become something of a rarity, I believe. Published by Blackwell, while he was still a student at Oxford.'

'Good. When you meet him, you must be sure to take it along for him to sign.'

'At our first meeting, Mr King?'

'Yes. That's the kind of thing which flatters his vanity.'

'But do you really think –?' He broke off.

'Yes?'

'Well, do you really think –? I cannot help feeling that Mr Hunter is merely being kind out of – of friendship for yourself.'

'Of course not. Henry is not that sort of person. If he cannot do a thing or does not wish to do it, then he says so '

'I do not like to trouble such an important man about my trivial affairs.'

'Henry enjoys helping others. I'm sure that he will be able to do something for you. He has an immense amount of influence.'

'I fear that you may have made me sound more interesting to him than I really am. He will be disappointed.'

'Nonsense!' This defeatism was beginning to exasperate me. 'Like many people who themselves possess charm, Henry is extremely susceptible to charm in others.'

181

'But I have no charm at all, none at all, Mr King.'

'Of course you have. You'll be a great success with him. You wait and see.'

I arranged with Kuroda to meet Henry and me at the lecture and then to go on to dinner with us at a Japanese-style restaurant, to which Kuroda himself had introduced me several months before. But when the lecture started, I noticed that Kuroda was nowhere in the crowded hall.

Henry lectures impromptu. When on form, he is brilliant; when not on form, he becomes discursive and repetitious and tends to speak with his eyes closed for several sentences on end. On this occasion he did not close his eyes once. As soon as he had finished, he was surrounded by a crowd of chattering and giggling students, many of whom were asking him for his autograph. My Japanese secretary approached me:

'Professor Kuroda has just telephoned.'

'Professor Kuroda? Why didn't you call me?'

'It was in the middle of the lecture. Unfortunately he is sick.'

'Sick? What's the matter with him?' I had seen him only that morning.

'His stomach. He said he was sorry not to have been at the lecture.'

'And is he coming now?'

'He was not sure. He asked me to tell you and Mr Hunter to go on to dinner. He will come to the restaurant if he is feeling better.'

Unfortunately Kuroda has no telephone.

'Is he really sick?'

'That is what he said, Mr King.'

'Did he sound sick?'

'Did he what, Mr King?'

'Oh, all right. Thank you.'

Henry was reading one of his poems to the students. When he had finished, he gave the book back to its owner and then turned to me:

'Well? Ought we to be going?'

'Kuroda has ratted.'

'The professor?'

'He telephoned to say that he was ill. His stomach. I don't believe it for a moment. He has the digestion of an ostrich.'

'And like an ostrich he wants to put his head in the sand at the prospect of meeting me. Can't you give him a ring?'

'He's not on the telephone.'

'Well, I suppose that I *could* see him tomorrow.'

'Before eight-thirty?'

'Yes, it would have to be before eight-thirty. A ghastly time.'

'If I haven't succeeded in getting him to you now, there's little chance of getting him to you at an hour like that.'

'Well, I'm famished. Let's go, shall we? Goodbye everyone. See you all some time, somewhere. . . . Delightful crowd. Really delightful. Now I mustn't get to bed too late tonight. You mustn't lead me astray, promise. But I *was* told in Tokyo of a little bar somewhere behind the station – I'm sure that you know it. . .'

It was about twelve o'clock when I got home, having left Henry drinking in the bar with a companion whom, at that moment at any rate, he obviously preferred to myself. I felt restless and exasperated, and but for the lateness of the hour, I should have gone over to Kuroda's house to see what had become of him. He had, needless to say, failed to appear at the restaurant. Since I knew that I would not sleep, I first polished a Sendai chest I had bought the day before, and then, still wakeful, decided to go for a walk with the dogs, inevitably making my way along the canal which flowed past Kuroda's house.

To my disappointment not a single light showed; he must be asleep. And since he rarely went to bed before two or three, perhaps, I suddenly thought, his illness was genuine. How dreadful if I had been angrily accusing him of having let me down when all the time he had been in pain or discomfort! Should I ring the bell? If he had had someone else living with him to answer it, I should certainly have done so.

I walked on, up into the hills, and such was the beauty of that night, unspoiled by the usual humidity of the Japanese summer, that I was at last able to forget my annoyance and disappointment. I let the dogs off their leashes, an act forbidden by Japanese law, and walked at ease, without being tugged along behind them. When I returned along the canal, I heard the sound of Japanese clogs clattering invisible ahead of me in the surrounding darkness and silence: surely one of the loveliest as well as one of the most sinister sounds in the world. Suddenly all three dogs had bolted off, unheeding of my shouts to them. Approaching closer I saw them jumping up around a small figure, clad in a summer kimono, who was attempting to fend them off with the towel and enamel basin which he was carrying with him, apparently on a journey to or from the Japanese bath.

'Ben! Arabella! Come here! Come here at once! Puppy-chan!'

The dogs turned their heads momentarily, they even wagged their tails; but they did not come to me. I peered into the darkness. 'Professor Kuroda!'

'Ah, Mr King – it is you. I was afraid that like Actaeon I was about to be dismembered by these beasts.'

'Are you all right?'

'Oh yes, indeed. I don't really think that they would bite me. They know me by now.'

'I mean, your stomach.'

'Oh, that.' He was obviously embarrassed. 'Yes, thank you, yes. It was only a temporary indisposition. I am afraid that I must have been indiscreet in the quantity I ate at lunch. Yes, thank you. I am now much better. In fact, fully recovered – as far as anyone of my age can be said fully to recover. I am sorry that I was unable to be –'

'It was very naughty of you. After I had taken all that trouble. And now, unless you go to see Mr Hunter early tomorrow morning – before eight-thirty –'

'Before eight-thirty!'

'He must be at the airport at nine.'

'Oh, I couldn't possibly disturb him at such an hour. Out of the question. I am really *extremely* sorry –'

'But don't you understand – this was to be your chance! He would have done something for you, I'm sure of it. Perhaps he'll even do something now in spite of never meeting you, but it's far less certain. Far less certain.'

'Yes, I see that. Of course.' He used his towel to mop at his forehead and neck. 'I am very much to blame.' Then he peered up at the moon, as he had peered up at it, seemingly so long ago, on his first visit to my house. ' "On such a night," ' he began.

'Don't you *want* to go to England?' I cried out in exasperation. 'Don't you want to go?'

'Ah,' he said, slipping an arm through mine. 'Let me walk with you to your house.'

'I don't believe that you really want to go at all. Do you?' I challenged him, knowing that I was showing to him a brutality which I had never shown before and guessing its effect on him, and yet not minding. 'Do you?'

'I *did* want to go,' he said. 'Really, I did.'

'Why the past tense?'

'The past tense?'

'You now have doubts?'

There was a silence. He pressed my arm gently: 'Yes,' he said at last. 'Yes. Yes, I do have doubts. I am so afraid that – that I might not measure up to what England requires of me.'

'Is that all?'

'All?'

'Or is it' – suddenly it was lit up for me – 'is it that you are afraid that England might not measure up to what you require of it?'

'What do you mean?'

I repeated the question.

Suddenly he giggled. 'Yes, that too,' he admitted. 'I have my England – the England in which my Japanese friends laugh at me for living – but would I – would I find it over there? I used to think that I should. But as it came nearer and nearer to me – England, I mean – I began to feel more and more doubtful. Your party – those people. . . . Oh, they were very nice people, such nice people, please do not think that I am criticizing them. But somehow – well, *not* what I'd expected. They alarmed me, you know. That was when I first started to think about this – this problem,' he concluded with a rueful smile.

'I see.'

'Mine is the England of Jane Austen, and Wordsworth and George Eliot and Thomas Hardy and – and even' – he giggled again – 'Mark Rutherford. I – I don't want to lose that England. Is that very foolish of me?'

I thought. 'No,' I said.

'Then you are not so terribly, terribly angry with me.'

'No. Of course not.'

'But disappointed?'

'A little.'

He sighed. 'Yes, and I am also disappointed. But a smaller disappointment is preferable to the risk of a larger one.' Again he pressed my arm. 'So I don't think that I shall trouble your kind Mr Hunter so early tomorrow morning.'

'As you wish, Professor Kuroda.'

His eyes twinkled. 'After my indisposition, I need a good night's sleep.'

1962

The Goat

All that summer Okuno was making his film about the goat, and since I had lent him some of the money with which he hired both his camera and cameraman, from time to time when I had a weekend free I used to make the journey, occasionally by car over the narrow dust-choked roads but more often by train, to see how he was progressing. I liked Okuno, although he often exasperated me with the intensity of his youthful egotism and his total lack of humour; and even more I liked the small, lackadaisical seaside resort, tumbled down before a crescent of blazing sand, which he had chosen for his location. The inn at which we stayed, an airy, wooden box, used to susurrate and creak around me as I lay awake, neither desiring sleep nor feeling any need for it. We all of us seemed to be devoured by the same dry excitement, as though a fire were crackling through us: an excitement which would leave me as soon as I returned to the heat and humidity of my office in Kyoto, to drowse, sodden with sweat and exasperated, over the correspondence which had piled up in my absence. 'I feel that this will be my break-through,' Okuno would say, greedily sucking at one of the innumerable cigarettes which he would hold between his middle finger and thumb, in such a way that the finger of his right hand and even the palm were orange with nicotine. We all felt the same; and we were right. *The Goat*, shown in small art cinemas first in Japan and then in America and Europe,

186

made none of us any money, but it made for Okuno the reputation which has already begun to set him apart from the rest of us. Jay Oppenheim, the American who was his constant companion throughout the filming, now says bitterly that he 'used' us; but that is not how Okuno looks at it: it is he, in his view, who is used by his talent, as a furnace is used by the fire which it contains. If others are consumed in the process, then he is hardly to be blamed.

After an indifferent Japanese-style dinner of titbits of vegetable and fish, both of them usually raw, followed by bowls of glutinous rice served with acrid pickles, the rest of us would lie out on the *tatami*, the light off so as not to attract the mosquitoes which bred uncontrolled in the small stagnant pools dotting the garden beneath us. But Okuno, even after innumerable cups of saké, would never relax. Either sitting hunched over the inevitable cigarette, at which he would gulp like a baby at the bottle, or striding up and down the room, the whole house creaking and shuddering beneath his tread, he would hold forth in his idiosyncratic yet miraculously fluent English. Jay, who looks like a pansy prize-fighter, with a pulpy battered face and hands far too large for the wrists from which they dangle as though they were boxing gloves, would from time to time catch my eye, smile and shake his head. 'Some kid!' I would imagine him saying, even if he did not actually speak the words, in his husky, falsetto voice. Old Nakamura, who had worked with a number of famous directors until his growing alcoholism made him too unreliable, would probably be asleep, his sharp chin piercing his chest to transfix him to the beam against which he was slouched. The boy – I knew him only as Shin-chan – would be seated with his bare legs crossed and his skinny muscular arms hugging himself as though in some perpetual inner agony which gave to his face a look of premature ageing and anxiety.

The story of the film was a simple one, which I myself had elaborated, without conviction, to Okuno one evening at my house. He had soon forgotten that; the story became inalienably his, and I was willing to yield it to him, hating it increasingly the more he talked about it. As I now recount it, I cannot even remember which were its original elements and which were the additions made by Okuno or one of the others during those long evening sessions of ours.

A group of children from two poor families who live in the same shack together and make a living by cultivating seaweed, find a goat which has strayed, dragging its tether and pin, down on to the beach, to rout in a pile of garbage. At first they are frightened of the goat and one of them even suggests setting on to it their dog, a shaggy, ravenous beast perpetually chained outside the shack to warn off thieves. But slowly the goat wins them over. The old grandfather, the patriarch of the two families, makes an attempt to milk it, but either the goat is dry or he lacks the necessary skill. The children are then told to take it or drive it away: there is no food for it; it maddens the dog, which never ceases to snarl and wrench at its chain; if found, people may think that they have stolen it. The children pretend to get rid of the animal, but in fact they take it up into the scrub on the hills above the beach and there construct for it out of brushwood a shed in which to shelter at night. Secretly they go up to visit it every day, carrying for it vegetable peel, armfuls of grass and anything else they can scrounge. Their lives are now centred on the goat; for it all sacrifices are made, to it all affection is given. Slowly it becomes for them a kind of a god so that at last they even erect for it at the entrance to its shed a rickety Shinto *torii*, made of roughly cut lengths of bamboo bound together with straw.

One day, however, the goat is discovered by its real owner, a maker of brooms and brushes who lives in the nearest village. Furious, he accuses the children of stealing the goat, demolishes and burns both shed and *torii*, and threatens them with the police. They are disconsolate. Often now, at night or early in the morning, they creep up to visit the goat tethered outside his hut, taking it scraps secreted from their meagre meals. Then the grandfather and their parents learn what they are doing, and they are beaten and forbidden to go again. But still, surreptitiously, they slip away.

One morning, at dawn, they are woken by a bleating near the shack followed by a frenzied barking. Joyfully they rush out, and there, totally unconcerned, its flanks sleek in the early sunshine, they find the goat once again routing in the pile of garbage. Hitching up his long underpants the grandfather appears, his eyes rheumy from sleep and his chin covered in white bristles. 'What's all this?' he demands. 'What's that beast doing here again?' They explain that they have had no part in its return; it has come of its own accord. 'Well, get it away from here!' They do nothing. 'Go on – get it away! Get it away!' He advances on the goat, waving his arms at it and from time to time hitching at his underpants. He makes hoarse sounds; he claps his arthritic hands. Suddenly the goat rears up on its hind legs and, as though in a formal dance, lowers its head and makes as if to butt him. 'So you would, would you!' Again he advances, attempting to grab the horns. One strikes him on the knee. In a fury, he goes over to the dog, now hurling itself about on its brief length of chain, and stoops to unleash it. The children run to prevent him. But with a bound the dog hurls itself on the goat, sinking its teeth deep into its neck. Somehow the wretched animal manages to free itself and strikes the dog a glancing blow with its horns before it waddles off down the beach. Again the dog attacks, this time driving the goat in panic into the sea. The children, fully clothed, race into the water after it, but out and out it swims, too swift and too far for them to follow, until all at once it sinks and is lost to sight. Days later its swollen corpse is washed up on to the beach, and the film ends with the children holding an elaborate funeral service before burying it on the hill-top where its shed and the *torii* used to stand.

In filming this story, which might so easily have been both senti- mental and melodramatic, Okuno succeeded in creating a childhood world perfect in every detail. His actors were drawn from the inhab- itants of the small seaside resort. The children he selected from a group which he had found playing baseball on the beach, and it was in his handling of them that he showed, as all the critics agreed, his genius as a director. There were five of them: the two youngest, who were intended to be four and seven, plump and fresh-cheeked, with thick, coarse hair cut in a straight horizontal line over their fore- heads and across the backs of their necks; the three eldest at once skinny and muscular, their movements alternating between a mar- vellous animal grace and a touching peasant awkwardness. The old grandfather was in fact the owner of the inn at which we stayed; the two sets of parents were a fisherman and his wife and the local schoolmaster and his wife, a beautiful girl from Tokyo. I never tired of watching Okuno coax and bully what he wanted out of all these diverse people. The goat was a white Saanen, brought from the mountains, a magnificent animal with topaz eyes, delicate hooves which it picked up and placed with the fastidiousness of a geisha walking down a muddy lane, and a huge udder which would swing from side to side as it trotted along beside us. To watch a relation- ship develop between it and the children similar to that in the film was astonishing. Often after the shooting for the day was over, they could be seen either wandering with it on the hills in search of forage or seated on the ground beside it as it grazed or rested. Even Okuno, Jay, Nakamura and the boy seemed to have developed a tenderness for the animal, grooming it, stroking it, carrying it pails of water or mash, and delighting in its caprices.

'Natural' was a word of which Okuno was especially fond, 'real' was another; and these are the two qualities of *The Goat* which the critics have invariably praised. 'No, no – it must not be faked, not faked!' he would cry out, clutching at his head, which was strangely narrow at the temples and then bulged outwards like a pear. 'Make it real – real!' 'Making it real' involved all of us in endless pains and trouble. For example, the beautiful girl from Tokyo had feet which, it was obvious, she tended with care. 'Not a fisherwoman's feet,' Okuno complained as soon as he saw them. And he then insisted that she should tramp around barefoot until the pale flesh had become sun-burned and the nails had cracked and split. At one end of the beach he found a real shack, long since abandoned, and he then went round the village to collect a debris of moth-eaten blankets, soiled strips of matting, a table with a broken leg, chipped cups and rice bowls and an ancient oil stove, with which to fill it.

He drove us all relentlessly – even I, on my visits, would be ordered to fetch this or that for him, to give advice on technical matters about which I knew nothing and to lead around the goat. Often he would be abusive – '*Baka!* Idiot!' he would scream at one of his actors, at Jay, Nakamura, or Shin-chan. 'No, no, NO!' Sometimes he would catch hold of one of us and by force impose his will upon us. 'Here! Here! That's right. No, not like that! Like this! This!' But towards the five children as towards the goat he showed a tenderness which never failed to impress me.

'Christ – he's impossible,' Jay would mutter to me. Nakamura, sweating under Okuno's sarcasms or rage, would gulp surreptitiously at the bottle of Japanese whisky which accompanied him everywhere. Shin-chan would hug himself yet more tightly. Although I had no part in the film, Okuno hated it if ever I absented myself. 'Where did you go?' 'I was swimming.' 'Swimming! But we have work, much work! How the goddam can we finish this movie, if every person goes off to swim?'

One afternoon, as he was nearing the end of the film, I drove out from Kyoto, to find him sitting on the beach, morose and preoccupied.

'What's the matter?' I asked.

'It's that goat.'

'The goat?'

'Yes, goddam.' He sucked at the stub of his cigarette, wriggling his bare toes, to which sand was sticking.

'Oh, that goat!' said Jay. 'Don't talk about it!'

'Well, what's the matter with it?'

'We shoot the scene with the dog,' Okuno said. 'Not good, not bad. It attacks the goat, see, and we get some shots before the goat turns, see, and the dog runs off. With cutting that will be OK, very OK. Then we tie a rope and pull the goat out into the sea. That's OK, very OK. But that goddam goat can swim, she can swim better than any of us.'

'It was a nightmare,' Jay said. 'Could we get that goat to drown? Not on your life. Nakamura here –' Nakamura was as usual asleep, a thread of saliva glistening in the sun as it stretched from his lower lip to the collarbone of his bare skinny torso – 'hit it with an oar, oh hit it and hit it. No good. Shin-chan swam to it and tried to pull it under with the tether. No good either. You can see the mark on his shoulder where a horn got him. We tried everything, but everything.'

I stared at them appalled. 'Are you out of your minds?' I asked.

'Well, it was pretty gruesome,' Jay confessed.

'That poor animal. . . .'

'Anyway it's still alive,' Okuno grunted.

'But I've never heard of anything so revolting. No, really, Okuno!'

'And how do we film the last scene, eh? You tell me,' Okuno said, suddenly tense as he leant towards me. 'Tell me.'

'What scene?'

'He asks me what scene! The scene where the tide washes the body of that goddam goat on to the beach, and the children go down and carry it up to the hill-top and bury it. Remember?' He was suddenly vicious. 'How about that?'

'Well, you could somehow fake it,' I said.

'Fake it! Fake it!' Now he was as furious as myself. 'In this picture there is no faking, we have no faking.'

I got up disgusted. 'If there were such a thing as the RSPCA in Japan, you would all be in gaol.' I strode off down the beach; at that moment it never occurred to me that none of them could possibly know what the initials RSPCA meant. After a few paces I halted and turned: 'And I suppose those wretched children had to watch this whole revolting business?' No one answered.

After I had swum far, far out, to lie on my back, arms outstretched, in an attempt somehow to relax and to prevent my body from still quivering with rage, I returned, not to where Okuno and his party were still sprawled on the beach, but to a point farther up. Some time I should have to collect my clothes, but not now. Later. After they had gone. It was against Jay, I remember, that my fury was chiefly directed. The others, after all, were Japanese, and at that moment that seemed to me some kind of excuse; but Jay was a westerner, a person like myself, with approximately the same values and the same kind of upbringing. I was forgetting that, in fact, Okuno and I were far closer to each other, once the superficialities of national behaviour had been stripped away.

The sand was hot and abrasive to the soles of my feet; I felt as if I were picking my way over a bed of powdered glass, fragments of which would, from time to time, lodge under my eyelids or prick my cheeks and forehead, as the damp afternoon wind began to strengthen. I crossed to a place where a stream split the hillside and spurted out, over a low lip of rock, to fall in a shallow pool. There were some stunted trees around this pool, and as I neared them, I heard first the clank of a chain on a bucket and then the goat's nervous bleat. The chain had got twisted around and around the pin so that the animal, wild-eyed and flanks heaving, could move only within a radius of inches over ground which it had already trampled to mud. Its coat, usually so sleek, now stood up in matted tufts, with burrs, strands of seaweed and earth sticking to it. There were two gashes, one on the neck and the other on the back, no longer bleeding but encrusted with flies. As I neared the animal to unwind the chain, it at once lowered its head. Inch by inch I approached, holding out one hand and making placatory noises. Eventually I managed to touch the pin, pull it out and disentangle the chain, the goat rearing away frantically with each new length of freedom. That done and the pin again secured – I had to use a large, flat stone to hammer it in for lack of a mallet – I scrambled up the hillside and began to break off branches from a chestnut tree, since I knew that it liked this fodder. Greedily it snatched at the armful I set down. While it munched, I bent down and with infinite caution began to pull away the burrs and seaweed from its coat. And that the children should have seen that, I thought. Horrible. Vile. Finished, I perched myself on a rock and stared at the animal. At first, seemingly unconscious of my continued presence, it went on with the business of jerking nervously at the leaves and consuming them with the sound of flames tearing through paper; but then, all at once, it poked its head up at me, to return my glance. The curious eyes, set flat in the narrow head, were totally expressionless; but finding that for some reason I could not hold their gaze, I jumped up and wandered off.

*

'I'm going to leave tonight,' I told Okuno stiffly, when we met in the hall of the inn.

He raised his thin eyebrows. 'Tonight? But why?'

'In disgust.'

He considered that for a moment. Then he drawled: 'It is necessary from time to time to do disgusting things to achieve artistic success.'

'No.'

'Yes, of course.' He gave a smirk, which I realize now was a symptom of unease, but which at the time exacerbated my annoyance.

'Anyway I want to leave. I – I have things to do in Kyoto.'

'You came by car?'

'No.'

'Then I am afraid you must wait till morning. Last train left' – he looked at his watch – 'five forty-five. Now it is six-twenty.'

'There must be some way of –'

'I think you must wait.'

'But, hell, I don't want to wait! I don't want to have anything more to do with you all! I'm sick of this film of yours, sick of your – your egotism and – and cruelty – and – and. . . .' I turned on my heel and rushed upstairs to my room. Unfortunately a Japanese sliding door cannot be slammed as satisfactorily as a western one, and I felt foolish as I repeatedly jerked it across until I managed to calm myself sufficiently to coax it shut. Even then, however, I could hear Okuno's voice from the other room down the passage, coming to me through the fragile barrier of plaster, paper and wood: '. . . Very strange . . . the heat . . . hysterical. . . . The goat. . . . Be over it tomorrow. . . . Tomorrow . . . shoot it again. . . . The goat. . . .'

Solitarily I sulked; solitarily I read a book until the maid came in to ask me whether I intended to join the others for dinner; solitarily I ate my dinner in my own room, gulping from a toothmug the luke-warm gin which I had brought with me from Kyoto. Then, the light out so as not to attract the mosquitoes, I sat for a long time gazing at the crescent of sand with the pale sea beyond it, the evening air unpleasantly humid on my bare arms and face. Shortly before nine o'clock, unwontedly sleepy, I decided to go to bed.

I was woken soon after dawn by the children's voices; and though it was only five-thirty, two hours before I usually got up, so far from feeling any annoyance, I was oddly exhilarated. I got up off the *futon*, the breeze from the open window no longer sticky and hot but miraculously dry and cool as it fluttered the summer kimono in which I had been sleeping. The whole shabby room was adrift in the glow of the rising sun, and for a moment I thought how beautiful it was: the graceful bamboo which supported the *tokonoma*, the lustre of the beams, stretching along the ceiling; the *tatami* mats, perfect in their proportions and the white squares of the paper screens perfect in theirs. What had been the matter with me the previous evening? It had been foolish of me to make a scene of that kind, however repellent the incident which had goaded me into doing so. That was the trouble with living in that perpetual grey-green miasma in Kyoto: everything slowly sweated out of one, oozing through one's pores in a dank, acrid discharge – all initiative, all energy, all toler-ance, all understanding, all sympathy, all resilience – until the only emotions of which one remained capable were exasperation and disgust.

The children's voices were growing shriller and louder; evidently they were excited about something – probably they were having one of their swimming contests or quarrelling about the baseball which they played throughout the day, however oppressive the heat or early or late the hour. I crossed slowly to the window and stood there, leaning against its side.

Ah, there they were! So far away; and yet, from the sound, they seemed to be just below the window. They had the goat with them, yes. I could glimpse first one of its horns and then a leg through the children hemming it around. All at once, something flashed above them; glittering in the sun and then flickering downwards as, in concert, they let out a curious, swooning wail. Again that glitter. Then the tight knot they had formed was loosened and unfolded, and they were running in different directions to return with sticks and stones hastily grabbed off the beach beyond the hovel. They began to shout in unison, '*Washoi, washoi!*' – the cry of the ecstatic devotees as they circle in their ritual dances at Shinto festivals – advancing on the beast, which lay twitching on its side, its coat smeared with blood, and in a wild euphoric frenzy hurling at it their missiles, belabouring it, and at last leaping on it to crush it deeper and deeper into the sand.

The boy Shin-chan, an excellent swimmer, towed the goat out, two inflated rubber tyres attached to it, and Okuno, in a rowing boat with Jay and Nakamura, was able to complete his film. The last scene, when the cadaver is washed ashore and the children hold a funeral service for it, was, all the critics agreed, the most moving of all. The children, as I myself witnessed, actually cried without any prompting or coaching: cried wildly, bitterly, inconsolably, gulping, keening and throwing themselves about. There was, as Okuno had always planned, nothing faked about it, nothing faked at all.

1962

The Festival of the Dead

Out of the pearly distance of the lagoon the first ship of the day announced its approach with a jaunty mountaineering song played over its loud-speaker system. The song grew louder and louder, thrown back and forth between the hills above the town of Amano-Hashidate and those above the village to which it was making its way. There were no passengers, the crew were half asleep. After the first few days of the summer school, when Harriet would first wake to this din and then lie listening to it rigid with fury, she had learned from exhaustion and habit to sleep through the next hour and a half until half past seven. But this morning she at once jumped up from her mattress on the floor and hurriedly began to dress. Through the paper-thin walls on either side of her she could hear her neighbours doing the same. Two of the women course members were talking together below her window – in English she was amused to note, as they had been urged to do throughout the past four weeks.

'The sun is shining for our departure. It was raining when we came.'

'You will be pleased to see your family again, Mrs Namba.'

'But I feel as though I were leaving a family here.'

'All good things must come to an end.'

While she brushed her hair, Harriet continued to listen to this stilted conversation. In spite of the discomfort of sleeping six to a room, the inadequacy of the food and the unremitting study of a foreign language, it was obvious that all the Japanese would regard this period, to her a disagreeable but financially necessary interruption to the routine of her life in Kyoto, as one of intense happiness. Harriet found this both encouraging and vaguely sad.

'Good morning, Mr Makino. Bright and early, I see.' Mrs Namba's voice seemed to parody Harriet's own; she had been in Harriet's class, its most eager and least intelligent member.

'Good morning, ladies. Up with the lark!'

'The early bird catches the worm. In this case the boat.' The two women could be heard tittering at the joke of the elder of them.

'We are hoping that you will sit with us on the train,' the younger said boldly.

'Thank you. But I'm afraid that that's impossible. I must see to the clearing-up. I shall be busy all today. I plan to leave tomorrow.'

Makino had spent four years in New York, and his full, deep voice might have been an American's. Harriet peered sideways out of the window in order to see him. He was a man in his fifties, squat and sturdy, with crisp grey hair, a neat moustache and eyes in which, even when he was laughing, there seemed to lurk an unfathomable sadness.

'Your wife will be pleased to see you,' the unmarried of the two women said. She was lame, the explanation no doubt of why someone so pretty had remained single into her thirties.

'East, west, home's best,' said Makino.

'You are right,' Mrs Namba agreed. 'But we have all felt at home here.'

Harriet had once seen Makino's wife when she had come down for the day on a visit, but he had introduced her to none of the staff and had not even allowed her to enter the hotel in which the summer school was accommodated. She was unusually tall for a Japanese woman, and when she walked it was with one hand on his arm, her head lowered and tilted slightly sideways. She looked frail and much older than her husband.

'Home is where your heart is,' the younger woman pronounced, and the two women went off into giggles once again.

When Harriet strolled out towards the jetty, it was already piled high with luggage. She looked for Makino but he had disappeared. Everyone was in a state of excitement, even those course members who had been most silent and reserved now chattering vivaciously to each other, with occasional squeaks and titters.

197

'A photograph! A photograph, Miss Monks!' A young man went down on one knee, while the people around Harriet froze into rigid postures, staring unsmiling into the lens of the expensive Canonflex. Harriet wondered, as she had frequently wondered in the past, what was the point of having a camera with speeds up to 1/1000 of a second if one treated it as though it were a pre-war Brownie.

'Now don't move, don't move!'

'Ch-e-e-e-se,' hissed a youth whom she had never liked into her right ear. Everyone shook with suppressed laughter as the shutter clicked.

'Professor Terada, Professor Terada! Please come and be photographed with Miss Monks.'

'Delighted.' The professor bowed to Harriet. 'Bright and early, Miss Monks!'

'The early bird catches the worm. In this case the boat,' Mrs Namba said, edging her way into the photograph.

'May I fetch your luggage, Miss Monks?' one of the youngest of the male students asked when the second photograph had been taken. He had been assiduous in his attentions to Harriet ever since she had appealed to him to rescue her bathing-towel from the roof below her bedroom window.

'Oh, I'm not leaving now. I just got up to say goodbye to you all.' The Japanese were impressed by this; during the course of the summer school Harriet had often complained to them, half in joke and half in earnest, about having to rise so early.

'You are very kind,' said one girl, and 'You are very thoughtful,' another added breathlessly.

'And when will you leave, Miss Monks?' Professor Terada asked.

'Tomorrow morning. I've made no definite plans. I want to see the O-Bon Festival here. This evening is the great occasion isn't it?'

Professor Terada nodded. 'The Festival of the Dead,' he said.

'Do you have such a festival in England?' a woman asked.

'No, not really. No, we don't.'

'No,' croaked a catarrhal voice. 'In the West we leave the dead to bury the dead. Far healthier.' It was Leonard Blond, the other non-Japanese instructor, folded up as usual into his shabby raincoat with his pointed chin on his narrow chest, and his pointed nose rheumy and blue in spite of the warmth of the August morning. He had a rucksack slung over one shoulder and behind him one of the course members carried his two scuffed and battered suitcases. Harriet, who disliked Leonard, was sure that the student had not

volunteered to carry the suitcases but had been asked to do so and
had been too polite to refuse. Throughout the summer school
Leonard had shamelessly got the Japanese to run errands for him,
to carry his text-books and even to lend him money. At his remark,
everyone looked vaguely embarrassed: was he joking or being
serious? It was a question which they were often obliged to ask
themselves when they were in his company.

'Good morning, Harriet,' he said. 'You've forgotten to do your
face. But it looks just as nice like that.'

'Thank you.'

'You are travelling with us on the boat, Mr Blond?' an elderly
teacher asked. He alone of all the course members had become
attached to Leonard, and Leonard's contemptuous behaviour
towards him seemed only to intensify his devotion.

'On the boat, yes. But I doubt if many of you will be on the same
train as myself.' Leonard discharged his nose like an antiquated
arquebus into the grubby handkerchief which he had plucked from a
pocket of his raincoat.

'You are not returning to Osaka?'

'Yes, I am returning to Osaka.' Often when he was asked a question by his pupils, Leonard would say: 'Now I'm glad that you asked
me that.' Harriet wondered why he did not say this now, since on
this occasion it was so obviously true. 'But I doubt if I am going the
same way as the rest of you.'

'Ah, Mr Blond has found a short cut.'

'Mr Blond has been consulting his time-table.'

'Tell us the way, Mr Blond!'

Leonard shook his head, his handkerchief still held to the tip of
his nose. 'No, no, certainly not. I've found a most ingenious method
of arriving in Osaka eight minutes before any of you. But I've no
intention of telling you how it's done. I'm looking forward to a
morning without your company.' Once again everyone became
uneasy, in the uncertainty of whether he was joking or not. 'Now,
Harriet – to you, in the strictest secrecy, I might perhaps be persuaded to divulge the itinerary to be followed. On condition that you
promise not to chatter to me during the journey. I want to write up
my diary. It's days behindhand.'

'That's sweet of you Leonard, but as a matter of fact I'm not
leaving until tomorrow morning. I want to see the O-Bon Festival.'

'The Festival of the Dead,' Professor Terada said.

'You'll be here all alone then? What bliss – after these weeks of never being alone for a moment. I wonder what you'll do with yourself when you haven't any students to ask you every five minutes to explain the present continuous or the use of the gerund?'

'You will not be entirely alone,' Mrs Namba intervened. 'Mr Makino will still be at the hotel. He says that he must stay to clear up.'

'Ah, that explains it,' Leonard said. 'That explains everything.'

'Explains what?' Harriet almost demanded. But she restrained herself. She, too, like the Japanese on so many other occasions, now had cause to wonder whether Leonard had spoken in jest or earnest.

As the ship disappeared into the mist at the further end of the lake, there was a knock at Harriet's door. She had been watching the ship from her window, the jaunty tune growing suddenly melancholy as it receded and faded. So it was all over at last; what had seemed endless had come to an end, and all the people with whom she had lived so intimately, hearing all their most secret functions through the paper-thin walls, burdened with their confidences and jostled by their identities, had once again become the strangers they had been four weeks ago. But strangely she felt a pang of regret when she had expected only relief.

'Come in!'

'The maid wishes to know whether we're going to have breakfast together or whether you prefer to have it separately. We're the only people left.'

'Well, why not together?'

'Why not? I'll go and tell her. With your permission I shall eat my usual Japanese-style breakfast.'

'And I shall eat my usual western-style one. With your permission of course.'

When Makino had gone, Harriet hurriedly began to make up her face, remembering what Leonard had said to her. She was a tall woman of thirty-six, with long straight black hair worn to her shoulders, a pale, oval face and a deceptive air of lassitude. This was the first time she and Makino had ever been alone together.

When he returned Makino seemed to be not in the least embarrassed by their proximity. She noticed his freshness and cleanliness, things at which she had marvelled throughout the course, since she herself had difficulty in ever finding time to wash and iron her clothes. His white shirt was crisp, the creases in his trousers sharp. Had he paid one of the maids to do his laundry and pressing for him? Or had he, like Leonard, bullied and inveigled some of the women members into taking on the task?

'You always look so neat and spruce,' she said as she seated herself on the floor opposite to him and knocked with her spoon on the shell of an egg, which, as on every other of the summer-school mornings, was both soft-boiled and cold. 'It always amazes me. I suppose that one of the maids has fallen for you.'

'Oh, no. I wash and iron my clothes myself.'

'How unusual for a Japanese man!'

'All students wash and iron their clothes for themselves. They can't afford to send them to a laundry.'

'But you're not a student and besides you have a wife.'

'I am not a typical Japanese.' He smiled, displaying his small, even teeth under his clipped moustache. 'Not at all. I do many things in the house. I learned that in the States. And besides my wife's not strong. She has a weak heart.'

He raised his lacquer bowl of bean-soup to his mouth and began to drink it with a series of loud sucking noises.

'At any rate you're a typical Japanese in the way you drink your soup,' Harriet said.

'I'm sorry.' He lowered the bowl.

'Why be sorry? No, no. Please go on. It doesn't worry me at all. I was only joking.'

'Ah, this sense of humour,' he said, fishing in the bowl with his chopsticks and eventually raising a slimy fragment of seaweed. 'This English sense of humour. It's so difficult for us. When are you joking? When are you not joking? I wish that you could teach me.'

'Often we don't know ourselves.'

There was a silence. Suddenly he looked up to say: 'Mr Blond – has he gone to Osaka or Tokyo?'

'To Osaka, I think. He was so absurdly pleased with himself because he had found some secret way of getting there eight minutes before anyone else. I've no doubt he'll have to make half-a-dozen changes and travel part of the way in a goods train. You know, the extraordinary thing is that he can't speak a word of Japanese and yet he can read the names of even the most obscure places in those time-tables of his.'

'Then he will travel to Tokyo later?'

'No, I don't think so. I don't know.'

'But you teach at Tokyo university?'

'Hm, that's right. But he teaches at some small university outside Osaka. I can't even remember its name. It's a mission university, no

201

one has ever heard of it.' Suddenly she had got the drift of his questions and she found herself beginning to blush. Inevitably, as the only two westerners on the course, she and Leonard had gone around in each other's company. Often he had annoyed her with his tendency to take her on one side or to come between her and the Japanese with whom she was talking, in order to whisper to her remarks, usually derogatory, about their colleagues, their students or Japan and the Japanese. But surely Makino could not have failed to see that in fact her fellow countryman filled her with nothing but a mixture of boredom and contempt?

'Mr Blond is a highly intelligent man.'

'Not really,' she said, enjoying his shock at the kind of blunt contradiction which no Japanese woman would ever venture.

'He's a writer, isn't he?'

'He likes to call himself one. He hasn't published a story – and probably hasn't written one – since he left Oxford half-a-dozen years ago.'

She knew that she was being ungenerous and malicious; but she was determined that Makino should be under no misapprehension.

'Would you like me to ask the maid to bring you some more toast?'

'No, thank you.'

'But you've eaten so little. Please have my apple.' She refused; he pressed it on her. Eventually she took it.

Munching, she said: 'I think that the course has been a tremendous success, really I do. You know, before I came here I never thought of Japan as an *efficient* country. One somehow doesn't think of the East as being efficient. It was such a surprise to find that the Japanese are in fact far, far more efficient than the English.'

'Now you're flattering us.'

'No, I'm not flattering you. I mean it. I'm not a person who flatters.' Why was it, she wondered, that one could never say anything favourable about the Japanese without their suspecting one either of insincerity or of irony? 'You worked very hard,' she said. 'You must feel you need a rest now.'

'Next Monday I must start the preparations for our second summer school on Mount Rokko. I'm sorry that you felt that one summer school was enough for you.'

'Yes, I feel sorry too. . . . You know, I enjoyed this far more than I expected.'

'The students very much appreciated all you did for them. The course would not have been the same without you.'

'It's nice of you to say so.' Embarrassed, she got up from the floor and began to search for a packet of cigarettes. There were no cupboards in the room, and her belongings lay either jumbled up in her two suitcases or stacked around the walls.

'You have a gift for teaching. A real gift. I've directed these summer courses for the last nine years, and you're the best instructor we've ever had.'

'Oh, nonsense. I find that hard to believe.'

'It happens to be true.'

'You never smoke, do you?'

He shook his head. 'I used to smoke – twenty a day at least. Then a doctor friend of mine at Kyoto University Hospital showed me some statistics and I gave up at once.'

'You must have a lot of will-power.'

'If it's a question of life and death. . . .' He got up. 'Well, I suppose that I must go up to the school and check the inventories before the workmen begin to pack.'

'Can't I be of any help?'

'No, really – it's very kind of you.'

'But I'd like to help.'

'You too need a rest. I have lots of helpers – some student teachers provided by the education board. Besides' – he smiled – 'the inventories are in Japanese.'

'Well, in that case. . . .'

'Thank you for your company.' He gave a formal bow at the door.

'Thank you for yours,' she said, parodying the bow in return.

Harriet had promised herself that she would spend the day doing a number of things for which she had had no time during the four weeks of the course: there were letters long overdue, clothes to be mended and a lecture to be prepared for the following week. She began on one of the letters, to her widowed mother in Hastings.

Dearest Mother,

It's terrible of me not to have written to you for such ages and ages. I don't know what you can think of me, especially as you are always so good about writing yourself. I never even wrote to you on the anniversary of Daddy's death. But that doesn't mean that I was not thinking about you. I was – a lot. It's just that a

course of this kind is so *unremitting* – one never has a moment to
oneself, not a single moment.

Actually it was not nearly as bad as I had expected. You
remember how I dreaded it and only agreed to come because I
had been so extravagant during my Hong Kong trip and needed
the money. The students – I call them students but most of them
were middle-aged teachers of English – were really awfully sweet
and everything was run most efficiently. The director was a man
called Makino. I'd been warned that he was rather of a terror – very hard-working himself and determined to see that all
his staff worked equally hard. But to me he was always as nice as
could be. In fact, he always seemed to be worried that perhaps I
might be doing *too* much. . . .

At that point she stopped and stared out of the window. The
lagoon was no longer milky and vast as in the early mornings; it had
grown narrower, even the trees which lined its farthest shore seemed
to be within easy swimming distance, the water below the window
was a dank yellowish-green on which tossed a scurf of melon rind,
vegetable peel, cartons and bottles. A hot wind was blowing, and
now, still accompanied by the same jaunty mountaineering song,
the little white-and-red steamer was once again making for the jetty,
so many people on board her that it seemed miraculous that she did
not capsize. Harriet watched them get off: the old village women,
knock-kneed and pigeon-toed in their soot-coloured kimonos; the
couples who, unlike young couples in the West, never linked arms or
held hands; the schoolboys and schoolgirls in their dingy black
uniforms with their glittering cameras slung about them. They
would all make their way up the mountain behind the hotel and from
the summit would look at the view of Amano-Hashidate solemnly
from between their legs, as Japanese had been doing for generations.

Harriet got up, yawning and stretching. She would finish her
letter some other time, when it was cooler and quieter and when she
herself felt less restless. Tying under her chin the straw coolie-hat
presented to her by one of the course members when she had complained of the glare on the beach, she made her way downstairs.

It was as if from habit that she found herself walking not to the
tree-shaded cool of the causeway that separated the lagoon from the
open sea, but instead up the street, flanked with shops which sold
gimcrack souvenirs, dried fish and soft drinks, to the parched
square of baked mud at the far end of which stood the school. But

this morning there was not the usual crowd of course members to offer to carry her brief-case, to ask her how she had slept, or to beg her to explain this or that problem in their text-books. Having always wished that she could be left alone for at least that ten minutes of the day, she now found herself missing their company. For the first time she was conscious of people staring at her – especially those who had obviously come from the country. People must have stared at her in the same way during the weeks before, but the course members had shielded her. Naturally self-conscious, she began to hurry along, her head lowered.

It was a curious sensation to be walking across the playing field, her feet scuffing up the dust, and then all at once to hear her own voice:

'I wandered lonely as a cloud
That floats on high. . . .'

It was the poem she had been asked to tape-record in the first week of the course; she had forgotten all about it. How awful she sounded! Like one of those derisive imitations of an English accent to which American teachers sometimes treated their Japanese students. But who had preserved the recording? And who could now be listening to it? Through the open window of the room which the staff had used as their Common Room she all at once saw Makino, seated at the long table which ran down its length, his chin cupped in his left hand and his right hand on a knob of the tape recorder open before him. He was alone and he was unaware that she was watching him from outside.

Harriet walked to the window. 'How dreadful that sounds! How can you bear to listen to it?'

'Not dreadful at all. You have a very beautiful voice.' But he at once turned off the tape-recorder, rising in confusion as he did so.

'Do I really sound like that? I hope not.'

'We've checked all the inventories. Now we're waiting for the truck. The others went across for a drink but I decided it would be better to rest in the cool here.' Evidently he felt that it was necessary to explain why he should be listening to her voice alone in the Common Room. 'I wanted to test the tape-recorders. One of them – the one borrowed by Mr Blond – isn't working. I'm glad that I found that tape. I didn't know that you'd made it.'

'It was after my lecture on Wordsworth.'

'I shall keep it for myself.'

'Oh, don't do that for heaven's sake!'

'Did you come for something?'

205

'Oh, I just came up to see if you needed any help. I had nothing to do.'

'That was very kind of you.'

She at first held his glance; then she turned her head away with a faint sigh and gazed towards the distant sea. 'Are you sure that there's nothing I can do to help?'

'Nothing. . . . Let's go and have a swim before it gets too hot!' he added, as though on a sudden impulse. 'How about it?'

'Fine. But can you – can you get away?'

'I think so. I don't have to load the truck myself, the young people will do that for me. And they don't really need me to supervise them. Let's go across and tell them.'

As they walked from the hotel to the causeway, Makino was taciturn. Harriet tried a number of topics with him – the summer school, his years in the States, his interest in linguistics – but all of them soon died. Yet, unlike most Japanese men, he did not seem to be in the least embarrassed or shy in her company. He walked fast, striding out beside her, so that she had difficulty in keeping up with him although her legs were longer than his. Eventually she said: 'My goodness, you're turning this into a race!'

'Sorry.' He shortened his stride. 'Was I going too fast for you?'

'You always seem to be in a hurry. Don't you?'

'That's because I always have too much to do.'

At each end of the causeway the crowds were always thick, but if one walked for ten minutes one could be sure of having the beaches on either side almost entirely to oneself. 'Over there seems all right,' Harriet said. 'There's no one in sight. And I can undress behind those bushes.'

'This is only the third time I have swum this year,' Makino said when, having changed, they began to pick their way down to the sea over the gritty, burning sand.

'Don't you like swimming?'

'Yes, swimming is my favourite sport, but every afternoon here I had to deal with administration – it was the only time when I could be sure of not being troubled.'

'I've swum every day since I arrived here.'

'But you're not at all sunburnt.'

He halted and for a moment they inspected each other. Like many middle-aged Japanese men but few western ones Makino was still without any superfluous fat. His shoulders were powerful, his waist narrow below a torso smooth but for a fine ridge of hair which ran from his chest to his navel. It was unfortunate, thought Harriet, that his muscular legs should be both crooked and too short; and yet, in some curious way, this defect seemed to add to his attractiveness.

'Oh, I never lie in the sun. I go so red. And besides it gives me a headache.'

'In America I had a girl-friend who was crazy about the sun. I was afraid that she would die of sunstroke. She was a blonde but by the end of the summer she looked like a negress. In Japan we think that a dark skin is ugly. Japanese girls are very careful not to get burned.'

Since it was only a few years since Makino had been in America Harriet assumed that he must have met the American 'girl-friend' after his marriage.

'Did your wife accompany you to America?' she asked disingenuously a few minutes later, as they splashed together in the shallows.

Makino shook his head. 'My scholarship was too small. And besides we thought that she would be lonely there – she can't speak any English. So she stayed in Kyoto and looked after our little son.'

'For four years?'

'Yes, for four years.' He sighed. 'It was a long time.'

At that he struck out and away from her, swimming with an apparently effortless speed, his feet churning up the water in an opalescent cloud behind him, until he had almost vanished from sight. Harriet was a good swimmer, but she could not possibly hope to keep up with him; nor did she dare to go so far away from the shore. Instead she swam with a few leisurely strokes until she was out of her depth and then turned over on her back and floated, eyes shut, for minutes on end. The water lapping gently around her head made a sound in her ears like the rustle and crackle of tinfoil. She felt strangely remote, self-contained and relaxed, and yet exhilarated.

Suddenly it happened. On her bare left shoulder a needle seemed to plunge deep, leaving a fearful aching aftermath. She gave a gasp; then with flailing arms, she made in panic for the shore. 'Makino-san! Oh! Oh! *Makino-san!*' But at first he was too far out to hear her. Standing with the water up to her knees she tried to peer round at her shoulder, using her right hand to pull the shoulder forward. All she could see was a small red spot, nothing more. But the ache continued.

'Makino-san!'

At last he heard her, or at least saw her frantic waving. Even faster than he had left her he now hurtled back. 'What is it? What's the matter?'

'Something stung me. Here. On my shoulder. I can't think what it was. It's so painful.'

'Where? Let me see.' He put his hand to the place.

'It's not a sea-snake, is it? Is it?'

She had heard of people who had died from sea-snake bites: not admittedly in Japan, but in Singapore and Penang.

'No, no, of course not.' He laughed.

'Then, what can it be? It's so painful. It can't be a scorpion, I suppose? A sea-scorpion? People have told me about them in Japan. The pain gets worse and worse.'

An old man trundling before him a cart loaded with soft drinks was approaching and Makino shouted out to him in Japanese. Slowly he lowered the cart and limped down to the beach. Makino spoke to him in Japanese, the old man peered at Harriet's shoulder.

'He says that it's nothing serious. It's a kind of stinging fish. They're very common here in the bay at this season. That's one of the reasons why the local people seldom go into the water after the fifteenth of August.'

'Is he *sure* that it's nothing else?'

Makino again questioned the old man.

'Quite sure. He says that the best thing is to put on some saké – and to drink some saké as well. If you don't like saké I imagine that any alcohol will do as well. Come – let's go back to the hotel at once. No need to put on our clothes. We shall want a shower anyway.'

As they hurried back to the hotel, their clothes over their arms, Harriet complained: 'It gets worse and worse.'

'Poor thing. Yes, the old man said that it *is* very painful. But truly it's nothing serious. You musn't be frightened.'

She had thought him unsympathetic before; but now he spoke with obvious concern for her, taking her by the arm and guiding her over the pebbles and through the bushes.

'You wait here,' he said, when they had reached her room, 'and I'll go and ask the landlord for some alcohol. I'll only be a moment. Why don't you sit down?' He turned at the door. 'Better now? Better?' She nodded her head, and although in fact the pain was growing increasingly intense, forced herself to smile.

When he returned, he was carrying a tray on which were two glasses, a half-bottle of Japanese whisky, two bottles of soda water, an opener, some ice in a chipped tea-cup and a small pot of ointment.

'He says that this ointment is specially for that kind of sting.'

Harriet peered into the pot as Makino unscrewed the lid. Its colour was purple and it smelled vaguely of fish.

'What can it be?'

'I've no idea. But let's try it. Turn round.'

His hand was rubbing her shoulder, the ache had now become like the raging of an abscessed tooth. She felt his bare, muscular leg against the back of her knee. Then suddenly she had either turned involuntarily or he had whirled her round to face him and they were clutched in each other's arms.

Less than an hour later he left her room. 'I must go back to the school. They'll be wondering what has happened to me.'

'Will you be coming back for lunch?'

'No, I'm afraid not. I have to have lunch with Ito-san.' This was the headmaster of the local primary school in which the classes and lectures of the course had been held. 'I'm sorry.'

'Must you really go to the school now? Surely they can manage on their own?'

'Yes, I think that I must go.' She was both astonished and abashed by his cool, even chilly self-composure, as he began first to gather up his things over one arm and then to replace on the tray their empty glasses, preparatory to taking them out with him. 'Are you sure that you wouldn't like me to leave the whisky with you?'

'Quite sure.' She was now crouched on the floor, watching him. It was odd, she reflected, how much more disreputable one felt in that position than on a bed.

'And the sting? How is it? Still painful?'

'Oh, that.' She had forgotten all about it. 'Yes, it's all right, thank you. It seems to be wearing off.'

'Good. Then I'll leave you now.'

'Come and see me when you return.'

He gave a formal bow. 'Would you like me to go with you to the festival?'

'Please. Of course.'

Again he bowed. 'Goodbye.'

'Goodbye.'

Somehow the day passed. The sting all at once again became a persistent throb and when she examined it with the aid of a mirror from her handbag she saw that the flesh was growing puffy and red.

She wrote letters; she even began to prepare her lecture, sitting at the open window and from time to time looking out at the crowds waiting for the little steamer below. The maid had brought her her lunch, consisting of a watery curry, a bowl of rice and an apple. She ate some of the rice, devoured the apple and left the curry untasted. Late in the afternoon she wandered along the beach and then, making a wide detour, returned by way of the school. But she could not find Makino anywhere, the school seemed to be deserted and all the equipment used during the course had already been removed. The tracks of a lorry could be seen deep in the dust, and embedded in one was one of Makino's notices. 'Course members are reminded that it is not permissible. . . .' She could make out the opening words printed in the violet ink he usually used. She retraced her steps to the hotel, lay down on the floor of her room, on the rumpled cushions which still remained there from the morning, and at once, in spite of the continued throbbing of her shoulder, went off into a deep sleep.

It was dark when she awoke and Makino was at the door, again with a tray on which he had glasses and whisky. 'Oh, I'm so sorry. I thought that the room was empty when I could see no light.'

She groaned and sat up, clutching at her head. The throb from her shoulder seemed to have moved up into her temples. 'What time is it?'

'Nearly eight o'clock.'

'Oh God!'

'I came up once before. But when I saw that there was no light I went away again. The maid has dinner ready.'

Harriet rose unsteadily to her feet. 'I feel awful. I must look awful. Let me wash and change. Then I shall be better.'

'I'll come back in twenty minutes. Take a drink if you want one. Would you like me to pour one out for you before I go?'

'You don't have to go, silly. Sit down and talk to me.'

But totally ignoring this invitation, Makino went to the door, gave his formal little bow and said: 'Then in twenty minutes. The maid is in rather a hurry. She's afraid of missing the festival.'

'Oh yes – the festival. We mustn't be late for that.'

But he had vanished even as she was speaking to him.

Twenty minutes later he returned, followed by the maid, who began to set out the food. The maid looked morose, no doubt because of the lateness of the hour, but after Makino had joked with her for a while her plain, peasant face, spherical except for the sagging jowls, began to clear and brighten. Harriet recalled how

210

during the summer school Makino would soothe angry students or placate disgruntled ones merely by a few good-natured words.

'I shall be glad to prepare a meal for myself at last,' Harriet said, chewing on a rubbery piece of cuttle-fish.

'Do you cook?' He seemed astonished.

'Of course. Every Englishwoman cooks these days.'

'But I thought that you must come from a very aristocratic and rich family,' he explained seriously.

Harriet laughed. 'I don't know why you should have thought that.'

'We all of us thought that. All of us at the summer school. We decided that you were of a different class from Mr Blond.'

Leonard never tired of informing the Japanese, in the course of ordinary conversations, in his classes and even during his lectures, that his origins were working class. 'Well, yes, *that* perhaps,' Harriet laughed, once again feeling that she was being ungenerous and mean.

'Class in England is very difficult for us to understand.'

'We English also have difficulty in understanding it.'

At this point the maid interrupted them, as she was to continue to interrupt their conversation throughout the meal. How old was Harriet? she asked Makino in Japanese. When Harriet replied tartly that that was something which western women preferred not to reveal, the maid found this so funny that she giggled behind her raised kimono sleeve, her dewlaps shaking, for several seconds on end. Having at last recovered from this paroxysm, she asked, again through Makino, whether Harriet could guess her own age in turn. Harriet replied in English: 'Oh, at least a hundred,' wishing that the woman would realize that it was not necessary for her to provide entertainment for them as maids in Japan habitually provide entertainment for the guests they serve, but would merely leave the food, all of which was in any case cold, and go about her business. Wouldn't she like to leave for the festival? Harriet suggested to her. But the maid replied that it was no trouble at all to remain until they had finished and that the Englishwoman and Makino must not worry themselves on her account.

She next began to ask Makino about his family, and Harriet then saw that she had her uses. Was he married? she queried. And how long had he been married? And how old was his wife? When the maid next asked if Makino had any children, he replied abruptly that he had none. The maid blinked her eyes, the lashes of which were coated in white powder, and protruded her lips in sympathy. She was also childless, she said, although she had been married twice.

'Why do you tell her that you have no children?' Harriet asked Makino in English. 'You told me that you had a son earlier today.'

'I *had* a son – once.'

'Oh, I see.'

'He died while I was in America. But it was really the war. Not enough food. He got tuberculosis.' He gave her the information in a dry, emotionless tone of voice; then, picking up a bowl of mountain potato and holding it to his chin, began to shovel the glutinous mess into his mouth with his chopsticks.

The maid leant over to whisper something to Makino behind her raised hand.

'She wishes to know if you have ever been married,' Makino said.

'You know the answer to that.'

'Do I?'

'Of course you do.'

When the meal was over and the maid had carried out the dishes, bowls and glasses, Harriet crossed over from the other side of the table in order to seat herself beside Makino.

He smiled at her; then, putting his small, well-manicured hands on the table before them, he said: 'Oughtn't we to be going to the festival? It will have started already.'

'Just let me finish my cigarette.'

'You oughtn't to smoke so much.'

'I know.' She put her head on his shoulder. 'It's so difficult ever to be alone with you. All through the summer school I always hoped that we should find ourselves alone together, but then on each occasion those wretched students would gather round. Or else Leonard would turn up. Even on our excursion day – do you remember? – when we began to walk to the lighthouse, those two girls overtook us. And now this evening we have to have that maid with all her silly questions.'

'To be alone in Japan is very difficult. Do you know, when my wife and I first married – it was during the war, we were very poor and half the houses in Osaka had been destroyed – we used to share a room with my parents. Can you imagine – a young married couple . . .?'

'I know so little about you. I wish that I knew more.'

'Come. We must go.' He was growing restive.

'Yes. I suppose so.'

They had decided that it would be quicker if they were to walk to Miyazu, the centre of the festival, over the causeway rather than follow the road all the way round the lagoon by bus. Where there had been crowds and the noise of cars and transistor radios and the weaving hither and thither of excited children, there was now a complete desolation. Once someone churned past them on an antiquated motor-cycle; once a stray dog, grey and huge, loped across their path, making Harriet clutch at Makino's arm as it appeared out of the shadowy bushes before them. That was all.

'In Japan it is always either crowds so dense that they suffocate you or a total absence of people. I should love to have lived here in the Meiji period when the country was virtually empty.'

Makino put an arm round her shoulder – her bad shoulder but she said nothing about it, even though the contact renewed the ache – and then put his cheek against hers.

'The endless has come to an end,' she sighed.

'What do you mean?'

'The summer school. There was a time, about two weeks ago, when it seemed to have gone on forever. Didn't you feel that?'

He shook his head.

'Why did you come to Japan?' he asked after a silence. 'Tell me.'

'Oh, I don't know. Oh, yes, I suppose I do! It was Mifune – seeing him in a film. *Rashomon*, it was. I came to Japan because I imagined that all Japanese men would look like Mifune. You're the first I've met who does.'

'No one has ever told me before that I look like Mifune,' he said seriously.

'Haven't they? How odd! You do, you know.' She kissed him on the cheek.

'The festival has begun. Look!' Ahead of them a rocket soared up through the pale grey sky and opened out like a Japanese umbrella, dripping first a golden and then a crimson rain. 'We shall never get there in time.'

'Oh how sad! I so much wanted to see it.'

'You can see the lanterns from here. Don't let's walk any more. Let's sit here on this jetty. We shall see just as well.'

'Yes, let's do that.'

They sat and then lay on the hard, moist concrete, while the rockets continued to fizz and expand above them.

Suddenly Makino jerked up. 'The first of the lanterns,' he said, fastening the buttons on his shirt. 'They have begun to float them on the water.'

'Where?'

213

'Over there. Look.'

Far off, where the bay narrowed to a point, a single light had detached itself from the lights which lined the shore and had begun to bob outwards on the water. Others followed it, first singly, then in twos and threes, and finally so thick that the distinction between land and sea was obliterated. 'Oh, beautiful!' Harriet's cry was involuntary. She caught Makino's arm. 'I'm glad that we're here and not with the crowds. Aren't you?'

Without looking at her, he said: 'Those are the souls of the dead. They return, you know, on this day. In Japanese homes we light lanterns to guide them back. Then, when the time comes for them to return to the other world – to their own world – in certain parts of the country we float these lights for them on the sea or down our rivers. This must seem a strange thing to you,' he added on the apologetic note which Japanese so often assume when discussing customs in which they themselves believe or half-believe but which they think will appear ludicrous to foreigners.

The lanterns, carried out on the tide, were now filling the whole of the farthest end of the bay. Endlessly they advanced, the forerunners already passing the place where Harriet and Makino were standing and then moving on into the wider and wider darkness of the open sea to the north.

'Have you ever been to Kukedo?' Makino suddenly turned to her to ask.

'Kukedo? No. Where is it?'

'Near to Matsué. They have there a cave which they call "The Cave of the Children's Ghosts". It's one of the most beautiful places in Japan. Far more beautiful than here. Totally unspoilt. There's the sea and on one side of it these marvellous sandy beaches and on the other side of the bay mysterious caves going back far into the hillside. The people there – the country people – believe that at this time of year – during the festival of O-Bon, the Festival of the Dead – all the dead children come back to play in one of the caves. There's a mound of sand at its entrance and they say that the next morning you can see on it the faint marks of innumerable children's feet. That's what they say. You go into the cave – it's rather frightening, you know, so dark after the glittering sea outside – and everywhere you look you see, well, kinds of altars made of pebbles and stones piled on top of each other. Memorials to these – these dead children. And then you slowly make out in the gloom – your eyes are beginning to get accustomed to it – all the things that have been piled up before those altars. Dolls. Broken toys. Rusty pop-guns and tricycles and – and, oh, all that kind of thing. And clothes. Tattered shirts, sneakers, mildewy jumpers and socks. They've all been put out there, you see, for the children when they come back, when they're *supposed* to come back. It's oddly moving, you know. You tell yourself that it's all nonsense, sentimental nonsense. But it – it moves one.'

He said all this with his face still turned to the sea. Harriet could make out his profile clearly now; it was glowing in the reflected light from the innumerable lanterns. And then she suddenly glimpsed the tear glistening like a bead of glass in the corner of the only eye that was visible to her. At the sight of it she simultaneously felt horrified, wanted to comfort him, and recalled, hating herself for doing so, a remark which Leonard Blond had once made to her about the Japanese: 'You think that they're made of granite. And then you turn up the granite slab and you find this huge, oozing slug of sentimentality quivering underneath.'

'I must go there one day,' she said. 'To Kukedo. Is that what it's called?

'Oh, it would probably mean nothing to you.'

'Why should you say that?'

'A Japanese superstition. Like this one here now. It has its *aesthetic* appeal of course. But how can it have anything more for you?'

'Oh, don't be foolish. Death is something universal, it's not something exclusively Japanese, you know. And loss, bereavement, they're also. . . . Oh, well, never mind.'

He had turned even farther away from her so that all she could see was the back of his head and his chin. In silence they both gazed out before them. The whole of the bay now seemed to be alight; but then, gradually, as though flames were sweeping across a forest, leaving behind them a charred desolation, the end nearest the shore began to blacken under the harbour lights at the same moment that far out the open sea caught fire. Harriet felt a burden of unshed tears weighing on her eyelids. 'It's a wonderful idea. The dead passing out like that into the darkness. Wonderful.'

But as she spoke, Makino moved away from her into the massed shadows of the trees behind them. Peering, she saw that he was removing his trousers, then wrenching off his shirt, then finally kicking off his shoes and tugging at his socks. 'What are you doing?' she cried. He did not answer. Running past her, his naked body

215

gleaming in the rosy reflection off the waves, he plunged and vanished from sight. 'Makino-san! Makino-san!' She wailed his name. Far out he reappeared, a dark blob among the lanterns. Wildly she looked around her for someone to call. Then she saw the rowing boat, tethered to the end of the jetty some twenty yards away from where she was standing, and she began to run towards it. She jumped in, it almost capsized. 'Makino-san!' she called again. She grasped the oars, which were clumsy and heavy. Then she realized that she must cast off the rope.

With difficulty she at last began to propel the boat out towards the open sea. The lanterns were bobbing all around her and from time to time she would strike one with an oar, causing it either to capsize or to go out with a sizzle and a splutter. Like putting out a soul, she thought, in panic. Wildly she looked around. But now she could no longer see him. Everywhere there were the flickering lights, the darkness beyond the lights, the darkness advancing behind the lights. He had become a part of the darkness, the flames had consumed him. She buried her face on the crossed oars in front of her and burst into a paroxysm of tears. Soon she was crying softly as though to herself, her grief welling out of her in an effortless stream, while the boat pranced and whirled in the criss-cross currents and the lanterns bobbed around her, their dazzle blurring through her tears.

Suddenly she felt the boat tipping to one side. It was, for some reason, a moment of sheerest horror. Then a face appeared, hair over the eyes. She stared at it.

'Why did you do that?' she burst out at last. 'Why? Why? I thought that you . . . I thought. . . .'

Panting, Makino flopped over the side of the boat and lay there, his pale face upturned to her gaze.

'Idiot!'

He said nothing. He closed his eyes.

'Are you all right?'

'Yes.'

'But what were you trying to do? Did you go completely mad? I thought that you'd drown. I was terrified.'

'Sorry.' He gulped. 'I thought that I'd drown too. The currents here. . . .'

'Idiot!' she cried again. 'Why? Why?'

'My boy,' he said between chattering teeth. He turned his head away so that she could no longer peer, with her devouring love and her devouring curiosity, down into his eyes. He raised an arm and covered his face with it. Still gazing down she saw, with an extraordinary distinctness as though in a dream, the black hairs growing on the upraised arm and then the lines on the half-open palm above it.

'Dearest,' she said. 'Dearest.' She knelt in the boat beside him, oblivious of the water which began to seep on to her skirt. All round the lanterns were still bobbing; even the sky now seemed to be reddening with them. 'Dearest.'

She put her arms round his dripping body, feeling his heart thudding against her eager fingers. But when she attempted to grasp his hand, repeating 'Dearest, dearest, dearest,' it was cold, crinkly and unresponsive to her touch, and when she attempted to put her lips to his, he jerked his body away from hers like a stranded fish, with a strange, inarticulate exclamation of anguish or disgust.

1960

Indirect Method

This is a room. What is this?

It is a room.

This is a hotel room. What kind of room is this?

It is a hotel room.

This is an expensive room – the most expensive room in which I have ever stayed. Is this room expensive?

Yes, it is expensive.

Direct Method. Liz hears Mildred's voice or the ghost of Mildred's voice (so long silent, letters to Canada unanswered, perhaps Mildred dead) teaching her pupils in the dining-room.

Who is Mildred?

Mildred is the teacher.

She is (was) also the lodger, who had come out to Japan with an Air Force husband, had abandoned him or been abandoned by him (the story changed as rapidly and inexplicably as her spirits would soar or sink) and had then set up as a freelance teacher.

Direct Method. But Mildred said that people as indirect as the Japanese did not take to it. They preferred word-for-word translation. Fish have neither hands nor feet – *Sakana niwa te mo ashi mo arimasen*. That kind of thing. Mildred swore that she had seen that sentence in a course for beginners prepared by some Japanese professor. But so many of the strange or exciting things that Mildred

218

related had happened only in her imagination. Perhaps (Tom and Liz sometimes speculated) the marriage to the Air Force officer had also happened only there.

This is a room. This is a hotel room. This is an expensive room.

There are two beds, each neatly folded down to make a white sandwich-like triangle at either corner. There are two armchairs and two bedside tables, each with a lamp on it and each with a Gideon Bible in its drawer. In the bathroom there are two face towels and two bath towels and two glasses which have a paper seal over them, like the paper seals over the bidet and lavatory bowl.

I expect you wish to be left alone, Professor Ito told her down in the lobby. The truth is that Professor Ito wished to leave her alone, because he wished to get back to his laboratory, even though it was already past nine. You must be tired and tomorrow your programme is a busy one. He finds it hard to adjust to the fact that the young, untidy woman with all those children, who used to work up at the Baptist Hospital, should now be a leading authority on diabetes. In the past he patronized her, as he patronized her husband, also a doctor. He wants to continue to patronize her but feels, baffled and slightly exasperated, that he can no longer do so.

Liz does not really want to be left alone, because to be alone, except when she is working, is something to which she is not accustomed. If the room were less expensive, she might hear sounds from the rooms on either side of her: the flush of a lavatory, the throbbing of a radio, voices raised in anger or in love. But this is an expensive room.

The walls are covered in shimmering grey silk, so that, in the lamplight, they look as if cooling water were trickling down them; but, in fact, the coolness comes from the air-conditioner grille, from which a strand of pale blue ribbon streams outwards to show that it is functioning. There is a darker grey silk covering the lampshades, and the thick carpet is of the same colour. There is a crimson and white *toile de Jouy* on the chairs and the curtains and the headboards of the beds are of the same material. The design, of a woman on a swing, her skirts billowing up around her, while a courtier kneels and plays some kind of stringed instrument, suggests a Fragonard.

Liz begins to unpack. She has travelled on the bullet train from Tokyo and she feels as though she herself had been shot by some invisible gun through all those hundreds and hundreds of miles, to arrive, blunted and bruised, on this target. She feels no hunger, only an insistent thirst. In the bathroom she has seen a little spigot, with assurances in Japanese, English, French and German, that the water is both drinkable and iced. She breaks the seal of the glass and fills it. Then, in the room with no climate, she drinks the water with no taste. The air is filtered, the water is filtered. The cold rim of the now empty glass against her lips, she stares at the television set. It has a blind across it, not of the *toile de Jouy* but of a crimson velvet, as though something obscene might be going on, unseen, on its screen.

She will ring Yamada-san, she will ring Mrs Payne at the Baptist Hospital, she will ring the Bensons, she will ring Yoshiko. . . . No, she will do none of those things. Not yet. But she will ring Osamu.

The telephone has the texture and colour of mother-of-pearl. Oh, Osamu, she used to say, do please try to get this number for me. These Japanese phones drive one round the bend. But this one works perfectly. It is a woman who answers ('*Moshi! Moshi!*') and of course that must be Osamu's wife, whom Liz has never met but whose colour photograph she has seen, beautiful in a kimono with a dragon writhing up one side.

One moment! Please!

Osamu's wife, Noriko, must know who she is. She sounds excited.

Mrs Butler. . . . Osamu is giggling with pleasure. You have come at last!

This was our houseboy. Who was he?

He was your houseboy.

He learned English by the Direct Method. He learned it by talking it to us and the children. He did not learn it from Mildred or any school.

Osamu wants to come round to the hotel immediately; but Liz still has that feeling that she has been fired from a gun, it is now almost ten, and she knows, because he has written to tell her, that he now lives in a remote suburb out near Arashiyama. Tomorrow, she says. And he says, Yes, tomorrow, he will call in on his way to the office.

That means, since this is Japan and not England, that he will call in at half past seven.

You can have some breakfast with me.

He is not sure about that; but he will call in.

They sat at the breakfast table and Osamu sat with them. That was in the last months, not when he first came to them and sat in the kitchen. Even when he sat with them, he liked to have rice and pickles for breakfast. The pickles had a pungent, slightly rotten smell that Tom would say, in private, put him off his food. Osamu also made himself soup for breakfast, pouring hot water on to powder from a packet and then slurping it noisily. Tom said that that slurping put him off his food too.

Liz replaces the telephone on its cradle. There is a throbbing at her temples and, though she has just drunk that glass of iced water, her mouth and even her throat already feel dry. It must be the air conditioning. Or nerves. Only now does she notice that, under a bank of drawers of the built-in furniture, there is a small refrigerator. It will be stacked with bottles that she will never open.

The *toile-de-Jouy* curtains are drawn back, in such perfectly symmetrical folds that either the maid must have have spent minutes arranging them like that or else they are never closed. Beyond them, instead of an ordinary window, there is an exquisite *shoji* – a frame of delicate blond wood, each of its squares filled with a nacreous paper that perfectly matches the telephone. It is so silent in this room that she wonders what lies behind the *shoji*. Some miniature garden, devotedly tended by a wizened man with the legs of an ancient boiling fowl? (Osamu raked the garden with fierce rhythmical strokes.) Some tributary of the Kamogawa river, with a hump-back bridge and willows drooping their splayed fingers along its margins? (Osamu, flushed and slightly unsteady from two whiskies, leant beside her over the parapet, squinting down into the barely moving water.)

Liz crosses to the window. PLEASE DO NOT OPEN. The prohibition is there in English and, of course, like every other instruction in the room, also in Japanese, French and German. But she must get it open, she must see what lies behind it. She struggles and at last, squeaking in its grooves, the *shoji* begins to slide away.

Four – five? – feet away from her is a high, totally blank wall. She puts her head out, twists it uncomfortably, tries to crane upwards. There is a plume of smoke at the top, which uncurls and then slowly dissipates. She looks down. Far below, there is a cobbled alley, but she cannot make out where it comes from or where it goes.

She pulls the *shoji* back again. She must forget that she ever disobeyed the prohibition to open it. She must forget that blank wall and the strange plume of smoke at the top. She must forget that alley, which seems a passageway too narrow for anything but rats. She must still imagine that miniature garden or that tributary of the river or even a view of distant Mount Hiei, where Osamu pointed, Look, Mrs Butler! A monkey! Many monkeys! and there they were, grey and shrilly chattering, as they swung themselves from liana to liana and from branch to branch.

She must keep calm. She must have no claustrophobia. No one could stifle in a room like this, so long as that pale blue ribbon streams out from the grille of the air conditioner.

This is a room. What is this?

It is a prison.

No, this is a room. This is an expensive room. What is this?

It is a prison.

Osamu wore wooden clogs, an open-necked aertex shirt (one of Tom's cast-offs) and a pair of jeans with a St Martin label. He wears black brogues, a network of tiny cracks across their insteps, a blue pin-stripe suit, the trousers of which are short enough to reveal his dark-blue hose with their scarlet clocks on them, and a white polythene shirt with a dark-blue tie, the knot of which has the explosive appearance of a bud that is about to burst open. Osamu had hair cropped so close to his head that you could see the scalp. His hair is now brushed back from an incision-like parting and it is heavily greased. Osamu was handsome. He is handsome.

You have not changed at all, he says. Fifteen, sixteen years! Just the same!

But they have both changed. Her hair is greying and she has an air of quiet authority that he finds as disconcerting as she finds his sudden attacks of giggling.

Have some coffee. Tea? Something? Anything?

But he shakes his head and looks at his watch, as, across the table from him, she fiddles with the cutlery. He is afraid of being late at the office, though he was often late for her and Tom.

He now asks about Tom and the children, laughing incredulously when she tells him that Anna is married and has a baby, that Adrienne is now at Oxford, and that Jerry now plays cricket for his school. All these things have been recorded in the occasional letters she has written to him. She now wonders if he has ever read those letters, as she has always read his.

He looks again at his watch. It is a multifunctional, digital one, and she knows what Tom's verdict would be on it: Vulgar. It has a gold bracelet but she doubts if the gold is gold all through.

Mrs Butler. . . .

She smiles and corrects him: Liz.

Liz. . . . But he finds that difficult. He has to go, he says. He has to open up the office, it is he who has the keys. No, no, she must not get up from the table, she must continue with her breakfast.

But she follows him out into the foyer, where he tells her: I will see you on Saturday. A statement, not a question. He adds: Unfortunately, every weekday I am busy.

I am busy on weekdays too. Professor Ito has already given her her programme, a sheet for each day, with the sheets all stapled together inside a cardboard cover to make what looks like a paperback.

I will bring my car and we can go wherever you wish.   -

Your car! You have a car now?

He giggles. Very old, he says.

Osamu usually drove the car for them, because Tom hated negotiating those narrow alleys, and she had still to learn. He liked to drive fast, to prevent bigger cars from overtaking, to overtake bigger cars. He had a number of minor accidents, until Tom threatened to deduct the cost of the next from his wages; but each repair bill was far in excess of what they paid him for a month.

She presses a handkerchief to her upper lip, saying: So early in the morning and yet already it is hot.

He tells her to please go back to her breakfast but, tactless, she insists: she must see this car of his.

In the hotel car park there are a number of American limousines among the new or almost new Toyotas and Datsuns and Hondas. A Japanese, in a gleaming white, short-sleeved shirt, jeans and rubber gloves is washing down a bronze Rolls Royce with a CD number-plate.

Osamu repeats: My car is very old.

It looks to her like any car in any street in London; but then, scrutinizing it more carefully, she sees that, yes, there are signs of rust here and there.

It is all I can afford, he tells her.

I can't see anything wrong with it. We have an absolutely ancient Mini to run around in. She does not mention that she and Tom also have a brand-new Peugeot.

I will call for you on Saturday. About eleven. A statement, not a question.

Lovely. A statement too. It is really for him and not for Professor Ito and his colleagues in the medical faculty of Kyoto University that she has come all this way.

*

Osamu's wife is wearing a peach-coloured kimono. She totters towards Liz, knees close to her and hands clasped before her, and then, eyes lowered, she bows. Her face is too long and too aquiline to be beautiful in the West but Liz knows that here it is beautiful. She has an air of extreme fragility and yet of – no, not unbending, but bending strength. There is a little girl of four, with her hair cut straight across her forehead, and she too is wearing a kimono. There is a boy of seven, who is wearing patent-leather shoes with straps across the instep, black velveteen shorts and a red-and-black spotted bow tie. The boy has his mother's aquiline features.

Osamu continues to giggle with a mixture of embarrassment and pleasure. Liz has presents for all of them: a Pierre Cardin scarf for Noriko (presumably it is only on special occasions that she dresses in kimono); a doll for the little girl; three models of vintage cars for the boy; and for Osamu a cashmere pullover. It is difficult to tell if any of them, other than the little girl, is pleased. Perhaps the other three are burdened with that terrible Japanese problem of obligation and its return. Perhaps, as they appraise what Liz has insisted that they must unwrap, though it is not the Japanese custom to do so in front of the donor, and as they exclaim How beautiful! and How kind!, they are secretly trying to calculate: How much could this have cost? The little girl rocks her doll in her arms, peering down at it as it opens and shuts its blank, blue eyes.

Osamu explains that his wife speaks little English.

Never mind, you can translate for her.

Sukoshi, sukoshi, says Noriko – meaning Little, little.

They stand awkwardly for a while in the foyer, as though not knowing what to say or do next. Liz eventually suggests that perhaps the children would like an ice-cream or some lemonade and Osamu and Noriko some coffee or tea.

But: Let us go, Osamu says.

He then addresses Noriko in Japanese, in a low, hissing voice, his head turned away from Liz. Noriko nods calmly, smiles, bows.

They will stay here, Osamu tells Liz. They will wait for us.

But wouldn't they like to come too?

It is better if we drive alone. The children may get tired or sick. My wife will take them into the garden. Have you seen the garden of the hotel?

She resists the temptation to tell him of what lies behind that exquisite *shoji* of her room. Not yet, she answers.

It is very beautiful.

224

In the car park, he walks over, not to the car in which he first came to see her, but to a large gleaming Datsun, that looks as if it had just come out of a showroom window. He fumbles with the key, as one does when unlocking a car door unfamiliar to one.

But this isn't. . . . She oughtn't to have said that; she realizes her mistake even as the words emerge.

He flushes: My car has broken down. It is always breaking down – I told you it was old! And so I have borrowed this car from – from a friend.

This, of course, is not true. He has hired it, because he feels that for her, a foreigner and a famous doctor, a guest of the university, to travel in that beat-up old car of his would cause a terrible loss of face: for her and so for him and perhaps even for the university, if anyone were to see her in it and recognize who she was.

It's a super car.

She gets in. How much can he have paid for it? His salary cannot be large. But it would make things worse to offer to pay a half share herself.

We shall go to the house. A statement, not a question.

The house is the house in which she and Tom and the three children and this businessman, who was once simultaneously their houseboy and a student, all used to live. Muriel also used to live there but somehow Liz tends to forget that. The house stood in a fashionable suburb of the city; but because of the construction of a ring-road through it and the destruction of some of the older mansions to make way for apartment blocks, it is no longer fashionable.

They drive slowly and the only words they utter is when one or the other of them points to some once familiar landmark.

What happened to the Servite Mission? Liz asks.

It has moved. Too big a house, too little money.

Oh, look, there's that bar where we used to eat that awful spaghetti when I was too lazy to cook!

It is now a very expensive restaurant. Western style.

Well, that spaghetti certainly wasn't western style, was it?

Do you remember the bath-house? Osamu points.

Late at night, as she sat reading a book in the sitting-room or lay beside Tom in the bedroom, she would hear the clatter of the Japanese boy's *geta* as he returned up the road from the bath.

And the dog pound? Now it is Liz who points.

Osamu went to the pound and found their labrador there. He never liked dogs but the children had been fretful all day because of its loss.

They begin to drive down the road leading to the house. It seems narrower, dustier, and more untidy than she remembers it, and the trees seem much taller. The wooden fence round the house was solid and high. Now it dips crazily in places and at one corner there is a hole in it, which has been plugged with a ball of rusty barbed wire. Liz begins to feel slightly sick and slightly frightened. She has seen over one of those dips that the garden is a wilderness. It is as if all that work that she and Tom and Osamu put into it must have been an illusion – like those dreams she sometimes has of working out intricate formulae, unrecallable when she wakes.

Osamu stops the car and she suddenly notices that he has about him a breathy excitement, as though he had reached the top of some peak and the air were too strong for him. He gets out and then he opens the door for her and reluctantly, her face ashen and pinched, she descends. He takes her arm, but only lightly, in order to guide her over the unevennesses of the road and then up the unevennesses of the broken steps. There are a number of bells, instead of the single brass one that Osamu used to polish with so much care and pride, and these bells are all of different shapes and sizes, with nameplates beside them, some in western letters and some in Japanese characters. He hesitates and then – just as she is saying Do we want to go in? – he presses one of the bells. Miss McCready, he says. But she has already seen the name, the only neatly written one among them.

Miss McCready opens the door, using her left hand while her right arm, perpetually trembling, is pressed into her side. There has been a sound of shuffling before she has appeared and Liz, being a doctor, knows that that is what is called festination and that Miss McCready is probably in the first stages of Parkinson's disease. The old woman scowls at Liz, still incapable of believing that that scatty English-woman who was always late for something or forgetting something at the Baptist Hospital, is now famous. Miss McCready was matron at the Baptist Hospital, where she had more power than any doctor; but now she has retired – though she still sometimes goes up there to 'help out', as she puts it, or to 'interfere', as the nurses put it.

Oh, my! she cries out, and her left hand flies to her mouth. Liz had never heard any other American woman say Oh, my! except in the cinema and here is Miss McCready, with her high colour and her high bosom, and her high hair-do, a ziggurat of greying plaits, saying it again, after all these years.

Osamu explains that Mrs Butler would like to see her old home and Miss McCready says, Well, she's very welcome to see my part of it! though there is no welcome in her tone. A tabby cat, long-backed and bushy, has now whisked out from the door behind her and stares at Liz with what seems to be an equal lack of welcome.

Liz wants to tell her, Oh, please don't bother, I'd rather remember it as I knew it, but Osamu is nodding to her to go in and Miss McCready is already shuffling off, with the cat rubbing itself against her calves as it zigzags behind her.

The house was huge and rambling, part Japanese and part western in style. A Japanese psychiatrist built it in the thirties, living in part of it and keeping his patients in the rest. It should have been an unhappy house, since it must have contained much unhappiness; even the psychiatrist had been lost at Guam, leaving behind a wife, who later killed herself, and an embittered mother, who was their landlady and obviously loathed them. But now, with curtains and plywood doors marking off the territories of the various tenants, it seems strangely shrunken.

This was once their sitting-room – an airy, uncluttered Japanese-style room, where they would force their awkward western guests to squat by the open windows in the summer or around a charcoal brazier in the winter. But the *shoji* have now gone from the windows and in their place are modern aluminium frames and glass; and a one-bar electric fire has superseded the brazier. There is a room divider, with a few books and old copies of the *Reader's Digest* and *Time* magazine on its shelves, along with a clutter of Japanese dolls and old postcards, propped up at random, and pottery of no value. On this side of the divider there is a bed, which also serves during the day as a divan, a crocheted rug thrown over it; two armchairs, sagging in the middle; a black-and-white television set. On the other side, there is a sink and a cooker and a pedal bin and some shelves with pots and pans and stores on them. Miss McCready was excessively tidy and clean. Miss McCready now lives in a mess of cat's hair and cat's smell, dust, worn linoleum, and a bed obviously unmade under its crocheted cover.

A panic seizes Liz as she looks around her. She is surrounded by fragments – the *tokonoma* still remains and, yes, that little window beside it does not have an aluminium frame like the rest – but she cannot get the fragments to fit. It is as though a precious cup had been smashed and she held certain of its jagged pieces in her hand but not all of them, and then tried to recreate, not the cup – that was impossible – but just her memory of it.

Miss McCready grudgingly offers some Nescafé but Liz, unable to speak, shakes her head. Miss McCready then suggests that she might ask some of the other occupants if they would mind if Liz looked over their apartments and bed-sitting rooms; but Liz shakes her head at that too. The garden, yes, the garden – that is really what she would like to see.

Oh, the garden. . . . Miss McCready sighs. Well, you know how it is? If everyone is responsible, then no one is responsible. She can no longer do anything about it herself – she just isn't up to it any longer – and, since that nice French student left, well, the place has just gone to rack and ruin. Jimmy prefers it like that, of course, it's his jungle now, but still – she shakes her head, so that it seems to tremble in precise time to her hand – it's sad, really sad. It has taken Liz some time to realize that Jimmy is the cat.

Eventually Osamu and Liz go out into the garden, while Miss McCready, Jimmy held under her chin with her left hand, while the right arm goes on trembling, watches them balefully. She never liked Liz, never trusted her, schemed against her and gossiped about her. Oh, she always had a good conceit of herself, that one, and no doubt has an even better one now!

Osamu and Liz walk through the waist-high grass and brambles to the pond. They look out over it, its surface now tented with a thick, matted green, with a gaze of identical sorrow. This was how the pond had been when first they had come; but then Osamu said that he would clean it out and they would have goldfish in it and water lilies and other aquatic plants.

Tom took the children to the annual fair at the Baptist Hospital but, though Liz ought also to have gone – Miss McCready noticed her absence and remarked on it more than once – she said that it was much too hot and that in any case she had to wash her hair and mend some socks and do a number of other things. Osamu announced that he was going to clean out the pond. It was something that he had been planning to do for weeks but somehow he had never got round to it, so enervating was that long, humid summer.

Liz had washed her hair and then, leaving the mending and all the other little chores, she had settled down on the verandah with a novel and a thermos of iced lemonade; but she knew later, though not at the time, that all this had really been only a pretence and a pretext. She could not see the pond from the verandah, since it was round at one side of the house; but eventually she got up and, book in hand, she strolled under the trellis of rambler roses and over the yellowing lawn, until there she found him, thigh-deep in the pond.

He was hacking and tugging at its vegetation with an extraordinary savagery, his hand raising a bill-hook and whirling it down, time and time again. His near-naked body – he was wearing only a *fundoshi* or loin cloth – was smeared with a mingling of sweat and mud, and mud even caked his eyebrows and hair.

She looked at him appraisingly and he looked up at her, the bill-hook raised. Neither of them smiled.

I hope there are no leeches in that water.

He laughed. Probably he did not understand what leeches meant. How about a drink? That must be hot work.

He hesitated; then he nodded and clambered, dripping, out of the pond.

He sat on the log of a tree that they had recently had to have cut down – the centre of its trunk had contained a greenish, friable substance that disintegrated into dust in one's hand – and she went indoors to bring out a tray laden with the gin fizzes that he had now learned to like. The mud was almost dry on his squat, muscular body when she came back. He looked like some aborigine, perched there on the log.

They began to drink in silence, he still seated there and she standing; and then, when he had almost finished, she put out a hand to him, effortlessly, as she had so often dreamed of doing and thought that she would never dare to do. So easy! She put out a hand to him and he took the hand in his own mud-smeared one and she drew him to his feet and they walked like that, hands held, she always a little ahead of him, back into the house. . . .

Osamu tugs at a plant growing at the edge of the pond. It is fleshy, with a purple shine along its sharply serrated leaves, each like a miniature saw, and it resists him by slithering from his grasp time and time again. He laughs, looking down at his hands which are now covered in an evil-smelling glue. He takes a handkerchief from his pocket and wipes them.

All that work. . . . And for nothing.

Well, it was beautiful for a while. Do you remember the water lilies? She remembers the water lilies, stiff and waxen, and how he would wade among them, raking away the slime.

She has an impulse to hold out her hand to this thick-set business-man in his businessman's suit, as once she did to the muscular, near-naked student; she wonders how he would react. But then they both stroll, separate from each other, back towards the house.

Miss McCready gives them a baleful stare, as she stands on the verandah, her left hand shielding her small, extremely blue eyes.

It's so sad about that pond, Liz says.

It's so sad about the whole garden. But I'm beyond it. Seventy-six last birthday. And that Belgian slug upstairs – Miss McCready raises her voice, instead of lowering it, as she looks up to the balcony above her – knows of no exercise other than lifting a beer mug to his lips.

They go back into what was once the sitting-room. Osamu and Liz lay there, the *tatami* matting smeared with mud and Liz smeared with mud, until, suddenly, in terror, they heard footsteps above them. Mildred, whom they had supposed still to be out, must have come home earlier than expected. Then Osamu ran to his room and Liz ran to the bathroom. What's all this mud doing here? one of the children eventually asked; and Liz then explained how the labrador had leapt into the pond with Osamu and must have brought it in.

You must find it strange to return after all these years, Miss McCready says.

Very strange.

You haven't changed. It is clear that she feels that people ought to change. Especially Liz.

Haven't I? I feel that I have.

In the car, before he starts up the engine, Osamu takes some paper tissues out of the back pocket of his trousers and again carefully wipes whatever is left of the greenish stickiness of the pond plant off his hands. Then he presses the starter. Interesting, he says.

Sad.

Liz can feel the tears, unshed but waiting, pricking at the corners of her eyes. She turns her head away from him.

While Noriko prepares the lunch in the apartment, Osamu and Liz go out for a walk with the children. Osamu is reluctant for the children to come and Noriko, speaking in a low voice to him while her eyes gaze at Liz with a gentle sweetness, seems to share that reluctance. But the children are insistent, the little girl even setting up a low keening when it looks for a moment as though her brother will be taken but she will be left behind.

Oh, do let both of them come. Why not? Liz intervenes.

Do you really want them to come? Osamu finds it difficult to believe this.

Of course.

She and Osamu walked this path once before with some children, but then they were hers, not his, and it was night. Tom was away in Tokyo, standing in for an American doctor on furlough, and because it was so hot and humid in the Kyoto house, they had decided to go out and see the cormorant-fishing on the river at Arashiyama. The forest was thick on either side of them, so that it was difficult to tell how much of the fatigue that all of them felt was due to its pressure and how much to the pressure of the atmosphere.

Now it is all changed; there is no path and no forest attempting to obliterate it. Instead, there is a paved alley between the block of apartments from which they have come and the other nine making up the complex belonging to the firm for which Osamu is working. Liz feels a desolating sense of loss. It's all so different, she says. I can hardly recognize it.

Osamu stoops and picks up the little girl, who is already wailing that she can't keep up with them. Japan is changing, he answers. He is proud of a change that makes it no longer necessary for students like himself to do menial jobs for foreigners like Liz and Tom in order to make their way through college.

The little boy edges towards Liz and then, suddenly, to her amazement, she feels his hand in hers. It is a curiously rough, cold little hand, with nails that, though scrupulously clean, would be thought in need of cutting back in England. It might almost be the claw of a bird. She smiles down at him but he turns his head away, as though fearful of smiling back at her.

Well, the river is the same, with a leaden haze over the forest on either side of it and a few bathers in its waters. On either bank there are still bamboo rectangles raised up on stilts, canopies of straw above them, where people squat for refreshments; there are still omnibuses, with neatly groomed girls in uniforms officiously blowing whistles to summon errant passengers; there is still that sense of barely checked, menacing wildness – as though suddenly a typhoon might snap off the tops of the trees, a tidal wave might submerge the pleasure craft, or a volcano might erupt from one of the mountain peaks.

They hired a boat, because at that period it cost only a few shillings to do so. Night had fallen and all over the vast expanse of the river there were other boats, their cormorants, perched on their prows, silhouetted, like sinister heraldic emblems, by the braziers flaring beside them. The children were delighted; Adrienne even wanted to stroke one of the birds but Osamu told her not to, the bird might attack her. Each bird had what looked like a collar round its neck and Osamu explained that this was a device to prevent it from swallowing any fish that it caught. All this is only for tourists, he said. The men do not make money from the sale of the fish but from the hire of the boats. The oars creaked, the birds emitted a guttural sound that seemed to be a distorted echo of that creaking. One of the three men in charge of their boat banged with an oar on its side.

Suddenly Osamu, realizing that the children were totally absorbed in the spectacle of the chained, gagged birds diving for fish, turned to her: Why cannot I come to England?

Oh, Osamu! Why! We want you to come, of course we want you to come, but what sort of life would you have over there? You don't want to be a houseboy for the rest of your days – even if we could afford to employ you. Tom's right. It's much better for you to take this job with this pharmaceutical company that he's found for you. You don't want to cut adrift from your family and – and your whole *life* out here in Japan. It would be hopeless.

She, too, was hopeless. In eleven days they would board the P & O liner in Kobe and she would probably never see him again.

Osamu sighed. She took his hand in hers but quickly he withdrew it. One of the children let out a squeal. Rockets were whizzing up into the leaden sky and then falling, in innumerable torrents of green, red and gold over the river and the forests on either side of it and even the mountains beyond.

They are standing on the precise spot where they disembarked from the boat under that continuing rain of coloured fire. Liz wonders if Osamu remembers. The boy lets go of Liz's hand, which has been sweating from the contact though his has remained strangely dry, and runs down to the water's edge. He kneels and stares at something – it looks like no more than an upturned tin – in the shallows. Osamu, seeing what he is doing, shouts something angry and the boy gets up. He is dirtying his beautifully pressed shorts and his long stockings.

They're such gorgeous children, Liz says.

He clearly does not like her saying that. Perhaps, like many Japanese, he is superstitious and fears that some malign fate may exact retribution. He looks at his multifunctional digital watch and tells her that it is time they went back, since Noriko said that the meal would be ready at half past one.

The children, hers not his, ran ahead of them, half excited and half fearful, up the path that wavered through the forest crowding in on either side of it. Snakes, monkeys, wild dogs, wild cats! Or ghosts! They had been told by Osamu that you could always recognize a Japanese ghost because it had no feet. To frighten themselves like this only intensified the memory of the pleasure of watching those strange, cruel-beaked birds dive for fish and then, so unexpectedly, that downpour of fire all around them. Liz turned to Osamu and put her hands on his shoulders. No one behind, no one in front. A miracle in Japan! She kissed him, holding him close to her, as though she were the man, confident and strong, and he the woman, shrinking and pliable.

Osamu lifts up the little girl, who has been wailing fretfully. She smiles at him, the tears still on her cheeks, puts out a hand and tugs at a lock of his hair. He does not mind, because when a child is young it can do what it wishes in Japan. It is only when it is older that it must learn self-control and circumspection.

The table is laid as it might be in the West, with knives and forks and spoons and a cruet stand and white napkins fringed with lace. There are flowers on it and chairs around it. Osamu explains that Noriko has been taking lessons in western cookery. Liz wonders if she has been taking these lessons against the coming of this English-woman who once employed and loved her husband.

There are lamb chops, which are pinkish at the centre because they have not been cooked long enough, and potatoes that have been cooked so long that they have been reduced to a watery flour. There is a bottle of acid red wine which, Liz notices, Osamu does not offer to Noriko. Later, there is a lemon chiffon pie, the top of which tastes as if it were indeed made of chiffon. But all this does not matter. With a mingling of pain and tranquil consoling pleasure, Liz realizes that Osamu and Noriko are totally happy with each other. Noriko may complain laughingly that her husband is always coming home late, because he has to stay up so many nights playing mahjong with prospective customers – whom he must usually allow to win. Osamu may complain that, though Noriko has a degree from Doshisha Women's College in history, she prefers to look after the house and children than to get a job. But they are only teasing each other, there is no acrimony in all this, neither wants the other any different – in the way that Liz and Tom so often want each other different. Liz now feels that, though she is sitting so close to Osamu and though the little girl is sitting between Osamu and Noriko, yet the husband and wife are somehow merging into each other, even as she looks at them and listens to them. Their bodies are coalescing, their faces are becoming superimposed on each other. She wonders if anyone has ever felt the same thing about herself and Tom. Perhaps Osamu did, so many years ago. It is all so different now.

They drink coffee out of thimble-like cups of Kutani china. Liz has never liked modern Kutani china, usually so bright and over-decorated; but she feels no inclination to find fault with it this afternoon, any more than with the sports pennants hanging on either side of the door (Osamu played football for Kyoto University), the two garish dolls, one male and one female, each imprisoned in a cell of glass on either end of the mantelpiece, or the view of the Houses of Parliament – in fact a dishcloth once sent by her as the kind of present that can easily be parcelled – which has been carefully pinned above the upright piano.

It is at this piano that the little boy, in his black patent-leather shoes and his spotted bow tie, now seats himself at his father's bidding. There is a hush, the little boy is nervous. Then, as he strikes the keys, legs dangling several inches from the floor, Liz realizes that what he is playing, with several wrong notes, is 'God Save the Queen'. When that is over and she has congratulated him and Osamu has patted his square, closely cropped head and Noriko has kissed him on the cheek, Liz knows, as one always knows in Japan, even though no word has been said, that it is time for her to go.

Noriko and the children accompany her and Osamu down into the courtyard, where the car is parked. Noriko is going to bow her fare-well, but on an impulse Liz goes forward and kisses the Japanese woman, an arm thrown around her shoulder. The Japanese woman is plainly surprised but she is also pleased. Liz wonders if Osamu has ever spoken about their love-affair in that distant past. She doubts it. But the Japanese can convey and intuit so much without any words and Liz knows that Noriko knows and, more important, feels no resentment.

You have such a happy family, Liz says as the car begins the journey along the broad, blaring highway to Kyoto.

Yes. We are happy. He says it simply. A fact.

It was right that you didn't come to England with us. *We* were right – Tom and I. Though I wanted you to come.

But Osamu makes no answer to that. Perhaps he has genuinely for-gotten that he ever begged them to take him; perhaps it is less embar-rassing to pretend that he has forgotten. I wish to see England, he says. One day.

Oh, do come and stay with us! We'd love that.

Of course. Thank you. I think that in maybe five years my firm will send me.

Yes, it has all been mapped out for him, as for every other employee of the company. They all know how many years it will be before, on some pretext or another, they are dispatched to the West.

I *have* enjoyed this day!

I am sorry that Tom-san could not come with you.

Yes, he so much wanted to come. But they'd only pay my fare, not his. And it's now become so expensive out here in Japan. Unbelievable!

Do you remember when we could stay for one thousand yen in a Japanese inn?

Yes! With breakfast and dinner included. That used to be – oh, about a pound.

Tom said that Osamu had better drive her and the children to Amano-Hashidate and he would follow in the train the following day. Otherwise they might be charged for the unused rooms. There were three of these rooms, divided from each other by *fusuma* that could be pulled back, fragile on their grooves, to make a single room, beautiful in all its proportions, that looked out over still, smoky expanses of water, divided by a causeway. The first room, which was large, was for Tom and Liz; the next, which was larger, was for the children; and the small one, little more than a vestibule, was for Osamu. When they arrived and Liz saw the tiny room, she said, Oh, I do hope this is big enough for you, and Osamu, surprised, replied that it was a four-and-a-half-mat room and that, when he was a schoolboy, he had shared just such a room with his younger brother.

That night she went to him, tiptoeing through the room in which the three children slept, with the moonlight powdering their upturned faces with a grey, luminous dust. She slipped off her kimono, as, from the floor, he held out his hands to her. But, just as she was about to kneel down on the *futon*, she saw what looked like a ravelled piece of black string on the whiteness of the pillow. Her hands went to her mouth when the string suddenly wriggled. She pointed.

Osamu leapt up, naked, from the *futon*, seized one of the transparent, plastic slippers provided by the inn, and began to hit out wildly. It was a *mukade*, he said, and Liz knew that that meant a kind of poisonous centipede, though until now she had never seen one. Long after the insect was no more than pulp on the *tatami*, he went on beating at it, as she had seen Japanese women, their faces flushed with a kind of obsessive malevolence, pound away at rice in

235

a pestle, in order to reduce it to a pulp for rice balls.

There was a wail from the next-door room. He had woken one of the children. Liz slipped back into her kimono, slid the *fusuma* open and whispered: It's nothing, go back to sleep, don't worry. Then she whispered to Osamu that it was all too difficult, every sound could be heard, she must return to her room. The sight of that naked figure slashing out at the insect with flushed face and flailing arm, had filled her with more dread than the wail of the child. Yet a *mukade*, it was well known, could cause death with its sting, and it was natural enough that Osamu should have been so violent.

What happened to Mrs Budden? Osamu suddenly asks. He means Mildred.

Liz explains that she has lost touch with her, letters have not been answered, perhaps – who knows? – she may be dead. She went back to Canada to live with a sister and, after all, she was no longer young even in those far-off times when she occupied the two top-floor rooms as a lodger.

Liz wonders why he should suddenly ask about her. Except that he was always convinced, however much Liz herself might pooh-pooh the idea, that Mildred knew about them. She watched, she listened: he was sure of that.

Osamu laughs: Direct Method, he says.

Yes. She believed in the Direct Method.

They reach the hotel and they are now going to say goodbye. They will not see each other again for – well, all those years that will elapse before Osamu's service to the Company is rewarded with a visit to England. He puts his hand in his pocket and he takes out a small, beautifully wrapped package.

A souvenir, he says.

What is it? I know I shouldn't open it now but may I break all the Japanese rules and do so?

He nods, smiling.

She sits down on a chair in the foyer and, her fingers trembling and clumsy, unties the ribbon and peels off first the layer of wrapping paper and then the tissue paper beneath it.

I remember that you collect them.

It is a Chinese snuff bottle, carved out of tourmaline in a pattern of water lilies. As she looks at it, she thinks of the pond and of the near-naked figure emerging from it, daubed with mud, with the fleshy pink-and-green lilies opening their mouths around him.

She and Tom no longer collect snuff bottles, because soon after

236

their return from Japan they were so short of money that they had to auction off their whole collection. But she does not tell Osamu this, of course, as she begins carefully to rewrap the bottle first in its tissue paper and then in its wrapping paper and to retie the ribbon around it.

Tom will love it, she says. How kind you are!

No obligation now weighs on him: not for the Pierre Cardin scarf, not for the cashmere pullover, not for the doll, not for the three model vintage cars, not even for the hours – so few! – that she lay with him. This is a museum piece and he has paid it all off, the whole debt. She can understand why, though they are about to say good-bye, he has the air of a man who has just emerged from a law court, unexpectedly acquitted.

Dear Osamu. . . .

Well. . . .

He gives that embarrassed giggle. Then he says that he must get home, he is sure that she has many, many things to do, he hopes that she will enjoy the rest of her trip and that she will come back soon to Japan. She planned to ask him up to her room but now she knows that it would be humiliatingly pointless to do so.

The lift-boy glances down at the package in her hand, no doubt wondering what this grey-haired foreign woman has bought or what she has been given. The package feels extraordinarily heavy to Liz, as though it were some huge stone that she had balanced in her palm.

She goes into her room and she puts down that terrible weight and then she goes over to that blond frame of wood covered with nacreous paper. She stares at the notice: PLEASE DO NOT OPEN.

This is a room. What is it?

It is a prison.

No. This is a room. Repeat.

It is a prison.

No, no. Let me give you the Japanese equivalent. This is a room – *Sore wa zashiki desu*.

Indirect Method.

She was about to force the *shoji* apart again but now she leaves it.

1978

A Scent of Mimosa

It was long past midnight when the municipal Citroën dumped the four of them outside the Menton hotel. Tom, the youngest and most assertive of the Katherine Mansfield Prize judges, grabbed Lenore's arm and helped her up the steps. It was Lenore, thirtyish and thinnish, who had that year won the prize, given by the municipality. Though they had never met until the start of their journey out to the south of France together, he was always touching her, as though to communicate to her some assurance, at the nature of which she could still only guess. As they followed behind, Theo and Lucy, the other two judges, maintained a cautious distance from each other. There had been some acrimony, many years before, about an unsigned review in *The Times Literary Supplement*. Lenore could no longer even remember which of the two had written it and which had felt aggrieved.

In the hall they all stared at each other, like bewildered strangers wondering what they were doing in each other's company so late at night, in an unknown hotel, in a foreign town.

Tom broke the silence, swaying back and forth on his tiny feet: 'Well, what's the programme for tomorrow? Christ, I'm tired!'

Lucy hunted for one of three or four minuscule, lace-fringed handkerchiefs in the crocodile-leather bag that dangled from her wrist. When travelling with her stockbroker husband she was used

238

to more luxurious hotels, more powerful cars and more amusing company. 'Apparently we're going to be taken up into the mountains for another banquet.' She held the handkerchief to the tip of her sharp nose and gave a little sniff.

Theo, who was almost as drunk as Tom, wailed, 'Oh God! Altitude and hairpin bends always make me sick.'

'Well, there'll be plenty of both tomorrow,' Lucy replied, with some relish.

Lenore gazed down at the key that she was balancing on her palm. 'The ambassador told me that he would be placing a wreath on some local war memorial. Tomorrow's armistice day, isn't it?'

Lucy, who had been affronted that the prize-winner and not she had been seated on the New Zealand ambassador's right, exclaimed, 'What a dreadfully boring man! Nice, but oh so boring!'

'Oh, I thought him rather interesting.' Lenore was still secretly both frightened and envious of Lucy, who was older, much more successful and much richer than herself. 'Some young New Zealander's going to meet us up there, the ambassador told me. In the village. He's coming specially for the Katherine Mansfield celebrations.'

'I suppose if your country's produced only one writer of any note, you're bound to make a fuss of her,' Tom commented.

'Well, we'd better get some sleep. If we can.' Lucy began to walk towards the lift. 'The beds here are horribly hard and lumpy.'

Tom again held Lenore by the arm, as he shepherded her towards the small, gilded cage. So close, she could smell the alcohol heavy on his breath.

Lucy got out first, since on their arrival together she had managed to secure for herself the only room on the first floor with a balcony over the bay. Bowing to Lenore, she sang out, '*Bonne nuit, Madame la Lauréate!*'

Lenore gave a small, embarrassed alugh. 'Good night, Lucy!'

Theo got out at the next floor, tripping and all but falling flat, with only Tom's arm to save him. He began to waddle off down the corridor; then turned as the lift gates were closing. '*Bonne nuit, Madame la Lauréate!*'

Lenore and Tom walked down their corridor, his hand again at her elbow, as though once more to assure her and perhaps also himself of something that he could not or dared not put into words. They came to her door.

'Well. . . .' He released her and clumsily she stooped and inserted the key. 'Tomorrow we'll drive up into the mountains and watch

239

poor Theo being carsick and meet the ambassador's young New Zealander. And, of course, hear lots and lots of speeches.'

She opened the door; and at once, as though frightened that she would ask him in, he backed away.

'Well, *bonne nuit, Madame la Lauréate!*'

'*Bonne, nuit, Monsieur le Juge!*'

She shut the door and leant against it, feeling the wood hard against her shoulder blades. Her head was throbbing from too much food and drink, too much noise and too much French, and her mouth felt dry and sour. What would each of the others be doing now that they had separated? She began to speculate. Well, Lucy would no doubt be taking great care of each garment as she removed it; and then she would take equal care of her face, patting and smoothing, smoothing and patting. Theo, drunken and dishevelled, his tiny eyes bleary and his tie askew, would perch himself on a straight-backed chair – he always seemed masochistically determined to inflict the maximum of discomfort on himself – and would then start work on the pile of postcards that he had rushed out to buy as soon as they had been shown into their rooms. The postcards would, of course, arrive in England long after his return. Someone had told Lenore that he had a wife much older than himself and a horde of children and stepchildren – six? seven? eight? – to all of whom he was sentimentally devoted. And Tom? Tom, she decided after some deliberation, would walk along to his room, wait there for a few minutes, and then take the lift downstairs again and go out into the night, wandering the autumnal streets in search of a – well, what? She did not know, not yet; any more than she knew the nature of the assurance that that constant touching was designed to convey.

The bed was soft, not hard and lumpy at all as Lucy had complained, too soft, so that its swaying was almost nauseating. Perhaps poor Theo would be bed-sick and would have to take to the floor. . . . She shut her eyes and yawned and yawned again. . . . She was asleep.

When she awoke, it seemed as if many hours had passed, even though the dark of the room was still impenetrable. Her body was on fire, the sweat pouring off it, her head was throbbing and she had an excruciating pain, just under her right ribs as though a knife had been inserted there and was now being twisted round and round. The central heating was always turned too high in these continental hotels; and after having eaten and drunk so much, she ought not to be surprised at an attack of acute indigestion. She threw back the sheet and duvet and then, after lying for a while uncovered with none of the expected coolness, she switched on the bedside lamp and dragged herself off the bed. For a long time she struggled with the regulator of the radiator that ran the whole length of window; but the effort only made her sweat the more, it would not budge. She would have to open the window instead. Again she struggled; and at last the square of glass screeched along its groove and she felt the icy air enfolding her body.

From her suitcase she fetched a tube of Alka Seltzer and padded into the bathroom. It was as she was dropping two of the tablets into a tumbler of water, the only light coming through the half-open door behind her, that suddenly she felt a strange tickling at the back of her throat, as though a feather had lodged there, coughed, coughed again, and then effortlessly began spitting, spitting, spitting.

Giddy and feeling sick, the sweat now chill on her forehead and bare arms, she stared down at the blood that had spattered the porcelain of the basin and was even dripping from one of the taps. She felt that she was about to faint and staggered back into the bedroom, to fall diagonally across the bed, her cheek pressed against the thrown-back duvet. Oh God, oh God. . . . She must have had some kind of haemorrhage.

She lay there, shivering, for a while. She would have to see a doctor. But how could she call one at this hour? The best thing would be to go along to the room of one of the others. But she shrank from appealing to either Lucy or Tom. It would have to be Theo.

She got off the bed, still feeling giddy, sick and weak, and went back into the bathroom to wash away the blood. This time she turned on the light. The two tablets of Alka Seltzer were now dissolved; but, with an extraordinary hyperaesthesia, she could hear the water fizzing even when she was still far away from it. She approached the basin slowly, fearful of what she would find in it: the trails and spatters of blood on the glistening porcelain and over the tap. But when she was above the basin and forced her eyes down, there was, amazingly, nothing there, nothing there at all. Porcelain and tap were both as clean as she had left them after brushing her teeth.

It was cold and damp by the mountain war memorial, a lichen-covered obelisk, one end sunk into the turf, with a stone shield attached, bearing names that for the most part were Italian, not French. The mayor, cheeks scarlet from the many toasts at the banquet and medals dangling from his scuffed blue-serge suit, stood before it and bellowed out an oration to which Lenore did not listen, her gaze tracking back and forth among the faces, mostly middle-aged and brooding, of the handful of villagers huddled about her. Lucy had retreated into the back of the municipal Citroën, saying that she was certainly not going to risk a cold just before she and her husband were due to set off for the Caribbean on a holiday. Theo was holding a handkerchief to his chin, as though he had an attack of toothache, his tiny eyes rheumy and bloodshot. Tom, who had been chatting to their dapper young chauffeur in his excellent French, now stood beside the man, faintly smirking.

At last the oration ended and the ambassador, grizzled, grey-faced and grave, walked forward with his wreath, stooped and placed it against the tilted obelisk. An improbable girl bugler, in white boots and a miniskirt that revealed plump knees at the gap between them, stepped proudly forward and the valedictory notes volleyed back and forth among the mountains. Again Lenore felt that tickling at the back of her throat; but now it was tears. She always cried easily.

Suddenly she was aware of a smell, bitter and pungent, about her; and she wondered, in surprise, what could be its source. It was too late in the year for the smell to come from any flower at this altitude; and it seemed unlikely that any of the village women – with the possible exception of the girl bugler – would use a perfume so strange and strong. She peered around; and then, turning, saw the tall young man with the mousy, close-cropped hair and the sunburned face, his cheekbones and his nose prominent, who was standing a little apart from the rest of the gathering. A khaki rucksack was propped against one leg. Their eyes met and he smiled and gave a little nod, as though they already knew each other.

The ceremony was over. In twos and threes the people began to drift away, for the most part silent, and silent not so much in grief as in the attempt to recapture its elusive memory. The young man, his rucksack now on his back, was beside her.

'Hello.' The voice was unmistakably antipodean.

'Hello.'

'You won the prize.' It was not a question.

'By some marvellous fluke. I've never had any luck in my life before. Everything I've achieved, I've had to struggle for.' She gave an involuntary shudder, feeling the cold and damp insinuate themselves through the thickness of her topcoat. 'You must be the New Zealander.'

'*The* New Zealander? Well, *a* New Zealander.'

'We heard that you were coming.'

'I always try to come.'

The ambassador was approaching, still grey-faced and grave. 'Your New Zealander has arrived,' Lenore called out to him.

'*My* New Zealander?' He looked at the young man, who held out his hand. The ambassador took it. 'So you're from back home?'

The young man nodded, at once friendly and remote. 'Wellington.'

'What brings you here?'

'I wanted to be present at the ceremonies. I was telling Miss Marlow, I always have been.'

'Then you're a fan of K. M.?'

'Oh, yes.'

Lenore was becoming increasingly bewildered. She turned to the ambassador. 'But didn't you say . . .? Didn't you tell me last night – at the banquet – that you were expecting a New Zealander?'

'I?'

'Yes, surely. . . .'

'But I'd no idea this young man would turn up. None at all.'

'But I'm sure. . . . Didn't you . . .?'

'We've never set eyes on each other. And we know nothing about each other. Do we?' He appealed to the other man.

'Nothing at all.'

'Anyway' cold and tired, the ambassador began to move away – 'it's been nice to meet you. What's your name?'

'Leslie.' It might have been either surname or Christian name.

'We'll be seeing you again?'

'Oh, yes. I'll be at the prize-giving ceremony tomorrow. As I said, I've been at every one.'

Lenore and the young man were now alone by the lop-sided war memorial. Far down the road she could make out Theo, shapeless in his ancient overcoat, a cap pulled down over his bulging forehead, as he urinated against a tree that soared up into the gathering mist and darkness. Tom was climbing into the car beside Lucy; Lenore could hear his laugh, strangely loud.

'How are you going to get down to Menton? Would you like me to ask if we can give a lift?'

'Oh, that's very kind of you. But I think I'd like to stay here a little longer.'

'Here?' She could not imagine why anyone should wish to stay on in this cramped, craggy village, with all the inhabitants drifting back into their homes and nothing to see in the coagulating mist and dark and nothing to do.

He nodded. 'She came up here. She was driven up here by Connie and Jennie.'

'Oh, yes, they were the ones who lent her the Villa Isola Bella, weren't they? Connie was the aunt.'

'Well, cousin really.'

'I didn't know she'd ever been in this village. I know the journals and the letters pretty well but obviously not as well as you.' Suddenly she did not wish to let him go; this imminent parting from a total stranger had become like the resurgence of some deep-seated, long-forgotten sorrow. 'Can't we really give you a lift? We can squeeze you into our car.'

He shook his head. 'I want to stay here a little. But I'll be down. We'll meet again?'

'Perhaps this evening you might join us for dinner? We have the evening free and we thought that we might all go to a fish restaurant in Monte Carlo. Lucy – she's one of the judges – says that Somerset Maugham once took her there and it was absolutely fabulous.' 'Fabulous' was not Lenore's kind of word; it was Lucy's. 'Do try to join us.'

'Perhaps.'

'Please! We'll be leaving the hotel at about eight-thirty. So just come there before that. It's the Hotel du Parc. Do you know where it is?'

He nodded.

'How will you get down to Menton? There can't be a bus now.'

'Oh, I'll manage.'

'Lenore! Time we started back!' It was Tom's peremptory voice.

'I must go. They're getting impatient. Please come this evening.'

He raised his hand as she hurried away from him, in what was half a wave and half a salute. Then he remained standing motionless beside the war memorial.

Lucy said fretfully, 'We want to get down the mountain before this mist really thickens.'

'I'm sorry. But that was. . . . He was from New Zealand.'

'Is that the one you told us about last night?' Theo asked, wiping with a soiled handkerchief at eyes still streaming from the cold.

Lenore nodded, 'Yes, I did tell you about him didn't I?' She all but added, 'But the funny thing is that the ambassador pretended that he'd said nothing to me at all about his coming.' Then something made her check herself.

It was as though, walking over sunlit fields, she had all at once unexpectedly found ahead of her a dark and dense wood; had hesitated whether to enter it or not; and had then turned and in panic retraced her steps.

'Well, he's obviously not coming.' Lucy drew her chinchilla coat up over her shoulders and got to her feet. The two men also rose.

Lenore sighed. 'No, I suppose not.'

'He probably decided there were more amusing things for a young man to do on the Côte,' Theo said.

'I can think of less amusing things too,' Lucy retorted tartly.

'Perhaps he hadn't got the money for a slap-up meal.'

Of course, of course! Tom was right. Lenore saw it now. What she should have said was, 'You must be my guest, because I want to spend some of my prize money in celebration,' or something of that kind. She had spoken of the 'fabulous' restaurant to which Lucy had been taken by Maugham – enough to put off anyone who was travelling on a slender budget. Of course!

Once again Tom tried to take her arm as they emerged into the soft November air; but this time she pulled free with a sharp, impatient jerk.

The next morning they were driven out to Isola Bella, the villa on the steep hill where Katherine Mansfield had lived for nine months in a fever of illness and activity. The villa itself was occupied; but the municipality had made over a room on the lowest of its three levels into a shrine. A bearded French critic, who was regarded as an authority on the English writer, explained to Lenore that an outhouse had been converted into a lavatory and shower, in the hope that some other English or New Zealand writer might soon be installed in what was, in effect, a tiny apartment.

'But Katherine Mansfield herself never lived here?'

He hesitated between truth and his loyalty to his hosts. Then: 'Well, no,' he agreed in his excellent English. 'Katherine lived above.' (He invariably referred to the writer merely by her Christian name.)

'And probably she never even came down here?'

Again he hesitated. 'Possibly not.'

Lenore wandered away from the rest of the party, up the hill to the rusty gates that led to the main part of the house. Ahead of her, as she peered through the curlicues of wrought iron, stretched the terrace on which the invalid would lie out for most of the day on a chaise longue spread with a kaross made of flying-squirrel skins brought home from Africa by her father. Oh, and there were the mimosa trees, like elongated ferns – Katherine Mansfield had described how she would lie awake at break of day and watch the shafts of the rising sun shimmer through them. All at once, Lenore could smell the tiny yellow flowers still hanging from the fragile racemes. Though infinitely fainter, a mere ghost, it was nonetheless that same odour, pungent and bitter, that had enveloped her up in the mountains. But surely, so high up in the mountains, no mimosa could grow or, if it did, could come to bloom in November? As she breathed in the scent, deeper and deeper until her lungs began to ache with it as they had done that first night in the hotel, she thought once again of the New Zealander and wondered what had happened to him. She had hoped to see him in the town early that morning as she had wandered alone about it, pretending that she was in quest of presents but in reality in quest of him; but he had been nowhere. And now he had not turned up at the villa, as she had also hoped that he would do. Perhaps he had already moved on, with his exiguous rucksack, farther up the coast; perhaps she would never see him again.

Suddenly she wanted a spray of the mimosa. She rattled the gate and the rusty padlock swung from side to side, with a dry sound of scraping against the bars. The occupiers of the house must be away. But she tugged at the bell, hearing it tinkle from somewhere out of sight. No one came. She thought, If he were here, he could climb over for me. He'd find some way. She hoisted herself up with both hands, feeling the flaking metal graze a palm. But it was useless.

'Can I help Madame?'

It was the French critic, stroking his beard with a narrow, nicotine-stained hand.

Lenore explained what she wanted; and then he too tugged at the bell-pull and even shouted out in French. No one came. Oddly, she could no longer smell that pungent, bitter odour, not since he had come.

He shrugged. 'I'm afraid that I am too old and too fat to climb over for you. Perhaps if you come tomorrow, the owners will be here.'

'We're leaving tomorrow morning.'

'Then. . . .' Again he shrugged. When he had first seen her, he had thought her a dowdy, insignificant little woman, and had hardly bothered to speak to her. But now he experienced a sudden pull, as though a boat in which he had long been becalmed had all at once felt the tug and sweep of the tide. Now he too grabbed her arm just above the elbow, as Tom had kept on doing until that rebuff of the previous night. 'Let me assist you down the hill.' How thin the arm was, how pathetically thin and fragile – the arm of a child or invalid. He felt excited at the contact.

'I have given most of my life to Katherine,' he told her, as they began to descend. It was not strictly true, since he had given much of his life to other things: to the editing of a magazine, to the collection of Chinese works of art, to women, to eating and drinking. But at that moment, when his fingers felt the delicate bone inside its envelope of flesh, he not only wished that it had been so but believed that it had been so. 'In a strange way you remind me of her, you know.'

In the Town Hall the audience for the prize-giving ceremony was composed almost entirely of elderly men in dark suits and elderly women in hats. Lenore had been told that she would have to make a small speech of thanks in French after Lucy had spoken, also in French, on behalf of the judges. Lenore had never made a speech in her life, let alone a speech in French, and she dreaded the ordeal. The hall was stuffy, its radiators too hot even on this autumn day. She felt headachy, sweaty and vaguely sick, as she listened, in a kind of trance, first to the orotund platitudes of the mayor, then to the clipped phrases of the ambassador and finally to Lucy's few witty, lucid comments. In rising panic she thought, If he were here, if only he were here! In one hand she was clutching the typescript, the French of which Lucy had corrected for her.

She heard her name and then one of the French officials was giving her a little push from behind, his hand to her shoulder. She rose and, as she did so, she felt the room revolve first gently and then faster and faster around her. She clutched the back of her chair, staring up at the face of the mayor on the dais above her. All at once she could smell, far stronger than ever before, that pungent, bitter odour of mimosa. It was all around her, an enveloping cloud. She moved forward and then up the steps, the French critic putting out one of those long, narrow hands of his to help her.

She was handed an envelope, cold and dry on her hot and damp palm, and then she was handed a red leather box, open, with a bronze medallion embedded in it. Whose head was that? But of course – it was Katherine Mansfield's, jagged prongs of fringe across a wide forehead. She looked down and read: *'Menton c'est le Paradis d'une aube à l'autre.'*

The mayor was prompting her in a sibilant whisper, perhaps she would wish to say a few words?

She turned to face the audience; and it was then, as she moistened her lips with her tongue and raised the sheet of typescript, that all at once she saw him, standing by himself at the far end of the hall, one shoulder against the jamb of a closed door and his eyes fixed on her.

She began to read, at first all but inaudibly but then in a stronger and stronger voice. Her French was all but perfect; she felt wholly calm.

In the premature dusk, they talked outside the Town Hall, pacing the terrace among the stunted oleanders.

'You saved my life,' she said. She felt the euphoria that precedes a bout of fever. 'I can't explain it but I was, oh, petrified, I felt sure I could not say a word, and then suddenly I saw you and all at once. . . .'

'I like that story of yours. Very much.'

'Oh, have you read it?' She was amazed. The story had appeared in a little magazine that, after three issues, had folded and vanished.

'Yes. It was – *right*. For her, I mean. It's the only story that she herself might have written, of all the ones that have ever won the prize.'

'That's a terrific compliment.'

'I mean it.'

'I'd hoped that perhaps you'd have joined us last night.'

'Well, I wanted to,' he said, with no further excuse.

'And then I thought that I might see you at the villa.'

'I've been there many times.'

'But not this time?'

He did not answer; and then she began to tell him about the mimosa on the terrace – how she remembered reading about it in the journals and the letters and how she had wanted a spray, just one spray, but there had been no one at the house and the gate was padlocked. 'If you'd been there, perhaps you could have climbed over. But none of our party looked capable of doing so.'

'I'll get you a spray.'

'Will you? Can you?'

'Of course.' He smiled. His teeth were very white in the long, sunburned face.

'But we leave early tomorrow.'

'What time?'

'We must leave the hotel at ten for the airport.'

'Oh, that'll give me time. Don't worry.'

Boldly she said, 'Oh, I wish there were no banquet this evening! I wish we could just have dinner alone together.'

'There'll be other times,' he said quietly. 'Anyway, I won't forget the mimosa.'

'Promise?'

'Promise.'

After that Tom was again calling and the cars were starting up and people were shaking her hand and saying how glad they were for her and that soon she must come back to Menton again.

When she looked round for the New Zealander, she found that he had vanished.

Lenore was back in her dark, two-roomed Fulham flat. At the airport Lucy had been whisked off by her husband in a chauffeur-driven Daimler, barely bothering to say goodbye. Theo had explained that it would be impossible to fit any more passengers into his battered station-wagon, already packed with his wife, a number of children, a dog and a folding bicycle. Tom had said that it looked as if the friend who was supposed to meet him must have got held up and he'd wait around for a while. So Lenore had travelled alone on the bus. She had felt chilled and there was again that pain, dull now, under her right ribs.

She shivered as she stooped to light the gas. Then she remained kneeling before it, staring at the radiants as the blue light flickering up from them steadied to an orange glow. He had failed to keep his promise and she had no idea of where he might be or even of what he was called - other than that either his surname or his Christian name was Leslie. It was hopeless. She got up, with a small, dry cough, and went into the bedroom. There she hauled her suitcase up on to the bed and began to unpack it, hurriedly, throwing things into drawers or jerking them on to hangers, as though she did not have a whole empty evening ahead of her and a number of empty days after that. At the bottom of the suitcase she came on the typescript of her speech - she crumpled it into a ball and threw it into the wastepaper basket - and the red leather box, containing her trophy. She pressed the stud of the lid and lifted it upwards with a thumb; and, as she did so, it was as if she were releasing from it the smell, pungent and bitter, that soon was all around her. She gave a little gasp; the pain in her chest sharpened. Looking down, she saw the spray of mimosa that lay across the medallion.

She took the spray in her hand; but it was dry, dry and faded and old as though it had lain there not for a few hours but for many, many years. 'Leslie.' She said the name aloud to herself and then, with no shock and no alarm but with the relieved recognition of someone lost who all at once sights a familiar landmark, she remembered that yes, of course, Leslie had been the name of the beloved brother killed in the war, whom Katherine Mansfield had always called 'Chummie'.

She touched the arid, dead raceme and some of the small, yellowish-grey blossoms, hard as berries, fell to the carpet at her feet. They might have been beads, scattering hither and thither. Three or four rolled back and forth in her palm. She felt a tickle at the back of her throat; it must be pollen, she decided wrongly.

Then suddenly the concluding lines of Katherine Mansfield's sonnet on the death of her brother, read long ago and forgotten, forced themselves up within her, like the spurs of a plant, buried for years, all at once thrusting up into the light of day.

> *By the remembered stream my brother stands,*
> *Waiting for me with berries in his hands . . .*
> *'These are my body. Sister, take and eat.'*

She gave another little dry cough, and tasted something thick and salt on her tongue. The scent of mimosa was already fading as those blooms had long since faded. But she knew that it would come back and that he would come back with it.

1972

So Hurt and Humiliated

At twenty-two Rosamund Dangerfield was a girl for whom everything had always gone well. Yet there were times when she had to
admit to herself a certain dissatisfaction which she could not
explain. There were even times when she caught herself in the
strangest of fantasies; of being humillated, or in pain, or profoundly
unhappy. All this was morbid, she knew; and yet that year in Greece
such thoughts continually oppressed her, so that when she met
Costa Arslanoglou she had the feeling of having come to the mouth
of a dark tunnel which she had often already explored in her dreams.

He was a tall youth, with curiously light blue eyes under the
darkest of eyebrows, features almost monotonous in their grave
regularity, and a sinuous grace of movement which would have
made him conspicuous anywhere but in the Eastern Mediterranean.
He was wearing a cream silk shirt with a 'Lord Byron' collar that
revealed the gold chain he wore round his neck. His shoes were of
white suede, and his belt was of crocodile. He gave an impression
both of wealth and of unreliability; and Rosamund could not help
comparing him with Robert Burnett, in whose office she met him,
since Robert was so obviously both reliable and poor.

'And here is Colonel Dangerfield's daughter,' Robert greeted her
as she came in from the library. 'Hello, Rosamund. Mr Arslanoglou
had been asking about his examination board for his scholarship. So

251

I told him that your father would be the chairman, and that I have nothing to do with it. . . . Mr Arslanoglou, Miss Dangerfield.'

As he introduced them, he made a gesture with his plump hands which looked as if he were passing invisible plates between them. His ordinary, decent face was red and shiny with the heat, and even the cow-lick into which he brushed his sandy hair seemed to be damp.

'How is it we have not met before, Miss Dangerfield?' Arslanoglou asked, as he bowed over her hand.

'Should we have met?'

He laughed. 'Why not? Anyway, I hope we shall meet again.' He looked down at the gold watch on his wrist: 'I must go, Robert. I have to play tennis with the daughters of the American admiral. Do you play tennis?' He turned back to Rosamund, and as the light of the setting sun fell on his cheekbone the skin looked so smooth that she wondered if it were perhaps powdered.

'Sometimes.'

'Then we must play together.'

'Really, what impudence!' Robert exclaimed, as soon as the Greek's footsteps on the stone passage outside could no more be heard. His face expressed the mixture of bewilderment and hurt feelings which seemed to be his most usual response to the events at the Institute. 'Do you know why that chap came to see me?'

'No.' Rosamund shifted a pile of exam papers and perched on Robert's desk. 'Why?'

'He's in for a Council scholarship. So, as he sings in my madrigal group, he thought he would persuade me to give him a helping hand. Extraordinary, isn't it?'

Rosamund laughed, but she realized that Robert, who was fiddling with the tops of the pens and pencils that stuck out of the pocket of his crumpled linen jacket, was far from amused.

'I find it sickening. I don't want to see the chap again – even though he has got a damned good voice.'

'But surely, Robert, there's nothing wrong with that sort of thing in this country. Everyone does it.'

'Not in this Institute.'

'No, of course not. But it's silly to feel aggrieved if someone makes a mistake. Daddy's always having to return presents. I was pretty sick the other day, I can tell you, when he made me refuse a bracelet.'

'Oh, I suppose you're right.' A drop of sweat ran down Robert's cheek and trickled on to his collar. 'I know Costa's one idea is to get himself to England. And really he's the best of this year's candidates.'

'I should have thought he was rich enough to go to England without Council help.'

'Rich? Good God, no! He's nothing but a clerk in a coal business.'

'But I thought – he *looks* so –'

'Oh, like all of them, he puts all his worldly wealth on his back – or into his teeth.' Robert's teeth, which were blue where they had not been stained brown by his pipe, had obviously never received the same lavish treatment. 'I can bet you that there was probably a lunch of bread and olives under that expensive belt. No, Costa's not rich. But you'll find him wherever the rich go.'

They continued to talk about other subjects, until the bell rang for Robert's class; then Rosamund wandered out into the heat of the afternoon. She walked the few yards that separated the Institute from the Yacht Club but, seeing her friends seated in groups of five and six under the gaudily striped umbrellas of the terrace, she merely waved back to them as they waved to her and continued on her way. Soon the road up which she was drifting petered out in a jungle of barbed wire, corrugated-iron sheds and piles of rusty tin-cans. Three old women, shrouded in black, sat and gossiped in the doorway of an old Army Nissen hut and hid their faces behind dirt-seamed hands as they saw her approach. A goat was cropping the yellow vegetation that sprouted in a dried-up water course while, nearby, a couple of half-naked boys rolled in the dust. They seemed to be wrestling; but as Rosamund walked past them she realized to her horror that they were doing something else. Then all her desire to explore this part of the town – it was called Tomba, because there was a tomb on the hill, supposedly of a Macedonian king – suddenly died within her. She became aware of the flies that she had repeatedly to brush from her lips; of an odour, sweet and clinging as chloroform, that tainted the air; of the hostility or the weary indifference on the faces of those she passed. Hurrying now, she stumbled over the stones of the unmade road as she returned to the Yacht Club.

Yet her dissatisfaction persisted. Here she was, a week later, with three pink-faced young men who worked under her father, and two girls, one from the Institute and the other from the Consulate. She knew that if she said something intended to be funny, the others would laugh; probably they would be genuinely amused – it was not hard to amuse them – but even if they were not amused, they would laugh nonetheless. She would dance with Willy, the young lieutenant who was differentiated from the two pink-faced young men by his small, clipped moustache, and she knew that it would be easy to arouse him to a pitch of physical excitement that he would find almost intolerable. When she wanted the orchestra to play the Greek dances which the Greeks never wanted, she would only have to mention this fact and the dances would be played. Such was the importance of Colonel Dangerfield; and, to be fair to herself, such was her charm.

One of the other young men was telling a long and confused story about a trip he had made into Yugoslavia, when the back axle of his car had broken, and the girl from the Consulate was repeating: 'Oh, but how awful! How too, too awful!' She had only come to Greece from South London two months ago, but she had already mastered the idiom, if not the accent, of this set.

A hand rested lightly on Rosamund's shoulder: 'Mademoiselle.' She turned round and looked up; Arslanoglou was behind her. 'May I have this dance?'

'Will you excuse me?' Rosamund said to her party. She knew that as soon as she had left the table, they would all forget the axle broken in 'Jugland' and start questioning each other about the Greek stranger. They would remark on the flashiness of his white shark-skin dinner jacket and on the blood-stone which he wore in a ring on his little finger. She would be lucky if the word 'gigolo' were not used.

'You looked so bored,' Costa said. 'And I was bored too.' There was a kind of sensual languor in his voice. 'Were you bored?'

'No, of course not.' Rosamund, never disloyal to her friends and countrymen, all but snapped out her answer.

They danced on in silence; and really, she thought, how wonderful it was to be partnered by someone whose hands were not sticky, whose feet did not shuffle, and whose breath did not hiss audibly in one's ear. Yet at the same time she felt the kind of sickness that overcame her when she spent too long in the sun; the same kind of sickness that she had experienced that afternoon when she had hurried back from Tomba.

'Do you like this?' Costa was asking.

'Yes. Do you?'

He grinned. 'Just the job.' The phrase, which she knew he must have picked up during the British occupation, seemed to have acquired an even more jarring vulgarity when spoken by him. 'I love everything English, you know. Your English waltzes – your English books – your English food –' He looked down at her and squeezed her hand as he added: 'And, of course, your English girls.'

Really it was insufferable; and yet, spoken in that sensuously languorous voice of his, the words had a power to which some mysterious part of her being was forced to respond. She felt revulsion, certainly, and even a kind of horror; and yet she was being drawn into the tunnel with a no less certain fascination.

'May I not have the next dance too?'

'No, I'm sorry. You see, I am with a party of friends.'

'Ah, those young officers who dance in their walking shoes – and the women with too much powder on their faces?'

She turned away at this insolence, but he caught her arm and said: 'Then another evening you must come out with me. Yes?'

'Oh, I don't know.'

'I shall telephone you.'

Colonel Dangerfield did not like his daughter to go out alone or with strangers. Once, during the civil war, someone had fired a shot at him in a restaurant, and since then he had received a number of those threatening anonymous letters that are so freely sent in Greece. He was a man apparently hearty and careless, but in fact of an almost morbid sensibility, and it was now fixed in his mind that the town was full of people determined to 'get' either him or his daughter. Rosamund was his only child, and he lavished on her the affection which an inner timidity prevented him from bestowing on his men. People said that he was 'friendly' and 'charming'; but they realized, after they had known him for a little, that his friendliness and charm were no more than an effort to keep on good terms with a world which he both disliked and dreaded.

On the night that Rosamund was invited out by Costa Arolanoglou, the Colonel insisted that his driver should take her to the Anglo-Hellenic League, wait there for her and then drive her back.

The evening began with Costa indulging in a kind of banter which perpetually hovered on the verge either of insolence or impropriety. Rosamund told herself that conversation of this kind often passed for wit between Greek men and women, and that she was being insular to resent it. They were sitting alone together at a table in a corner of the square, high-ceilinged room, and from time to time they would get up to dance to the clatter and twang of an ancient cottage piano. Few people whom Rosamund knew came to the League, which was considered socially inferior to the Yacht Club, and since Costa's conversation revealed a persistent, if muted, snobbery she could only suppose that he had brought her here because it cost so little. At ten o'clock, however, Robert appeared in dusty grey flannels and open-necked khaki shirt, a pipe in his mouth, and joined them while his wife danced with a teacher from the Institute. He was obviously surprised at finding Rosamund with Costa.

Soon after he had sat down, one of his students, a beautiful girl, walked past and said good evening both to him and to Rosamund. Costa looked after her and then, turning his glass of 'ouzo' in the fingers of his left hand, he murmured a word in Greek; his enormous, dark eyes under the gracefully arched eyebrows were fixed on the drink.

'What did you say?' Robert asked in incredulity; he spoke Greek fluently.

'Oh, nothing.' Costa now looked up at them and laughed. 'I know that girl.'

'You had no right to say what you did.' Robert tweaked the bulbous end of his nose between his finger and thumb – a gesture habitual to him when he was annoyed or nervous.

'Oh, everyone knows that she does as much business as the Corinth Canal,' Costa said airily.

There was a silence during which Robert's face reddened; then he pushed back his chair, said a curt 'Good night, Rosamund,' and made his way back to his own table.

'Oh, you English – you are so *prim*! But I love it; I love your primness; yes, really, I love it. And probably our Mr Robert Burnett knows that girl better than any man in this room.' At this point Costa smiled at Rosamund and, unbelievably, gave an outrageous wink.

'I think I must be going.'

'Going!' He looked at his watch. 'But it is not yet eleven.'

'The car is waiting, and I musn't keep the driver up too late. . . . My father is very strict.' As she added this, she felt guilty of a disloyalty to the tall, white-haired man with the broken nose and the shrapnel-marks on his cheek, who, at this moment, sat in his study reading Palamas as he waited for her return.

For a while Costa and she argued, until, with a shrug of his shoulders, he gave way and helped her with her coat. But when they were out in the street, he said: 'Just come and look at the sea. There is a full moon; the water will be beautiful. . . . Look, your driver is sleeping. Why do you want to wake him? He is probably dreaming of his sweetheart, who is waiting for him on some far-off island. Yes' – he peered into the Daimler – 'he is even smiling as he dreams.'

Rosamund knew that the driver was already unhappily married, but she did not spoil the illusion.

'Oh, very well,' she said.

The sea was indeed as beautiful as Costa had said. Here along the quay, the air was heavy with the aroma of lemons piled high on the bobbing caïques. From the deck of one caïque a cigarette glowed; from another floated a song, followed by gusts of ribald laughter. The moon was low, the sky full of stars.

'Do you think that same moon is shining over England?'

'Why not?' Rosamund answered tartly. 'There is only one moon, isn't there?'

'Ah, you are so unromantic,' Costa sighed, taking her hand in his. 'But I am Greek, and I am romantic. And I would like to say to the moon, "Moon, little moon, take a message for me to England. As you shine over the green meadows, tell her that a Greek, Costa Arslanoglou, dreams much of her, and loves her, and will come one day to visit her." ' The extravagance of this apostrophe seemed absurd to Rosamund; and the absurdity seemed somehow to be increased by Costa's pronunciation of the first syllable of 'meadow' to rhyme with 'bead'.

But there was nothing absurd about the kiss that then followed, on the vast, deserted quay, with the lights winking out of the darkness, the air heavy with the scent of lemons, and the body of the young Greek crudely insistent through his summer clothes.

They walked back to the car in a silence which Rosamund only broke as he opened the door for her: 'Can't I give you a lift? Do you live far away?'

'Yes, far away. I shall take the tram.'

'But surely – where do you live?'

'Oh, in one of the suburbs. You must go alone like a fairy princess, in your carriage. The tram is good enough for me, a mere mortal.'

When the car was moving, nausea suddenly swept over Rosamund in wave after choking wave. She looked for her bag to get herself a cigarette; and when she found that she had not got it with her, it was a measure of her distrust of Costa that she should, for a moment, imagine that he had taken it. Then she realized that she had probably left it at the Anglo-Hellenic League, and she called to the driver to take her back.

On their return journey they passed the tram stop and Rosamund saw that Costa was still waiting; he had lit a cigarette, and his shark-skin dinner jacket gleamed through the darkness. The bag was, as she had expected, by their table at the League, and now once again the powerful car was carrying her to her home. This time there was a tram at the stop, and Costa was boarding it; he did not hurry, but took a last puff at his cigarette, threw it into the gutter, and then swung himself on to the platform. Rosamund first waved, but he obviously did not see her; afterwards she turned, as the car swept past, and looked from the back window.

Across the front of the tram was the single word 'Tomba'. Sparks scattered down from the long metallic arm as the mustard-coloured box lurched through the darkness.

When, two days later, Rosamund was again driven down to meet Costa at the League, he at once said: 'Look, this League is so boring. Let us walk up to the old fortifications and watch the sun set. There is a tavern there where they play Greek music and do the old Greek dances.'

'It sounds marvellous. But really I don't think we'd better. Daddy fusses terribly, and he's told the driver that he's to see that I spend the evening here. The driver isn't even allowed to go away and come back.'

'But that's absurd!'

'Is it? Yes, I suppose it is.'

'Look – wait a moment!' Costa made for the car.

'What are you going to do?'

He gave his brilliant smile as he replied: 'Just wait and see.' He had drawn out his wallet.

He and the driver whispered together, Costa leaning in at the window of the car, for a few seconds; then he returned to announce: 'Well, that's all right.'

'All right? What do you mean?'

'How do you say in English – "money always talks".'

Rosamund made as if to go to the car; her mouth was already open to tell the driver to stay, to order him to give back Costa's bribe, and to threaten to report him to her father. But with the gentlest of swerves the gleaming grey and black Daimler had already turned the corner and had passed from their sight. And, in her heart, Rosamund knew that she was glad that this had happened.

Strangely, their path to the fortifications was that up which she wandered on the day she had first met Costa; and since she now guessed that he must live here at Tomba, it was with difficulty that she restrained herself from asking him to show her his house. But she knew, as they passed these endless avenues of corrugated-iron shacks, that he would feel ashamed if she did so; perhaps he might even imagine that she had returned that night in the car deliberately to spy on him. 'Oh, how ugly it is here,' he kept exclaiming. 'How ugly it is!' He wrinkled up his nose in what she could only suppose was a genuine disgust; and then she pitied him both for his poverty and for having to maintain this pretence of riches.

All at once they were passing the dried-up water course where she had seen the two half-naked boys; and though such frankness would, in the past, have been wholly alien to her nature, she now began to tell him of her experience. She told it, not as a joke, but as something squalid and shocking; and therefore she felt it insensitive of him both to guffaw and then to exclaim: 'Poor devils!. . . You see they are too poor to have any toys with which to play.' Once again he had revealed the thread of peasant coarseness which seemed to her so often to run through the characters of even the most civilized Greeks.

Perhaps it was her annoyance at this remark that made her feel, when they at last reached the fortifications, that the view was not worth the climb; or perhaps that evening the sunset, usually so magnificent over the bay, was in truth a disappointment. There were wisps of grey cloud, tinged at the edges with the dullness of copper, but the sun itself was lost, and Olympus drifted in an ever-deepening haze. A wind had risen to parch the already dry skin and to whirl dust into the eyes and on to the lips. Within the fortifications there was a stretch of baked mud where some youths were playing football. Rosamund and Costa stopped to watch them, but there was something oppressive in their tattered clothes and savage, absorbed faces under darkly matted hair, and soon they hurried on.

What came next had all the hideous fascination of Rosamund's half-waking fantasies. At last she had reached the end of the tunnel, and as she lay, eyes wide in horror, under the shadow of a ruined buttress, while far off she could hear the football still thudding back and forth in the dimming light of evening, it seemed to her that she had known and suffered all this before and that, in some strange way, this experience now, for all its overwhelming horror and pain and beauty, was but a copy or a memory of another experience, at another time, in another place.

As they walked back down the hill, Costa said: 'Tomorrow I have my board.' He put his arm round her.

'What board?'

'For my scholarship to England. Don't you remember? Your father will be chairman.'

'Oh, yes, yes.'

'Wouldn't it be wonderful if I could win? I hear that next month you and your father will go. That is true, is it?'

'Yes. We shall go.' She felt a curious disinterestedness; but she did not yet know if this were the disinterestedness of extreme happiness or of extreme despair.

'I *must* win the scholarship. Otherwise I should never see you again, after you leave.' Suddenly she realized that as they walked, arms linked, his body was trembling. 'You will speak to your father, won't you?'

'Speak to him? What do you mean?'

'Oh, you know how to do it. Tell him how much I want to visit England – tell him that you like me. If you do like me,' he added with a grin.

'But, Costa, you don't understand –' She stopped, dismayed both at his inability to understand and at hers to explain.

'You want me to come to England, don't you?'

'Yes, of course, but –'

'Well, then, speak to your father.' As he spoke these words his voice was gentle and pleading; and yet the pressure of his arm about her waist seemed to express all the desperate urgency of a life-time.

'You're home very late.' Her father rose to his feet as she came into the study; but before he accepted her kiss, he was careful to slip a used envelope between the pages of his book, so that he could again find his place. 'What have you been up to?' His scarred face, with its broken, boxer's nose would have looked brutal in the transverse beam of the reading lamp were it not for the diffidently unhappy expression of the small green eyes. 'What have you been up to?'

'It's only just eleven o'clock, father.' She felt afraid to place her lips on his forehead, as though, from the mere touch of them, he could guess that another's lips had rested there. 'What have you been doing?'

'Oh, I drowsed off while I was reading this book.' He gave an involuntary shiver, although even in a dressing-gown and pyjamas, one could not feel cold on a summer night like this. 'I must get up early tomorrow, I have this wretched board.'

'What board?'

'Oh, it's these Council scholarships; they always get an outsider to be chairman. Damned nuisance really.'

'I think that must be what Costa was talking about.'

'Costa?' He reopened his book and looked down at the page, as though he were quickly reading something of importance; then he gazed up at her: 'And who is Costa?'

'This Greek I was with tonight. He's trying for a scholarship. Costa Arslanoglou.'

'Oh, I see.' He laughed, and closed the book with a snap. 'Has he been making love to you in order to get a scholarship?'

'What on earth do you mean? No, of course not. You know that we spent the evening at the League.' She was afraid now and wondered whether her father knew about the bribe to the driver: the man might, conceivably, have confessed.

'Don't take it so seriously,' the Colonel reassured her. 'Can't you see a joke? . . . Who is this Arslanoglou anyway?'

'Oh, I don't know. He's a friend of Robert Burnett; he sings in his madrigal group. He seems extremely intelligent and charming. I should have thought he was very much the kind of person it would pay the Council to send to England.'

Colonel Dangerfield smiled; it was a lop-sided smile because of the tautness of the skin where the shrapnel had marked him. 'That we shall see tomorrow, shan't we?' He went and fastened each of the study windows with an unhurried deliberation, and then turned back to her: 'Well, good night, old girl.'

'Good night, father.' Again her lips touched his forehead; and again she suffered the irrational dread that by this contact she would betray all the events of the evening.

Colonel Dangerfield went out and Rosamund could hear him whistling softly to himself, 'Leise, leise', as he climbed the stairs to bed.

Costa was alone on the terrace of the Yacht Club. He sat on one chair, his feet were on another, and his right arm dangled over the back of a third. Every five minutes he would take a sip from his glass of Coca Cola. He wanted it to last him until he went home to dinner.

'Costa!' Rosamund had stepped off the yacht of a friend and now ran over. But as she approached, in white shorts and blouse, she noticed how slowly he removed his legs from the chair; how slowly and how faintly he smiled; and how reluctantly he heaved himself up to greet her. 'How did the board go?'

He looked at her, and his face seemed yellow and strained. 'Sit down,' he said quietly; and when she had done so, he added in the same quiet voice: 'You did not speak to your father.'

'But, Costa, I did.'

The skin of his face looked as if it might crack as he smiled again and answered: 'I do not believe you.'

'I swear, Costa, that when I got in last night –'

'What does it matter? He did everything to humiliate and hurt me. He wanted to make me look a fool, and he succeeded.' He laughed, and took a sip from the misty glass before him: 'That is the English way. It did not surprise me.'

'But, Costa –'

'Oh, let us talk of something else. What will you have to drink! A Coca Cola?' He clapped his hand for the boy. 'Don't worry – I shall get to England somehow. Yes, I shall get there in the end.'

It was in silence that they now sipped their drinks; and Costa, who had trained himself to linger for an hour over each such glass, finished this one within five minutes. He got up to go, explaining that his mother expected him home to dinner: 'I shall telephone,' he said. But the call never came.

Two weeks later the mission on which Colonel Dangerfield had been serving was recalled to England, and finding himself put on the retired list, he bought a house and some acres of land in the West Country. After some argument, he allowed Rosamund to take a one-room flat of her own in a London block where one of his sisters already lived, and to start work as apprentice to an antique dealer in the Old Brompton Road. With a mixture of relief and nagging dissatisfaction Rosamund resumed the threads of her old life: the parties in Kensington and Regent's Park; the afternoons swimming at Roehampton; and the uneasy weekends in the country with her father.

A month after she had returned to England, she received a picture postcard from Rhodes, with the words 'All the best' and a signature which at first she could not read. It was a measure of her dissociation from her whole life in Greece that it was not she, but a friend, who eventually deciphered the scrawl as being 'Costa'. That same night, however, Rosamund had a dream of lying in the shadow of the fortifications – this time, alone – while, nearer and nearer, she could hear the football thud. Soon it would strike her, and when it did so, some terrible disaster would follow. But the next day that dream was soon forgotten, and Costa was forgotten with it.

Another postcard came many weeks later: 'How are you? I think that soon I shall reach England. It will be wonderful to see you again', and to this one she sent back a few conventional words. Then a letter came; but it was no more than the communication of an acquaintance to an acquaintance, and Rosamund answered on the same detached note. But now as she moved through her crowded agreeable life she seemed more and more to sink back into that old fantasy of hers of humiliation, or pain, or profound unhappiness; and she no longer knew whether it was with dread or with longing that she thought of these things.

One evening, when she had raced back from her work to change for a party, the telephone rang and she heard a voice say: 'Is that Miss Dangerfield?'

'Yes.' It was not Costa's voice; it was a voice brisker and far more matter-of-fact, it had the trace of a Cockney twang. And yet even at that moment she divined that it was connected with Costa.

'This is the Immigration Officer, Dover, speaking. I wonder if you can tell me – are you expecting a visitor from Greece?'

'Well, yes . . . in a way. . . . Do you mean Mr Arslanoglou?'

'Yes, that's the gentleman. Is he going to stay with you?'

'Stay with me?' Rosamund was a fundamentally honest person; and when such people are taken off their guard, they always speak the truth. 'Oh, no – that would be impossible. There'd never be any suggestion of that, I think.'

'Oh. I see.' There was a momentary silence at the other end, while Rosamund tried to picture to herself the man to whom she was talking. 'Mr Arslanoglou insisted that he would be your guest while in England. . . . I'm going to be frank with you, Miss – Miss Dangerfield. The fact is that he's arrived here with only four pounds and nine dollars in his pocket, no return ticket, and no other visible means of support. Actually this is not the first lie in which we have caught him out – he had six hundred Greek cigarettes in his bag, none of which he declared. I'm going to admit to you that we regard him with some suspicion.'

'But I can assure you, he's entirely honest – entirely respectable.'

'Well, the position is this. We obviously can't let him into this country unless somebody is willing to guarantee his fare back to Greece. Are you prepared to do that? It involves a sum of about thirty pounds.'

For a moment Rosamund thought: her allowance was decent, even if not lavish, but she lived well and seldom saved more than a few pounds a month; obviously she could not ask her father to help with a loan; but if she did not do so, she would entirely use up her balance at the bank. 'The money will have to be deposited with us,' the voice now added.

'Yes, very well. Yes, I'll do that.'

'First, however, we shall have to check on some other details in the gentleman's story. Have you any idea why he should come to England?'

'I suppose he'd like to find some work over here. That's what I gathered from his letters.'

'Some work?' A sharp upward inflection. 'Yes, I see. Because his visa is made out for "business purposes". That, of course, we must check. . . . Well, anyway, thank you, Miss Dangerfield. We'll get in touch with you tomorrow morning about the deposit.'

Rosamund did not go to the party; instead, she lay on the divan which at night became her bed, and smoked cigarette after cigarette as she stared out of the window at the lights of the Thames. There was already a touch of autumn in the air, and some dead leaves had blown in through the window and scraped along the parquet. Over and over, she repeated to herself the conversation with the Immigration Officer, and each time she found in it some new insinuation of his or some new clumsiness of her own. Costa had intended to come and live with her, and she had repudiated that suggestion; and in doing so she had repudiated, once and for all, that evening among the ruined fortifications which (she at last realized) had become the watershed from which her whole emotional life would henceforth always flow. Cigarette after cigarette burned away between her nerveless fingers while she thought now of the two half-naked boys struggling in the dust; now of the moon shining on the vast, empty quay; and now of no more than a gold chain resting on a strip of bare sunburned flesh.

Next morning the Immigration Officer was again on the telephone. 'I'm afraid we can't let that Mr Arslanoglou in – in spite of your kind offer to guarantee his return fare. Frankly we now regard him with the greatest suspicion. We checked up on that "business visa" and as far as we can make out he has no business here whatever. He can't tell us what firms he has come to see. He can't even give us any reference except you. . . . It seems altogether pretty fishy to arrive with only four pounds and nine dollars in one's pocket, no return ticket, and a number of lies. We don't like the man, and we don't like his behaviour.'

'And where is he now?'

'Oh, we've sent him back to France.'

Four weeks later a letter arrived for Rosamund. There were no words of thanks for her offer to guarantee the thirty pounds, and no regret for having told a number of foolish falsehoods. There was not even an explanation of whether Costa had, in fact, intended to come and live with her, so that she could never really know the extent of what she had lost through a life-long habit of honesty. All that the letter contained were a number of reproaches; but it was hard to tell whether these were intended for her or the Immigration Officer or the English in general:

'. . . You know how much I love England,' the letter concluded. 'You know I have always thought only of coming to visit her. And then to be treated as a smuggler and a spy! I no longer understand the English, and I no longer trust them. I do not wish to have anything more to do with them. I should have learned my lesson when I failed to get the scholarship, but I was foolish, and now I have to learn it again. Never have I been so hurt and humiliated in my life.'

As she cried on her bed, grief brought a lucidity during which Rosamund wondered whether Costa would ever learn his lesson; and whether he had even for a moment guessed the extent to which the hurt and humiliation were not his, but her own.

1950

Sundays

'Did you remember to bring the Sundays, darling?'

'No, I left them on the plane.'

'Fuck!'

A few moments later a boy joined the man and the woman in the garden of the villa. 'Did Daddy remember to bring the Sundays?'

'No, Mark, your father did not remember to bring the Sundays. In spite of my reminding him on the telephone last night.'

'Oh, fuck!'

'You mustn't use that word, Mark. You know I've told you not to use that word. It's an ugly, inexpressive word that suggests a certain poverty.'

'Well, you're always going on about how poor we are.'

'I meant poverty of imagination and vocabulary.'

'I suppose I could get into the car and drive all the way back to Milan before shaving or having any breakfast or unpacking, and say to someone at the Alitalia desk, "Please could I have the Sunday papers that I left on the plane because my dear wife and my dear son seem to be unable to survive without them." '

'I hardly think that'll be necessary, though it's generous of you to offer. We'll survive.'

'You could get them in Como, Daddy. They'll probably have them in Como by now. They usually do by Monday.'

'Daddy is not going to waste a lot of petrol by going into Como. If you want them that badly, then you can go into Como yourself.'

'*I* don't want them that badly. I thought that you did.'

Mrs Newman listened to her daughter, son-in-law and grandson from the half-open window of her bedroom, as she sat before her dressing-table mirror, bunching up handful after handful of her dry wispy hair and stabbing it with hairpins. She held two hairpins between her teeth and another rested in the soft fleece of her bedjacket, where it had fallen unregarded. Her eyes ached as though from the flash of those swords striking against each other down there in the garden, among the deck-chairs and the breakfast crockery and the sleeping dogs.

'There was something I particularly wanted to see in the *Observer* supplement, Mummy. It really is too bad!'

'Well, you can't, that's all. There arc at least a hundred paperbacks in the sitting-room that you can read.'

'I've read them.'

'Not all of them. Don't talk nonsense. Or, if a book is beyond your powers, how about some weeding?'

'I thought that Giovanni was supposed to do the weeding.'

'Giovanni can't do everything all the time. Even if we do pay him more than anyone else ever paid any gardener on Lake Como.'

'This coffee's cold, Ellen.'

'Well, of course it's cold, darling. We had breakfast ages ago.'

'Couldn't you make some more? Or is that asking too much?'

'Oh, do make it yourself. You can see I've settled down to sunbathe.'

'That's a nice welcome when I've flown all the way over here to be with you for less than a week.'

'Oh, Christ, I feel depressed!'

'No boy of fifteen has any right to feel depressed. At your age I didn't know the meaning of the word. Depressed! Why, you've got *everything*!'

'You've got to admit, Jack, there's something terribly lowering about this lake.'

'Then why the hell did you decide that you must have a villa here? For God's sake, surely it isn't unreasonable of me to expect some hot coffee when I arrive here all the way from London for less than a week.'

'*I* decided that I must have a villa here? I did no such thing. I said that it would be nice to have some kind of retreat in Italy. It was you who then, in your infinite wisdom, picked on this hole.'

The swords flashed on in the sunlit garden beneath her; but she looked out over them to the calm lake, iridescent scarves of mist draping its further corners and trailing over the sides of the mountains. There were three tourist buses far down there, outside the Hotel Bellevue, and if she screwed up her eyes against the low morning sun, she could see women in brightly coloured frocks and men in brightly coloured shirts and trousers clambering aboard. She remembered the clop-clop-clop of hooves up and down what had not then been a highway but a narrow winding road. She remembered the small, bow-legged hunchback, like some wizened former jockey, who sold rose-scented nougat from a funny little stall on wheels. She remembered a parasol that she had lost, forgotten on the boat most probably, its handle the head of a swan carved in ivory. She remembered the sweating, hairy men who played *boccia* on the green space beyond and behind the hotel and how they would stare at her or any of the other foreign women, their loud, angry-seeming voices (of course they were not really angry) falling away as they did so.

'You remember nothing. *Nothing*. I've only to ask you to do something for you to forget it.'

'I have more important things to remember than the Sundays. Such as earning enough money to keep you and that bone-idle son of yours in luxury in this villa. Not to mention your mother.'

'My bone-idle son – or, rather, *our* bone-idle son – has just finished a strenuous term.'

'I'll believe in that "strenuous" when I see his report.'

The swords continued to flash and the ache between her eyes gathered itself into a tighter and tighter knot. Mrs Newman splashed some eau de cologne on to a handkerchief and held it first to one and then to the other shrunken cheek. The flesh tingled comfortingly. Then she sighed, picked up her bag, grasped her stick with its rubber ferrule. She had had another better stick, the handle of which seemed to fit itself exactly to her small, arthritic hand, but the boy had broken it while using it for some undivulged purpose – bird-nesting? nutgathering? – in the woods above the villa.

Out in the garden she kissed her son-in-law – this stocky, blue-chinned, balding businessman whom she always felt, even after all these years, to be a stranger. At such times he always put a hand on each of her shoulders as though he were about to force her to her knees in submission to his will. His cheek tasted rough and salt on her lips.

'Daddy forgot to bring the Sundays.'

'Now, look here, I don't want to hear another fucking word about those fucking Sundays.'

'Must you use that word in front of mother?'

'It can't be the first time she's heard it in this household.'

'Where are you going, Granny?'

'For a stroll. Just for a stroll.'

'For heaven's sake, mother! Why do you want to go out for a stroll? It's going to be a scorcher. We don't need the Sundays to tell us that. Come and sit down here in the garden with us.'

'Make yourself some coffee, mother. And make me some too while you're about it, since neither this wife nor this son of mine seems disposed to do so.'

'God, what a depressing morning!'

'No woman with as little to do as you has any right to feel depressed. If you were Giovanni's wife, you would be taking in other people's washing.'

'And if I were his daughter, I'd be walking the streets of Milan. Yes, I know.'

Mrs Newman let herself out of the rusty iron gate with its enamel plate '*Attenti ai cani*', even though the two dogs did nothing but sleep and eat, and then began the slow descent down the cobbled *muletiere*. Whoever had constructed it had obviously misjudged the extent of a human pace. To go from each level to the next, it was necessary either to take a giant stride or to take one normal step followed by a child's one. Behind the high wall, trailing its wistaria (it was strange that wistaria no longer seemed to have any scent) she could hear the scrape and clash of those three swords against each other.

An old man in boots and a shiny black alpaca coat, a sack over his shoulder, was mounting towards her. He paused, a hand pressed to the small of his back, and beamed at her, revealing chipped, nicotine-stained teeth. '*Buon' giorno, Signora.*' His breath wheezed and whistled. Before Giovanni, it was he who had tended the garden as he had done for more than forty years; but there had been angry words, most of them unintelligible to him though he had understood their gist, and he had never come back. The family told all their neighbours that he had let them down disgracefully; but since he had been owed several thousand lire, which they had made no attempt to pay him, he might have said the same of them.

'*Buon' giorno, Bruno,*' Mrs Newman replied. She would have liked to have paused for a little to have a conversation with him in her execrable Italian but loyalty prevented her. 'Must you talk to that horrible old man after the way that he's behaved to us?' her daughter had once demanded viciously when she had come on the two of them exchanging a few words by the gate.

The little hydrofoil – her son-in-law had laughed at its 'thoroughly pretentious' name, *La Freccia delle Azalee*, 'the arrow of the azaleas' – was skimming across the lake. It was not really graceful but it looked graceful from here – like some swan, she thought fancifully, flying low above the water. She wondered if she would reach the quay in time, the boat must be early; and then, as she hurried on, the toe of her left shoe caught against a cobble and she fell heavily against the wall on that side. Now that she was old, she noticed that she bled easily. Where the rough stones had grazed her forearm, small beads of crimson were already beginning to swell. She held a handkerchief, drawn from the waistband of her dress, to them, her lips drawn in, in frowning concentration; and so intent was she on doing this that at first she was wholly unaware of the throbbing of her ankle. But the throbbing intensified; and as she walked on, leaning heavily now on the stick that fitted so uncomfortably to her hand, it was as if, somewhere in her ankle, two small bones were rasping against each other. I wonder if I've broken something? But if I have, surely I couldn't go on walking?

The boatman saw her hobbling down the steps and, because they were early, he decided to wait. But she did not know that and so she hobbled even faster, waving her stick to catch his attention and even calling out in her heavily accented Italian, '*Aspetta! Momento! Vengo!*'

She bought her return ticket and the boatman held out a hand to her, the palm dry and calloused, to help her along the narrow gangway. She gasped, '*Grazie! Grazie mille!*' and made her way into the stifling cabin, which was full of Italian women with baskets and children, a group of local schoolboys sprawled out over the seats and puffing ostentatiously at cigarettes even though a notice said '*Vietato fumare*', and about a dozen young German tourists in the skimpiest of clothes. She looked round for somewhere to sit and a beautiful German girl, with a skin so translucent that the sun slanting through the porthole seemed to shine through it to the perfect bones beneath, got up and pointed: '*Bitte.*' She was wearing the shortest of shorts, ragged at the ends, and a blouse that obviously had no brassière beneath it.

'Oh, no, my dear. . . .' Mrs Newman said, feeling strangely

breathless at the nearness of the girl's youth and health and beauty.
'Please.' This time it was said in English.

At that, Mrs Newman sat down. She let her head fall back on the
greasy rest behind it, oblivious of the handkerchief, now encrusted
with dried blood, that was wrapped about her forearm, of the throbbing of her ankle and of the shouts and scuffles of the schoolboys.
She loved the eagerness and freshness of that girl and her compan-
ions, their solemn faces suddenly lighting up as the sun picked out
now one stretch and now another of the lake, making it flash with
fire. '*Schön! Wunderbar! Sehr schön!*'

Once the girl turned and smiled down at her and between them
there was suddenly this strange complicity, though they had never
seen each other before and probably would never see each other
again. The breeze was cool on her bare arms and her throat and her
forehead. She could see the Hotel Bellevue through the porthole and
she remembered once again that rose-scented taste of the nougat and
the sweating, hairy men with their swelling forearms, their loud
shouts and laughter and the frank, almost brutal way in which they
stared at any of the foreign women who passed. The three tourist
buses had gone.

It was hot when she stepped off the boat, the boatman again
holding out to her that dry, calloused hand. He had long drooping
moustaches and hair parted as though by an incision down the
centre of his skull, like some Edwardian masher in the Hotel
Bellevue all those years and years ago. '*Buon' divertimento*,' he
said, which amused her. What sort of '*divertimento*' am I likely to
find at my age? she felt like asking.

She inquired at the first kiosk, to which they usually went, but the
woman shrugged her shoulders from inside her little box and then
said that either the Sundays had not come or else, with all these
foreign tourists, they must have sold out. She seemed neither to
know nor to care. Mrs Newman said, '*Grazie*' with a slight inclination of her head; but the woman had returned to her reading of *Oggi*
and paid no attention.

The street up to the cathedral seemed far longer than she remembered it and there were so many people walking along, often arms
linked or pushing prams or leading the large dogs that had recently
become so fashionable. It was hard to avoid them and they often
made no effort to avoid her. The handkerchief slipped off her forearm. After she had picked it up, stooping with difficulty on the
crowded piazza, she decided not to replace it, since it must have

271

gathered dust. She stuffed it into her bag. The dried blood had made it as crisp as a dead leaf.

She at last reached the kiosk by the cathedral. The Germans had got there before her and she waited patiently while they flicked over a magazine full of photographs of nude women and giggled and commented noisily. One of the boys would snatch the magazine from whoever was holding it and then it would be snatched in turn from him. They jostled and pushed each other while the girls looked on with indulgent smiles. At last Mrs Newman was able to get at the Sundays and paid out what seemed to be an exorbitant price for them. Almost two pounds, she reckoned. Then she began to hobble back. Yes, definitely, quite definitely, her ankle was swelling. But she had the Sundays, that gave her a quiet feeling of triumph.

She sat on a stone bench on the quay, a thin, bent, not particularly attractive old woman in a pink shantung dress, a pink straw hat and old-fashioned strap shoes, waiting for the hydrofoil to come skimming, an ungainly metallic swan, over the glittering water towards her. She did not look at the papers, which were far heavier than she had imagined to be possible. Instead, she stared at the lake, which seemed to widen as the sun mounted higher and higher above it, the mountains receding further and further into the pale blue sky, the villas and churches and little clusters of red-roofed houses receding further and further into the dark green foliage. She remembered a little *vaporetto* and a party of six of them, all young and all English; and how they had laughed at her because she had complained of feeling seasick on the short journey from the Hotel Bellevue to Como. A child with a hoop stopped and stared at her with a kind of brutal curiosity; and she stared back and then gave a tentative smile, which the child did not return. The child's mother screeched, laden with parcels, '*Mario! Vieni qua!*' and, with dragging footsteps and many backward glances, the child moved away, the hoop in one hand and the stick in the other.

Again the boatman helped her aboard. He said something about her returning very quickly and she felt too tired now to explain about the Sundays. So she just gave him a smile. After the confusion and noise of the journey out, the boat was now empty except for a couple, as old or older than herself, who sat very stiff, their arms close to their sides, without ever looking at each other or speaking to each other. Both wore black; the woman even had on black stockings and the man a black tie. Perhaps they were returning from or going to a funeral.

The *muletiere* seemed so steep, each cobble glistening, as though it were wet, in the sun that now shone full over the water, that she decided, having taken one or two steps, to turn back and take the road instead, even though it was longer. But she had forgotten that the road had no pavement; so that each time a car whooshed past, she found herself cowering against the wall. It was silly of her, she knew that; there was plenty of room for the two of them. But she could not help herself, the reflex was too strong.

Suddenly she thought, Why shouldn't I try to hitchhike? From time to time her grandson did so, when he was too lazy to climb up from the beach or the shops to the villa. She halted and, when a little red beetle of a car, a Fiat 116, chugged round the bend below her, she made a vague poking gesture up the hill with her forefinger. The car screeched on. But the van that followed stopped. It belonged to the butcher, who, according to Mrs Newman's daughter, always put up his prices for them because they were foreigners. He was a stout, jolly man. She noticed that there were reddish stains round and under his fingernails, of blood she supposed, and that he smelled of raw meat. He asked where she had been and, when she told him, he said, '*E bello il giro*' and she said, Yes, yes indeed. She still felt too tired to try to tell him about the Sundays in her halting Italian.

'Where *have* you been, mother? You got us worried. I do wish you wouldn't just wander off like that.' Her daughter still lay out on the deck-chair, her arms and legs and bare midriff glistening with oil.

'To Como.'

'To Como!' Her son-in-law also lay, almost naked, out in a deck-chair. From inside she could hear that her grandson was playing one of his records. 'For God's sake, turn that down, can't you?' his father bawled.

'I got the Sundays for you.'

'Don't shout at him like that! These *are* his holidays, you know.'

'If he'd play something half-way decent! The Beatles would just be tolerable. But that crap hour by hour!'

There was the screech of the needle being jerked across the record; it sounded to Mrs Newman like someone tearing silk. The boy's face appeared, congested with rage, at the window. 'Can't I ever do anything I want to do?'

'Not if it conflicts with your dear father's wishes.'

'It's time you grew out of the Bay City Rollers. That's for kids.'

'I suppose you want me to listen to Beethoven symphonies all day. Not, I notice, that you've ever bought any.'

'Well, it would be an improvement.'
'Oh, do leave the poor boy alone!'
'I got the Sundays for you.'

No one seemed to hear her. The boy's angry face disappeared from the window. Her daughter replaced her mask over her eyes with a hand glistening with oil. Her son-in-law chewed on his pipe and squinted down at his detective story. She put the Sundays down on an empty deck-chair and went into the house. She knew that none of them would pick them up; none of them would even glance at them. But, strangely, instead of feeling disappointment, she felt an exhilaration. I got them. It wasn't so difficult. In fact, it was rather fun. Quite a little adventure. The nicest day since, oh, I don't know when at this villa.

She put the stick back in its stand, glanced briefly at the graze on her forearm and then hobbled down the hall to the kitchen. As she expected, her daughter had put out the potatoes for her to peel. She always hated to have to do the potatoes herself and she had established this pretence that her mother enjoyed doing them. Mrs Newman began to peel, oblivious of the throbbing of her ankle; eventually the doctor would be summoned and would have to bind it up for her. As she peeled, she sang in a slightly cracked but still firm and true voice: 'Vilia, oh Vilia. . . .' Yes, it had been a lovely morning. She couldn't remember such a lovely morning for a long, long time.

Out in the garden her daughter, son-in-law and grandson – the boy had given up the record-player – listened for a few seconds. Then her son-in-law said: 'Mother seems to be in a very jaunty mood all of a sudden,' and her daughter said: 'I wonder what she's got to be so happy about.'

1976

The Soutane

When the Abbotts came out of the hotel, Lucy called to a plain fifteen-year-old child with thin legs and arms protruding out of a blue cotton frock: 'Oh, Stella, aren't you joining us?' The girl sprawled in a deck-chair reading one of the tattered comics which Lucy had found, when unpacking for her, in a vast bundle, fastened with a hairy length of string, at the bottom of her suitcase.

'Do you want me to join you?' the child asked vaguely.

'Do as you like.' It was hard for Lucy to forgive a daughter who, so totally without distinction, had one day swum too far from the shore of the Cornish village where they were holidaying and, being rescued by her elder brother, then convalescent after a year in a sanatorium, had involuntarily caused his death.

'Then I think I'll read,' the girl said.

As the Abbotts trudged along the mountain path, they neither of them said the things they were thinking: how futile it had been to bring Stella from England to the Dolomites when all she ever cared to do was to sit and read that kind of rubbish; how charmless she was; and how unjust they each secretly thought it that, instead of her, the brilliant, athletic boy who had for sixteen years beguiled them with his showy, almost hysterical charm should now be dead. They seldom spoke about him, but that he obssessed both of them was evident from the incident which now followed.

This was a walk they had never before taken, but many times they had wondered who could live in that square, many-windowed pink house which stood desolate among the 'Ore' – strange-shaped rocks thrusting like so many rust-stained excrescences out of the soil, as though beneath a skin of grass, crops and trees some disruptive poison continually fretted. From this distance it appeared as if some kind of black hangings had been suspended from many of the window-sills of the house, and Lucy suggested that they might be there for mourning. She had been thinking of death, and the spectacle of these blobs of darkness against the sunny pink façade intensified the mood of heaviness that had settled on her as soon as she had left the hotel.

But when they approached nearer to the house they saw that what they had thought were hangings were in fact garments, put out to dry. As the wind nosed itself into their clammily sagging folds, they would make a slapping noise against the pink stucco. There was no other sound, except for the ghostly twitter of a bird, probably a lark, far, far above them.

The Abbotts walked on as the path took them, round the apparently deserted house and so on, twisting between the rust-covered boulders, until they came to a small hill from the other side of which they could hear voices, sudden, yelping cries, the crunch of feet on gravel, and weaving with these common, human sounds an odd, intermittent twanging as though, many times magnified, a harp string were plucked. Breasting the hill, they were astonished to find a playing field with innumerable soutane-clad figures kicking foot-balls, hitting tennis-balls to each other, or wandering in conversation. The twanging noise was being produced by two figures at a little distance from the others, each clutching what appeared to be a tambourine. A black ball volleyed between them, and the two black-robed figures – they were no more than boys – raced tirelessly from side to side, striking it with broad, sweeping movements.

'How hot they must become,' Lucy said, and Henry made one of his jovial, crude jokes about 'the odour of sanctity'. 'How on earth can they move in those extraordinary garments?' Lucy continued, as plaintively as if she herself were being made to chase a ball in yards of black, clinging gaberdine. 'That building must be some kind of monastery, don't you think?'

One of the two players had now begun to trot away, and for a moment the Abbotts turned to watch him as he skidded down an incline, briefly crossed himself before a wayside shrine, and then, cutting across a meadow, made for the pink house. Meanwhile, the other boy pocketed their ball, threw down his tambourine, and negligently threw himself beside it. He had straight, fair hair, the clumsily large hands and physique of a peasant, and a face with high cheekbones and a broad expanse of forehead gleaming with sweat. He lay utterly relaxed, his arms outstretched and his eyes screwed together against the acute dazzle of the afternoon sun. He appeared to be unaware of the two middle-aged Americans, the robustly handsome man and the no less handsome woman, who stood so near watching him

Lucy said: 'He reminds me somehow. . . .' She was thinking of their son who after a game of tennis would lie like that on his back, with the sweat glistening under his fair hair; and though, feature by feature, the peasant boy with the clumsy hands and the black, much-patched boots was wholly unlike that other boy in his blazer and flannels, a resemblance persisted.

'Yes, I thought for a moment . . .' Henry said.

The boy's companion was now trotting back with something – a box, it seemed – under one arm. As he passed the shrine he once again made a little bobbing curtsey and crossed himself before hurling himself up the slope down which he had before slithered. Some yards away he fumbled with the catch of the box and, drawing out a banjo, arrived breathlessly thrusting it at his friend.

The fair boy sat up, crossed his legs before him, and then, having strummed a few notes, began to play, not inexpertly, 'Home Sweet Home'. It was a strange scene: the soutane-clad figures shouting and gesticulating in the distance as they pursued their thudding foot-balls; the two cross-legged boys, one no less absorbed in assimilating the trite melody than the other in producing it; and the American man and woman still standing some twenty yards away with faces averted in a pretence of not listening. For a moment the cloyingly sentimental melody had revived in both of them, almost as acutely as at their first hour of loss, a memory of their boy; it was all but unbearable.

When the notes ceased, Henry walked uncertainly towards the musician. 'Where did you learn that?' he asked in Italian.

The boy looked up and smiled. He had a faint golden down above his upper lip, candid eyes set wide in his almost square countenance, and a nose which, like his ears, seemed surprisingly fine and delicate in a face otherwise so roughly modelled. He explained without any shyness: he was Italian, yes, his family came from Pola, but as a refugee in Naples he had worked as a mess-boy for the Americans, and when they left, one of them had given him this banjo. From them he had learned a little English, he added, and in Africa he had learned more.

'In Africa?' Lucy queried.

Yes, in Africa; he was a missionary. They were all missionaries, and every two or three years they were sent back on holiday. The *collegio* – he pointed to the square pink house – had been built for that purpose. Actually, he had been in Africa for only seventeen months, because – he looked rueful – he had contracted amoebic dysentery and out there it was almost impossible to get rid of the bug.

They talked like this for a time, while the other boy, squat and dark, with a frizz of black hair, remained silently gazing into the banjo on the grass beside him. From time to time he would put out a hand, the back raw as if it had been chapped in a high wind, and would pluck out a note. Then he got up, and still staring down at the banjo, clumsily excused himself before wandering towards the footballers.

'Have we frightened away your friend?' Lucy asked.

'He's shy.'

'Do you have to play in that?' Lucy pointed at the soutane, and made a grimace.

The boy laughed: 'We get used to it.'

'But it seems so pointless,' she almost exclaimed.

After a few more minutes of conversation, Henry said: 'Well, we'd better be getting along. See you some time again,' he added casually.

'I hope so.' The boy again picked up his instrument. As they walked away, they heard him twang his fingers across it three or four times. But then there was silence; and when they looked back, he was once more lying outstretched, with his large-boned peasant's body open, under its soutane, to the dazzle and heat of the sun.

All that walk they could not cease to talk of him. Obviously he was older than he looked, they decided, but how extraordinary that a boy like that, so healthy and normal and *ordinary* – they repeated that last word many times – should become a priest, and a missionary too, coming here to be cured of his dysentery and to play at ball in that absurd, suffocating garment before going back to God knows what hell in the tropics.

The next afternoon, although they had by now ceased to discuss

278

him, they again, as if by mutual consent, took the path to the playing field. Stella came with them. The boy was in the same place, sitting cross-legged with the ball and the two tambourines beside him; but when they approached, he at once jumped up, brushing the dust off the back of his soutane with both large hands. This time he spoke to them in English, explaining eagerly that on Saturday afternoon Father somebody-or-other would be giving a lecture at the *collegio* on the mission's work in Africa, and wouldn't they care to come? There would be slides, he added, turning to Stella who had picked up one of the tambourines, and also a real Negro missionary, one of their converts.

'What is this?' Stella asked, turning the tambourine over and over.

'It's a game.'

'A game?'

'In Pola we call it *tamburello*.'

'Show me.'

'Darling, perhaps . . .' Lucy said.

But the boy was quite willing, and soon Stella was running about on her lean, brown legs, shouting, laughing and every now and then tripping on some obstacle, a stone or a tuft, while Lucy and Henry watched her in amazement. All these holidays she had been silent, almost sullen, and they wondered now if, during the long period during which Henry's diplomatic work had forced them to abandon her to relatives, some radical change, until this moment hidden from them, had been taking place.

After their game she whispered to Lucy: 'Can't we ask him to tea?' and Lucy doubtfully passed on the invitation. But he was sorry, the boy said, that was against the rules, for such things one must first get permission. Another time, Henry said. Yes, of course, another time, another time, Lucy said.

From then on they saw much of him. At the lecture Stella, looking over her shoulder, spent more time watching him operate the lantern than watching the screen. Together they read her comics, and he would laugh boisterously, bringing the palm of his hand down, slap, slap, slap on to his knee, as he threw back his head. One day they all went up the Paganella, the nearest of the mountains, in the *funivia* – an iron cage which dangled from a cable with eight people inside; and all at once Stella was afraid, but instead of her mother it was him that she clutched, burying her face in the crook of his arm and reiterating 'Save me, save me', while Lucy said with an edge of asperity to her voice: 'Don't make such a scene, dear. What on earth are you afraid of? We're perfectly safe.' Later he and Stella bounded from rock to rock in search of the edelweiss they had been told could be found there, and now it was Lucy's turn to be anxious: 'Oh, do be careful! Henry, tell the child to be careful.' Always the boy wore that cumbersome soutane and his agility in it never ceased to amaze them.

They continued to discuss him and sometimes, on such occasions, Stella would be present, listening but saying nothing. They would like to have asked him why he had become a priest, but some scruple, they could not have said what, prevented them from doing so. Lucy was particularly obsessed by the subject; but when she thought about it or talked about it for long, she would experience a sudden, unfathomable weariness, not of the flesh, or of the bones, or even of the mind, but of the spirit itself. She would lie awake, gazing out of the window at the Brenta, blue and chill in the moonlight, and her whole being would seem to breathe forth in the sigh that she drew as yet again she repeated to herself: 'I don't understand it!'

'I don't understand it!' After that afternoon on the Paganella, she brought the phrase out at dinner. 'There he was, leaping about from rock to rock like any ordinary boy of his age. It's not as if he can have any feeling of vocation, how can he? Just an ordinary boy,' she repeated. 'There are hundreds like him.'

'It beats me,' Henry said.

Stella suddenly said, putting her knife and fork down on her plate: 'I can understand it.' It was the first time she had ever joined in these discussions. Her eyes were bright, her hands were trembling as she pressed them down on the table, and all at once a flush swept over her and no less suddenly ebbed, leaving her face drawn and white.

Lucy said, controlling herself with difficulty: 'Perhaps he's confided in you.' Stella did not answer and Lucy pursued: 'Well, has he?'

'If he had, he wouldn't want me to tell – would he?'

Obviously the child was being impertinent. Lucy laughed and said: 'Do hurry up with your fish. You're keeping us waiting.' But at that moment the resentment which had for so long worked beneath like some disruptive poison burst explosively upwards, and its impact stunned Lucy, like some physical blow.

That night Henry found his wife standing in her dressing-gown before the open window of their bedroom, with some photographs in her hands. 'You know they *are* alike,' she said, and there was a strange dreaminess in both her voice and expression. 'There is some resemblance.' She showed him two photographs side by side – one of the young peasant with the tambourine in his hand, and the other of a youth lolling beside a tennis-court in white shorts and an open-necked shirt.

Next Saturday was a *festa*, and the Americans persuaded the boy to get permission to drive with them in their Buick to a lake a few miles from the village. 'Bring your bathing costume,' Lucy said, and he laughed in his boisterous way and shook his head, so that she assumed that was not permitted. It was a day without a cloud, the air sweet and fresh and yet inducing a mood of almost autumnal languor in the older woman as they drove away in the car. The boy, too, was taciturn, almost morose, and she wondered if he was offended at something or was not feeling well. She glanced back at him over her shoulder and noticed how he sat, hunched forward in the seat with his hands clasped before him. But 'Oh!' he exclaimed in rapture when, coming round a bend of the mountain road, they saw the lake before them, a violet gold-fringed eye, winking up out of the darker violet of the surrounding slopes. '*Ma bello, bello,*' he reiterated: and indeed it was beautiful, this long solitary expanse of water under the cloudless sky. '*Bello,*' he kept saying, and each time she heard the word Lucy felt her spirit leap unaccountably within her, as if at some victory.

He lay on the sand, in his black soutane, trickling sand between his large peasant fingers, while Lucy and Henry bathed. Stella had refused to go in – 'Too cold,' she objected – but it was obvious that she had only said this because she had wanted to be with the boy. When Lucy came out of the water, she stood before him in the sunlight, with the drops sparkling on her still beautiful thighs, and said: 'Why don't you go in?'

'Because it is not allowed.'

'No one will see you,' she said. 'And anyway, what harm is there in it? It's wonderful,' she said.

The boy was silent, still trickling the sand through his fingers, and Henry said: 'You can have my bathing trunks. I've had enough for one day. Persuade Stella to go in with you. She's only waiting for you to give her the lead.'

The sand continued to trickle; until, suddenly, the boy leapt to his feet and strode over to the car where the others had changed.

They had none of them ever seen his body under the soutane, and now, as he hurled himself at the water, its beauty amazed them. His skin, though so long shielded from the light, was naturally brown; his shoulders broad; his hips narrow. Watching him as he swam out and out, Lucy felt as she had felt many years ago when a car she was driving had failed to respond to the steering wheel. Then there had been a crash, she had almost been killed. But now the boy, suddenly turning over to swim on his back, began to call out: 'Stella! Stella! Aren't you coming to join me?' His teeth flashed brilliantly, the arm he waved caught the golden sunlight. Lucy lay down on the sand, the minute grains clinging to her moist flesh and costume, while shudder after shudder passed over her body. She closed her eyes, she put an arm over them, while that intense weariness she had so often experienced during these days left her weak and dizzy.

All that day he laughed and joked with an almost hysterical abandon. Again and again he and Stella dashed into the water; again and again they ran races, scattered the fine sand. Then they would ravenously munch slices of bread crammed with *mortadella*. Only when the sun was declining behind the mountains and a chill breeze sprang up did he at last put on the soutane. Then, all at once, he became grave again, and this gravity, put on like the black habit, seemed also to communicate itself to the others, so that it was in silence that they began the drive home. As the lake disappeared, black now except at its farthest point where the sun made it golden, the boy announced: 'I am going away tomorrow.'

They all expressed consternation. 'I didn't tell you, because I didn't want to spoil our day. Tomorrow twenty of us go to Rome. The next week, Africa.' They asked a few questions and he answered them, all four speaking as though their words had to be dragged up out of some unfathomable well of despair. They reached the hotel, and he said: 'I'll come to say goodbye tomorrow.' He had already told them that his bus left at six in the evening. 'You have been very kind.' He did not shake hands and he did not once look back as he walked away from them down the hill road.

But the next day passed and though they sat on the terrace waiting, the three of them in silence, holding books they pretended to read, he never came back. At a quarter to six Lucy rose: 'Well, if we're going to see him, we'd better walk down to the *collegio*. Obviously he couldn't get away.' Her husband had risen too, and she now turned to Stella: 'Coming?'

'No.'

'He'll think it odd if you don't.'

'I don't want to come.'

Outside the *collegio* they found the bus, once red but now yellow with dust; the boy they could not find. All the members of the *collegio* appeared to have turned out, a number of inquisitive *villegianti* were there, with perambulators, dogs and children, and, in the centre of all this confusion, the mayor himself stood. Peering, one by one, into the dust-stained windows of the coach, Lucy at last saw him. He sat alone in a pose that was strangely tranquil and relaxed amongst all that excitement. She had walked down here in the secret hope of finding him broken, reluctant, even rebellious; she had wanted him to grieve or cry out against his exile. And, instead, there he sat with his hands in his lap and that expression of eager, yet patient, resolve on his face. Henry was going to tap on the window to attract his notice, but Lucy caught his hand. 'Better not,' she said; for she knew now that the boy, too, had passed, like her son, into a region, terrifying and strange, where her love could no more reach him.

They walked back in silence, and found Stella in her deck-chair before the hotel. 'Did you see him?' she asked; she looked terribly ill.

'Yes, we saw him.'

The girl's mouth opened and then shut. 'He loved me,' she said at last.

And for Lucy the knowledge of that truth was the bitterest thing of all.

1949

Unmaking

There were fourteen main bedrooms, each with a bathroom and each with a balcony that fringed the gleaming eyeball of the lake. There were two dining-rooms, one for when the Principessa was alone and one for when she was entertaining, a *salotto* and a *salottino*, a billiard room, a ballroom, a music room, a library and a room, its walls covered in crimson damask, with nothing in it but four card-tables, inlaid with mother-of-pearl and banded with brass, and the sixteen lyre-backed chairs that went with them. There were long, high-ceilinged passages, a labyrinth of them, with carpets, to which age had given a silvery patina, stretching down their centres. Each morning the thirty-two-year-old half-wit son of the Principessa's personal maid would push a carpet-sweeper, as though it were a toy horse, up and down them. From time to time, smiling or even giggling to himself, he would vary his usual sober pace with a sudden frenetic whoosh. There was no vacuum cleaner in the whole villa, just as there was no central heating, no wireless, no gramophone.

It was said that there were ten miles of walks in the grounds. Over the centuries this or that Principe or Principessa had thought, 'I'd like to see the view from that point' or 'It's a nuisance to have to walk round these rocks'; and at once *contadini* would be ordered to hack, hew and heave. Then someone would say, 'Oh, but the ladies must have a handrail' or 'Oh, but the old folk must have some steps'; and at once handrails were erected and steps were laid out. There were artificial grottoes, dripping moisture from what looked like artificial moss and ferns. There were tunnels and ruined towers, seldom entered because they were reputed to be the haunts of bats, and a number of 'dependencies' which housed poor relations, the bailiff and his family, estate workers, footmen and guests of whom the Principessa preferred not to see too much. Surmounting it all was a ruined chapel, dedicated to the Madonna of Montserrato; but after a landslide had obliterated the three young labourers who had been excavating yet another walk beneath it, it was now inaccessible except to the more adventurous of the children of the *contadini* who, finding a vertiginous foothold now here and now there among the boulders, would shin up to it as an act of bravado. Old Bruno, who had once been one of the three coachmen and was now one of the two chauffeurs, would shake his head and say that the chapel had become an evil place – *un posto cattivo*. But he never specified.

All these things, except the chapel and the remoter dependencies, the Principessa insisted on showing personally to the short, jolly, sweating German major and the tall, frigid, frowning lieutenant who accompanied him. '*La Principessa parla Tedesco?*' the major had inquired with an execrable accent. '*Disgraziatemente, non,*' she had answered, even though that was not true. '*Allora. . .?*' The major did not feel equal to carrying on his negotiations in Italian. '*Inglese?*' suggested the lieutenant, who was examining a signed photograph of Queen Mary in a silver frame. 'Well, yes,' replied the Principessa with a little smile. 'Good,' said the major, who had once been a Rhodes scholar at Oxford. The lieutenant was now busy examining a signed photograph of the Duke of Aosta, also in a silver frame.

'I am not tiring you, Princess?' The major was solicitous, even though he had not guessed that this tall, erect, white-haired woman, with her smooth, rosy cheeks, her strong clear voice and her firm gait, had already passed her eightieth year.

'Not at all, thank you,' she answered.

As she opened one door after another – 'This is another bedroom', 'This used to be a nursery', 'This is only a box-room' – the major would advance straight to the tall windows, disregarding everything around him, would throw their halves open on to the narrow ledge of the balcony and would then step out, exclaiming, 'Beautiful!' or 'Magnificent!' or 'Splendid!' It was always left to the lieutenant to count the beds, to pull open drawers and to peer into the shadowy recesses of cupboards or of bathrooms in which huge old-fashioned bath tubs and bidets and throne-like water closets loomed up whitely. From time to time he would make some note on a sheet of paper attached to a clipboard.

In the lower, formal garden, the major snatched some lavender and, crushing it in his strong, stubby fingers, held it to his nose. 'What do you call this in English? I can't remember.' 'Lavender.' 'And in Italian?' 'Almost the same. *Lavanda*.' 'It sounds more beautiful in Italian. Everything is more beautiful in Italian.' From time to time he would stop, as so many of the villa guests had stopped before him, at some particularly breathtaking view of the lake or of the mountains and, like them, he would then exclaim, as on the balconies, 'Beautiful!' or 'Magnificent!' or 'Splendid!' Meanwhile the lieutenant, whistling under his breath, would scuff the gravel with one of his dusty boots or test the solidity of a handrail or the firmness of a flight of steps.

'Your family has lived here for a long time?'

'The Comadini have been here since the fifteenth century. It's thought that the original villa may have belonged to Pliny the Younger, as you probably know.' Of course the major knew nothing of the kind. 'There's a letter of his. He describes the villa as – let me remember – "supported by rock, as if by the buskins of the actors in tragedy" and goes on to say that he therefore calls it "Tragedia". His villa by the water he called "Commedia".' For the first time that afternoon the major ceased to smile. In their English versions he had no idea who Pliny the Younger was or what a buskin was.

'So much history,' he sighed.

'Yes, so much history,' she echoed with a flash of pride.

Later, in the *Salotto*, seated in a straight-backed chair covered in a tooled Spanish leather, with the two officers enfolded (somehow to their disadvantage, each of them felt) in the embraces of two deep armchairs before and below her, the Principessa poured out tea from burnished silver into handleless cups of the finest porcelain. There was a faint smell of methylated spirit from the blue flame of the warmer; there was a faint smell of hay from the China tea. The 'cookies' – the Principessa used that word, not 'biscuits', when she offered them – were friable and lemony. They lay nestled in the folds of a heavy, lace-fringed napkin, which in turn rested on a silver dish.

'So what do you think of the villa?' she prompted with the faintest irony.

The major cleared his throat, reddening beneath his tan. 'Seldom have I seen. . . . Indeed, never. . . . Beautiful.' He heaved himself out of the armchair, as though out of a bath, and crossed to the window. The vast eyeball of the lake looked up at him; he looked down. 'This is very . . . distasteful,' he said. He meant it. He turned: 'In a war . . . and now that, in the south, the Italians . . . our former allies. . . .'

'But of course. Let me give you some more tea.'

He shook his head with an odd, almost angry vehemence. 'Now that we are consolidating our position in this area, we need a house like this. For our headquarters.'

The Principessa nodded, her cup held between both her fragile hands. 'So you told me.'

'We shall take the utmost care. You may rely on that. The utmost care. Nothing will be damaged. We shall all be officers. We shall be' – again the blood rushed up under his tan, again he cleared his throat – 'most happy to employ all those whom you employ.'

The young lieutenant coolly put out a hand, took a sugar lump and placed it between his teeth. He began to suck, while still holding on to one end of it. The major and the Principessa both saw him but only the major was discomforted.

The major took two paces away from the open window and then two paces back to it. 'Of course you may stay on here, Princess. There is no danger, none at all, that we should ask you to leave. But you understand – most of the rooms. . . .'

'But of course!' He was relieved, if also puzzled, by her laughter.

'Your own suite of rooms. . . . There was, if I remember, a – a little study. . .? Or perhaps we could spare you that little sitting-room. The – the. . . . What did you call it?'

'The *salottino*.' The Principessa shook her head. 'No, I shall be quite happy in my own corner of the villa. Thank you all the same.'

'It would be difficult to offer you the music room – the piano. As you know, we Germans, like you Italians, love music. . . .'

'I never go into the music room now. Not since my husband's death.' She wondered what these Germans would have made of Guido, ceaselessly hammering out first ragtime and then jazz on the vast Bechstein grand that, because of the damp from the lake, was always in need of tuning.

'Ah, the Prince was musical!'

The Principessa gave her small, ironic smile. 'You might say that.'

The lieutenant glanced obtrusively at his watch and then tapped it with his forefinger, glancing over to his colleague. The major rose.

'On Monday afternoon – if that will suit you, of course, Princess – an advance party of us will come to make the final arrangements. Then on Tuesday. . . .'

'You had better have a word with Franco.'

'Franco?'

'The majordomo. He'll look after you. But of course if there is more that I. . . .'

'We shall try to make as little trouble as possible for you, Princess. No more than is absolutely necessary.'

In the long hall, hung with its murky portraits of centuries of Comadini – the Principessa had not accompanied them there – the major turned to the lieutenant. 'To have grown up in such a place!' he exclaimed in a tone of wonder.

The young lieutenant shrugged, drew a crumpled packet of cigarettes from a pocket of his tunic and stuck one in his mouth. He had been wanting to smoke throughout the visit and it baffled and annoyed him that he had not been able to bring himself to do so.

That evening, with the assistance of Franco, her personal maid, Ida, another maid and the lanky young footman who had been rejected for service because of his weak lungs, the Principessa moved into her suite of rooms all that she would require while the Germans were in residence. There were so many things of which she no longer made any use – the musty-smelling books in the library, the table of embroidery silks beside her high-backed chair in the *salottino*, ivory-topped walking sticks and parasols covered in brilliantly coloured satins, the baskets and leads and collars of dogs long dead and buried – but which she now felt an overwhelming sadness at abandoning, even if only temporarily. But when Franco, white-haired and distinguished as any ambassador, advised her that they must lock up or hide this or that, she gave a fatalistic shake of the head. 'We must trust them,' she said; and by that she meant 'We must trust Providence.' Nonetheless, long after she had retired to bed, the old majordomo, the footman and the two maids busied themselves with packing up and transporting to cellars, outhouses and the empty dependencies scattered about the woodland everything that seemed to them to be particularly precious.

The old fear any change, however small, since it prefigures that greatest of all changes so near to them. But after that first overwhelming sadness, the Principessa felt strangely light-hearted as she took off her numerous rings and brooches and, with the assistance of the agitated maid, began to undress.

'Ah, Principessa, what a terrible thing to have happened!' Ida's hands trembled clumsily.

'Worse things are happening all over the world.'

Ida nodded. Her son, older brother of the half-wit, had been reported missing on the Russian front, just as the Principessa's only son had been reported missing at Caporetto so many years before.

'It'll all pass,' the Principessa said, slipping her arms into the sleeves of her silk night-dress with a small shudder of her ancient body.

'It'll all pass,' Ida repeated after her.

The Principessa lay in the dark, unable to sleep.

Her whole life, up to the moment when the two Germans had been announced to her, had been an infinitely laborious process of remaking. What had been ugly, crude, cheap, common, vulgar had, over a whole lifetime, been remade into the elegance, luxury, beauty, grandeur, distinction that this ancient villa symbolized. Few remembered it now but it was she who had bought back the whole estate: the villa itself from a Milanese industrialist on the point of bankruptcy; the dependencies from their humble inhabitants at grossly inflated prices; the strips of land from the *contadini* whose families had farmed them for generations. And it was she who had then put together all these separate fragments, like some skilled artisan mending, with infinite patience, a shattered work of art. Her husband, the Principe, had not cared for his lost patrimony. He was happy enough to live on her money in the Rome apartment in the Via Quattro Fontane, to play his bridge, to visit his mistress, to exercise his giant poodle, to go to nightclubs, to hammer out jazz on the piano. The Comadini name meant nothing to him; he was totally ignorant about the Comadini history. 'I am more Comadini than you,' she would tell him; and he knew that she was right and never contradicted her.

But the irony (of which only a few people were aware) was that she had not even been born Italian. Her mastery of the language, which she spoke so beautifully, was only another part of that whole laborious process of remaking – as was her acquisition of all the elaborately arcane forms and fashions of a class at first remote from her. She was like some upstart who seizes a throne and then rules with what seems to be an inherited finesse and assurance. Even some of the noblest of the nobility were a little in awe of her. She had so much more style, so much more authority and, most important of all, so much more money than themselves. That money, the black river on which all her gay, glittering, splendid edifices floated, had also been remade. Only a few people, most of them very old, were now able to trace it back to its source in America. Everyone else assumed that it was Comadini money, since there had been a long period when the Comadini had been some of the richest people in the world. Virtually no one knew of the Estonian Jew who had fled a pogrom in which his father and mother had been killed; who had arrived in Brooklyn with his ailing wife and infant daughter, unable to speak a word of the language of his country of adoption; and who had then, with a remarkable persistence, made a fortune from the garment industry, exploiting other emigrants less enterprising and ruthless than himself. There had eventually been a move from New York to New Jersey; and the child – to his grief his only one – had there been dispatched to Miss Dana's school in Morristown, where she mixed with the daughters of no less successful steel-makers, railroad tycoons, cattle barons, bankers and brokers. The unpronounceable Jewish surname was adapted into a pronounceable Gentile one.

Her mother by now had died, like some species no longer able to adjust to the ever-accelerating process of evolution. It was the girl's father who took her to London, Paris and Rome; and it was he who arranged for an eminent Swiss surgeon, long before the phrase 'plastic surgery' was known to the world, to break her nose brutally, as another stage, perhaps the most painful of all, in that whole lifelong process of remaking. (In later years people would often remark on the 'aristocratic distinction' of the Principessa's nose.) Then he set about marrying her off. There was an English baronet who all but took her and then decided not to – instead marrying, not one of his own kind, but, more humiliatingly, a Gaiety Girl. Next there was a Romanoff prince; but rumours, which the millionaire at first discounted, of a life of 'degeneracy' became too insistent. Finally, in Rome, the last of the Comadini met, in both senses, his match. She had always striven to placate and please her father, usually with no success; but at last, shortly before his premature death from a heart attack, she had succeeded in doing so by this most awe-inspiring of dynastic alliances.

As she now reviewed this whole process of remaking, so arduous that it sometimes seemed to her that she herself had built the whole villa and laid out its gardens and woodlands with her own bare hands, the Principessa now felt a tranquil satisfaction. Her head and shoulders propped up on pillows each of the whitest and crispest Irish linen, with the princely monogram stiff in a corner, she smiled into the darkness. Even that plump, sweating major had not supposed for one second that she was anything other than what the world had for so long accepted her as being: Italian; Gentile; aristocratic. 'It'll all pass'; but what she had remade, first at the command of her father, then at his prompting and finally as a propitiary gesture to his shade, would not pass. This riffraff might briefly occupy the villa, their boots trampling noisily up and down its corridors, their jeeps grinding noisily up and down its drives, their harsh, guttural voices echoing noisily up and down its stairwells. But it was *they* who would pass.

Carlo had always been something of a fool; it never ceased to amaze the Principessa that he had finally succeeded in getting where he was. When his father, like her son, had been killed in the First World War, she had taken his mother into service as a laundrywoman and had allowed her and the baby to establish themselves in three cramped, low-raftered rooms under the roof of the villa. Instead of playing rough, noisy games with the other children on the estate, Carlo, a sickly boy with pitifully thin arms and legs and an overlarge head perpetually tipped to one side as though it were too heavy for the support of his neck, would follow his mother everywhere with a lamblike bleating of '*Mamma! Mamma! Mamma!*' He was later teased and bullied at the local school for his inability to master even such elementary skills as throwing a ball overarm, riding a bicycle or flirting with a girl. Later still, when he worked briefly in the villa as a footman, his sleepy, faintly insolent inefficiency got on the Principessa's nerves. Eventually, his mother dead, he left the villa and the village first for Milan and then for Rome. And now here he was, back as the Fascist boss of the area.

Since his return, he had made it a habit to call from time to time on the Principessa, his dark suit or his uniform well pressed, his shoes or boots gleaming and his nails manicured to a pinkish gloss. He had acquired weight, both of body and of authority; in his sallow, hooknosed, narrow-browed way he had even grown handsome. In the winter the two of them would sit before the log fire, drinking the China tea that smelled of hay; in the summer they would sit out on the terrace, he with a Campari soda and she with a fresh orange juice in a slender glass pearled with moisture from the ice cubes in it. There was still deference in his treatment of her; but the deference was that of a man to a woman, of someone young to someone old, and not of an inferior to a superior.

When the footman had placed the silver tea service before the Principessa – because of the imminent arrival of the Germans, they were meeting for the first time in her boudoir – Carlo rose, tiptoed to the door and made sure that it was shut. Really, thought the Principessa, despite all outward changes he's remained as essentially silly as he always was.

'I'm horrified by this news.'

'Why? What's happened now?' She was thinking of the armies pushing up inexorably through the south of Italy.

'The villa, the Germans.' He spoke in a hoarse undertone, as though behind one of the tapestries or inside one of her cupboards some German eavesdropper might be lurking.

'Oh that!' She picked up one of the friable, lemon-flavoured 'cookies' and bit into it. 'Oh, I'll survive that. After all, I've survived a great deal in a long life. Those that I've so far met seem pleasant enough. The Germans are usually, well, correct, if nothing else. Aren't they?'

He shook his head gloomily; and she remembered, for a brief irrelevant moment, that child's head lolling to one side and that baa-like 'Mamma! Mamma! Mamma!'

'After all, what can they do to harm an old woman like me? I'll hide away in these quarters here until the time comes for them to move on. It can't be long now,' she all but added and then checked herself, remembering who this new Carlo was.

'Principessa, you could be in danger.'

'Danger!'

'I oughtn't to be saying this to you. If they knew in Milan or if the Germans here knew. . . . But I owe you a debt. A great debt. And I've not forgotten it. Never.' Emotion made his voice swell and tremble.

'Debt? What do you mean, Carlo?'

He looked affronted and aggrieved, not realizing that she had been kind to so many dependants of the villa not out of any spontaneous impulse but merely out of obedience to the Comadini code. But then he told himself that she was old, old, and that her memory was probably failing. Patiently he reminded her of what she needed no reminding: 'You took us in, my mother and me. After my father's death. You paid for my mother's funeral. For my education.'

'Oh that! But that was nothing!' She was totally unaware of her cruelty.

He leant towards her, brown hands clasped tightly in each other. The light from the lamp beside him – the heavy lace curtains of the boudoir excluded almost all the daylight – gleamed on those square fingernails buffed to an opalescent pink.

'You're in danger, Principessa. I know what I'm talking about.'

'Oh, don't be so silly!'

But he persisted: 'In the past – before the Germans came – there were rumours about you. About your ancestry. And so on. But it was easy for me, in my position. . . .'

'What rumours?' She imagined the sleepy, faintly insolent young footman grubbing about among her papers; forcing locked drawers to do so; listening at doors when she spoke to her lawyer from Milan or her financial adviser from New York.

He faltered, hardly daring to put the rumours into words.

'Well?' she demanded.

'You are, of course – were, of course – American. We're at war with America, Principessa. I don't have to tell you that.'

'I've been an Italian for many, many years. For more years than you have lived. My only son died for Italy at Caporetto.'

He inclined his head, with a sigh. 'Still. . . .' He began to tinkle the spoon round and round the cup on the spindly table before him. The Principessa felt an urge to put out a hand to stop the ceaseless movement. He had always had the knack of getting on her nerves. Then he went on in a hoarse whisper totally unlike his usual firm, commanding tone: 'There's the other matter, too, of course.'

'The other matter?'

'These rumours . . . rumours. . . .'

'Yes?'

'Well – about – about your race, Principessa.' He could not bring himself to say 'Jewish' or 'Jew'.

'Oh.' She sucked in her cheeks, so that the smooth, rosy cheekbones suddenly became more prominent and the lips were bunched into an ugly knot. So the sleepy, faintly insolent footman had been more observant than she had ever imagined possible. 'I see.'

'To me of course all that's nothing. Of no importance at all. To most of us Italians, as you know. . . . But these Germans. . . .'

293

She stared at him with a kind of inquiring disdain: Who are you? What are you? What are you doing here in my house and my boudoir? He wriggled in the constriction of his dark suit, putting two fingers inside his stiff collar.

She gave a little snort at the back of the 'distinguished' nose which, more than half a century before, that eminent Swiss surgeon had brutally smashed with a little hammer. 'What can they do to me?' she demanded. 'Whatever I may or may not be.' She was, he saw, going to admit nothing.

Resentment at her ingratitude and contempt suddenly swelled in him. 'There are camps. You must have heard of them. Even people as distinguished as yourself, as rich as yourself. . . .' (He almost went on, 'As old as yourself.') 'They have no pity. None at all. Believe me.'

'Oh, my dear Carlo. . .!' It was the same tone, contemptuously amused, that she had used when her dead husband had confessed some new folly to her – an unpaid tailor's bill, the purchase or crashing of yet another sports car, the acquisition or ditching of yet another mistress. She put down her cup and, picking up the small, lace-edged linen square in her lap, she dabbed at her lips with it.

'I'm being very serious, Principessa. Your situation could be very grave indeed.'

'Nonsense!' She was getting to her feet; she was taller than he, even when he too rose and faced her. 'Anyway – what do you imagine that I can do about it?'

'You must get away. As soon as possible.'

She stared at him, incredulous.

'Yes!' His was now the insistence of a parent to a disobedient child. 'You've no time to lose.'

'Oh, really, Carlo! Do you expect me to leave my villa, my village, my people, my whole life here. . .? You must be crazy! At my age? Do you realize that I'm eighty-three?'

'Principessa – please go! While you still have a chance. I'll see to it' – again his voice assumed that conspiratorial whisper – 'that no one stops you. You could slip over the mountains to Switzerland. Others have done it, you know that. Or the lake. . . . But once the Germans are settled in. . . .'

She gazed at him with exactly the same expression – unimpressed, pitying, sardonic – with which she used to receive his or his mother's tales of how the other children on the estate had been bullying him. Then she shook her head. 'It's out of the question.

294

Quite out of the question. And I'm sure not even necessary. But thank you, Carlo – thank you all the same.'

After he had gone, his face flushed with chagrin, she thought cynically to herself: He's afraid, that one. He always was afraid. A coward. A mean little coward. He knows the war is ending. He already sees himself hung up by the heels in the market square. He wants to earn some credit with me and with every other decent person.

It was a squat closed van, such as might be used to transport a cow to the bull or a pig to the slaughter-house. The tyres were thick, their treads worn, and the black paint was pocked and scored. Looking down at it from above, she thought: It might be a hearse. Ida stood fearfully beside her, her eyes raw from weeping.

There was a knock at the door of the boudoir and the German major, sweating even more than usual, was outside. He clicked his heels and bowed. 'We are ready, Principessa,' he said in a small humbled voice.

'I really can't see why Bruno shouldn't drive me in one of the two cars – instead of having to travel in *that*.'

'I'm sorry, Principessa.' He genuinely was sorry. 'Shall we go?'

She pointed to a small, crocodile-leather suitcase, surprisingly heavy because of its silver fittings. Many years ago her husband had shot the crocodile. It was almost as though she expected the major to carry it; but from behind him a private soldier, with a soft doughy face and hair the colour of lard, stepped forward. She heard the scrape of his hobnailed boots on the elaborate parquet but it meant nothing to her, as once it would have done. Ida gave a little sob.

On the wide staircase the major leant towards her. 'You understand, don't you, Principessa? All this is nothing to do with me. But soon you will be back. This evening. Tomorrow at the latest. Just a simple interrogation. There has been some mistake.'

She could see faces at the windows round the courtyard: some, frightened or grief-stricken, of the servants; more, inquisitive or apathetic, of the Germans. She raised a valedictory hand to the servants and nodded, now in this direction and now in that.

'I shall see you this evening,' the major said, as though to reassure himself, rather than her. 'Or tomorrow.'

She shook his hand, feeling it pulse oddly, as though it were an imprisoned bird, in her firm grasp. 'Thank you.' She knew that this silly, anxious man meant well.

He helped her up into the van and then, taking the old-fashioned crocodile-leather suitcase, with its faded gold monogram, from the soldier, handed that in too. There were two soldiers inside, at either end of a hard bench. She sat on another hard bench opposite to them. She did not mind the hardness; she had always chosen upright chairs without upholstery. For a brief moment she glimpsed Ida's face, convulsed by grief and terror, behind the major's shoulder; she heard a long animal wail, like the wail that her beloved saluki dog used to give when she went out and left him behind her. Then the doors of the van crashed shut and someone outside drew across the bolts.

The two soldiers opposite stared down at their clumsy boots, deliberately avoiding her calm, candid gaze. The van began to throb; then, with a crunch of gravel, it swayed round in a circle and began to move forward.

She could see nothing now but the two soldiers, a squashed cigarette butt between the feet of one of them and, high above their heads, a patch of moving, changing green, crisscrossed by wire netting. But she knew the winding drive so well that at no moment was she in any ignorance of her whereabouts. Now they had taken the hairpin bend where, last year, torrential rain had brought a boulder thundering down; now they were passing the little chapel, with its elaborate stucco work and its Luini, too soft and sentimental for her taste, of a Mother and Child; and now that sudden lurch of the van to the left must mean that they had swerved to avoid the wood piled there from the fallen chestnut tree. Finally they were making the detour round the kitchen gardens to pass the row of *contadini* dwellings. She wondered if any of the *contadini* were watching the van as it passed; she wondered how many of them regretted its passing.

She had felt a stoical calm and patience till this moment; but as the van turned out from the drive on to the main road, gravel giving way to smoother asphalt, she was surprised by a sudden access of joy, as though the thin, sluggish blood in her eighty-three-year-old body had suddenly started to flow more copiously and faster through her narrowing arteries. All that she had remade, so laboriously and at so much cost, through more than half a century, denying all the deepest needs of her nature, had in a single week been unmade again; and though the stones of the villa might still go on standing – as a hotel, as a hostel, as a rest home, as a conference centre – it too had been unmade as effectively as if those Germans had exploded a bomb in it.

But, strangely, she felt no grief or rage or fear but only this exhilaration. Almost a century before some obscure Estonians had been driven out of their burning hovels; and now she, bearer of one of the most distinguished names in the whole world, was being driven out of a palace contaminated by alien presences. The thread, winding back from the vast estate on the promontory to the little village in the marshes, so long ago and so brutally and so decisively severed, had now been knit together again. She could feel it all in her hands, a complete, integral spool. She smiled across at the guards, who at once looked away.

1978

The Silence is Rest?

My dear H.

I write this last letter to you; but since our names begin with the same initial, perhaps in a sense I am also writing it to myself. People have so often remarked how alike we are. So often you have seemed to hold up a mirror to me – or, more accurately, I have seemed to hold up a mirror to you. But, in reflecting you, with all your natural decency, goodness and, above all, normality, this glass of fashion that I have absurdly been supposed to be has, I am afraid, proved a distorting one.

You have always believed everything that I have ever told you; but on this occasion, such is your loyalty, I have no doubt that, after my death, you will pretend not to believe what I am about to confess to you here. So it will happen that, despite my urgings that you should tell my story, you will tell, not it, but a travesty of it. It will, of course, be out of character for you to lie, but you will prefer to lie than to commit the disloyalty of being truthful.

Apart from my mother, you are the only person that I have ever really loved; and, whereas my intense love for her has been a hatred no less intense, my love for you has been, from first to last and from last to first, wholly unalloyed. But I have not merely loved you, as I know that you have loved me; I have also been in love with you. That will shock you, I think. I remember with what indignation you

298

reported to me those 'scurrilous rumours' that I had, during my days – and nights! – as a student in Germany, been more friendly than I should with R. and G. You merely assumed that I had got into the wrong kind of set, whereas, in fact, I had got into the right one – for me.

There is a divinity that shapes – or misshapes – our ends. That divinity (if He or It exists) also misshapes our beginnings, so that I cannot remember when I did not think of the ideal partner in my life as being, not a woman, but a man; and I can hardly remember when I did not think of that ideal partner as being yourself.

. . . Oh, am I being honest? Though I have never been honest before, I must be honest now. There was you, yes, there was you; but there was also *her*. No, not, as you in your innocence will assume, poor, silly, demented O., but my mother. I must have loved her to distraction – mustn't I? – to have done what I did. Yes, I *was* mad, though not in the sense that you and everyone else suspected me of being and as O. eventually became.

Let me start from the beginning, let me try to get it all into order. I don't want this story to be like one of those so-called masterpieces of dramatic literature in which confusion is worse confounded by the superimposition of this text on that (first quarto, second quarto, first folio, and so on).

I suppose it was all commonplace enough, though you – yes, I come back to that noble, shining innocence of yours – will not think it so. The ardent husband is at first away at the wars and then, when he returns, he is too often preoccupied with his manifold responsibilities. The even more ardent mother, living in a society in which any kind of infidelity would be, well, not perhaps unthinkable but certainly unactable, pours into the fragile vessel of her only son all the passion welling up within her. He shares her bed at that age when children are supposed – how wrongly! – to be innocent; and then, for fear of what people may say, he merely shares her room. Through half-closed lids at night, he watches her unbraid her hair and slip out of her clothes; and in the morning he stands over her as she makes up that smooth, voluptuous face. (No wonder that, in later years, he should have such a horror of women painting themselves.)

Then, as old age approaches and his younger brother takes from his shoulders so many of the burdens that previously distracted him, the father becomes aware again of this still youthful, still beautiful woman, whom he had almost forgotten. He experiences an

Indian summer of concupiscence; and guessing – as you never guessed – both the oddity and the intensity of the relationship between his wife and his son, he turns against the boy. The boy is first banished from the bedroom; then he is even banished to a university in another country, on the pretext that he cannot receive an adequate education in his own. In his vacations, the young man (no longer a boy) sees, disgusted, the way in which this aging, raging martinet treats his beloved mother like some tart in a brothel. He stands at the door of the bedroom now forbidden to him and he hears those sighs, groans, gasps, whimpers, cries. He stands there and he even seems to smell the rank sweat of the enseamèd bed in which they disport themselves. (The wrong word, that – disport. What they do together seems more like work than sport.)

So it is that, like his mother, he begins to think the unthinkable; and so it is that, unlike his mother, he finally begins to act the unactable. No murder was more premeditated – no wonder that you, my mother, my uncle and even my father himself would so often urge me not to brood, not to keep myself to myself, not to wrap myself round in what seemed to you all to be a cloak of impenetrably inky melancholy. *I was working it out!* But how were you to know that?

Between his ferocious bouts of passion, my father, exhausted, would drop off, wherever he happened to be: at the dining table; while going through his papers; while watching a play or listening to music or even talking to someone. 'He's failing,' my uncle would confide in me, shaking his head as he tried to conceal his pleasure – for, by then, he was already taking on himself many of my father's duties. That cunning old man, P., who had taught my father everything he knew and still treated him like some dim-witted pupil, would tell me that he was worried – 'It's not like your father to show this kind of lethargy. I think that we should call in some medical help from Germany.'

It was I who had already called in some medical help from Germany – while I had been studying there. I had had to pay for it, I'm afraid, not in a way that I should really have wished and certainly not in a way that you could possibly have approved. Yes, R. and G. procured the poison for me – as medical students, they found that easy enough; but, in return – well, it was useless for me to say 'man delights not me' (though you always delighted me), since they insisted on their reward of (to use an even more hackneyed quotation) their pound of flesh.

300

So there it was, that little bottle which I carried around with me for days and days on end. It gave me such an amazing sense of power. I could kill anyone with it – my mother, my uncle, P., O., myself or even you. Then, one drowsy afternoon of midsummer, I found him lying out in the orchard, giddy with wine and God knows what filth had been going on in that bedroom upstairs (she, my mother, still lay up there). He touched his heart – I shall always remember that gesture, the blue-veined, wrinkled hand resting there, as he looked up at me with those small, porcine eyes of his, the jowls quivering loosely and the belly tautly upthrust. A satyr, that's what he looked like – though I know that in the absurd eulogy I spoke over him after his death I described him (what hypocrisy!) as 'a Hyperion'. He said that he must have eaten something that had disgreed with him; and then he belched. That revolted me even more. I thought of that blue-veined, wrinkled hand resting, not on his chest, but between her legs, and of his foul breath exploding in her face. That did it for me. You've always said that my besetting fault is that I can never make up my mind but I made it up there and then. I said I'd got something that might help him – a new medicine that I'd brought back with me from Germany. He knew how far German medicine was in advance of ours. I'd go and fetch it. He grunted assent.

I carried the glass of water, with the few colourless, odourless, tasteless drops in it, back to him, down through the lush weeds, hearing them (extraordinary hyperaesthesia!) swish at each of my steps. The glass was cold, my cheeks were burning. He was asleep again by the time that I reached him, but I shook him roughly by the bony shoulder and then I shouted, 'Father!' He started up, momentarily terrified, as though from a nightmare and jerked my arm, so that some of the liquid jumped from the glass and splashed a cheek and trickled into a hairy ear. 'Drink this,' I said. He put a hand to the ear. 'My ear is burning.' 'Drink this,' I repeated. He drank.

So simple, so easy. His heart must have been worrying him for a long time, everyone said – *you* said, my unwitting accomplice; *she* said, for whom I had done it; *he* said, who was so soon to take her away from me. Only one person suspected all might not be precisely as it seemed to be, and that was old P. People have always dismissed him as a bore and a buffoon; but he could not have survived all those years first as my grandfather's chief adviser and then as my father's and now as my uncle's, if he did not possess antennae infinitely more sensitive than those of others. Yes, he suspected something all right;

and, misinterpreting my pretended interest (after all, I had to conceal my love for *you*) in that plain, plaintive, dotty daughter of his, he put her on to me – to try to get some kind of confession out of me. But I was well able to deal with her.

. . . Yet still he persisted; so that, in the end, well, I had to finish him off too. By then R. and G. had turned up, supposedly summoned by my mother and my uncle to discover whether I was in the throes of a nervous breakdown or not, but in fact summoned by him. He had put them through it, as only he knew how. Very gentle, very gentlemanly, very insistent – a steely menace under all that assumed fatuity. He broke them, it could not have been hard. Perhaps he blackmailed them. The other O., always his creature, may have given them away. After all, he too is 'not the marrying kind' (as P., with his love of euphemistic clichés, might have put it). I was rather sorry to have to kill the old boy, because in an odd sort of way, though I baited and teased him, I rather liked him. Well, no, not *liked*, but admired. There was such a fund of sense to him. When you thought about it, his advice, though at the time it might seem pompous and sententious, was always so *good*. Yes, really. You were wrong to laugh at him behind his back and I was wrong to encourage you.

. . . And then there was O.'s breakdown and her suicide – I regretted that too. *Regretted* – that's inadequate to express it. It haunted me. Poor, foolish girl. I told myself that her life had not been worth much but somehow, when my mother told me how it had happened – that ghastly drowning, all entangled in weeds, the slime on her face – I almost screamed with the horror of it all. She is always eloquent, my mother. I must have got my eloquence from her!

Yes, ah yes, my loved mother, my loathed mother. . . . How could I have guessed that, having done that *thing* – somehow, even now, I find it difficult to write the word 'murder' – I should not have her to myself, to myself alone? How could I have guessed that I had done that *thing* – that murder – merely in order to hand her over to someone younger, more lusty, and far more lustful than the brute from whom I had delivered her? I had never realized before the extent of the resemblance between them – my father and my uncle. I did now. I would see him staring at her, in precisely the same way, the small eyes curiously youthful in the lined, bearded face; and there would be in them the same strange vacancy, like that vacancy in O.'s eyes when they dragged her out, dripping and mud-smeared, from the brook. I would watch them mount the stairs to the bedroom, as she and my father had so often mounted them before; and as my mother and father then, so now they would clutch at each other even before they were wholly out of sight. As in that agonizing past, so in this even more agonizing present, I would creep up a few minutes later and would stand outside that door and would again hear those sighs, groans, gasps, whimpers, cries and again would seem to smell the rank sweat from the enseamèd bed in which they disported themselves. (That odd epithet again – why do I repeat it?)

Uncannily, it was as if my father had come back to life; and had come back with all his ailing, failing vitality renewed. I once even called him 'Father', by the same strange slip of the tongue that had once made me address O. as 'Mother'. I should have to kill him all over again, I decided; and perhaps, this second time, when they buried him, before old Y. had time to scatter the coffin with earth, I'd plunge a stake through his heart, to make sure that, vampire-like, he did not rise up again and yet again, to take from me what was rightfully mine and mine alone.

So I began to plan it – and, in planning it, I made use both of you and of that ridiculous crowd of second-rate actors who happened, by some improbable stroke of luck, to appear on the scene. I wanted to get it about that it had been my uncle who had murdered my father; and who would be more convincing as the disseminator of such a monstrous lie than you, who were known never to tell anything but the truth? If somehow people could be made to believe that my uncle had done away with my father in order to usurp both his estate and his wife, then they could also be made lenient to me if, in killing him, I seemed merely to be carrying out an act of filial piety.

That resemblance – that's what I counted on. The two brothers looked so alike. I told you and I told my uncle and I told many other people, rich and poor and high and low, that I had had visions of my father; and they all – yes, you included – would try to look as though they believed me and yet, involuntarily, would make it amply clear that they did not. I was deranged, that was their secret conclusion. One night – do you remember? – I came in from the cold night air and rushed, in pretended terror and distraction, into your bedroom and cried out, 'He's there! He's out there!' You tried to calm me down but I went on repeating, 'No, I tell you, he's there! Out there!' So eventually, to humour me, you got up and went out and up the winding stairs; and because you were my friend and because, unlike the others, you could still only half-persuade yourself that I was out of my mind, you half-believed – you did, didn't you? – even though a rational part of your mind kept insisting that No, it was out of the question, no traveller returned from that undiscovered bourne.

Then, as soon as you were out of sight, I rushed to the room in which my uncle and my mother slept in that mountainous bed, festooned with faded damask. He was far less inclined to humour me than you had been – my mother lay in the bed, her hands clutching the lace-fringed sheet that she had drawn up around her trembling nakedness, as he stood in virile fury beside it; but eventually he pulled on some clothes and muffled himself in a coat and scarf. 'I'll catch my death,' he muttered. Oh, I liked that phrase, I liked it!

Well, it was he whom you saw, and not my father, his brother; but already you had half-believed me – hadn't you? – and now, glimpsing that shrouded shadow, gigantic against the moon, you completely believed me. You, too, had seen my father. I was not mad, after all. After that, other people thought that they had seen him, because human suggestibility is as vast as human stupidity and human cupidity and human guile.

. . . Everything seemed to be going so well, so very well. But then – I lost heart. Or nerve. Or belief. I don't know. It wasn't conscience that made a coward of me but simply an immense weariness, as of someone lost in a desert who suddenly prefers to lie down and die than to trudge on thirstily to an oasis that may only, after all, be a mirage. I had been so sure of what I wanted – her love, your love, each exclusive to myself – and now I became no less sure that these two things were impossible of attainment. Even with my uncle dead, as my father was dead already, she would always find some-one else, who would never be I; and you had already found your Felicity, so aptly named for you and so inaptly for me. All my planning, my striving, my simulation, my dissimulation seemed at a stroke – the stroke that killed the old man as I lunged at him – weary, stale, flat and unprofitable. I wanted to be done with it all. I want to be done with it all.

But, in part at least, I am an actor – which is why I immediately found some kinship with that ridiculous troupe, ranting and posturing through the pathetic little drama that I wrote for them. As every actor knows, a great play must end with a holocaust of every-one of importance. It is only the unimportant who survive. (In that, art does the precise reverse of imitating life, since in life it is generally the unimportant who are the first to go to the wall – and to their deaths.) I wanted this drama of mine to end in such a holo- caust, because – what hubris! – I wanted that it too should be great. The actor in me demanded that – demanded the plangent rhetoric of dying speeches, the stage laden with corpses, the gore and groans and gaspings, and the horrified, gaping faces of the super- numeraries, each hoping (God knows why) that one day it will be he or she, not standing there unharmed in the crowd, but writhing there, poisoned or disembowelled or pierced to the heart.

So I have planned the final tragedy – for this must be a tragedy – as I planned all the events that went before it. As I am part an actor, in addition to being a real man – that man who was (already I am writing in the past tense) your closest friend – so I am also part dramatist, moving all of you, yes, you too, around in the toy theatre to which this great globe itself seems suddenly, absurdly to have shrunk. How tiny, how silly, how trivial it seems! But, within the convention of this toy theatre of mine, I want it all to be *dramatic* – however tiny, silly, trivial.

I have cunningly filed to a point the button on one of the swords and I have tipped the point with that same poison that I poured, stealthy drop by drop, into the glass of fresh, ice-cold water that I carried out through the swishing weeds to my father as he lay grunting in sleep in the orchard. (The heavy apples flashed with fire, as the sun, piercing the thunderous branches, shone on them.) I have smeared the same poison over the smooth surface of the monstrous pearl – indeed, a pearl of great price, since what could be more precious to me now than the gift of death, whether my own or others'? We shall all die – my mother, my uncle, that silly, hot- tempered brother of O.'s. And I. I, too. I, of course. To die is what the leading actors in a tragedy must expect.

But you will not die. Though you are a notable, not a nonentity, in this story, in your case alone the action will follow the rules, not of drama, but of life. You will be spared, you will survive – to tell the tale. But *will* you tell it, *will* you? Oh H., be sure to tell it as it really was, as I have told it to you now, and not as you would like to persuade yourself that it was. Forget your Felicity for a while and concentrate only on *me* and on what *I* felt and what *I* planned and what *I* did. Can I rely on you for that? I always could rely on you. I must be able to rely on you now.

It is almost time. You will come for me and we shall go in to them together and then, after a time, you will come out again, one of a crowd of horrified and yet exalted survivors and spectators – like those people who pour, horrified and yet exalted, out of a theatre at the close of some masterpiece of tragedy. Men must abide their going hence, even as their coming hither. But, for me, the going hence does not seem much of a journey – indeed, one no further than from *this* room to *that*.

I am ready now; and the readiness is all – or nothing.

Ah, H., H. . . . .

The rest is silence; and – I hope, I hope – the silence is rest.

1982

His Everlasting Mansion

Come not to me again, but say to Athens,
Timon hath made his everlasting mansion
Upon the beachèd verge of the salt flood. . . .
                              Timon of Athens, V.i.

Filth of the world, a world of filth. The detritus of cans, bottles,
wrapping-paper, melon-rinds, orange-skins, lettuce-leaves, fish-
bones, rags and condoms lies, spread out and stinking, on the ash-
grey sand under the huge evening sun and clogs the five rickety steps
that lean away, no longer passable, at an angle to the jetty at which
no boat ever moors. A valise – its last journey, like my own, long
since done – nudges the lowest step of all, the labels of luxurious,
far-off hotels (Ritz, Carlton, Ritz-Carlton, Waldorf, Astoria,
Waldorf-Astoria) peeling away from it like shreds of scalded skin. A
woman's satin shoe, heel-less but with the diamanté still aglitter
within the rusty circle of its buckle, bobs just out of reach. A newspaper, streaked with grey-green lichen-like stains, shows the face of
the famous and infamous general, shunted from siding to main line
and then back to siding like some locomotive of antique design but
violent power. In the 'good' years, that were bad, I entertained him
on my yacht, even larger than his, and in my house, far more
resplendent than his palace; and in the 'bad' years, that were no less

307

bad, I attempted to appease his fractious exile by ordering that money should be transferred from one numbered Swiss bank account to another. Now I reach out for him, leaning out over the filth of the world, the world of filth, the fissured concrete of the jetty grating on my knees through my threadbare jeans and my scrawny arm extending splayed fingers on which the nails, uncut and dirt-seamed, curve like the talons of some bird of prey. The dog watches. I grasp. I gasp. I pull. But the section of newspaper held in my hand dissolves into a scum; and when I seize another section and another section, they too dissolve. The general's face splits precisely where the trim moustache divides, and then once more splits across those small, wary eyes, which are now gazing up at me as though yet again to beseech me, *Save me, save me.* But I no longer have any wish to save him, even if I could do so.

I shall walk my little island, last and least of the many that once I owned, kicking out indiscriminately at the cans, bottles, wrapping-paper, melon-rinds, orange-skins, lettuce-leaves, fish-bones, rags and condoms. If there were human bodies, dead or alive, I should kick out at them too. But at the dog, the once magnificent boxer, his sides now fallen in, his tail broken and his eyes red-rimmed, I never kick out. He is my sole companion, if one excepts the silver-fish, the spiders, the flies, the mosquitoes, the fleas, the bugs, the cock-roaches and the wasps that inhabit, along with the dog and me, the dry husk of my hut.

I shall slip off my shoes, trodden down at the heels and their ravelled laces long since abandoned, to paddle in that filth of the world, that world of filth, as once I would swim in it, swallowing, effortlessly and with no sense of nausea, all the nameless horrors that floated on its tide. Puffing, I shall mount the symmetrically rounded hill and, tiptoe, shall reach up, the dog patiently watching me out of his red-rimmed eyes, to pluck from one of the stunted trees a green apple that, as I bite into it, fizzes a corrosive vinegar, or from another an olive that, grating against my rotten teeth, seems to be all stone. I shall prostrate myself on the soil beyond the symmetri-cally rounded hill and, the dog beside me, shall join him in lapping at the brown, brackish water that has collected in the interstices of a gully. Then, perched on a rock, with that filth of the world, that world of filth outstretched before me and the dog outstretched behind me, I shall once again regurgitate and chew the bitter cud.

A shepherd boy, I raced headlong down a mountain side with a crumble and crackle of stones, to the city fermenting as relentlessly with its filth as this sea all around me. I, too, was in a youthful ferment of ambitions, schemes and plots. I had only one thing, myself; and I must have everything. That one thing I sold: my youth to the ageing women, their steps dragging under the weight of their furs and satins and their arms limp under the weight of their encrusted, clanking bracelets; my strength to the ailing men, yawning and sighing away their lives behind nails buffed to a shiny pink; my enthusiasm to the effete women, men, half-women, half-men who had as little zest for the haggling of the market-place as for what it offered. Then I bought: ruined warehouses and ruined businesses, trinkets, pictures, carpets, flesh; and, finally, those scraps of paper, at first meaningless to me but later to be prized more highly than anything that I could touch or see or tread or fondle. I glittered, a column of gold smelted from an accumulation of numberless impurities.

Soon there were villas, chalets, apartments and mansions; Rolls Royces, Cadillacs and Lamborghinis; Titians and Poussins and Picassos. The dry husk of my life became loud with its human silverfish, spiders, flies, mosquitoes, fleas, bugs, cockroaches and wasps. Film stars, with opulent breasts and long, wet hair would clamber out of my swimming-pools, reaching up to clasp the hand that I chivalrously held out to them. On the deck of my yacht a long since senile statesman would suck, a swollen baby, at the teat of a Romeo and Giulietta that I had plugged into his mouth. A world-famous painter, inwardly furious but outwardly grateful, would listen, head bowed, to my ignorant criticism of the churning impasto with which he had depicted the sea around one of my many islands. A Nobel prize-winning novelist would drawl, eyes narrowed over the champagne goblet raised to an ill-concealed grimace: *Ah, but you really are astute! How cleverly and how cruelly you put your finger on precisely what is wrong with my writing!*

Always there were the presents: the ties that I would toss contemptuously to my valet to keep for himself; the watches (Omega, Piaget, Longines) that I would drop negligently into the calloused palm of this or that of my deck-hands; the cigarette-lighters and cigarette-cases and cigar-cutters, all gold of course, that would clutter up my drawers until someone had the initiative to steal them. Those who lavished these gifts on me knew all about investment. With a wide gesture they flung their bread on the waters of my generosity and with an even wider gesture they scrabbled both it and its accumulations back. *Oh, but you shouldn't. . . . Oh, but I couldn't.* . . . But I did; and they could. One of my secretaries, a youth etiolated from the hours that he spent in a shuttered room at a typewriter, fell in love with the daughter of one of my associates. *I've nothing against the lad, oh nothing at all. But he must see, you must see.* . . . *One day my daughter is going to be an extremely rich woman.* . . . *Well* – I laughed – *let me make him an extremely rich man. How much should I settle on him?*

Your bounty is as boundless as the sea. That was the Nobel prize-winner, smugly sure that I would not know the origin of the quotation. He intoned the pentameter as he accepted the cheque that would lubricate his passage out of one failed marriage and into another. But my bounty, like this boundless sea about me, was one soiled with the filth of the world, a world of filth. I had descended that remote mountain side with a crumble and crackle of stones, and it was those same stones, obdurately unbreakable like myself, that I had wielded with my scratched, bleeding, aching hands to gouge out the channel through which this 'bounty' now flowed to irrigate their parched and stunted lives. It was a bounty not of love but of hate.

I hated them for the nurseries in which they had been pampered; for the schools in which they had been taught to quote from Shakespeare; for the horses on which they had hunted and hacked; for the servants whom they had always so effortlessly commanded; for their titles and commissions and degrees. I hated them for their delicate complexions, their soft hands and softer voices, their assumptions of command. I hated them, I despised them. *How far will you go? How far can I go? Will you allow me to give you this and this and this? Will you continue to entreat me for loans, advice, gifts, invitations? Will you beg me to take anything from you – your wives, your daughters, your sons, even yourselves – provided that I stretch out a hand to save you?* Oh, how I loved to witness the humiliation which you imposed on yourselves! It reminded me of the story, told to me by the Nobel prize-winner, of that vulgar nineteenth-century French *parvenu* whose mistress became more and more outrageous in the extravagance of her demands. At her insistence, he bought for her a Rajah's diamond and then invited her to dinner, in order to present it. Behind a screen in the lofty dining room he concealed some of her most intimate 'friends'. The banquet *à deux* was resplendent and she was resplendent. A gold dish was brought in, covered, and taken to her. The waiter raised the lid. The plump cocotte gaped, wrinkling her little nose. There, embedded in excrement, glittered the Rajah's diamond. *If you remove it with your teeth, it is yours*, her lover told her. *But mind – no hands.* She half-rose from the table, tore at a handkerchief, shrilled at him, burst into hysterical weeping. Then, when he remained unmoved, she seated herself again, with the same resolution with which her chambermaid mother would apply herself to some inevitable, if revolting, duty. She lowered her head. A lock of hair fell forward. Nose, lips and one cheek all became smeared. Then, as she triumphantly extracted the Rajah's diamond between those large white teeth, she heard a cachinnation from behind the screen. . . . A *parvenu* myself, I know exactly how that French *parvenu* must have felt.

Soon, most of my wealth consisted of scraps of paper hoarded away in banks all round the world; and then, all of a sudden, an icy gust of wind swept through country after country and bank after bank, and those scraps of paper were scattered in all directions. It was not, I thought, impossible to retrieve them, indeed it should be easy – since my famous 'bounty' must have made me innumerable affluent and powerful friends. To some I sent emissaries; to some I went myself. *Ah, my dear fellow, if only you had asked at some other time. Nothing would give me greater pleasure but with this recession. You must know that I. You must realize that we. There's no one in the whole world that I'd more like to. If last month. If next month. Last year. Next year. The truth is. Skint. Cleaned out. Not a bean. But surely if you asked. But surely if you approached. But surely.* Like that newspaper by the jetty, disintegrating fragment by fragment as I tried to grasp at it, so my fortune and my friendships disintegrated at one and the same time.

If I now went into those clubs where once I had been welcomed with enthusiasm, eyes slid away and, in many instances, even the owners of the eyes slid away too. If I entered those hotels (Ritz, Carlton, Ritz-Carlton, Waldorf, Astoria, Waldorf-Astoria) where once an obsequious manager would himself conduct me to my suite, now a wary desk clerk, riffling through his register, would tell me, *Sorry, sir, a muddle, there doesn't seem to be, there isn't.* The telephone in my mortgaged palace became preternaturally silent, having once rung continuously throughout the day. My former secretary cut me, as he strutted past me in the street with the wife whom I had bought for him. My mantelpiece was now bare both of ornaments and of the invitations that this man would once take so much pleasure in propping up along it. The Nobel prize-winner wrote a *nouvelle* about a vulgar upstart who cheated and lied himself to a fortune and then, one morning, woke up to find that it had gone. The painter gave an interview in which he expatiated on the lavish hideousness of the houses in which I had entertained him. The drooling baby-politician took his next cruise as guest of one of my rivals. When I rang up the whore whom I had set up in a duplex across the road from me, I could see her sauntering through lighted rooms in her negligée even as her maid lisped that Madame had gone away on holiday and no, she had no idea when she would be back.

I sold my last picture and I planned my last party, taking into my confidence only my majordomo – once a peasant like myself, from the village next to mine. He alone had remained faithful to me; and it was he who supervised the hanging of my garden with thousands of fairy-lights, the setting of the tables and chairs under the resin-scented trees, with the sea glittering behind them, and the delivery of the heavily embossed invitations to all those people whose lives and mine had once been lapped together in those priceless sheets of paper now lost on the ravaging wind. There was general amazement, consternation, embarrassment and joy. *The old boy has somehow pulled through. One must hand it to him. Well, one always knew. Trust him to have a trick or two up his sleeve. One might have guessed.* The uninvited telephoned with invitations of their own, to remind me of their existences. My whore, following the custom of my affluent past with her, instructed her *couturier* to send me his bill. (*I'm sure you wouldn't want me to disgrace you.*) The Nobel prize-winner forwarded a copy of his latest book specially bound for me in the softest calf. The painter had one of his churning pictures of the sea around one of my houses delivered to me. The baby-politician's wife telephoned to say that he would be staying with me on the night of the party – though he had not, in fact, even been sent an invitation.

Under the thousands of fairy-lights the hired waiters moved among these hired guests. A number of *paparazzi* had gate-crashed, as had a famous tennis-player and a couple of pop-singers. (*We knew that you had really meant to ask us.*) Flash-bulbs exploded as now this celebrity and now that linked an arm in mine or threw an arm around my neck. Chained in his kennel, my sleek boxer – the same dog that now lies outstretched beside me, his shrunken flank heaving like a dilapidated bellows and an opaque eye upturned to the sun – began to howl with an eerie persistence; but no one seemed to hear him.

Eventually the guests sought out their place-names at the tables set out, their napery glimmering and their cutlery glittering, under the thousands of little lights dangling from the resin-scented trees. *I'm sure I should. How strange that you and I. Oh, change the cards. Here, here, we're here! No, there!* The orchestra on the flower-wreathed platform on the brow of the hill swayed into a waltz. *Lehar! Strauss! But the Elder, not the Younger! But Richard, not Johann!* The hired waiters gravely made their way out of my palace, along the winding paths, towards the hired guests. They held aloft, on gloved palms, gold dishes like that gold dish that the *parvenu* Frenchman had had presented to his cocotte. Other hired waiters processed towards the hired guests with bottles wrapped in napkins. *I'm sure it must be Strauss. But the Elder, not the Younger. But Richard, not Johann!* The waiters ceremoniously removed the lids of the dishes, the waiters ceremoniously tilted their bottles. The guests stared, tittered, were aghast. Into each dish had been stuffed wads of Monopoly money of enormous denominations. Out of each bottle poured, not champagne, but nuggets of chocolate encased in golden foil. Unreal, totally unreal, the counters that I could never redeem. But it was a joke, of course it was a joke! Some of them began to laugh, others were smiling; but when – the once baying dog now on a leash at my side – they saw me, above them and above the abruptly silent orchestra, on the bare, brown hill, also laughing, laughing, laughing, their own laughter and smiles ceased. Singly or in groups, they began to rise. A woman with improbable orange hair scrabbled under her table for a high-heeled satin slipper with a diamanté buckle. Under one of the swaying bulbs the general's face seemed streaked with a green-grey lichen, like his face in that newspaper photograph. The Nobel prize-winner staggered against a spindly chair and sent it crashing to the ground, there to shatter, with the same unforeseen violence with which his literary reputation was soon to topple and shiver to fragments. The painter was short-sightedly examining one of the foil-wrapped nuggets, as though he still half-believed that they were made of solid gold. My whore had seized a handful of the Monopoly money (notes for £5,000, £10,000, £20,000) as though she still wholly believed that it was bankable. The dog gave a yank at his leash of plaited crocodile leather and reared up, fangs bared. Again and yet again he bayed, menacing and eerie. The general was one of the first to run. Then everyone was running. Still, still I laughed; and in wilder and wilder frenzy the dog still jerked at the leash now held in both my hands,

313

repeatedly hurled himself forward and kept up that baying.

In a spluttering little caïque, stinking of sheep, diesel oil and vomit, the dog and I came to this island, clambered up the five rickety steps – they were then still passable – and made our way up to the husk-hut crepitant and murmurous with its insect life. The dog hunted through the sere bush, his coat growing mangy and his flanks lean, his eyes sinking within their red rims as a cobwebby penumbra settled on them. I bit on the vinegary apples, I tried to bite on the stone-like olives. I even grubbed for roots and rooted for grubs. The majordomo had begged to stay with us but I had not let him. He had stood at the stern of the caïque, his wide peasant hand shielding his narrow peasant face from the glare, as he gazed motionless at us, the hoarsely panting caïque carrying him off through the filth of the world into a world of filth.

Months later, the majordomo returned in a smartly gleaming motorboat, with a panama hat jauntily tilted above his narrow peasant face and an ivory-headed cane in his wide peasant hand. Some of the scraps of paper had been wafted back. They had settled, they had multiplied. An oil-prospecting company in which, as a kindness to the son of one of my hired friends, I had invested a few thousand pounds, had struck it rich. My whore had been decapitated in a motor accident, hastening from one millionaire lover to another, and, her will unchanged since our separation, had left me the duplex that I had bought for her. A luxury hotel was being built on the stony ground of the smallholding that, for all my then wealth, my father had bequeathed to me, his eldest son, on his deathbed. But, perched on this rock, the dog panting on his side beside me, I was totally uninterested in the majordomo's excited gabble. Later, other, bigger vessels came to the rickety jetty, with uniformed crews and gleaming brass-work and awnings under which their owners and their owners' guests could shield their delicate complexions from the sun. But the dog only bayed and I only laughed, as they interceded with me to give up all this nonsense and to return to 'civilization', told me of some fool-proof investment (*Out of our long-standing friendship I want you in on the ground floor*), or bleated about 'temporary' difficulties, a nasty little hitch or the sluggishness of cash-flow. Still perched on this rock, I watched them as, amazed, disconsolate, despairing or angry, they chugged, chugged back through the filth of the world into a world of filth.

My hatred and contempt for them had once been merely the obverse of my love and admiration for my own self. Oh, how I had loved and admired myself for my unbounded energy, my pristine youthfulness, my unwearying resourcefulness and my extravagant bounty; and how much easier it had been to love and admire myself for all these things if I could also hate and despise them for their effeteness and their senility and their ineffectuality and their avarice. Look here, upon this picture, and on this. (The Nobel prize-winner would be amazed to hear me quote those words.) But now my hatred and contempt for them have long since become an integral part of my hatred and contempt for myself. Call me not by my name but, if you must call me anything, in the language of my country call me 'Misanthropos'. The dog lies beside me and in his company I shall for a while live a dog's life – since that, despite what people say, is preferable to the life of a man. Together, he and I shall lap from the same stagnant puddle and together we shall scratch ourselves from the bites of the same fleas. We shall even defecate the same parasites. Perhaps we shall die together. Yes, I am sure that we shall.

Above the last of my mansions, on the last of my islands, there writhes a fig tree long since dead and even longer barren. One day I shall have learned again to love myself enough to throw over the strongest of its branches the rope that the dog drags around with him, and to hang first him, so humane in his simple bestiality, and then myself, so beastly in my complex humanity. When that hour comes, these scraps of paper, as illusory as those other scraps piled high in innumerable banks in innumerable cities of the world, will have to stand as my gravestone.

But there is time enough for that. Of time, as of the filth of the world and of the world of filth, there is always enough.

1983

FOR THE BEST IN PAPERBACKS, LOOK FOR THE

In every corner of the world, on every subject under the sun, Penguins represent quality and variety – the very best in publishing today.

For complete information about books available from Penguin and how to order them, write to us at the appropriate address below. Please note that for copyright reasons the selection of books varies from country to country.

In the United Kingdom: For a complete list of books available from Penguin in the U.K., please write to *Dept EP, Penguin Books Ltd, Harmondsworth, Middlesex, UB7 0DA*

In the United States: For a complete list of books available from Penguin in the U.S., please write to *Dept BA, Viking Penguin, 299 Murray Hill Parkway, East Rutherford, New Jersey 07073*

In Canada: For a complete list of books available from Penguin in Canada, please write to *Penguin Books Canada Limited, 2801 John Street, Markham, Ontario L3R 1B4*

In Australia: For a complete list of books available from Penguin in Australia, please write to the *Marketing Department, Penguin Books Australia Ltd, P.O. Box 257, Ringwood, Victoria 3134*

In New Zealand: For a complete list of books available from Penguin in New Zealand, please write to the *Marketing Department, Penguin Books (N.Z.) Ltd, Private Bag, Takapuna, Auckland 9*

In India: For a complete list of books available from Penguin in India, please write to *Penguin Overseas Ltd, 706 Eros Apartments, 56 Nehru Place, New Delhi 110019*

A CHOICE OF PENGUIN FICTION

Maia   Richard Adams

The heroic romance of love and war in an ancient empire from one of our greatest storytellers. 'Enormous and powerful' – *Financial Times*

The Warning Bell   Lynne Reid Banks

A wonderfully involving, truthful novel about the choices a woman must make in her life – and the price she must pay for ignoring the counsel of her own heart. 'Lynne Reid Banks knows how to get to her reader: this novel grips like Super Glue' – *Observer*

Doctor Slaughter   Paul Theroux

Provocative and menacing – a brilliant dissection of lust, ambition and betrayal in 'civilized' London. 'Witty, chilly, exuberant, graphic' – *The Times Literary Supplement*

July's People   Nadine Gordimer

Set in South Africa, this novel gives us an unforgettable look at the terrifying, tacit understanding and misunderstandings between blacks and whites. 'This is the best novel that Miss Gordimer has ever written' – Alan Paton in the *Saturday Review*

Wise Virgin   A. N. Wilson

Giles Fox's work on the Pottle manuscript, a little-known thirteenth-century tract on virginity, leads him to some innovative research on the subject that takes even his breath away. 'A most elegant and chilling comedy' – *Observer* Books of the Year

Last Resorts   Clare Boylan

Harriet loved Joe Fischer for his ordinariness – for his ordinary suits and hats, his ordinary money and his ordinary mind, even for his ordinary wife. 'An unmitigated delight' – *Time Out*

A CHOICE OF PENGUIN FICTION

Stanley and the Women   Kingsley Amis

Just when Stanley Duke thinks it safe to sink into middle age, his son goes insane – and Stanley finds himself beset on all sides by women, each of whom seems to have an intimate acquaintance with madness. 'Very good, very powerful . . . beautifully written' – Anthony Burgess in the *Observer*

The Girls of Slender Means   Muriel Spark

A world and a war are winding up with a bang, and in what is left of London all the nice people are poor – and about to discover how different the new world will be. 'Britain's finest post-war novelist' – *The Times*

Him with His Foot in His Mouth   Saul Bellow

A collection of first-class short stories. 'If there is a better living writer of fiction, I'd very much like to know who he or she is' – *The Times*

Mother's Helper   Maureen Freely

A superbly biting and breathtakingly fluent attack on certain libertarian views, blending laughter, delight, rage and amazement, this is a novel you won't forget. 'A winner' – *The Times Literary Supplement*

Decline and Fall   Evelyn Waugh

A comic yet curiously touching account of an innocent plunged into the sham, brittle world of high society. Evelyn Waugh's first novel brought him immediate public acclaim and is still a classic of its kind.

Stars and Bars   William Boyd

Well-dressed, quite handsome, unfailingly polite and charming, who would guess that Henderson Dores, the innocent Englishman abroad in wicked America, has a guilty secret? 'Without doubt his best book so far . . . made me laugh out loud' – *The Times*

FOR THE BEST IN PAPERBACKS, LOOK FOR THE 🐧

A CHOICE OF PENGUIN FICTION

Trade Wind   M. M. Kaye

An enthralling blend of history, adventure and romance from the author of the bestselling *The Far Pavilions*

The Ghost Writer   Philip Roth

Philip Roth's celebrated novel about a young writer who meets and falls in love with Anne Frank in New England – or so he thinks. 'Brilliant, witty and extremely elegant' – *Guardian*

Small World   David Lodge

Shortlisted for the 1984 Booker Prize, *Small World* brings back Philip Swallow and Maurice Zapp for a jet-propelled journey into hilarity. 'The most brilliant and also the funniest novel that he has written' – *London Review of Books*

Village Christmas   'Miss Read'

The village of Fairacre finds its peace disrupted by the arrival in its midst of the noisy, cheerful Emery family – and only the advent of a Christmas baby brings things back to normal. 'A sheer joy' – *Glasgow Evening Times*

Treasures of Time   Penelope Lively

Beautifully written, acutely observed, and filled with Penelope Lively's sharp but compassionate wit, *Treasures of Time* explores the relationship between the lives we live and the lives we think we live.

Absolute Beginners   Colin MacInnes

The first 'teenage' novel, the classic of youth and disenchantment, *Absolute Beginners* is part of MacInnes's famous London trilogy – and now a brilliant film. 'MacInnes caught it first – and best' – *Harpers and Queen*

A CHOICE OF PENGUIN FICTION

Money Martin Amis

Savage, audacious and demonically witty – a story of urban excess. 'Terribly, terminally funny: laughter in the dark, if ever I heard it' – *Guardian*

Lolita Vladimir Nabokov

Shot through with Nabokov's mercurial wit, quicksilver prose and intoxicating sensuality, *Lolita* is one of the world's great love stories. 'A great book' – Dorothy Parker

Dinner at the Homesick Restaurant Anne Tyler

Through every family run memories which bind them together – in spite of everything. 'She is a witch. Witty, civilized, curious, with her radar cars and her quill pen dipped on one page in acid and on the next in orange liqueur . . . a wonderful writer' – John Leonard in *The New York Times*

Glitz Elmore Leonard

Underneath the Boardwalk, a lot of insects creep. But the creepiest of all was Teddy. 'After finishing *Glitz*, I went out to the bookstore and bought everything else of Elmore Leonard I could find' – Stephen King

The Battle of Pollocks Crossing J. L. Carr

Nominated for the Booker McConnell Prize, this is a moving, comic masterpiece. 'Wayward, ambiguous, eccentric . . , a fascinatingly outlandish novel' *Guardian*

The Dreams of an Average Man Dyan Sheldon

Tony Rivera is lost. Sandy Grossman Rivera is leaving. And Maggie Kelly is giving up. In the steamy streets of summertime Manhattan, the refugees of the sixties generation wonder what went wrong. 'Satire, dramatic irony and feminist fun . . . lively, forceful and funny' – *Listener*

A CHOICE OF PENGUIN FICTION

Bliss Jill Tweedie

When beautiful Lady Clare La Fontaine marries for money, she enters a glittering world of luxury and corruption and discovers the darker side of sexual politics in Jill Tweedie's blockbusting, bestselling novel. 'Huge, vital and passionately written' – *Cosmopolitan*

Fair Stood the Wind for France H. E. Bates

It was France, and wartime – and not the moment to fall in love. 'Perhaps the finest novel of the war . . . a lovely book which makes the heart beat with pride' – *Daily Telegraph*

The Flight from the Enchanter Iris Murdoch

A group of people have elected ambiguous and fascinating Mischa Fox to be their god. And thus begins the battle between sturdy common sense and dangerous enchantment. Elegant, sparkling and unputdownable, this is Iris Murdoch at her best.

Very Good, Jeeves! P. G. Wodehouse

When Bertie Wooster lands in the soup, only the 'infinite sagacity' of Jeeves can pull him out. 'A riot . . . There are eleven tales in this volume and each is the best' – *Observer*

To Have and To Hold Deborah Moggach

Viv was giving her sister, Ann, the best present she could think of – a baby. How Viv, Ann and their husbands cope with this extraordinary situation is the subject of this tender, triumphant and utterly absorbing story. Now a powerful TV drama.

A Dark and Distant Shore Reay Tannahill

Vilia is the unforgettable heroine, Kinveil Castle is her destiny, in this full-blooded saga spanning a century of Victoriana, empire, hatred and love affairs. 'A marvellous blend of *Gone with the Wind* and *The Thorn Birds*' – *Daily Mirror*

FOR THE BEST IN PAPERBACKS, LOOK FOR THE

A CHOICE OF PENGUIN FICTION

Other Women   Lisa Alther

From the bestselling author of *Kinflicks* comes this compelling novel of today's woman – and a heroine with whom millions of women will identify.

Your Lover Just Called   John Updike

Stories of Joan and Richard Maple – a couple multiplied by love and divided by lovers. Here is the portrait of a modern American marriage in all its mundane moments and highs and lows of love as only John Updike could draw it.

Mr Love and Justice   Colin MacInnes

Frankie Love took up his career as a ponce about the same time as Edward Justice became vice-squad detective. Except that neither man was particularly suited for his job, all they had in common was an interest in crime. But, as any ponce or copper will tell you, appearances are not always what they seem. Provocative and honest and acidly funny, *Mr Love and Justice* is the final volume of Colin MacInnes's famous London trilogy.

An Ice-Cream War   William Boyd

As millions are slaughtered on the Western Front, a ridiculous and little-reported campaign is being waged in East Africa – a war they continued after the Armistice because no one told them to stop. 'A towering achievement' – John Carey, Chairman of the Judges of the 1982 Booker Prize, for which this novel was nominated.

Every Day is Mother's Day   Hilary Mantel

An outrageous story of lust, adultery, madness, death and the social services. 'Strange . . . rather mad . . . extremely funny . . . she sometimes reminded me of the early Muriel Spark' – Auberon Waugh

1982 Janine   Alasdair Gray

Set inside the head of an ageing, divorced, alcoholic, insomniac supervisor of security installations who is tippling in the bedroom of a small Scottish hotel – this is a most brilliant and controversial novel.

FOR THE BEST IN PAPERBACKS, LOOK FOR THE 🐧

A CHOICE OF PENGUIN FICTION

Family Myths and Legends   Patricia Ferguson

Gareth was just beginning to believe that he really enjoyed his relatives these days. And then Gareth's grandmother turns up in Gareth's hospital – and he is up to his upwardly-mobile neck in family once more. 'Great funniness and perception, and stunning originality' – *Daily Telegraph*

The Beans of Egypt, Maine   Carolyn Chute

Out of the hidden heart of America comes this uncompromising novel of what life is like for people who have nothing left to them except their own pain, humiliation and rage. 'It's loving, terrible and funny and written as deftly as stitching on a quilt . . . a lovely, truthful book' – *Observer*

City of Spades   Colin MacInnes

'A splendid novel, sparklingly written, warm, wise and funny' – *Daily Mail*. *City of Spades*, *Absolute Beginners* and *Mr Love and Justice* make up Colin MacInnes's trilogy on London street life from the inside out.

The Anatomy Lesson   Philip Roth

The hilarious story of Nathan Zuckerman, the famous forty-year-old writer who decides to give it all up and become a doctor – and a pornographer – instead. 'The finest, boldest and funniest piece of fiction which Philip Roth has yet produced' – *Spectator*

The Rachel Papers   Martin Amis

A stylish, sexy and ribaldy funny novel by the author of *Money*. 'Remark-able' – *Listener*. 'Irreverent' – *Daily Telegraph*. 'Very funny indeed' – *Spectator*

Scandal   A. N. Wilson

Sexual peccadilloes, treason and blackmail are all ingredients on the boil in A. N. Wilson's new, *cordon noir* comedy. 'Drily witty, deliciously nasty' – *Sunday Telegraph*

A CHOICE OF PENGUIN FICTION

Monsignor Quixote Graham Greene

Now filmed for television, Graham Greene's novel, like Cervantes' seventeenth-century classic, is a brilliant fable for its times. 'A deliciously funny novel' – *The Times*

The Dearest and the Best Leslie Thomas

In the spring of 1940 the spectre of war turned into grim reality – and for all the inhabitants of the historic villages of the New Forest it was the beginning of the most bizarre, funny and tragic episode of their lives. 'Excellent' – *Sunday Times*

Earthly Powers Anthony Burgess

Anthony Burgess's magnificent masterpiece, an enthralling, epic narrative spanning six decades and spotlighting some of the most vivid events and characters of our times. 'Enormous imagination and vitality . . . a huge book in every way' – Bernard Levin in the *Sunday Times*

The Penitent Isaac Bashevis Singer

From the Nobel Prize-winning author comes a powerful story of a man who has material wealth but feels spiritually impoverished. 'Singer . . . restates with dignity the spiritual aspirations and the cultural complexities of a lifetime, and it must be said that in doing so he gives the Evil One no quarter and precious little advantage' – Anita Brookner in the *Sunday Times*

Paradise Postponed John Mortimer

'Hats off to John Mortimer. He's done it again' – *Spectator*. A rumbustious, hilarious new novel from the creator of Rumpole, *Paradise Postponed* is now a major Thames Television series.

Animal Farm George Orwell

The classic political fable of the twentieth century.

CRIME AND MYSTERY IN PENGUINS

Deep Water Patricia Highsmith

Portrait of a psychopath, from the first faint outline to the full horrors of schizophrenia. 'If you read crime stories at all, or perhaps especially if you don't, you should read *Deep Water*' – Julian Symons in the *Sunday Times*

Farewell My Lovely   Raymond Chandler

Moose Malloy was a big man but not more than six feet five inches tall and not wider than a beer truck. He looked about as inconspicuous as a tarantula on a slice of angel food. Marlowe's greatest case. Chandler's greatest book.

God Save the Child   Robert B. Parker

When young Kevin Bartlett disappears, everyone assumes he's run away . . . until the comic strip ransom note arrives . . . 'In classic wisecracking and handfighting tradition, Spenser sorts out the case and wins the love of a fine-boned Jewish Lady . . . who even shares his taste for iced red wine' – Francis Goff in the *Sunday Telegraph*

The Daughter of Time   Josephine Tey

Josephine Tey again delves into history to reconstruct a crime. This time it is a crime committed in the tumultuous fifteenth century. 'Most people will find *The Daughter of Time* as interesting and enjoyable a book as they will meet in a month of Sundays' – Marghanita Laski in the *Observer*

The Michael Innes Omnibus

Three tensely exhilarating novels. 'A master – he constructs a plot that twists and turns like an electric eel: it gives you shock upon shock and you cannot let go' – *The Times Literary Supplement*

Killer's Choice   Ed McBain

Who killed Annie Boone? Employer, lover, ex-husband, girlfriend? This is a tense, terrifying and tautly written novel from the author of *The Mugger*, *The Pusher*, *Lady Killer* and a dozen other first class thrillers.

CRIME AND MYSTERY IN PENGUINS

Call for the Dead John Le Carré

The classic work of espionage which introduced the world to George Smiley. 'Brilliant . . . highly intelligent, realistic. Constant suspense. Excellent writing' – *Observer*

Swag Elmore Leonard

From the bestselling author of *Stick* and *LaBrava* comes this wallbanger of a book in which 100,000 dollars' worth of nicely spendable swag sets off a slick, fast-moving chain of events. 'Brilliant' – *The New York Times*

The Soft Talkers Margaret Millar

The mysterious disappearance of a Toronto businessman is the start point for this spine-chilling, compulsive novel. 'This is not for the squeamish, and again the last chapter conceals a staggering surprise' – *Time and Tide*

The Julian Symons Omnibus

The Man Who Killed Himself, *The Man Whose Dreams Came True*, *The Man Who Lost His Wife*: three novels of cynical humour and cliff-hanging suspense from a master of his craft. 'Exciting and compulsively readable' – *Observer*

Love in Amsterdam Nicolas Freeling

Inspector Van der Valk's first case involves him in an elaborate cat-and-mouse game with a very wily suspect. 'Has the sinister, spell-binding perfection of a cobra uncoiling. It is a masterpiece of the genre' – Stanley Ellis

Maigret's Pipe Georges Simenon

Eighteen intriguing cases of mystery and murder to which the pipe-smoking Maigret applies his wit and intuition, his genius for detection and a certain *je ne sais quoi* . . .